7 DAYS

A Dee Rommel Mystery

by
Jule Selbo

© 2025 by Jule Selbo

This book is a work of creative fiction that uses actual publicly known events, situations, and locations as background for the storyline with fictional embellishments as creative license allows. Although the publisher has made every effort to ensure the grammatical integrity of this book was correct at press time, the publisher does not assume and hereby disclaims any liability to any party for any loss, damage, or disruption caused by errors or omissions, whether such errors or omissions result from negligence, accident, or any other cause. At Pandamoon, we take great pride in producing quality works that accurately reflect the voice of the author. All the words are the author's alone.

All rights reserved. Published in the United States by Pandamoon Publishing. No part of this publication may be reproduced, stored in a retrieval system, or transmitted in any form or by any means—for example, electronic, photocopy, recording—without the prior written permission of the publisher. The only exception is brief quotations in printed reviews.

www.pandamoonpublishing.com

Jacket design and illustrations © Pandamoon Publishing
Art Direction by Don Kramer and Elgon Williams: Pandamoon Publishing
Editing by Tylee Ertel and Elgon Williams: Pandamoon Publishing

Pandamoon Publishing and the portrayal of a panda and a moon are registered trademarks of Pandamoon Publishing.

Library of Congress Cataloging-in-Publication Data is on file at the Library of Congress, Washington, DC

Edition: 1, Version 1.00
ISBN 13: 978-1-950627-76-9

REVIEWS FOR 7 DAYS, A Dee Rommel Mystery and other books in the award-winning series

Rich with Maine flavor, the fourth book in Selbo's Dee Rommel Mystery series (after *8 Days*) finds Portland private investigator Dee Rommel involved in what at first appears to be a simple domestic altercation at a local diner, where a disturbed woman named Gilli Wanz steals her purse. That incident and its surprising reverberations launch Dee into a complicated murder investigation that intersects with her own past. When Gordy, her partner and godfather, asks her to investigate the death of his friend, Frank—an environmental rabble-rouser whose death had previously been ruled a suicide—Dee must reconnect with her past lover and current detective on the case, Donato, to delve into the mystery surrounding Frank's demise. Between drug dealers, Forever Chemicals, Frank's children, and Gilli's criminal brother-in-law, the web of intrigue expands with each chapter.

A satisfying mystery with a tidy conclusion, *7 Days* delivers a compelling, twisty pursuit and appealing characters, portrayed through the eyes of a tough protagonist who's not afraid to follow her gut. This ex-policewoman has seen a lot, but she still nurtures a welcome hopeful streak: "I think the world's worth fixing," she says, when conversation gets bleak. Selbo's prose blends sharp dialogue, warm characterization, and striking Atlantic coast detail—from lobster shacks and locals whose favorite word is "Ahyup" to the 17th-century homes of swank Kennebunkport. Donato asks, preparing tea, "We doin' fancy or homey?"; one man Dee encounters is "all crusty teeth, nose hairs, and a real bad shave."

Ongoing series threads keep Dee from only living for the case. As she connects the dots, Gordy fights his own hard challenges with pancreatic cancer. Readers unfamiliar with the series will catch up quickly, as Selbo builds background hand in hand with suspense, dropping a slew of tantalizing clues that lead Dee and Donato on a treasure hunt. Readers who crave twisty intrigue with dark ties to the past will be entertained and onboard for future entries. - **Booklife Reviews**

"An exquisitely multi-layered plot that comes together seamlessly to deliver a spinetingling and startling climax. If you're missing Sue Grafton's Alphabet series, you'll want to read Jule Selbo's Dee Rommel books—they're as comforting as they are exciting!"—**Holly West, author of the Mistress of Fortune mysteries and the Anthony Award-winning editor of** *Killin' Time in San Diego*

"Underestimate Dee Rommel at your own peril. With 7 DAYS, Jule Selbo has written a tight, propulsive crime novel with a unique lead character who ranks right up there with some of New England's best crime creations. A worthy entry in the series!" - **Scott Lyerly, author of** *The Last Line*

"Portland, Maine is one of the characters of '7 DAYS', as strong as the protagonist, Dee Rommel, and she is mighty. In this fourth book in the series, Dee is still as tough as nails, but she is starting to reveal a softer, more sensitive, and vulnerable side where love and family come into play. Dee must tackle murders connected to farmlands, Forever Chemicals, and greed. '7 DAYS' is one week of building tensions - do yourself a favor, set aside a chunk of time when you pick this one up." - **Matt Cost, Award winning author of the Mainely Mystery series amongst others**

8 DAYS, A Dee Rommel Mystery

"Selbo paints a portrait of Portland, Maine so vivid, you can practically smell the salt air. And she populates it with a cast of characters as colorful as they are nuanced—her indefatigable sleuth Dee Rommel chief among them. '8 DAYS' finds Dee squaring off against a shadowy cabal who will stop at nothing to prevent their unspeakable crimes from being dragged into the light, resulting in a breakneck tale chock full of grit and grace." - **Chris Holm, Anthony Award-winning author of** *The Killing Kind*

"*8 DAYS* is a fantastic, suspenseful thriller that fans of Lisa Jewell and Lisa Gardner will enjoy." - **Kristi Elizabeth for** *Los Angeles Book Review*

"Jule Selbo never makes a misstep in *8 DAYS*; rock-solid writing and vivid characterizations lead the reader down a dark path of exploitation and deceit." – **Gillian French, author** *Sugaring Off* **and** *The Lies They Tell*

9 DAYS, A Dee Rommel Mystery

"Dee herself is shown to be a complex, prickly hero living with a disability and harboring a deep curiosity beneath a hard-bitten exterior. Readers will happily follow her down many rabbit holes. *9 DAYS* is a twisty, entertaining whodunit with sharp sleuthing and a lot of heart." – **Starred * Kirkus Review**

"Female investigator Dee Rommel -- wounded and vulnerable under her tough, don't-touch-me exterior, tenacious as hell in the pursuit of justice for her clients – is superb as the lead in this suspense-filled page turner. *9 DAYS* has it all – a compelling mystery, a ticking clock, and a cast of well-developed characters to both love and hate. Highly recommended." - **Kerry Anne King, bestselling author of** *Other People's Things*

"*9 DAYS* is my favorite kind of crime novel, a riveting story driven by fascinating characters with rich and twisty relationships. And Dee Rommel is my favorite kind of character, a sympathetic and relatable combination of thinking and action. This excellent Maine-based series extends the PI genre with grace and grit and class. Don't sleep on this one! - **Richard Cass, author of the prizewinning** *Elder Darrow Jazz Mystery Series*

10 DAYS, A Dee Rommel Mystery

In *10 DAYS*, Dee Rommel shows herself to be nervy and relentless and it becomes absolutely necessary to hang in for the grand finale. - **Toronto Star**

"*10 DAYS* is a complex, well-constructed mystery that hooked me on Day 1. Selbo's characters, good and bad, are emotionally satisfying. And the pacing of the plot is spot on and full of surprises." - **John Lansing, best-selling author of the Jack Bertolino crime series**
"In Selbo's punchy, vivid prose, Dee is hard-boiled when she needs to be, but her injury gives her a vulnerability and interiority that deepen her. *10 DAYS* readers will root for her as she steps gamely into every peril. An entertaining, richly textured suspense yarn with a spirited hero." – **Starred * Kirkus Review**

Dedication

To Mark for 10,002.6 reasons – I'll roundup and make it 10,003 reasons

7 DAYS

CHAPTER ONE
Monday

"Mom, who's harassing you?"

My mother is petite, every blonde hair in perfect pageboy place, and she has blue eyes that can change from registering kindness, impatience or challenge in an instant. Her tailored St. John suit speaks to the meticulous determination that's always present. At this moment, as a frothy Boston Pops rendition of *Jingle Bells* provides the piped-in noise for our elevator ride – there's a tightening around her mouth. She flicks her eyes at Chester. "You weren't supposed to say anything."

"It's not to be ignored, Gayle," he says. Chester's super-protective, has been since their wedding three years ago.

My mom shakes her head. "She doesn't need to get involved, Chester."

"Saying nothing is not a good option," I tell her.

My mother only comes up to my shoulder, but her height (and charm) cannot cover her tough lady grit. She's a top administrator of the Cancer Research Center of Boston, speaks at conferences around the world about the importance of research support and has a way of convincing big donors to open their wallets. "We're here to celebrate your birthday week, Dee. Let's have a wonderful lunch." We get off the elevator and step into the Executive Dining Room, she smiles at the other well-dressed executives that pass by. They all know her, she's one of the foundation's bigwigs.

Chester Forbright fits right in too. He's sixty-five, has movie-star gray hair and skin that's leathered from summer sailing. He's from an old (and rich) Boston family. This morning, we met in the lobby of CRCB and I handed him my regular offering – a trio of glazed maple Holy Donuts. We had moved to the VIP Visitors' Desk, handed over our winter coats to the greeter, got our VIP badges and headed to the bank of elevators. He dropped his bombshell. "Your mother doesn't want me to tell you what I'm going to tell you," he said. "But she's become the target of a cyberbully-"

"My mother?"

He continued, "I want to take advantage of your expertise. You told us, you and Gordy, have had cases in Portland."

"True." G&Z Investigations has been hired to flush out cyber-stalkers, cyber-bullies and cyber-haters who make harassment the reason they wake up in the morning. Some of our clients cite it in the workplace, some are parents who want to find out who's bullying their kid through devices like cell phones, computers, tablets, games, or through the endless list of apps that can be misused to persecute. I do a happy dance when we can get the cops and DAs on board and get cases before a judge who will hand out fines, restraining orders, and jail time. This is the kind of criminal activity people can't have expunged from their records; it'll show up when they apply for jobs or loans or try to get someone to date them. One of our clients was Kali, a twelve-year-old (her parents paid our fee) who had won a Maine Kids poetry contest; she'd inadvertently beat out a fifteen-year-old who thought the prize was her destiny. Bullying social media posts began, and Kali was having a hard time coping; she'd stopped eating, she started cutting herself and swallowed too many of her mom's sleeping pills. Luckily her parents found her in time. When the misguided fifteen-year-old was brought before a judge, she dared to give excuses and said Kali was being a 'baby'. The judge sentenced her to six months in Long Creek Juvie. A tragedy anyway you look at it.

But my mother? She was the least deserving of animus. And plus, I would think she'd be protected by the security forces at CRCB. "Mom, what's this person's problem with you?"

My mother moves ahead to chat with the maître d. The Center's private restaurant has hosted Nobel Prize winners, Paul Marks Award champions, important visiting cancer researchers, politicians, and big pocket benefactors. They've been feted and schmoozed here while enjoying the views of Head Island and Dorchester Bay. White tablecloths, crystal glasses, and in a salute to the upcoming holidays, pine wreaths hang on the walls. We're seated at a table by the window. My mother re-straightens the perfectly straight goldplate flatware.

"He's a young man who didn't get the promotion he thought he deserved, and he's acting out," she explains. "We don't need to discuss it. I'm sure things will settle down."

"It's unprofessional," Chester says. "What if he becomes dangerous? He doesn't belong in this foundation."

"Chester, please." My mom touches his arm. "It's not productive to form judgements like that." She looks at me, changes the subject. "You look very nice."

This morning, to make my mom happy, I'd ignored my jeans, turtleneck and down vest and put on the pinstriped Calvin Klein suit she bought me last year and repacked the necessary contents of my catchall into the Coach Tote that was also last year's birthday present. I figured they would also impress at the posh Boston law firm, Latvey and Key, when I arrived at my early morning deposition. The firm hires G&Z Investigations when they need an investigator in Maine to ferret out information for their clients and today, I reported our findings on a Massachusetts contractor who tried to cover up a second wife and family in Stockholm, Maine – a small town near the Canadian border. I spent a week there, got photographs and video, DMV registrations, and neighbors' testimonies. I'd even visited the school where the bigamist sent his second set of cute kids.

Chester won't be sidetracked. "Gayle, this needs to be nipped in the bud, let Dee use her skills."

She pretends not to hear him. "Dee, honey, think about this big birthday. Friday– four days from now."

"It means you're getting closer to sixty."

"Age is nothing. It's what you've done and what you plan to do." She sips from her crystal water glass. "I'm sorry I have to go to London tomorrow and I'll miss the exact special day."

"Don't worry about it." I get back on topic. "Tell me how – why – this harassment started."

My mom sighs. "He thinks I promoted Amy to head of the department because she's a woman. And because she's Asian American and gay. That I chose to tick the diversity boxes instead of merit."

"True?"

"No. Amy earned her position."

"Was he senior in the department?" I ask.

"No. Actually, he and Amy started in Partnership the same day. Two years ago." She raises her chin. "He says his discrimination claim will include my bias against him because he -medically- tips the obese scale. He also insinuates that he was discounted because his parents are farmers in Iowa and not Mayflower descendants."

Boston is full of ancestral pomposity. I point out the obvious: "Mom, you're not a Mayflower descendant. And I'm assuming this 'Amy' isn't either."

"The young man is grabbing at straws," she says. "I'm sure he'll realize that, and it will stop."

Chester (he *is* a Mayflower descendant) puts his veined and generous hand over her smooth, small one and looks at me. "She hasn't been sleeping."

My mother moves the water glass a milli-inch to the right. I look at her more closely. She does look tired.

"You have a Human Resources department," I say. "What's HR's take?"

"I haven't shared this with them."

"Have you mentioned it to one of your in-house lawyers?"

"I'm giving it a little more time."

"Why?" I ask. "Why are you giving this person so much leeway?"

Something else is going on. What isn't she telling us?

I press. "Doesn't Tucker see all your digital communication?"

Tiny Tucker's been mom's private assistant for the last ten years – he enjoys being called 'Tiny' because he's almost seven feet tall. His life consists of worrying about his two Great Danes and my mother – organizing her calendar, rolling her phone calls, apprising her of relevant news stories and international exchanges on cancer research.

"I have a private DM line for those reporting directly to me. I haven't gotten Tucker involved."

Is she identifying with this Iowa person? When I was twelve, my mom, who had grown up on a farm in central Maine, worked her way through college and law school and dedicated her workdays to non-profits. She'd turned around a few failing foundations in Maine, helped them gather large charitable donations and move forward to become viable research hubs. This led to her being head-hunted for the position at CRCB. She and my dad thought the opportunity and challenge were too exciting to pass up - and my mom *is* ambitious. She tried commuting, daily, from Portland to Boston. That became untenable so she rented an apartment in Boston and became a weekend mom, did her best to show up on Friday nights for my basketball games, my softball games, my weekend track meets. Family time was squished into Saturdays and Sundays. My dad thought she walked on water; he said he was fine with it.

I was more resentful.

"Done talking about it, honey." She forces light and bright. "Now, I insist. As per tradition, only memories of Dee's childhood are allowed for the remainder of the lunch. Oh look, here's our champagne."

The maître'd is moving towards us with a bottle. He expertly pops the cork, pours the golden liquid into our flutes. We toast each other. "To your birthday week, honey," says my mom. "This morning, I thought about your fourth, when we went tobogganing and you drank so much hot chocolate you were sick." She laughs. "Your poor stomach – and the diarrhea."

"Come on," I groan.

"Was it your sixth birthday when you took a header on the ski slope at Sugarloaf?"

"You always remember the good times, Mom."

'Birthday week' became a tradition because, once she took the Boston job, her travel schedule increased. Given a full week's window, she could usually guarantee she'd be in Portland for at least one celebratory day. There was the exception - my twenty-seventh birthday. My father had died six years previously, so it was just mom and me. She spent the whole week - seven days - with me; I was in a hospital bed, facing the below-the-knee amputation of my left leg due to an on-the-job injury and wondering about leaving the police force, wondering what the rest of my life would be like. She organized doctors and surgeons, screened visitors and got contractors into my apartment to get it ready for new and unexpected needs. At the end of the week, she went back to Boston for one day to gather work and clothes (letting Gordy do the sitting by the bedside stuff) then she was back in Portland and stayed on my couch for an entire month. We didn't talk much. She connected to conference calls and WebEx for work, took me to the docs and Portland Prosthetics Clinic, ordered in food and we watched a hundred National Geographic documentaries. Finally, I convinced her I needed to be independent, and she needed to get back to her Boston life.

My mom's still talking, "…how you played the second to the left daisy in the ballet recital when you were eight and told me, with great seriousness, that you'd done the dance classes only to make me happy, but the ask had become too big, that you hated twirling and mincing and would rather be on the kiddie basketball team. You insisted we take your tutu to Goodwill."

Salads arrive and are placed in front of us. My mom had made the executive decision (she tends to do this) and pre-ordered. Salad, because she eats like a bird, because she's concerned about Chester's weight, and because she knows I have a habit of picking up a half dozen Holy Donuts when I drive down from Portland; three for Chester and, as I drive, I devour the others.

She went on, ad nauseam. Skating on the thick winter ice on Goose Lake, snowball fights, roaring fires in the fireplace. Chester, finally relaxing, grinned because he could tell she was happy, going over old times. My mother and I take small sips of champagne – she's going back to work, and I want to be sharp at my upcoming appointment. Chester indulges, he enjoys being retired and using a private car service when traveling around Boston.

Mom and I finish the meal with black coffee. As we leave the restaurant, Chester kisses my cheek. "You'll do something about this, I know you will."

Tucker's waiting for Mom in the foyer of the 20th floor. She's surprised when I wave goodbye to Chester and step off the elevator with her. "Did you want to talk more, Dee?"

"No. All birthday-memoried out. Just gonna hit the restroom – then I'm due at my next appointment."

"Is this more G&Z work?"

"It's personal."

She raises an eyebrow. I know she's hoping 'personal' might mean romantic. "Is your friend and his motorcycle back in the country?"

"No, mom."

"He's... interesting."

Non-committal. She pats my arm. "Honey, coming home to someone can take the sting off a long day. I want that for you – if you want it."

She's hoping I'll clarify any feelings. "I gotta go, Mom."

She looks wistful, desiring a more intimate interaction.

But she knows we don't do that. I don't do that.

"Love you, honey." She walks with Tiny Tucker toward her office - he's leaning down to her, discussing her schedule for the rest of the afternoon.

Mom didn't share the name of her harasser, but she may not be aware of how easy she made it to locate him. Info dropped: Partnership. That's probably the Partnership Department. Amy's name. Gender. Tipping towards obesity. Iowa. I remember noticing the map of the floor next to the elevator - there for the Fire Department in case of an emergency. I check it. Partnership is on the west end, half a football field away from my mother's office. I stride down the hallway; my VIP badge gets me smiles and nods and invites no questions.

The Partnership area is relatively small. There are cubicles in the center for interns and newbies, they're empty now, employees are probably at lunch. Offices are against one wall; each has a view of high-rises across the street. The largest one has a small plate on its door - 'Associate Director'. Someone's at the desk. This must be competent Amy. The next office is being used by a woman with large glasses - she's in her sixties; the name plate next to her door reads 'Merri Light'. Another office is uninhabited at the moment, but the pink tissue box and pink cardigan on the back of the chair makes me think it might belong to the mid-twenties woman in the pink dress that I saw going into the restroom. There's one more office, at the end of the row. An Iowa State Fair poster is on the wall. The nameplate reads 'Liam Grimshell'.

He's blond, wears tortoise-shell glasses. He has that dissatisfied, slightly-pissed look that descends on persons who think they always get the short end of the stick. Maybe his co-workers don't include him in after-work-happy-hour gatherings or ask him to hang at the food trucks on the street at lunch. He doesn't have a gym rat vibe – more of a couch-potato and big-bag potato-chip-eater look. His suit jacket hangs on one of those wooden, free-standing valet forms – this guy eats large and doesn't like wrinkles.

I head to the common area behind the cubicles to a buffet with a Keurig coffee maker, stirrers, sugars, and creamers. I appreciate the many flavors of coffee capsules, make sure I'm half-hidden by a pillar and use my cell phone to call the Cancer Research main switchboard. I ask to be connected to Liam Grimshell's extension.

His phone rings. I can watch him as he answers it.

"Grimshell here." His voice is high, doesn't match his heft.

I choose a name that's not an easy one to remember and speak fast. "Hello, I'm Marianna Celeste Brightonbaum, I'm from a group that's been hired to explore - using Anti-Defamation League guidelines – any episodes of harassment in the company's workplace."

He looks confused. "From where?"

"Private firm." I babble as if I'm reading from a prepared script: "We're hired to go through employees' digital communications. As you know, businesses can access all company's emails, direct messages, et cetera to monitor inappropriate use - as well as an employee's access to social media platforms, political and pornographic websites. All communications on the company's devices are property of said company and, in hiring us, said company protects against lawsuits down the line. I've been asked to do random check-ins and quick surveys."

"Wait. I haven't heard about this, isn't this something we have to be told about?" There it is, that nod to feeling picked on, being ignored, left uninformed.

I put a coffee capsule into the Keurig, choose the six-ounce pour option. "This is our first week in the building, I'll need thirty seconds for the survey." I get a little chatty. "Can you believe people have a bad habit of using digital means to spew thoughts, opinions, and concerns they should share only with a therapist? Don't they know that loose lips, loose fingers, loose respect for each other – basically anything put into cyberspace - cannot be hidden anymore?"

He's frowning. "I'm very busy," he says. "Maybe another time."

I go on as if I didn't hear him. "Do you Insta-?" I ask.

"Yes," he says, flummoxed. "But not on the company's computer."

"Do you Flit? Flitter?"

"Not a lot."

"Do you Friendline?"

"On my personal laptop. Not on the company's time. Or server."

"Do you Squeak, Freak and Bleep?"

"Ahhh-"

"Don't be embarrassed, if you graduated from college within the last decade, it's understood it was a fad to become detestably malignant online and that a lot of people perfected the practice."

"I don't-"

"Have your bosses assigned the Anti-Defamation League survey that covers cyber-hate and harassment?"

"No."

"Take comfort in the fact that federal and state harassment laws are in place. State laws are unique of course, but Massachusetts takes them seriously. My boss says he hired me because I have a nose to sleuth and the passion to prosecute. In my last job, I had two resignations the first day."

"People resigned?" His voice is a notch higher.

"Must've figured out it was better to resign and not have inappropriate behavior on their permanent employment record." I clear my throat as if I'm caught by surprise. "Well, over my thirty seconds. Let me tick you off on my list. Your name is 'Madson Rippen', correct? Extension 462?"

Now he really looks confused. "No. This is extension 642."

"Oh, my bad. I was assigned the 400 extensions. You may or may not get another call from a colleague, like I said, it's random. Anyway, thanks for your time."

I click off, continue to watch him from my vantage point. He hangs up, drums his fingertips on his desk. Then he reaches for the phone, looks like he's going to make a call. To verify the call was legit? He hesitates and puts the phone back on its cradle.

Let's see if he's a smart guy.

He stands, moves to the window, looks out. Doesn't move for a whole minute.

7 Days

A worker is coming back from lunch and heading to her cubicle with a takeout bag in hand. I adjust my VIP badge, grab my paper cup full of coffee and a few packets of sugar. I smile as I pass her and head to the elevator.

I descend to the lobby, retrieve my coat. And leave the building.

CHAPTER TWO

"*Terminator?*" I ask.

"Cyborg."

"*RoboCop?*" I ask.

"Cyborg. That's a human connected to robotic devices that are controlled by their own brain."

We're in Hogan's massive workplace at Claren Tech, just outside of Boston. The center, once an exciting nerve center, is now a ghost campus. No driverless vehicles sprint from building to building, no forward-thinking scientific advancements are being celebrated, no buzzing at all. Only one building is active: Brad Hogan's Bio-Mechanics Lab.

He hasn't changed in the year and a half since I've seen him. His hair – the color of mahogany – still curls on the collar of his blue denim work shirt. He's got on pressed dark jeans, the bottom half of the fabric tucked under the remains of his legs. The white-ish scar is there, breaking through his left eyebrow and crossing his face from temple to ear. Wait, there *is* a change. His green eyes, flecked with gold, are not as angry and aggressive as when I first met him. There's a calm.

"*Avatar?*" I ask as I'm rolling up my wide-legged Calvin Kleins.

"Jake Sully? In human form, he's a paraplegic, but when he's part of the experiment – he travels out of body to become a Na'vi, so he's able to run, fly, spin, fight, fall in love while inside a ten-foot-tall, rainbow-colored body. So, no *real science* involved, more 'fantasy'." Hogan shakes his head. "And I don't deal with fantasy."

"Doesn't a lot of new science start out as fantasy?" I ask.

"Ahhh." He laughs.

I doff my LiteGood prosthesis. He commands his power chair over to his worktable. My C-blade is before him - state-of-the-art - made of ninety layers of carbon fiber, with a shock absorbent rubber sole attached to the bottom of its curve; its shape is perfect for long distance running. Strength and flexibility off the charts. The blade's attached to a suction socket specially built for my residual limb. The whole appendage was out of my price range (close to twenty thousand dollars) but it's a Hogan design and I'm his lucky guinea pig. He's specifically fashioned it for my six-foot height, my weight, and limb measurement.

When I told him I was planning on running the Boston Marathon next September, he decided I'd benefit from a customized vacuum pump. He points to the small device he's attached to a C-blade near the ankle complex. "The pump will force a greater evacuation of air between your stump liner and the upper socket wall, give you more suction," he says. "The added eight ounces of weight will be negligible, and it should give you a stronger sense of solidity. Let's see how I did."

I don the blade and move off the exam table, bounce so my weight descends on the appendage. This activates the vacuum pump; the socket tightens around my residual limb. I walk around the room testing it, getting used to it.

"What about *Blade Runner*? Gordy and I argued about what the robots are called," I say.

"Replicants," he says. "I know your next question. Are cyborgs and replicants the same thing? No. What's Darth Vader? These are favorite discussions at lunch here in the lab. What's Terminator? What's Number Six? What's Iron Man? Are cybernetic organisms all bionic?"

"I'll leave that discussion to you all." I head to the treadmill.

"Heard Gordy's under the weather."

I peel off my suit jacket. "A bit. He'll be fine."

The machine's cranking, I quicken my stride until I'm jogging. He's right - the vacuum pump addition makes my stride feel more solid.

I speak above my footfalls, above the hum of the treadmill. "Not sure I want to introduce AI into my body."

"My goal? Give amputees back a sense of wholeness. We're working on a new surgical method to implant bionic sensors at the time of amputation - so brain-to-muscle signals can be sent immediately, and the robotic appendage can react accordingly."

"That's sci-fi."

"No. It's near-possibility. Control of the appendage is the goal. You like control."

I laugh. "Most people do. I don't want a lot of neurolinks in me. Don't want someone to be able to access my brain."

He laughs. "That's the horror movie version."

I punch in commands to get the treadmill to slow and come to a stop. Next to me is a glass case, a series of tiny chips showcased on black fabric. "Those are the neuro chips that could make me bionic?"

He offers a hand, and I step off the machine. "Those are examples of what's being used in Scandinavia. So, people don't have to carry their gym cards or e-ticket train cards or office access cards; they get the chips implanted in their bodies. Machines read the chips."

"Not for me."

"Change can be good."

"Mmmm." I release the C-blade, hand it to him. "I'm at the track four times a week. Wendy's got me on a good mileage plan to get me ready for Boston."

"Keep sending me updates." He smirks. "Gordy had to tell me you passed the PI test."

"Yeah."

"Congrats. He was proud."

He glides his chair over to his worktable, sets the C-blade on a soft, non-abrasive cloth. "You should be good to go."

I don my LiteGood. I want to ask if he's a candidate for neurolink implants, but it feels intrusive. He's a private person, all I know is that ten years ago, as part of a Military Intelligence crew outside of Kabul, his vehicle ran over an IED stuffed with crap – literally. Taliban added feces and rotting animal innards inside the explosives so if the target didn't immediately perish, infection wouldn't be far away. Hogan was the only one in his truck who survived. He got airlifted out, weathered nine surgeries, spent the next year in the hospital, then dedicated his time to making life better for veterans in the same situation as himself.

We head out of the lab and the building, move through the too-quiet campus. "How's Lucy?" I ask.

His face lights up. "We're engaged."

"What? That's great!"

"She asked me first. I said 'no'."

"Why?"

"Wanted to give her the room to think about doing better."

I get it - the questions about attractiveness and acceptance, there's the desire to not be pitied. He wonders why Lucy Claren, an heiress - and a tech wonder wants to marry him.

"Have you talked to her?" He asks.

"No."

Lucy's reaction, after her kidnapping and then the rescue G&Z orchestrated, was to become isolated. But she's still on the list of America's most eligible bachelorettes, there are probably men lining up to get her attention.

Hogan continues, "She said she'd accept my answer, but she also built me a lab next to her in the new place, filled closets in her guest house with my clothes and added my name to her private jet roster. She made me promise to show up every Thursday for spaghetti night and presented me with a calendar of when we'd have kids."

I laugh. "She's become more assertive."

"She says she knows now that life's too short not to be."

"I guess."

"I had to agree." He grins. "Three weeks later, when she was dishing up spaghetti, I asked her. Got an immediate 'yes'."

"Congratulations!"

"I got a second chance. We figured, we both did. You and Gordy are invited to the wedding."

"Where will the happy event take place?"

"We'll let you know."

The Claren Tech secrecy. The laying low. Sharing their work only when they feel they can control *who* gets it, and control *how* it's used.

I get into my car. "I've seen you two together. It looks like a very good thing."

"I'm a lucky guy," he says, tapping the hood of my car. "Keep yourself open to new science, Dee. To future possibilities. In life and limb."

***

I'm on I-95, heading north. Not sure why passing the *Welcome to Maine - The Way Life Should Be* highway sign always makes me breathe easier. I tap on my dash phone, connect to my mother's home landline. Chester answers. "Hello, Dee. Your mother's changing for the evening, we're headed to the ballet. Should I tell her you're on the phone?"

"No need. Did she mention if another inappropriate message came in?"

"I asked. She said 'no'. Did you find out his name?"

"Yep."

"Tell me?" he asks.

"Not a good idea."

"At least tell me what you did."

"Better not get into details. Mom would know you're keeping things from her."

"Probably."

"For some reason she's being protective of him. You know why?"

"No." He sighs. "You're a good daughter, Dee. Are you back in Portland?"

"Not yet," I say. "I had an errand to do north of Boston, so I'm on the highway now."

A dark cloud has opened, and cold December rain plummets to the earth. My windshield is suddenly heavy with water, my wipers strain against the weight.

"Come down and stay a few days next time," Chester's saying. "I need a few killer backgammon games."

"I'll try. Bye." I click off.

My mother's inaction worries me. Why would she allow herself to be used as a punching bag by Liam Grimshell?

CHAPTER THREE

Another hour of driving and I'm passing South Portland's Maine Mall. It's just after nine and my stomach's growling. Sparrows, my neighborhood haunt, will be packed – it's Monday Night Football, the Patriots are playing – and I just want to eat and then hunker down in front of the fireplace in my apartment and start a *CanFindAnyone* search on Liam Grimshell.

But the refrigerator at my apartment is empty. For most of the summer, Reader had kept it full. Pickles, olives, usually roasted chicken. My mom's words play through my mind - the ones about 'coming home to someone can make a hard day seem less so'. Mmm. Food-wise, I guess that's true. Reader left in late August, said he wanted to get to Scandinavia in time for some touring before the first snowfalls. He'd asked me to take a few months off from G&Z Investigations and travel with him. I wasn't ready to do that, I had a private investigator test to pass and Gordy and I had cases to bring to conclusion. And I didn't want to miss Maine's autumn colors. I did go to Boston to see him off. That's where I met Brigid Berger. She looked like a female version of Reader - dark hair in a ponytail, long legs, toned and dedicated to adventure. Reader's Harley Road King, with batwing fairing and Ground Zero speakers looked good next to Brigid's Softail Deluxe, customized for a low ride. She explained she was a 'wanderer' too – and it turned out, (news to me) Reader and Brigid had a habit of meeting up in different places around the world. They'd done Thailand, Vietnam, Germany, Poland, Croatia and Greece. Now the plan was for them to get onto the cargo ship to Norway. Neither found luxurious accommodations necessary, all they needed was transport for themselves, their motorcycles, and berths with reading lights.

Reader's habit of sending postcards continued every week for two months, but it's tapered off. He didn't make it back to Portland for his uncle's annual Thanksgiving feast.

7 Days

He doesn't like to plan. He'll show up. Or not.

I take the first exit in Portland and a minute later, I'm looking at the rain falling in front of a neon sign in the shape of a giant fish. It belongs to Letty's Diner, a local eatery nestled on the Holyoke Wharf next to fishing boats and stacks of lobster traps. I hold my Coach Tote over my head as I rush inside. Allison, the waitress on the late shift, waves. "We're on last call. Usual?"

"Sounds good."

The home-cooking hangout is divided into two spaces - booths and a long counter on one side of a half wall, free-standing tables on the other. The side with tables is filled, someone's having a retirement party and they're on their final toasting. The counter's empty, and I land on my favorite stool. There's a mirror on the header wall and there's my reflection. I've replaced my Calvin Klein suit jacket with a fleece pullover, my hair's slipped out of its tie-back. Allison puts my fish plate in front of me: scallops, shrimp, oysters, haddock, and a side of home fries. A lot more filling than my lunch salad. I squeeze some Captain Mowatt's Canceaux Sauce over the whole thing.

"You're a worm," the woman in a booth behind me is saying. "Your neck's wet and Jello-ee slick and you have that mouth that's so little it's like you're hiding your tiny teeth and tiny tongue. You have a Voldemort nose."

Her voice is flat – and it carries. I look up into the mirror, catch sight of her. She's cubic. Square head. Flat hair that's been cut to frame a box-shaped face. The couple is too interested in each other to notice me.

"What's a Voldemort?" he asks.

She mimics him cruelly. "*Who's* Voldemort. Ahhgg. The villain in Harry Potter, stupid. He's got slits for nostrils," she says. "Worms don't have nostrils, but snakes do, so maybe you're a worm snake."

Allison's at the massive coffee urn, dumping the grounds into a compost bucket. Our eyes meet, she mouths 'weird' at me.

The guy looks up from the menu. "Gilli, did you take your meds? Sometimes you tell me you have, but really, you've forgotten. Finish your dessert." She's got a dish of ice cream in front of her. The strawberry frozen treat, surrounded by thick hot fudge, is melting and the spray of whipped cream on the top is about to topple.

Her oversized flannel bag is on the booth's table, leaning against the window. He reaches inside it and takes out a vial. "Babe, you're not eating your hot fudge." He extracts a gelatin capsule from the vial, dips it into the chocolate, holds it up between his fingers.

Gilli stares at the capsule. The thick chocolate drips off it. She opens her mouth, lets him put it on her tongue. He picks up his spoon, gathers ice cream and she lets him feed her. There's something going on under the table, some foot to crotch action.

"Ah Gilli, you are a vixen," he says. He doesn't notice Gilli wipe a napkin across her mouth and dispel the pill because he's waving to Allison. "Check, please."

Allison hustles over and drops it on the table. A hundred-dollar bill is offered, Allison dips into her fanny pack and makes change – three twenties and a few singles.

"Name's Nail." The man looks up at Allison. "Like hammer and nail."

Allison gives a practiced smile. "Have a nice night."

Gilli wraps a wool scarf twice around her thick neck. Her eyelids look heavy. "You're gonna slither out of here on your belly and worm your way into my place and into my refrigerator and my butter and my beer." She grabs hold of the table knife and jabs it at him. Not exactly playfully. Allison's tired of them. She goes to the wall, pulses the light switch. "Have a great night, customers. We're closing now and we wish you all a very nice evening."

The retirement party on the other side of the restaurant shuffles out. I don't recognize any of them – it's - December, not exactly tourist season, but Portland's been growing fast lately and new faces and new agendas have moved into town.

My eye catches an odd movement in the mirror. Did I just see Gilli slipping a Letty's knife, fork and spoon into her bag?

Nail stands and blocks my view. He *is* sort of snakey/worm-ish. Tall, thin, pasty-faced. Bone structure and muscles do not dominate – he's soft and 'dewy'. His mouth *is* small and pursed. He grabs his jacket; it's beigy-white, the color of a maggot. Gilli gets up too, she wears wool socks that go to mid-thigh, a mini-skirt that's tight on her wide hips and faux-leopard kick boots. Looks like she hasn't brought a jacket – must be one of those Mainers who won't wear fleece or down or wool if it's not twenty degrees below freezing.

Nail strides to open the door for her. "Gilli, you're over-tired. I'll drive."

"Fuck you," she says, grabs a plastic menu, hugs it to her chest and stumbles out.

They're gone.

Allison breathes a sigh of relief. "And someone told me a perk of waitressing is meeting all kinds of nice people."

"Must be the same person who told me relationships are good for you," I say.

"How come people can't just be nice to each other?"

Neither of us have a good answer.

I bite into my last diver-caught sea scallop. It's still warm. December's the start of scallop season, these were probably harvested from beds an hour or so out of the city. Tasty.

"Big plans tonight?" asks Allison.

I pay my bill. "Got some research to do. Some case files to read."

"I'm meeting people at Wandering Moose. Karaoke, if you want to join-"

I sling the strap of my bag over my shoulder. "Thanks. Not tonight."

Allison dances as she wipes down the counter. "I start with Cardi B, move on to Taylor Swift, and finish the night with Beyonce."

"Go kill it."

The vestibule of Letty's offers a last moment of warmth before stepping into the wet that's turned to an icy sleet that can prick flesh. I grab a knit hat and gloves from my bag, pull them on. It's a ten-minute drive to my apartment, eleven minutes to turning on the gas fireplace. Just need to get in the car and go. I slip out onto the concrete deck.

Gilli's got the hatch open on her electric blue Lexus GX. She's bending in, her short skirt is riding up, so I see the tops of her thighs - what the over-the-knee socks don't cover. She leans in farther; I see her flat butt cheeks and the lacy floss of the thong that travels up her crack. Nail stands close, he's checking something on his phone. Suddenly Gilli straightens, she's got a baseball bat in hand, she whips it back to gather power and *"Yeoow!"* She swings the bat and hits Nail on his shoulder.

"Crap!" He staggers. She's coming at him again – this time landing a wallop on his hip. This takes him to his knees - he steadies himself on the hood of my car. She's got another swing in motion, this one's headed to his neck, but he gets his arm up in time and the bat cracks against his lower radius. Did I hear a bone crack?

"Hey! Stop!" I grab my bag off my shoulder - pitch it so its weight flies. I hit my mark, the bag smacks Gilli's chest. Her chin flips back, the bat drops to the ground, clanks on the blacktop, and rolls towards me. I grab onto the deck's railing, shoot my LiteGood out to the side so I can bend to pick it up, cursing that both knees won't work the way they used to. I open the diner door and fling the bat into the vestibule.

"Allison!" I yell.

Gilli's huffing, pulling her hair back off her face. There's a wild look in her eyes. She picks my Coach Tote up off the ground, strides to her Lexus and hurls it into the back and slams the hatch shut.

"Don't fuckin' take my bag!" I yell and lumber towards the car.

She whips her head back and screams a series of vowels at high register. The high heels of her faux-leopard boots slip on the wet pavement as she plops into the driver's seat, slams the gears into reverse and backs up - fast. I lunge out of the way, lose balance, and land on my butt. Still screaming, Gilli steers out of the parking lot and takes a right on Commercial Street. She and my bag (with apartment keys, my car fob, cash stash, one credit card, notebook, Visine, hair band and ID) are gone.

Faauuuuck.

Allison's rapping on the diner's window – she's on the phone. She better be calling the cops. The wind gusts, a shard of numbing frost hits my eyeball. "Shit." I fast-blink to accelerate its melt. I'm close enough to the deck railing to grab hold and use it to hoist myself up and get my LiteGood under me. I hoof it to Nail's side. Sweat and ice pellets merge on his face, it's like a waterfall gushing down from the top of his bald head.

"I thought I heard a bone break," I say.

He's cradling his arm. "She gets upset."

"Your name's Nail?"

"Like hammer and-" The same half-joke, but this time his tiny mouth is not smiling.

"Nail what?"

"Parcell."

Allison pushes the door open. "Coming back inside?"

"Come on." I put my hand out to help Nail up and usher him inside. "What's Gilli's last name?" I want info before the cops arrive – maybe I can add to my chances of getting my bag back without going through paperwork.

"Wanz. That's with a 'z' at the end. W. A. N. Z."

I get Nail to sit in the first booth. "Address?"

"52 Kahta. On the second floor."

Kahta's a new street in midtown Portland. A few years ago, three blocks of down-at-the-heels apartment buildings were demolished, and thirty-two new condos replaced them. They sold fast – at over a million dollars per unit. Someone got rich and others became homeless.

"Why would she take my bag?" I ask.

"She gets upset."

I wonder if those words are inscribed in Gilli's high school yearbook, if they're on whatever resume she might have, if they're tattooed on her ass. Maybe it'll be on her gravestone.

***

Two police cars and a small ambulance are in Letty's parking lot. Three cops have come inside to get a bead on what went down, one officer is stationed at the entry to make sure no one else enters.

It's quickly determined the two cooks and dishwasher didn't see anything; they're allowed to go home. Elliot, the manager, who had been upstairs in the office going over the day's receipts and was thus unaware of the odd behavior inside and the kerfuffle outside, tries to be patient but he knows he needs to be back early in the morning and he's tired. Allison and I have already shared with Officer Pavin, one of Gordy's poker buddies. Officer Daewon Pocket (he's serious dating my friend Gretchen) is still with Nail.

"I'm not pressing charges," says Nail.

"You sure about that, sir?" asks Pocket.

"Why do you have an accent?" Nail asks.

"Born in Cuba," says Pocket.

"How long have you been a US citizen?"

"Ten years."

"So, you're a real cop?"

"Yes, Mr. Parcell, I am."

"You sure you know the American constitution and not the Cuban one?"

Pocket doesn't take the bait. "We'll get you to the ER, Mr. Parcell."

"Ten years. You shouldn't still have an accent. Did the government review your background thoroughly?"

Pocket's a patient guy but Nail's not making it easy. The medic gets Nail's good arm out of his jacket and carefully maneuvers the injured one out of the other sleeve. There are heavy sweat stains on Nail's shirt.

"We'll need an X-ray to see what's what," the medic mumbles.

Nail's squishy body stiffens against the pain. "I'm okay. I should go find Gilli. She'll need me."

"Not until you get this arm checked out," says Pocket. "We'll want an official medical report."

"I said I'm not pressing charges against my girlfriend," says Nail.

Pocket closes his notebook. "Might be time to re-evaluate that girlfriend status."

"Maybe she didn't take her meds on time. That's not a crime. She's really a very good person."

"This way, sir," says the medic.

Nail's eyes harden, not happy he can't get his way, but he capitulates. A minute later, he's wearing a Mercy Hospital knit hat, walking under a supersized umbrella, and allowing himself to be ushered into the back of the ambulance. The vehicle drives off.

Elliot and Allison execute closing-for-the-night details.

Pocket and I stand in the warm vestibule; he's on the phone. He clicks off. "The team at Kahta Street says there's no sign of Gilli Wanz. No car, no one in the condo."

"Damn."

7 Days

"I'll write up a report on your stolen bag," says Pocket. He tears a page out of his notebook. "Describe it, the contents."

He doesn't have to share that the chances of retrieval are low, that — statistically - under twenty percent of stolen bags and purses are ever found. Slash and grabs, snatch and runs are maddening. Not sure I've seen a bag-used-as-a-weapon-and-steal before. But there it is. My plan to head home, do some research on Liam Grimshell, and get some sleep has been upended. Now I have a credit card to cancel, an alert to my bank about the loss of my ATM card, and I'll figure out how to schedule a DMV visit to replace my license. The idea of someone being able to access my personal data stings. Shit. My keys don't have identity tags on them, but I'll still get locks changed. What else haven't I thought of?

Why would Gilli Wanz take my bag?

"You got a hide-a-key at your place?" asks Pocket.

"Gordy's got my extra set. Can you drop me there?"

CHAPTER FOUR

It's after ten, but there are lights on in the living room. As I climb the steps to the narrow porch, two dogs erupt into barking frenzies. Furry heads appear in the window; there's Bert – Gordy's gentle labradoodle - the other yipper is a brown and white spotted beagle. His name is Thor - he and Detective Robbie Donato are roommates. My chest tightens and it grates on me that I can still react like a crusher when our paths cross unexpectedly.

Marie, Gordy's main squeeze, peeks out the window. Her hair is up in a topknot, her glasses are down on the tip of her nose. "It's Dee," she announces and moves to the door. The smell of lasagna wafts over me when she opens it.

"Italian night?" I ask.

"Always," says Marie. Her pretty smile looks tired. "*Manga*?"

"Just ate."

Marie, not really listening, heads to the kitchen as the two dogs sniff my shoes and lick my hands. I buff their necks and step into the living room. There's Gordy and Donato, sitting side by side on the newly upholstered couch. The fabric is full of yellow and red roses and the two guys, dressed in winter-brown sweaters and corduroys, look a bit like tree trunks with heads.

"Hey Rommel," says Donato. He swallows the last bite of his lasagna.

Gordy grabs the remote. "Patriots - fourth quarter, two touchdowns ahead." He puts the game on mute. "How was Boston? The deposition?"

"Done and dusted," I say. "I texted you."

"Oh. Yeah. Saw that. Write it up."

"I always do."

"Give your mother a 'hey' for me?"

Gordy and my dad grew up together, were always best friends. When my mom entered the picture in college, they became a buddy trio. She appreciates Gordy, especially because he takes his godfather promises seriously.

7 Days

"She says 'back at ya' and to get a lot of rest." I decide not to bring up the harassment, figure I'll get more research on Liam Grimshell first, and not add to Gordy's list of things to think about. His new medication is in play; the previous one made him sleepy, this one's got him more restless, nosey, impatient and sometimes manic.

"What about Latvey and Key?" Gordy asks. "They have more work for us?"

"Didn't mention it."

"Those are the relationships you want to focus on - where the reliable money comes from-"

"I do the books, Gordy, don't need a business lesson."

He grunts.

"It's all good," I say. "We did excellent work, it was appreciated." I turn to Donato, "What're you doing here?"

Gordy gets defensive. "I'm allowed to have friends drop in to see me."

"Get up on the wrong side of the universe?" I ask.

Gordy grunts. Despite (or maybe because) of his curmudgeon persona, people get a kick out of hanging with Gordy. He was once the boxing champion of New England (had a famous right punch) then a boxing coach and mentor to a lot of community kids who needed to learn to defend themselves. Brawn, hating bullies, a stint in the Army as a security officer, plus an ability to read people and notice details led him to being a private investigator. He knows the ins and outs of Portland's history, politics, and people and has been privy to a lot of secrets. He has a reputation for keeping confidences. Makes sense he's got friends who appreciate him, some who owe him, a lot who have benefited from his knowledge and generosity.

"Wanted to do a Gordy-health-and-well-being check," Donato says. "I drove by and saw the lights on-"

I haven't seen Donato much this fall. He always has a heavy caseload and now, when he can take a day or two off, he drives to Philadelphia to see his son. The little guy must be seven or eight months old by this time.

"You fussin' over me too?" Gordy asks me.

He looks a bit grayer. Maybe it's the light from the stalled tv image. Maybe it is the new meds. Dr. Boroughs has been doing more tests. I push off the worry. "No, not here to see if you've eaten your pasta."

I fill them in on the whacko domestic squabble at Letty's.

"What the hell?" says Donato.

"You stayed clear of it?" asks Gordy.

"Well, I threw my bag at the woman to stop her beating up the guy. And she drove away with it – my bag. My keys are in it, and you, Gordy, have my extra set."

Donato's calling into the PPD station, wanting to hear any update on Gilli Wanz. He's told he'll be called back. "Yeah. Soon as you get something," he says and hangs up. He turns to me. "Who's on it?"

"Pocket," I say.

"Stay clear of it," says Gordy. "And your keys are in the same place." He waves to the cabinet that displays his grandmother's collection of Maine Watershed Pottery. Gordy never uses it but when Marie, who started redecorating when she moved in a year ago, suggested she could pack it up and store the four dozen pieces in the basement, he growled that some things were sacrosanct. Gordy'll put up with sitting on chintzy flowery fabric for Marie, but his grandmother's pottery stays put. I grab my keys from the square, green-glazed coffee cup on the second shelf. "Got 'em."

I'm almost smacked by the kitchen's swinging door. Marie's coming out with a plate covered in foil. "Take the lasagna home, *brava ragazza*, that's what refrigerators are for. When you heat it up, no microwave. Heat it in the oven."

"Sure." I choose the easy reply because Marie won't be at my place to see me eat it cold for breakfast. I head to the door. "Got some things I need to do. You all go back to the game."

Donato whistles for Thor. "Time for us to go too." The beagle, chewing on one of Bert's toys, bounces up. Donato unfolds his long thin body, stands, and pulls on his scarf and L.L. Bean He-Man jacket. He takes Thor's leash out of the pocket.

"Five minutes left in the game," says Gordy.

"I think we know who's gonna win," laughs Donato.

"*Buona notte, cose dolci*, young sweet things with your lives ahead of you." Marie already has the door open. "Good night."

We step out onto Gordy's porch; the door closes behind us.

Donato raises his eyebrows. "She couldn't get rid of us fast enough."

"She likes to have Gordy to herself at the end of the day."

The icy rain has stopped, and the night air's getting colder. "You hiding something?" asks Donato. "You sure you didn't get hurt?"

"Not hiding anything. Not hurt."

Donato puts his PPD cap atop his head to hold in some body heat, I plop on my red knit. Next are our gloves. He stomps his boots on the porch, waking up his legs. "Snow's coming, I predict it," he says.

"I could go for some." A mumbled statement that sounds inane. Damn.

"Wanna ride back to Letty's?"

"They've already closed the gate on the parking lot. Car'll be fine 'til morning. Just gonna walk home."

"Thor wouldn't mind a walk. How about we keep you company?"

It's so easy for him. So casual. I want to make it clear that being alone with him, like this, is not a big thing for me either. "Whatever." We walk as my hyper-sensitivity descends, that familiar, vulnerable feeling when I'm not prepared to see him. I watch what I say, how I say it, do my best to not look too interested, to not look weak. To make it clear that I absolutely accept the 'friend' status he relegated our relationship to when he found out his ex-girlfriend was pregnant, and he was going to be a father. "Have you seen Dude lately?" I ask.

"Came back from Philadelphia this morning. He's twenty-five pounds now. A bruiser."

"Chubby?" I stuff my gloved hands deeper into my pocket and wish I had a scarf.

"Christine likes to call him 'long'. As soon as he gets on his feet, I think she'll start saying 'tall'."

Donato's ex and mother of Dude (real name Cosmo, Donato prefers 'Dude') is a former Portland news anchor, now a prime-timer in Philly and newly married to a rich dentist who seems to put up with Donato's frequent visits. We turn on Congress Street, head towards the water. "Thor likes having a little brother?" I ask.

"They're pals. Already, they're pals." He's serious and sounds gratified as if this was a top priority.

A sliver of moon ekes through the clouds. We reach Eastern Promenade. Most people are cocooned in their homes, soft lights are in windows and tv screens are on. My apartment's two blocks away but Donato puts his hand on my elbow and guides me across the wide street that hugs the park. "Thor likes to run down the hill," he says, pointing to the slope that leads to the East End beach and the white caps on Casco Bay.

We pass the empty basketball court. When I was at the Police Academy and Donato was one of the instructors, we played on the same team. We perfected a pass assist that usually ended with my successful hook shot.

Donato lets Thor off the leash. The dog bounds down the hill, pivots and slips on the slick ground, bounds back up to us, pivots and slips, races back down and loses his footing, slides into a Civil War historic marker. He's stunned for a moment, then barks at the obstacle as if expecting it wants to play with him. When there's no response, he raises his leg to pay his respects.

"Congrats on passing your PI license test," says Donato. "Pat said it was a good party at Sparrows."

"Yeah. Got a Sherlock Holmes hat, a magnifying glass and a shoe made of gum."

"I was in Philly," he explains. "With Dude."

Had I expected him to show? Hoped for it?

It had felt like an accomplishment. I'd met basic requirements – being a US citizen, having a college degree. My Police Academy diploma and a year on the force helped expedite my application, but passing the written test, the firearms test, and getting the green light from the Maine State Police after they completed their background check felt good.

"All that's left is to save up for the surety bond and insurance. I gotta have that in place before I'm official."

"Big fees, I assume."

"Oh yeah." Bigger than I can swing at the moment.

"Most PIs I know take out a loan. Pay it off."

"I want to do it clean."

"Or you don't want to put a button on it. Feels too finite."

No comment.

"So, Gordy stays solo on the letterhead for a little longer."

"Not sure he's even considering an official partnership. Only thing that'd be different is I'd be able to initiate cases."

"He respects you. He relies on you."

Nice words but I deflect. "It's mutual, I guess."

There's a long moment. And a gust of wind. He unwinds his scarf and holds it out to me.

"No, I'm fine-" I say.

"Take it. I've got thicker skin. Besides, I need to talk to you about something." He drapes it around my neck. It smells like the soap and shaving cream he uses.

I back up a few steps. "Is it about the real reason you stopped by Gordy's?"

Donato smiles, it's crooked - one side of his lips rises higher than the other. "You don't miss anything."

"You have a 'tell'."

He narrows his eyes. "What is it?"

"If I told you, you might work on erasing it."

"I don't have a 'tell'. You just think you're smart."

"It's showing right now."

"Geez, Rommel, you never give an inch."

My mother suggested, when Donato and I were seeing each other for those short few weeks before he found out Christine was pregnant, that I mention he could call me by my first name. I never broached it then, and there's no reason to anymore.

"Okay. I did want to see how Gordy was, but I needed some insight too. On you."

"Me?"

"I wanted his opinion. If you'd want to hear this from me – or through the grapevine."

"Hear what?"

"Billy Payer asked for a meet-up."

A drumming explodes in my ears – my heart beats faster.

Billy Payer, a Portland bad boy, is serving a thirty-year sentence on three charges: for the murder of his brother, kidnapping me and the assault of one of my best friends. He's residing in the Maine State Prison in Warren, the state's maximum-security facility that houses Class A and B felons. It's not a warm and fuzzy place - over 400 guards keep tight tabs on more than 900 deserving-of-shit inmates.

"We decided you wouldn't want to hear it through any grapevine."

That pisses me off – that he and Gordy felt it was in their purview to decide what was best for me. "Last time I checked, I was a grown-up."

"No need to get on a high horse."

Now he's really annoying, but at least my hypersensitivity has flown. We're two pros with agendas, jockeying for information. "What about Payer?"

"Payer says he's got information on a case."

"What case?"

"Not at liberty to discuss."

Donato's all about protocol, all about being worthy of oaths and ethics and trust. In all areas of his life. Admirable, sure, but sometimes it's like a brick wall he's built around himself.

"That little bit of information feels like a tease," I say.

"Sorry about that," he says. "A case may be about to re-open, that's all I can say. But - okay. This is what I can tell you: Payer wants a deal. He says he'll share what he knows about the case if it gets him closer to a transfer to a prison in Florida."

"Florida? What does he want, a suntan?"

"The warden says Payer's been laying the groundwork for the last year – he went through the drug clean-up program, signed up to see a shrink, avoids socializing with the felons who used to be his mates. Keeps telling the admin he's turning his life around."

"Is he convincing anyone?"

"With yoga classes and Bible study? By seeking out Pell and PEP attention, by finding a prison in Florida that offers classes for a bachelor's degree in public welfare and social work?"

"Social work? Payer would never want to help anyone."

Donato continues, "He's even cultivated a pen pal - some professor in Tallahassee. She's in community development and has stipulated she's willing to act as a tutor and a kind of sponsor."

I bet. Payer has an angelic face, a hard body and dangerous charm. My friend Karla made the mistake of falling for the swagger; he beat her and arranged her gang rape. She's still living as a shut-in with her parents almost two years later, unable to engage in the world. I shake my head. "He's got a long sentence; he may not have all his teeth when he gets out. What's the professor's expectation?"

"She says it's platonic. That she's impressed with his dedication to change. And the fact remains, the prison admin has to show that it takes a serious look at a convict's interest in betterment and higher education. Transfers to a different institution can be part of that."

Damn. Payer's always angling.

We're leaving a lot unsaid. I did have to deal with the sadist. And afterwards, Donato sat at the hospital, by my side, for days. And then he put together an airtight case against Payer. We'd gotten him.

He continues, "Whatcha thinking?"

Do I think life would be better if Payer was out of Maine? There's something fine about that option. On the other hand, do I want him to feel trapped and future-less, cooped in a drafty prison that stinks of grease, toe-jam and farts and only be able to feel a few warm rays of sunshine during Maine's short, unpredictable summers?

"Have an opinion?" he says.

"Look, if you need Payer to break a case – you're gonna use him." Donato won't miss the chance. I understand him telling me is just about lightening a blow. I level my gaze at him. "But if his snitching earns him a trip to a sunnier prison - can you guarantee he'll get eaten by an alligator?"

He laughs. Snowflakes, wet and heavy, drub against our faces. Now that Donato's told me what he needed to tell me, it's silly standing in the elements. I point to my place. "I have work to do tonight."

"Better be careful. You'll turn out like me – all work and no..."

The unfinished sentence hangs. And he's standing too close. He steps back and whistles for Thor. The three of us head across the wide street to the large Victorian home that's been divided into apartments. Mine is the smallest and it's at street level (converted from the former kitchen and servants' quarters). "Whatcha working on?" he says.

"Not at liberty to say," I tell him.

He grins. "Ah, Rommel. You never quit." We stop at the spot where the public sidewalk meets the private brick path. A year and a half ago, I would've been inviting him in.

As if reading my thoughts, he mumbles, "I better get going, I'm going up to Augusta early to see the new forensic pathologist - early."

"'Cause of this about-to-be- reopened case?"

"With the changing of the guard in the morgue, things got slowed up."

"Okay."

"Then I'll head to Warren to see Payer."

"Well. Night," I say.

Thor yips, rises on his hind legs and leans his front paws on my thigh. I give him a good-bye scruff. "You're cold, aren't you, buddy."

Donato picks him up, holds him over his shoulder like he's burping a kid. Thor nuzzles into his neck. "Rommel, one more thing," says Donato.

"Yeah?"

"Hear there's a birthday coming up."

Is he referring to mine? Seems like it.

"No biggie," I say. "Everyone has one once a year."

"You have special plans? Your motorcycle guy coming back into town?"

The 'motorcycle guy' is the nephew of Pat, the owner of Sparrows, the neighborhood's eatery where I do most of my eating and drinking. The leather jacket, thick boots, ponytail, and Harvard educated motorcycle guy showed up in Portland just about the time Donato decided he only had room in his life for his work and his son.

I shrug. "Last time I heard from him he was riding around Scandinavia with a woman named Brigid."

"Oh? Brigid? That's okay with you?" He waits for more information. But it's none of his business. He continues, "Did he want you to go with him?"

"I've got responsibilities here."

"So you turned him down."

I change the subject. "Birthdays aren't that big for me. Gretch and I watch movies and eat junk food on our birthdays. It's our tradition."

He nods. "Traditions are good."

"That's why they're traditions, I guess. Night."

Placing my fine foot and my fake foot carefully on the walk is now a priority. When it's wet and wintry, bricks get slippery, and I don't want to risk a misstep when Donato and Thor are watching. I turn to look back – Donato waves and they walk off.

Three locks release the final barrier and give me entry. I re-attach the locks, pull my curtains closed - habits that started when Billy Payer first started targeting me. I hang my jacket on the hook near the door and realize I've still got Donato's scarf. I'll drop it off at the Middle Street station. He'll get it. Sometime.

* * *

The day's gone from predictable to shitty to shittier. All sorts of disturbing rubble's been piling atop each other, all in one long day. Liam Grimshell. My mother's caginess. Hogan's challenge to stay open about blending my body with the latest technology, reminding me to not get stuck. The sick vibes of Nail and Gilli. My stolen bag. Gordy looking grayer. Donato - how he makes me want more from him and how I resent that. His news on Billy Payer, the asshole with the sunny smile and black heart who enjoys creating terror and inflicting pain. Donato was simply a courtesy sharer of information – but it was more like a reminder that I can't control fate.

I flip the switch on the fireplace, the gas flares. No choice but to take things one at a time. First, make those tiresome calls to cancel my one and only credit card and put a hold on my ATM card.

Done.

I pour two fingers of Rittenhouse. The rye's perfume is bitter. Fits my mood. The short hallway leads to my chilly bedroom, and I adjust the thermostat and lean into the bathroom to turn the shower onto maximum heat – I want it to be steamy. I peel off my clothes, doff the LiteGood, place the prosthetic against the chair, hop to my waterproof iWalk and use it to roll into the stall. The water pounds and pesters the bumps of the day – the ones created by those who feel they have a license to act out on their own disappointment or narcissism or selfishness and make a mess of someone else's life.

I dip my head, let my long hair drape over my face, and allow the hard spray to slap against my spine. Gordy thinks I get too caught up in trying to fix the unfixable. He reminds me that logic and kindness and magnanimity are not dominating traits in many sections of humanity. My mother wonders why I won't embrace a more white-collar way to pursue justice, wonders why I won't avoid getting directly in the face of jackasses. "I admire you, honey," she'll say. "But you get pigheaded, sometimes you won't stop when you should. It's not too late to choose the law school track – you'd be just one step back from direct confrontation with that bad element you're determined to put in its place." My best friend Gretchen likes to please and make people *feel* better. She cautions me, all the time, about my desire to make people better.

I toss these observations around in my mind too often, nearly always as conversations between me and me because they take place when I'm home and alone.

My flannel robe is soft on my skin, the crutches hard under my armpits. The heat from the fireplace helps dry the un-towel-able dampness. My computer is on the coffee table in front of the couch, and I power it up and access the *CanFindAnyone* site. G&Z uses it for initial internet dives - to quickly identify basics like address, phone, place of birth, next of kin, emergency contacts, vehicle registrations, and other useful personal data on persons of interest.

Liam Grimshell: the name goes into the search engine. There are multiple people in America owning that name. I narrow the search with age, rosters of University of Iowa alumni (assumed from the poster in his office). I land on various images of Grimshell through the years: blond, freckled, always the tortoise shell glasses. No police record. No DMV violations. No missed rent. No reports of harassment. There's a mention of an MBA from University of Massachusetts, Amherst. A few more photos. Always that square face. Never a smile. Eyes that stare straight ahead, like he's sending a challenge to anyone who may underestimate him.

7 Days

Why would he think he could intimidate my mother? She's strong on all fronts, rarely shows weakness. Or is my assessment of her skewed? Is she not as impenetrable as I think?

She'll be out of the country for a week. Maybe, as she predicts, his hostility will abate.

That familiar desire - for a simple satisfaction of a day well-spent - eludes me. Too many tendrils of thought, too many uneasy worries.

I lean back, feel the heat. Sip the Rittenhouse and take in the apartment. Everything's as it was this morning, exactly as I left it. Another reminder of my mother's words. "Honey, having someone waiting at home for you can take the sting off a long day."

Thanks, Mom.

SEVEN DAYS

CHAPTER FIVE

"Want me to wait?"

Abshir had picked me up at my place at sunrise and we've reached Letty's Diner; my Outback is right where I'd parked it. I'd found my beloved blue and gold two-tone at Used Car Lot two years ago – it was pristine, had never been dented, and had a stellar health report. Since then, it's bravely met a few obstacles and crashes, but I've gotten its body smoothed out, its brakes fixed, its wheels changed and upholstery restitched.

"No need, I'm fine," I say to Abshir. "I'll head to the office - mostly paperwork today. Gordy will want to see that report on the insurance fraud for the Jyber Ink. You should get to class," I say.

"*Haa,* but nothing until ten o'clock today. Since we're here, I will buy some coffee beans. The office is low on supplies."

"Good plan."

The storm never materialized last night, but the freezing temps are a constant. Abshir pulls his knit hat lower to cover his ears, unbends his Gumby-esque frame out of the van and heads inside Letty's. Definitely, he could use some carbs. Gordy's hoping news on Abshir's application to UM Law School will arrive soon. They met, three years ago, at the university's Career Day and Abshir convinced Gordy to let him volunteer at the office – 'to see American justice close-up'. Gordy thought he was too hopeful, and told him private investigators, sometimes, had to use circuitous routes to achieve 'justice'. He thought Abshir would get disenchanted, but he stuck to his ask and showed up regularly to take on office tasks. We started to look forward to the Somalian treats his mother cooked for us on Fridays. And when Abshir proved his reliability, loyalty and quick-thinking, Gordy added research duties and simple surveillance assignments and put him on the payroll.

Having a lawyer (well, a law student) in the office could help keep us on our toes.

7 Days

I get out of the van and press 'open' on my extra fob. My car's lock clicks, and I grab the handle - it's stuck because there's a layer of frost over it. I dig my gloved fingers into the grip, give it a forceful tug. Another one. The thin ice crackles and I jerk the door open. I slip inside, get the heater going.

There's a ping on my cell phone. It's a seven a.m. text and selfie from Chester. He and my mother are settled into their spacious seats on the airplane headed to London and are blowing kisses. The text reads: "Happy second day of Birthday Week!"

How many times do I have to tell them it's no big deal?

* * *

Parking restrictions in historic Old Port start at nine, that means I have ninety minutes before I need to move my car halfway up Munjoy Hill to the residential area and free all-day parking. *Cawahawww!* A seagull, braving the weather, lands with a thump on the hood of my car and plops his icy rump on the warm metal. "Go! Get off," I yell. The seagull ruffles his wings, signalling a guano poop could be on its way - full of that nasty uric acid that burns through paint. I slap on the windshield – "Go! Go!" The bird gives me a malignant stare, calmly stands, and defecates. *Cawhaww!* I can translate: "Take that, bitch in a warm car." He notices a trio of brethren attacking a trash can at the end of the block. He flies off to fight for winter toss-aways and to complain that summer tourist season serves up better gastronomical treasures. I don't feel sorry for him at all.

I retrieve the microfiber cloth from the glovebox. *A hard, SLAP-SLAP-SLAP* on the driver's window startles me and I whip around. "What?"

This invader wears one thick mitten, a hoodie and a bulky plaid overcoat that hides his body. "It's me. Nail. It's very important I talk to you." The coat is buttoned at the top, the bottom half is open and shows his arm in a fiberglass half-cast. His unmittened fingers are red and grossly swollen. He points to his arm. "Fractured radius." He motions to his neck and shoulder. "Bruised clavicle but not broken." He points to his hip. "You should see the size of the bruise." His eyes are a light blue-white, almost colorless. "Let's go into your office. It's freezing out here."

I get out of the car and use the soft cloth to swipe away the soupy guano. "What's so important?"

His breath clouds in the cold air. "Gilli's not answering her phone. We need to find her."

"Last thing I heard is the PPD are on that."

"She hasn't come back to Kahta Street, the police say, and since I'm not pressing charges, she won't stay high on their 'find her' list."

Damn. And a stolen Coach Tote won't be a priority for the PPD either. I'll have to accept its loss.

"I know where she dumps stuff," Nail says. "Like bags."

Had he read my mind? "What do you mean?"

"I'll tell you. Inside. Where it's warm."

He sees me hesitate – pushes. "Don't you want your bag back?"

* * *

Minutes later, Nail's pushing the hoodie off his pale bald head and looking around the entry space of G&Z Investigation. "Better," he says. "Warm." He walks to the large window and clucks appreciatively at the foggy view of the Portland Pier wharf. "Lucky you."

I power up the computer, keep an eye on him. "How'd you find me?" I ask.

"I asked the cops. They told me you were police for a while, but you chose to be a P.I. because you lost part of a leg when you were pushed off a building by some guys."

"Let's stick to the location of my bag."

He pats at his large coat. "I borrowed these clothes from a pal this morning 'cause I couldn't get into the condo." He pulls the pants up; they're cinched at his narrow waist with a thin belt. "He's bigger than me but having everything loose is good when you're injured." He grimaces at his cast. "You know there're seven trillion nerves in our bodies? Gilli collected information like that. All seven trillion hurt and the only thing that will make me feel better is finding Gilli."

"Maybe she's avoiding you."

"We're committed. And besides, she doesn't like to sleep alone. Something happened to her."

"Did you talk with her friends?"

He snuffles. "She doesn't trust a lot of people."

I'm thinking that with her personality, she may not have friends. But maybe there are other reasons she's gone silent. "I noticed you gave her a pill last night, covered with chocolate. What kind of pills does she take?"

He shrugs. "Her doctor prescribes them."

"Do they affect her decisions? Maybe she needs to sleep off whatever-"

"She always takes them. Her doctor tells me to remind her."

The code on the office door sounds and Abshir enters. He carries his backpack and a bag of coffee beans. Nail pushes his narrow chest out. "Who are you?"

Abshir, surprised at the aggression, shoots me a look.

"You don't look American," says Nail.

I'd like to tell Nail he looks like an alien and no one's acting like a hater towards him. "Hey," I say. "Unless you're gonna come through with the promised information about my bag, you can leave. Abshir and I have work to do."

"What kind of name is 'Abshir'?" Nail asks. The tone is still unpleasant.

I walk past him, open the door. "Here's the exit."

"Settle down," Nail says, like he's got a right to give orders. "You're too hotheaded."

"Your presence is not appreciated," I snap. "And we can grab you by your fractured arm and forcibly show you the way out."

Nail's small mouth purses like he's sucking lemons, but he stalls his opinions. He uses his good hand to reach into his pocket and take out a roll of cash held together with a rubber band. "Here's a thousand. Does that buy a morning of looking for Gilli? A thousand dollars and your bag back. Deal?"

* * *

Turns out 'bag back' (and not having to tell my mother I lost last year's birthday present) clinched the deal. Nail is in the passenger seat of my

Outback, turned towards me so the seat belt is strained. "You have a confident persona," he says. "You make a person think you should be in charge. Did you cultivate that?"

I eyeball the rearview mirror. Abshir's following us. He's got time before class and the destination is on the way to the University - and since neither of us appreciate Nail's odd behavior, double-teaming felt right.

"You always carry lots of cash?" I ask Nail.

"There's more. I've got more."

I'd put Nail's money into the office safe and had him sign a limited-service agreement before we set out. I'm driving uphill from Commercial Street, and we reach Congress Street, the northwestern limit of the Old Port area "Now go downhill," says Nail. We head down towards the Fore River. "Turn right," says Nail. We drive through short, jagged streets dotted with make-do auto shops, metal mini-storage units, and small, uncared-for houses. "Turn." Nail points to a one-way called Horseshoe Lane. We pass a series of *No Parking* signs because, curb to curb, the lane's barely the width of my Outback. We pass a few small houses, partially hidden by overgrown hedges. At the end of the street, Nail nods towards an empty lot. "Go in here."

I park next to a late-model black Wrangler 4X. It looks too shiny for the surroundings. Next to it is a used Audi, it's got a few years, the silver finish is rusty and there are multiple dings.

"Gilli owns the block," says Nail. "She tore down a shack to make the parking area. She charges a monthly fee to her renters and has everyone else towed. She's a good businessperson."

I just want my bag back.

Abshir's van slides in next to me. I step out of the car, my boot crunches on an orange cap, the kind used on syringes. There's an empty three-needle package nearby. "Gilli know her parking lot's also being used as a shoot-up location?"

Nail kicks at a spoon and discarded lighter. "She's gonna be mad."

We walk in the middle of Horseshoe Lane because there are no sidewalks. How has this odd locale escaped the bulldozers that have become so popular in the city? Maybe two hundred years ago blacksmiths set up shop here and that's how it got its name. My dad was big on Portland's history.

He'd tell me how Market Street earned its name (that one's obvious) and Fish Pier (because the fish auctions took place there). I look up the hill to see the massive red brick Medical Center looming. My dad told me that the hospital had been built over the old Arsenal Street, named for a military weapon storage space that was there in the 1800s or so. Maybe Horseshoe Lane was the place the army's horses were shod.

Nail pushes through a wonky gate connected to a wobbly fence that frames #5. The house has a gray-brown, soggy look. "I'll get the key," he says and struggles around the side of the house.

Abshir clears his throat, keeps his voice low. "I would like to share an opinion."

"Go for it," I say.

"He does not seem trustworthy." To Abshir, that's the ultimate criticism.

"Let's see how it goes," I say. Curiosity has grabbed me.

I notice the movement of a curtain in a window next door. Fabric is pushed aside, and a sharp chin is revealed. The person turns his head to say something to someone in the room with him. The curtain closes.

Nail, carrying a small garden gnome under his arm, joins us. He places the gnome on the porch railing, pops open its belly and takes out a key. "I knew Gilli wasn't done with me, she was just upset. If she didn't want me to be part of her life, she'd move all our hide-a-keys."

"Neighbors are keeping an eye out," I say to Nail.

He sniffs. "Gilli's the landlord. And he knows I'm her guy. So, piss off, I say." Nail unlocks the door, glares at Abshir. "You wait on the porch."

"He stays with me," I say.

Nail sulks. "No pictures." He steps inside. "I gotta flip the alarm off, one second." He closes the door to prevent us watching him. "Okay. Done. Come in."

We step inside, there's a small hit of heat, just enough to keep the pipes from freezing.

"Whoa." I wasn't prepared for the interior.

The front room is packed with floor-to-ceiling wire shelving units filled with ceramic figurines - those slick pastel-glazed ballerinas, potbellied babies, and pleasant peasant girls you find in knick-knack stores. Gretchen's grandmother has a collection of the figurines and Gretchen's worried she's going to inherit the caboodle - every saccharine-faced, bonneted girl carrying a bouquet of flowers.

"I wondered who spent money on these things," I say.

He lifts his chin as if he's proud. "Gilli doesn't need to pay. She has talent."

"What do you mean?" Then I get it. "She shoplifts?"

"Sometimes taking things is the only way she can feel whole; fill the void she feels."

"It's also a crime," I say.

Nail shrugs. "Is it? If a person needs to do does something so they can feel good about themselves?"

Abshir mumbles under his breath. "So, if a serial killer does what he does to feel good - his murders are not crimes?"

Nail pushes his pale face towards Abshir. "Gilli's not killing anybody."

I've never seen Abshir coil as if about to strike. Nail seems to bring out people's desire to pound on him. I step between them. "We're here for one reason. My bag."

There's a thin pathway through the shelving units. Nail motions for us to follow him and we reach a hallway. There are open doorways to rooms. The second room holds plush animals and dolls. "Does this room fill the void of a crappy childhood?" I ask.

"Gilli's parents were rich farmers, they gave her everything," Nail says. "Feeling empty is not about *not* having things." He looks around, gives 'thumbs up' with his good hand. "She's organized. I tell her I'm proud of her for that."

"Did you tell the PPD to look for Gilli here?" I ask.

"I'm not gonna get my girlfriend in trouble."

The next room is filled with boxes of gauze, Band-Aids, bottles of mouthwash, toothbrushes, cough syrups and all things for self-care.

"Gilli worried about getting sick?" I ask.

"During the pandemic, she hated the empty shelves in the drugstores so she stocked up when she could."

"And made the shelves emptier for other people?" Abshir asks.

Nail takes a step towards Abshir. "Don't be jealous because she knows how to be prepared."

7 Days

Abshir breathes his opinion of Nail – this time in Somalian – to me again. I've gotten to know what *ma jecla isaga* means.

Next room: yoga essentials, dish towels, ceramic cups with cheesy sayings painted on them, bags of chips and nuts. All those things that are on that checkout aisle before you hit the cashier at the discount stores. Gilli must be a master of slipping things under her shirt, down a waistband, into the bottom of whatever bag she might be carrying.

"She thinks of others too," says Nail. "When she runs out of space, she gives it all to shelters and starts again."

I shoot a look at Abshir, hoping he won't comment on the odd psychology.

"Where's my bag?" I ask.

We arrive at the bathroom. It's lined with shelves of perfectly stacked toilet paper. Nail points to the bathtub - here it's a jumble. Hundreds of wallets, small purses, fanny packs, totes and backpacks fill it. My Coach Tote is on top of the pile. Next to it is the menu from Letty's.

"So, this means Gilli was here last night," I say. "Or earlier this morning." The inside pockets of my Tote are zipped. I open them: the keys to my Outback are still inside.

My wallet, with credit card, cash and driver's license is gone. "Wallet's gone," I say.

"What color is it?" asks Nail.

"Red."

Nail moves to the bathtub, shoves a few things around – he pulls something out. "This it?"

"Yeah." I grab it. My driver's license is half out of its sleeve, but nothing else has been touched.

Nail leans against the doorframe. "Sometimes Gilli just wants to teach a lesson. Like: if you're in a restaurant, don't leave your bag on the back of your chair, don't leave it under the table if you're gonna run to the bathroom, don't let your wallet fall out of your back pocket. Don't leave your gym locker - or your car - unlocked. She likes to teach stupid people lessons."

"You can't make stealing things sound like she's doing people favors."

"You should think more openly," Nail says. "Let people be who they are."

I hold up my hands, I've had enough. "I'm fine without your advice."

"Now you have your bag," he says. "We have to find her."

I groan. Technically, we'd agreed that if the bag was recovered, I'd deposit Nail's money and give him three hours of a 'Gilli-hunt'. I feel stuck. "Okay, you need to make a list of her haunts. You know what she likes, who she knows."

I move past him into the kitchen. There's a plastic bin full of mismatched forks, knives and spoons. Probably Gilli's collection from every eatery she's been in. I look out the window, see that the backyard is small. Garden gnomes of all sizes cover the lawn. No place for a grown woman to hide.

"She ever sleep here?" I ask.

"Gilli likes a nice bed," Nail says. "There's no room for one here."

We walk back down the hallway, step out the front door. Nail sets the alarm and locks up. "Wait here."

Abshir and I watch him clutch the gnome and walk around the corner of the house. There's a sound of a door opening behind us. "Hey. You look familiar."

The neighbor's stepping out onto the porch. He's gotta be mid-forties but the hair - pulled into a topknot - is an attempt at a young hipster look. His boots are new and so is the heavy Rolex on his wrist.

He shakes a smoke out of a cigarette pack, his voice has a three-pack-a-day rasp. "I look familiar to you?"

"No. You don't," I say.

"Why are you staring?"

"Didn't mean to look like I was," I say. "Wasn't, really."

He puts the cigarette between his lips, half-smiles. His teeth are grayish and he's missing a front incisor. "Yep," he says. "You look like someone I met once."

"I have no memory of that," I say. "Sorry."

A vintage Chevy is coming down the street, it slows in front of #7. Top Knot saunters to the curb, and the window of the car slides down so he can lean his elbows on the frame and dangle his hands inside. The conversation is short. The window slides up and Topknot pulls out a purple Fuji Instant mini camera, the kind that provides an instant print. He snaps a shot as he waves at the departing car. The instant photo is printed and slides out of the camera. Topknot pockets the picture and the camera and sashays his way back to the porch. He flicks a Bic lighter to flame, holds it to the cigarette still in his mouth.

Nail comes around the corner, stops and glares. "Gilli says 'no smoking' in the rental."

"I'm outside. Outside is where we're free to be who we really are."

Nail continues. "You should smoke more 'outside' than the porch."

Top Knot flicks his cigarette and Bic lighter – they land on the brown lawn, joining a thick scattering of other butts. "Rental agreement also says I can beautify the property."

Nail points out, "Gilli was thinking flowers."

"Not what I find beautiful."

I interrupt. "We're looking for Gillian Wanz. Have you seen her?"

"Nope," says Top Knot.

"Not last night or this morning?" I ask.

"Nope."

A slighter person opens the door, he's got on a blue flannel shirt and a shiny puffer vest. He's in his early twenties, has a delicate face - except for the sharp chin - the one I saw jutting through the curtain. "Rusty," he says. "Who was in the car?"

"Hop off my nuts, none of your biz," says Top Knot.

"Okay, Rusty, whatever. Let's finish what we started."

"Impatient. Impatient." Rusty takes out the mini camera, takes a photo of the guy.

"Don't do that."

Rusty clicks the camera and captures another picture. "Whiner."

They retreat inside #7 and the door slams behind them.

Nail dismisses them. "They're trash. Let's go find Gilli. I paid you for half a day, let's get started." He's already out the gate, heading to the parking area.

Abshir leans into me. "Shall I skip class?"

I shake my head. "You don't want your professors to regret those law school recommendations. I can handle this. It's only a few hours."

"Try not to kill him," Abshir replies.

CHAPTER SIX

Abshir drives off and Nail tells me to help him connect his seatbelt because of his injuries. I comply, hating how he expects the special treatment, but just wanting to get on with it. "Does Gilli have any other properties?" I ask.

"She likes to buy empty lots. For parking purposes because it's needed in Portland, and she can make money providing space for cars."

"What void does that fill?"

Nail points a finger at me. "When you are sarcastic and judge, you cut yourself off, give yourself permission to stay distant. Remember, there's always room to be a better person."

"If we're gonna spend half a day together, the rule is you don't tell me who I am or how I should act."

"What's wrong with holding the mirror up? What are you afraid of seeing?"

Self-important shit. Getting my bag back may not be worth this.

He's got his phone out, he punches in Gilli's number again. "She doesn't answer."

"Where does Gilli like to shop or get coffee or tea?" I ask.

"Few different places."

"Maybe there's an old boyfriend she could be staying with."

"No boyfriend except for me."

"Does she go to a gym?"

"There's one at her Kahta condo. Sometimes she feels fat, and I need to tell her she's beautiful. Yeah, maybe she's there."

We arrive at the new Kahta Condominium Complex and park in a guest parking spot at the rear of the development. We follow the signs that point to the Condo Clubhouse. Nail's breath clouds in the air. "Gilli leaves a condo key for me in a special place under a shingle, that's the one I use."

"You don't live together?"

He looks offended. "We do."

7 Days

"Why don't you have your own key?"

"As long as the hide-a-keys are where I can find them, that means we're good."

We pass through a hedge of junipers; the one-story gym attached to the clubhouse is ahead of us. I notice a dark splatter on the glass wall. It looks like a large bird has hit it and exploded like a water balloon full of blood and guts.

Nail rushes to the glass, screeching. "Gilli!" He stumbles, finds his footing and scrambles. "Gilli!"

What I thought might be splayed black feathers on the exterior glass is dark, human hair matted with blood and brain matter on the other side of the glass. The blood and guts are Gilli's. Her face is shattered – her cheekbone is crushed, her nose is broken, the bridge goes one direction, her nasal openings go the other. One of her eyes hangs out of its socket, the other has an opaque look, the cloudiness that comes with death. She's upright because her shoulder is pressed against the floor-to-ceiling window, and an arm hangs over the handlebars of an exercycle. It's a study in violence; a quick hit was not the goal - it looks like a punishment.

Glad I didn't have breakfast.

Nail's madly pulling at the locked entry door. It doesn't budge. He kicks at it. He hits his head against it – hard.

I call 911 as I lope past a sign pointing to the Manager's Office. I pound on the door. No one answers.

* * *

Nail, hoodie up, sits on a bench in the garden area, he cradles his injured arm and rocks back and forth. There's already a bruise on his forehead. I've given him my red scarf to wrap around his neck and chin, it's bright against his paleness.

I pop a piece of gum into my mouth to try settle my stomach.

"Do something," he says.

"The police are coming. Any idea who did this?"

"Do something," he screams. *"Don't just do nothing."*

"I know, it feels like we should be able to do something. But we have to wait. Could this be about something Gilli stole-"

"She *collected* stuff."

I'm not going to argue.

"She collected things. And information."

"Information? About what?"

His shoulders slump. *"You are useless. I am useless."* He hangs his head and collapses back on the bench.

"I'm going closer to the gym, I'll be back." I leave his side and get as close as I can to the gym to take cell phone photos. I don't step off the stone walk - PPD will look for footprints on the frosted lawn. I don't want them to find mine.

Finally, the sounds of sirens approach.

CHAPTER SEVEN

Half an hour later, police tape has been rolled into place. An officer leads a blubbering Nail to a small ambulance that has arrived, and a medic gets him a heat blanket.

Vera Sandrich, a newbie officer who likes to throw her weight around (she thinks that'll make her superiors take notice) tells me to step back. We've crossed paths in the past and I predict the relationship will never mature into a friendship.

I'm already behind the tape, but I shuffle backwards. "Do you know what time the PPD units left here last night? They wanted to interview the victim about an assault she committed."

No answer.

"Any news on possible time of death?"

Sandrich is not supposed to answer me, and she doesn't.

Dr. Stapler, the city-appointed coroner (also professor of forensics at the medical school in Biddeford) is inside the gym with the body. He'll make early determinations and make sure the body gets up to Augusta to the new Chief Medical Examiner.

Detective Preston Banford is inside too. He's been partnering with Donato for the last two years. Maybe since Donato's in Augusta today and then driving to the state prison to talk to Payer - this is Banford's first 'primary in charge'. He's my age - has the career I thought I was destined for. Detective Latifa Lavonna, in a camel-colored parka, is inside with Banford. She's back on the force after taking five years off to make sure her sons made it through high school without taking major missteps. She succeeded; her boys are in college. She spent six months getting back up to speed - mostly with the new tech and routines - then slipped her detective badge back into her inside pocket.

They're moving to the gym's exit. They push out the doors. Lavonna heads to the ambulance to talk to Nail and Banford beelines in my direction. His long, dark gray coat has some gravitas, but - maybe he could re-think the earmuffs. He opens his notebook, finds a fresh page. "How'd you end up here?" His voice is low and bass-y, every word sounds like it reverberates in his ribcage.

"Gilli Wanz's boyfriend showed up at our office an hour or so ago," I tell him, pointing to Nail. "He was convinced something had happened to her because she hadn't answered his phone calls. He said the police weren't taking his concerns seriously. He hired G&Z to look for her."

Our eyes stay on Nail and Lavonna. She's got her hands on her hips, doesn't look like she's taken a liking to him. "He's your client?" asks Banford.

"It looks like my job's over," I say. "Gilli's been found."

The gym doors open. Gilli's body, zipped inside a body bag, is wheeled out.

"She was the person who swung a bat at him and stole your bag?" Banford asks.

"You heard about that?"

"Where were you from midnight to six this morning?" His head is cocked, his eyes steady on my face.

My eyebrows shoot up.

"You had a beef with her," he rumbles. "Gotta ask."

"I was asleep. In my bed. Alone." I lift my tote off my shoulder, display it. "And I got my bag back. So, no more beef."

"How'd getting it back happen?"

I tell him about Nail leading Abshir and me to #5 Horseshoe Lane in the Libbytown 'hood. I give a description of the place and its contents.

He writes down the address. "Sounds odd."

"It is."

"You see any connection – from that to this?"

We take a moment to consider the possibles. Was Gilli killed for saccharine ceramics or stolen wallets or a stolen backpack? Maybe she had a habit of assaulting others with her bat and this was someone's revenge. Did this happen because of something in her past or present? Or was she in the wrong place at the wrong time? No answers are forthcoming. I continue. "Gilli must have dropped off my bag at Horseshoe sometime after she left Letty's last night and before she arrived at the Kahta Gym."

He pens another note. "Why'd you two show up at the gym?"

"Nail said she worked out here. It was a place to have a look."

"He's a live-in boyfriend?"

"Technically, even though Gilli had him use a hide-a-key."

"Hide-a-key?"

"She shows him the location of the key – he says as long as it's there, their relationship was copacetic."

"Is that odd too?" Banford asks.

I shrug. "Their arrangement. But, yeah, odd. His belongings and personal items are in the condo. They've been together for over a year; he has no other residence. I guess everyone's got their kinks."

Banford moves to his next question. "Why'd you park back here?"

"Nail told me to."

"Because, in doing so, he knew you'd have to walk past the gym and see the body?"

He's got a point.

Banford stomps his feet. I notice his suede Bucksports. Not the warmest or most practical winter shoes. Under his long coat is a suit and tie. He's neat and tidy and usually dresses to impress. Impress who, I wonder. He gives his notebook a glance. "Here's the timeline we're looking at. Last night, just before nine o'clock, the boyfriend…" he nods towards Nail. "… is attacked by girlfriend, Gilli Wanz, with a bat. He leaves Letty's Diner in an ambulance, he's checked in at Mercy's ER around nine-thirty, finally gets treated and leaves there around two o'clock in the morning. He asks to be dropped off at the Residence Marriott on Fore Street because going home to a pissed-off girlfriend wasn't the best choice. Uniform decides to make sure Nail Parcell gets to his room because he was…" He reads directly from his notebook: "On painkillers and acting 'loopy'."

"And after that, no one had eyes on him?"

"No," says Banford. "But he had sustained a serious shoulder injury, had a fractured right arm and bruised ribs. Those physical impediments probably preclude overpowering a girlfriend who outweighed him."

Nail had about six hours of unsupervised time – from the time he got into his hotel room and when he showed up at the G&Z office at eight this morning. No, wait; there's another point in the timeline. "Nail told me he went to see a buddy - to ask if he had a change of clothes for him."

"What time?"

"Didn't ask."

"Name of buddy?"

"Didn't ask."

Banford expels a very deep bass sigh. "Slipping?"

"I was only thinking of a stolen bag. Not murder."

He switches gears. "Hear of Gilli Wanz having any enemies in the Kahta Condo development?"

"I didn't know her."

"This Nail Parcell say anything about any enemies?"

"Not to me."

Banford points to a middle-aged man with a shaved head and a headband who's shivering in a worn wool jacket. He's standing near an iced-over garden fountain. "That's Mike, the manager of the development. He lives on the premises. We've already got his statement, his whereabouts during the night."

"And they were?"

He pretends he doesn't hear the question. "He did tell us residents use their condo key and a gym keycard, in tandem, to get into the gym."

"Okay."

Banford continues, "Your friend Nail have a gym card?"

"Didn't ask."

"It's a duo thing. You have to use the gym card and condo key at the same time."

"Gilli could've let someone in," I say. "Someone she knew. Or someone she didn't think was a threat."

"Thinking the same thing."

Lavonna joins us. "Boyfriend's agreed to come down to the station to talk, fill in some background. He says he'll take a hot chocolate and some toast." She rolls her eyes. "He's treating me like his maid."

"Don't take it personally," I say. "He's all sorts of politically incorrect."

Banford notices the news van arriving. "Media alert." Crews pile out, start setting up. Banford lets me know he'll want to talk later, but for now, I have permission to leave the scene. Part of me is good with not having to continue with the Nail and Gilli saga. Nail's hard to take and Gilli gives me the creeps – both alive and dead. But no one deserves to die and be left on display like that. A larger part of me can't help but wonder – who did this? When? Why?

The JawJive app on my phone zings as I get into my car. I open it, Gretchen appears on my screen. The rosey streaks in her hair match her fuzzy pink sweater and the walls of Doggie DayCare (her business). She's holding a small pug-faced client.

"Morning," I say. Can't believe it's still shy of eleven o'clock.

Gretchen gets right to the point. "Calling to confirm details for Friday birthday movie night. I got the old DVDs out and hooked up the player. Are we decided on *Saturday Night Fever*, *Barbie* and *Inception*?"

"Sure. Sounds good."

"I vote for starting with disco, move into the all-pink world, then the 'what the hell is life about?'"

"Always end on the uplifting question."

"You, okay?" she asks. "Sounds like you're in a mood."

She's been a feeler since grade school and uses her sixth sense to suss out emotional disarray. I tell her she empathizes too much. She says I need to do it more.

"Been a strange couple of days," I say.

"How was your mom?"

"Expected mom lunch but with a little bit of a twist. I'll tell you later." Don't want to get into Liam Grimshell now.

"Come by, cuddle a pup. You'll feel better."

"I've got to report to Gordy."

"Okay. Then later. One more question," she says. "Apple birthday pie from Two Fat Cats Bake?"

"Always."

The pug yips, he must agree.

7 Days

"Bloat city, here we come." She lets the dog wiggle off her lap and join the other four-legged beings. "Stop by," she says. "There's a bulldog here you'd love."

We click off. I notice a thick wad resting in the well of the passenger seat. Nail must've left it. I lean over and grab the red and yellow striped lump - it's a thick, double-weight hand knit mitten. The match to the one Nail wore on his undamaged hand. A small tag is sewn to the cuff. *Property of Dalton Guffman.*

I look up. The squad car, with Nail in the back seat, is driving off. But I see that Banford's still talking to the building manager. I don't need a reprimand for withholding evidence, so I make my way to Banford, hand him the mitten and point to the name tag. "Nail left this in my car. Pretty sure it belongs to a friend that he saw this morning. Could help with a timeline for Nail."

He takes the mitten in his gloved hand, drops it into a plastic evidence bag. He rumbles a 'thanks' and I head back to my car.

CHAPTER EIGHT

"Give this Nail maggot his money back, we can't bank a thousand bucks for a ten-minute drive that ends up at a dead body." Gordy's looking at my shadowy cell phone photos of slain Gilli. "Write it up - start with the events at Letty's, and end with this." He tosses my phone back to me. "Give the report to Banford. It's muck and we don't want to wade in and get stuck anywhere near it."

We're in Gordy's upstairs bedroom. He's settled under a flowery quilt. His computer is atop a pillow on his lap. A stack of files is on one side of him, Bert is on the other. The dog's wagging his tail and snoring. Must be a good dream.

"We're not invited into the 'muck'," I say.

"Good. We got enough going on." He hands me three files. "I want these cases closed."

"Can't wave a magic wand. But they're moving forward-"

Gordy grunts, unhappy. "Donato tell you about Billy Payer wanting to get a transfer?"

My stomach tightens. "Yeah."

"We're not getting into that mess either. Let the guy rot."

Just hearing Payer's name rankles me. "What's with you and avoiding untidiness?" I ask. "You used to like to dig in, clean up a little clutter."

He grouches, "Maybe I'm seeing that life – simply lived – is preferable."

"Was that on some Hallmark card?"

Before he can snark back, Marie hurries in, buttoning her winter coat. "Dee, *cara*, are you sure you can stay? Because I am counting on you."

"We'll be working," growls Gordy. "Don't get all smothering about it."

She kisses his forehead. "Then, *uoma dolce*, I will take this opportunity to drive to Boothbay to pick up work by my new artist. Very talented; he paints water like I have never seen. I will title the show 'Water as Seen by the Heart'. What do you think of that title, Dee?"

7 Days

"Catchy." I have no idea what it means but Marie seems positive.

She pats Gordy's shoulder. "I'll be back to make you a late lunch."

Her footsteps sound on the stairs, the front door opens and shuts. Bert raises his head. When he sees that Gordy is still in place, he settles back and closes his eyes.

But Gordy's at attention. Looks ready to bolt.

"What're you doing?" I ask.

He puts his finger to his lips, a sign for me to be quiet. "Is she all the way gone?"

I look out the window. Marie's backing her SUV out of the driveway. "Going," I say. The car heads towards North Street - the locals' choice to connect with Highway 295. "Gone." I look back at him. "Whazzup?"

He throws off the quilt, swings his legs to the side of the bed and slips his stockinged feet into fleece-lined Crocs. "She's going to Boothbay and back. That's a minimum of two and a half hours. And that's if she's NASCAR, which she's not. Let's get out of here."

"What? Where? Why?" What the hell?

"I'm not sitting on my ass for seven days."

"What's in seven days?"

"Grab my parka, get your coat on, bring your car up to the back - close as you can to the fence. Got too many nosey neighbors around here who are working from home these days, don't want anyone tattling."

Minutes later, Gordy's given Bert a Chunky Chewbone, slipped into his flannel-lined parka, grabbed a canvas duffel and settled in the passenger seat of the Outback.

"Is this a good idea?" I ask as I put on my seat belt.

"I'm the boss, so yes, it is. Drive down Commercial."

"Gordy. What's happening in seven days?"

"Drive."

I turn towards the Ferry Terminal and merge onto Commercial – the wide street closest to Old Port's wharfs. We pass the hotels, tourist shops, local bars, and clothing stores. A few bundled-up people hurry to get to their warm destinations. We pass the brick building that houses G&Z Investigation. Gordy takes it in, like he's starving for it. Maybe he is, he's been cooped up for a month, with Marie hovering like a mother hen. We pass the longstanding Lobster Shack, DiMillo's Floating Restaurant, and shops offering hand-hewn furniture and hand-blown glass. Mainers appreciate one-of-a-kind craft, it's even more coveted if it's created in a solitary endeavor in a barn or basement by someone whose favorite word is 'Ahyup'.

Gordy motions for me to turn onto one of the narrow brick streets that veer off the main drag.

"Park there."

We're at a side door of the Regency Hotel – the door that leads into the wood-paneled Armory Bar. The post-breakfast and pre-lunch Bloody Mary regulars sit on their favorite barstools. When Gordy enters, a cheer erupts; it's like the long-lost president of Good Conversation has resurrected.

"Gordy," I caution. "What does the doctor say about-"

"Five minutes," he grumbles.

Bartender John prepares Gordy's Bloody Mary. "Make my doc happy," Gordy says. "Hold the jalapeno." I want to add "hold the vodka" but Gordy gives me a look.

"You got it, big guy," says John. "Good to see ya."

I sit at the far end of the bar, let Gordy have his moments with his pals. He's given the center seat, people stand around him, lean into him. There's laughter, friendly disagreements, familiar guffing and guffaws. Gordy says the next round of jazzed-up tomato juice is on him.

John brings me a side of fries, leans over to me and whispers. "He's skinny but not looking that bad."

I nod. And don't mention that as we drove down Commercial Street, Gordy told me his doctor has made the decision to use a surgical robot to help 'open him up' – get a closer look inside his guts to figure out the reason for his physical decline. Gordy joked that he asked for a discount since they'd only have to look at one kidney - because two years ago, he'd given one to his brother. "I'll be on the operating table a week from today," he'd said. "Doc says there's a ball of lousy cells crowding in my pancreas, says he needs to make sure it's not setting up a man-eating residence in the nearby bladder or bowel. Big whoop."

Shit. It is a big whoop.

7 Days

I'd gripped the steering wheel. Mumbled a long line of curse words and pulled over to the curb. He frowned. "Why'd you stop? No need for any melodramatic 'not-fair shit'. Keep driving, we only have so much time before Marie gets back."

Stubbornly I kept my foot on the brake. "I'm re-evaluating our relationship. What else have you kept from me?"

"I'm the boss. I'm the godfather. I decide what's shared."

I got angry. About the cancer news. And about his gray pallor. About him — possibly - not being big, bullying Gordy forever. I'd asked why a doc and a robot needed to open him up, why they couldn't put a camera up his nose or down his throat or up his ass or do a million MRIs to get a look-around. He told me that had all been done while I was up north in Maine, checking out the bigamist. My anger escalated. "Didn't I have the right to know what was going on?"

He just said. "Drive."

The reason for his recent manic oversight is now clear, why he wanted to go through every office file and account sheet and quiz me on my knowledge of all things 'office'.

"Drive," he said again.

I did. And here we are. I haven't touched my fries. Bartender John's curious. "You want ketchup?"

"No. Thanks."

Gordy stretches the five minutes to thirty.

Finally, we're back in my car, and he tells me he wants to make a few more stops.

I pull into the parking lot of the Portland YMCA. Gordy grabs the canvas duffel from the backseat.

"What are you doing now?"

"Five minutes."

I've heard that before.

Gordy walks into the lively health club. I trudge behind, notice how slow he's moving. Inside, various languages swirl — Senegalese, French, Somalian, Russian, Spanish, English and more. The music from the Zumba class gives everything a rhythm - the whirring machines, the clanking weights.

Blue-haired, fully-dentured Flo gets up out of her reception desk chair and shuffle-steps over for a Gordy hug. He's been a fixture here – lifting weights on the premises three times a week for decades while serving as a volunteer coach in the high school boxing program.

"Brought what I promised, Flo," says Gordy. He takes a plexiglass cube from the duffel. Inside it is an ancient pair of boxing gloves from the eighties – chipped leather, wrinkled and probably smelly. Flo and I read the inscription on the silver nameplate: *Gordy Greer, 3-Time New England Boxing Champion.*

Flo has already made room in the trophy cabinet; she places Gordy's gift in a place of honor. She has tears of gratitude in her eyes. "Bless you, Gordy Greer. From all those kids who were snuffing powder up their noses or shooting into their arms, you gave them something else to focus on. The lives you saved." She kisses his cheek. "Bless you Gordy Greer."

We leave the building, walk back to my car. "Why are you giving those away?"

"You wanted my gloves?"

"Never thought about it," I say.

"You think you're old enough to start thinking seriously about what you want?"

"I want you to get off my back."

"I'm putting my life in order. You're part of that."

"You can't put me in order," I say.

Gordy grunts. "We have another stop."

He tells me to park on Pearl Street, half a block from the Courthouse. The security guards know us, Gordy's been a regular witness in the State and County courts for twenty-some years and I've had my share of time on the stand giving evidence. Tony Dotz, the head guard, signs us in. His polyester shirt with its epaulets and pocket trim is stretched over his balloon belly and tucked into thick-weave black work trousers. The butt of the pants is shiny from all the sitting he does. "Hey, Gord, cold one, huh," he says.

"Nothing ever gets by you, Tony," says Gordy. "Thought you were gonna retire."

"Six more months, champ. In time to sit on Higgins Beach with a dozen lobster rolls."

7 Days

We walk through security and reach the buffed granite hallways that lead to the courtrooms. Gordy waves to a few lawyers and a private investigator from Brunswick and stops to talk to a court stenographer. No one comments on his baggy sweatsuit and Crocs ensemble, or his week-old stubble or hair that's rivaling Gene Wilder's in the *Dr. Frankenstein* movie. His best fishing buddy (took over that role from my dad) attorney Wallace Walsh, comes out of a courtroom, smoothing down his combover. He's a warm, untidy man, doesn't care if he's consistently on Portland's 'worst-dressed attorney' list at the Lawyers Laugh Yearly Buffet. His scuffed winter boots have orange shoelaces, and his socks feature chipmunks.

"Bought the tv for the icehouse!" Walsh calls out and comes over to confer about how to hook up the latest perk in the ice-fishing shed - once Clary Lake has a four-inch crust of ice on its surface.

Gordy takes a small container of yellow tube-jig lures from his pocket. "Found these in an old bag. These'll get 'em."

They plan for the future. Does Walsh know about the scheduled surgery?

I park myself on a bench in the hallway.

Pancreas. Where the hell is that? What does it do?

Local news is on the flat screen attached to the wall. The sound is off. On screen is an image of a family, all in sporty down parkas, standing in front of the sign for Southern Maine's popular Croake Sports Park. The bold Chyron headline reads: 'Croake Tragedy. Case Reopened.'

Gordy notices the newscast. He and Walsh move closer. "That photo was taken years ago," Walsh says. "Frank and Vivian with the kids - at one of the winter openings of the park. Before Viv got sick."

Gordy turns to his buddy. "You ever buy how they listed Frank's COD?"

"Suicide?" says Walsh. "Seemed off to me."

Photos and videos stream show Croake Park's two hundred acres - rolling hills and paths through the woods and fields. There are images of Frank Croake as the consummate outdoorsman, showing off his cross-country skiing skills, snowshoeing with his wife, summer picnicking at the property's lake and hosting a 5K to raise money for an environmental cause.

The timeline of Frank Croake's death is interesting. His body was found two days after he and his son Cooper let the traditional balloons release to open his yearly fundraiser for Croake Camp scholarship kids. The body was propped up against Marker Six on the Sports Park's High Eagle Trail, a double-strength plastic bag was over his head and held in place by a thick wrap of gaffer's tape around his neck. That was just last week, a couple days after the Thanksgiving holidays.

Walsh continues, "They give any details about why it's being reopened?"

"Not yet," I say.

Tod Dotz parks his heft nearby, nods, causing his three chins to jiggle. "I knew Frank wouldn't take himself out."

"You knew him too, Dotz?" asks Gordy.

Dotz drums his fingers on his stomach. "Worked for him on and off after I left the PPD."

"Doing what?"

"Security stuff."

I go back to studying the family portrait on the screen. Looks like the kids have inherited their father's sharp chin and high forehead. Three family members are smiling – not the son. His eyes look blank and disinterested. And since it's the same face I saw this morning on Horseshoe Lane, my interest increases. Nail labeled him 'trash'. Not a title anyone in the Croake family would appreciate.

The news report emphasizes that Frank had multiple residences in the state and that he was a widower and lived alone in each of them - that there had been no one to notice Frank Croake was missing.

That sucks.

"What's up?" Oscar Herbstrom joins the group. I recognize his port and bling from the photos I've seen of him in the newspapers and local magazines.

Gordy nods. "Saying it's murder now, Oscar."

He sighs. "Well. Frank never liked it when the attention wasn't on him."

He should talk. Herbstrom's a short guy with attention-getting dyed hair (midnight black) he has a rooster-barrel chest, and he's stuffed into a navy silk suit. Today, he's added a bright yellow tie and a good-sized diamond earring in his left ear. The attention-getters continue with gold cufflinks, a super-sized gold wedding ring, and a heavy gold bracelet on his wrist.

Gordy gives him a sideways glance. "You get a new jeweler, Oscar?"

Herbstrom pats Gordy on the shoulder. "Old buddy, I'll tell you if you tell me where you get your Crocs."

"Not sharing my secret for dress-for-success."

Herbstrom laughs. "Forgive. Forgive." He struts off.

A few minutes later, Gordy, Walsh and I walk out of the courthouse. Gordy mumbles, "Frank loved every damn breath he took," he says. "Knew he couldn't've snuffed himself. He always had plans."

Walsh heads back to his office, we head to the car. I tell Gordy about seeing Croake's son this morning. And a top-knot-hair guy named Rusty – and how it was a weird feeling when this Rusty guy thought he recognized me.

"Where was this?"

"Those people renting #7 Horseshoe Lane. I told you-"

"Show me," he says. "I want to talk to Cooper Croake."

"You should be back in bed."

"Next time you say that you're fired."

"You can't fire me."

"I can," he says.

"Who'd do your legwork?"

"You wonder why I don't tell people about this surgery thing? Cause of stupid words like 'you should be in bed'. What do you know?"

I snap back. "What do you know? I bet the doc said to lay low, stay home."

"What does he know?"

I almost match his volume. "You know more than the doctor?"

"I know that adding memories is what life's about. Memories come from 'doing'. Sitting under flowery quilts and not making new memories is what it's *not* about. Doing things - including getting answers and knowing who killed a friend is what it's about. Put that in your 'don't know anything' and gnaw on it."

We get into my car. We slam the doors shut in unison. Stupid - wasting time spinning petty peeves. Gordy's known me since I was a kid, he's been around at birthdays, seen my wins and losses, witnessed my parents' odd marriage, knew my aspirations. He insisted, after my injury, that I didn't sit in my dark apartment, that I get my ass to the G&Z office to manage the books. He quickly engaged me in the puzzles and choices of his clients – some righteous and some piddling, some mysterious, and some outrageous. He'd known I'd get distracted and eventually become involved with unearthing facts that proved every action has consequences.

He lifted me out of a deep funk that could've stretched on. He *yanked* me out of it.

So. No more snarking. I take a deep breath. "Donato said he was just assigned a case that might get reopened. This has to be it. Did he talk to you about it?"

Gordy snaps his fingers. "Damn. That was the sneaky he was up to. I see it now. Last night, between Patriot plays, he slipped in a few questions about Frank 'cause he knew Frank and I had served on some town committees together. Close-the-file kind of questions, I thought. Asked if, after Viv died, if I'd been aware of any depression. Asked if I knew the family - if I was going to the memorial. Slipped in that he'd heard through the grapevine G&Z had done some work for Frank at some point, wanted to know if that was true. That kind of stuff."

"Did Croake hire G&Z?"

"Yeah. Five or six years ago. But I told Donato it was confidential."

"What was it?"

"When Frank's body was found, I had Abshir get the office file for me. Wanted to look at it again. He hired G&Z when you were still in the Police Academy. There'd been missing cash from the Sports Park office. Frank was worried it was an inside deal because knowledge of the business seemed necessary to pull off the steal. He had eighteen employees at the time, some full time, some part time. I talked to them all, peeled away at opportunities and motives. It got tough when things started pointing towards his son, Cooper."

The sharp chin at #7.

"Were you right?"

"Never knew for sure. But my opinion? Cooper - who was only about sixteen then - started running up a tab with a dealer when he was in boarding school outside Boston. Struck me as a bright kid with daddy issues who was making some bad choices. When I told Frank the way things were looking – he shut the investigation down, paid my fee, said he'd take care of it. Would never tell me the details."

"Didn't get the final story?"

"Naw. But I heard Frank told his son he'd turn him over to the police if he ever heard about him and drugs in the same sentence."

"Tough love," I say.

"Frank never shied away from taking the bull by the horns."

I tell him about Rusty Razer sauntering to the car, chatting with the driver in the rusted-out Chevy.

"You see any drugs – anything - exchange hands?" asks Gordy.

"No. Could've been a jaw about the weather. Could've been a hand-off."

We reach the crest of the hill, I turn the car towards the smaller, shorter streets in the Libbytown neighborhood. I continue. "The Rusty guy took a picture of the car; he's got a little camera he seems to like."

Gordy looks at the ragged brown lawns and rusted chain link fences. "Frank's kids thought he should share his wealth; he thought they should get educations and jobs. In that order." He takes a shallow breath; there's a wheezing sound to it. "I remember Frank saying the saddest day of his life was when he decided he'd failed as a father."

We're on Horseshoe Lane. Gordy tells me to stop. He takes a long look at the semi-dilapidated #7.

There's no movement. The curtains stay put. No lights are on.

"Want me to knock on the door?" I ask.

Gordy eyes the yellow police tape stretched across the porch of #5. "There's probably a patrol coming by on a regular. Let's not get on their radar." He signals me to go forward. "Keep driving."

* * *

Bert's nose is pressed against Gordy's living room window when we drive into the driveway. Bert barks, happy to see his guy. Gordy's cell phone vibrates, he looks at it. "Damn. Marie's just off the highway." He opens the car door. "I gotta get upstairs. You follow, we need to talk."

"I was parked on the street when Marie left, she's gonna know my car was moved. I'll get it back in place."

"I taught you well."

Three minutes later, I'm back in Gordy's bedroom. His fleece-lined Crocs are back under the bed, the quilts are arranged, a pillow is in place on his thighs and the laptop is settled atop it. Bert is nestled beside him. Gordy puts his fingertips to his face. "Cheeks still cold. Get a hot washcloth."

He buries his face in the steaming terry and comes up for a breath just as Marie's car pulls into the driveway. I grab the cloth, get it back into the bathroom just as the front door opens.

"I'm home!" Marie calls. "Coming up!"

I land in my usual chair.

Marie breezes in, puts her hand to Gordy's cheek and to his forehead. "You're a little hot."

"I'm fine," he growls.

"Dee, are you staying for lunch?" Marie asks.

I stand. "No, thanks." I notice a monthly calendar; it's opened to December. There is a large photo of a holiday tree in snow and next Monday is circled. Seven days from today.

"I can get omelets together quickly," says Marie.

"Gotta go. Stuff to do at the office."

"All right, sweetie." Marie goes to the hallway to hang up her coat.

Gordy grabs my arm, points to a reddish-brown accordion folder on the window seat and hisses, "Read that." The label on the top of the file: *Croake*. "Frank was a friend. If someone took him out, I need to know who."

Marie hustles back in, there's another kiss on Gordy's forehead. "Rest while I heat up the minestrone." She strides out; her footfalls descend on the carpeted stairs.

"Get to the truth," says Gordy. "Be my legs and ears and eyes."

I tuck the folder into my bag. "I'll find out what I can."

Marie's waiting for me at the bottom of the stairs. Her hands hang by her sides and the energy she usually exudes is gone. "I can tell by your face that he told you."

I nod.

7 Days

She breathes in, forces a smile and puts her hands on my shoulders. "Don't be afraid. He's *forte*, very tough." Marie's eyes show a determination - she's holding onto a world the way she wants it to be.

My voice is tight. "Is there anything I should be doing?"

"I will cook and clean and love him here. Whenever you can, come to sit and talk. He likes that."

I push my emotions deeper. "Okay."

"He's *forte*."

"Gotta go. Thanks."

CHAPTER NINE

I put the accordion folder on the bar top and order a Rittenhouse. Pat, the owner of Sparrows for decades, sets a glass in front of me. His dancing shoulder, a holdover from his fiddle-playing days when he traveled with a band, has slowed down, but not his ability to read people. "A little early? What's up?"

"Been an eventful day already."

He pours a healthy two ounces and plops a postcard on the bar. "Got this from my nephew. Norway. Front of the card's a photo of a motorcycle next to a famous ski jump in Oslo, it's on top of a mountain. You get one?"

"No."

"Doesn't say anything about when he's coming back. You know anything?"

"No."

"Anything to eat?"

The scent of chicken soup, grilled cheese sandwiches, chili, brewing coffee, pie, and other belly-fillers permeate the space. The lunch crowd is gone. Two octogenarians remain at a table, they're finishing a slice of chocolate cake. But food has no appeal. I'm digesting information.

"Let me think about it," I say.

"Okay. Wave at me if you decide." Pat moves off to the kitchen.

I open Google on my phone and bring up an anatomical drawing of the human body.

Pancreas.

My dad told me one night - I was fourteen and we sat by the firepit at the Goose Lake cabin having s'mores – that I was actually more marshmallow than graham cracker and it was okay to show the marshmallow sometimes. He said it was a stupid analogy, but thought it made sense because I pretended to

7 Days

be a hard-edged graham cracker most of the time. I told him he was like the chocolate – all gooey and too sweet. I knew, sometimes, he worried that our non-traditional family unit was not solid enough for me. I'd tell him having a weekend mom and bookworm fisherman dad was just fine. Besides, Gordy lived two blocks away from our home in Munjoy Hill and G&Z was a five-minute bike ride from there. I had my dad. Seven days a week. And Gordy. I always knew where to find one of them.

Pancreas is below the stomach, tucked above the small bowel. Works with the digestive system and endocrine system. Makes insulin, regulates blood sugar levels.

I continue to read that you can live without a pancreas.

If taken out due to disease or damage, a person can live. With proper medications and treatments.

What kind of treatments? What medicines? What if those cancer cells are aggressive and determined to find new places to nest in different areas of Gordy's body?

Web MD be damned. Don't get sucked in. Focus. Do what Gordy asked you to do. Fine. I'll make a list that centers on Frank Croake - an information-gathering plan: what I know now, where I can find out more. The 'whens', 'hows' and the 'why' possibilities.

Pat's back, he rings up the bill for the octogenarians. "You gonna be ordering take-out for Gordy?"

"Marie's serving him soup now. He's being fed."

"She's a good one."

Seven days. Gordy's operation.

Does Pat know? Gordy has eaten breakfast here most mornings for years and has helped Pat out. Especially when Billy Payer slammed Pat's head against the bar - three years ago – in a sociopathic, drunken frenzy and things got messy. Pat's nose is still crooked. The deep cut across its bridge has healed, but it's left a deep purple scar. But that scar doesn't mask the other mileage on his face – a roadwork of good humor, patience, and the enjoyment he gets from providing a gathering place for the neighborhood. Pat's demeanor is too every-day. Gordy hasn't shared.

The door opens. It's Carl; he's fifty-ish and has a round pink face that has never needed shaving. He lives two blocks away with his hairless pig. Gallantly, he holds the door open for a forty-ish, red-haired woman in a cherry-red puffer jacket and a pink wool tam on her head; she's smiling like she just won the best cheesecake prize at the State Fair. Carl is spruced up too, there's a clean white turtleneck under his wool jacket. Is this a relationship? Well, that'd be excellent - someone moving forward in life and proof that even guys with pet pigs can get a date. Carl waves to me, then calls to Pat. "Put Dee's next one on my tab." Trying to be 'Mr. Big' for his date. Good for him.

I let the Rittenhouse scorch my throat. I close my eyes; memories spark. White doctor coats. White walls. White antiseptic everything. My dad, on a bed on wheels, tubed and masked, his heart in crisis, being rolled down a white hallway. Unsavable.

There's a voice behind me. "Gordy said you might be here."

It's Donato. He looks at my glass, raises an eyebrow.

"Hey," I say.

"Just talked to Gordy on the phone. He said you had G&Z's Croake file."

"I do." My hand is firmly on top of it.

"That you'd share it," Donato prompts.

"Did he use that exact word? 'Share'?"

"Maybe it was an assumption on my part," he says.

"My assumption is you're the official lead of the re-opened Croake case."

"I am."

Of course, when opportunity is presented, Gordy will take advantage. He's sent over the best source, and he'll be expecting me to use it. "No one thinks it's a suicide anymore?" I ask.

"New evidence came to light."

"Now it's foul play? Something south of chance or massively premeditated?"

Donato avoids a direct answer. "To be determined. That's why I need to get up to speed on anything that could open a path – so if you'd hand over the file-"

"No strong lead yet?

"As I said, looking for one."

"Ahm." I take a sip of my whiskey. "Since Gordy's not feeling so spry, I'll have to use my own judgment as to what G&Z should share."

He looks at the Rittenhouse again. "You eat today? Have breakfast or lunch? Are you being a hardass because you're working on fumes?"

"I had some gum."

"You don't look like your regular self. Feeling off?"

"I'm not sick."

His sharp blue-gray eyes study me. He's daring me to fill the silence – to provide the lowdown. I've seen him do the same thing in his interrogation sessions, staring down a suspect and unearthing confessions. But I don't cave. I cock my head to look at him, pat the file. "A lot of times, the only bargaining power a person has is information."

"Did I do something to make you angry? Can I buy you a burger and make whatever it is better?"

"Frank Croake was a friend of Gordy's," I say. "Gordy wants to keep up with how the investigation progresses. Doesn't want to wait for the slow siphoning of half-assed news sources or rumors."

"I love the old grouch too, but Gordy's gonna have to be patient-"

"He doesn't want to-"

"Come on. You know procedure. He does too."

Since I haven't opened the file yet, I have no idea if its contents will be helpful. But, at this point, Donato's clueless too. I have a little bit of an edge. "I share. You share. To make Gordy happy."

"Geez, Rommel. Frank Croake is no longer with the world."

"Gordy doesn't lose interest in a friend after death."

He grunts. Probably in lieu of cursing me. "I'll get a subpoena."

"Maybe you can." I pat the file again. "You'd have to convince a judge this five-year-old document *belonging* to G&Z and protected by *our* promise of client confidentiality has information pertinent to what happened last week in the Sports Park. That you're not on a random fishing expedition."

I sense the wheels in his brain turning - his careful consideration wheels. He's weighing pros and cons, trying to predict Chief Harper's reactions (when I decided to go to work for Gordy instead of returning to the PPD, I became one of Harper's least favorite persons). Donato's also assessing what could create a problem down the line in gaining a conviction, in giving clean testimony in court. Right now, I don't care about Donato's fidelity to procedure. "You know it'll go no further than us," I say.

He still holds out. So damn risk averse. Professionally. And personally. The latter is what probably stings the most. If I call him on it, he'd probably point to my tendency to dive-in headfirst without thinking about the depth of the water. I push forward. "What did Billy Payer have?"

Donato looks over his shoulder. The octogenarians are on their way out. Carl and his redhead are sharing a cheese plate. The waitress is near the kitchen, talking to Pat's assistant cook. The rest of the place is empty.

"Guess I'm not getting an answer on that one," I say.

Donato leans over the bar, interrupts Pat as he loads bottles onto a bottom shelf. "Okay if we take the back booth?" he asks.

"All yours," Pat says. "Want iced tea or Allagash Light?"

"Tea. And two burgers. Medium. Thanks." Donato's got a hand on my back; he guides me to the booth. "I think you need a burger to wash down the whiskey."

We settle in Gordy's favorite spot. Pat sets Donato's iced tea in front of him and Carl's gift – the second pour of whiskey - in front of me. "Coleslaw or French fries?" asks Pat.

"Coleslaw," we say in unison.

Pat moves to the kitchen.

"Okay," Donato says. "This I can tell you. Payer was cagey. However, I think he could have something that's something - relating to the Croake case."

"Payer's full of shit."

"Sure."

"What does Payer think he'd get from you? A rec to the prison board? A contribution to his Florida fund?"

"One thing he wants I'm not willing to give."

7 Days

"What's that?"

"Doesn't matter. It's non-negotiable."

I know the look. The half-closed eyes and the set of his mouth. An answer to that question will not be coming. Donato's put on his alpha hat, what he does when he's sure he knows best.

He continues. "Mostly, I think he wanted to show off 'the new and improved Payer'. Nebbish haircut, ironed shirt, the mini-Bible in his shirt pocket. All repentance on display." He takes another sip of iced tea. "Your turn. Tell me something."

I can withhold too. "You told me something without really telling me anything."

He hates to be called on it. "Let me look." He reaches for the file.

I pull it out of his reach.

He tries a 'guilt' approach. "You're taking advantage of our relationship."

That hangs in the air a second too long, but I don't want to go into what 'relationship' he's referring to. I finally say. "I'm working for Gordy - he's my boss. That's priority." Unexpected emotion rises hot from my chest and my eyes fill. I dip my head, look away.

"Rommel. There's something going on with you. What is it?"

I clear my throat and slide to a new approach. "Maybe you'll find this worth attention. A body was found at Kahta Condo Complex this morning-"

"Yeah, yeah." Donato takes off his bill cap, tosses it on the booth cushion next to him. His sandy hair stands up in front. He shoves it to the side to get it to lay flat. "You're talking about the woman who was killed, the one who took your bag. That's bad, that's tragic, but Detective Banford's all over it so it's not taking precedence for me. I need to concentrate on Croake."

I fill him in on my early morning Horseshoe Lane jaunt - about Gilli's stolen loot in #5 and where I'd seen Cooper Croake on the porch of #7.

He's a bit keener. "What was he doing there?"

"Looks like he was making a deal with the other guy-"

"What guy?"

"Out-of-date topknot on his head, a little too smooth. Cooper called him 'Rusty'."

"Huh." Donato takes out his phone, punches in a text. "Banford's got a team next door at #5. I'll have him go over. Cooper hasn't answered his phone. We checked the Croake family house on the West End, he's not there. His sister's there – she came up from Connecticut. His phone lights up, he reads the text. "No one's at #7 at the moment."

"Gilli Wanz owned basically everything on Horseshoe Lane."

"Huh," is all he says.

I taste my whiskey, but the burn has lost its appeal. I need to keep the mind clear. A large group bursts into Sparrows, they're loud and boisterous; from their conversations, they're ready for a high-spirited pre-theatre dinner before the show at Portland Stage. They fill four tables, and their voices displace the quiet.

"Can we take this somewhere else?" Donato asks. "Maybe we should go back to Gordy's."

"Marie insists on him napping after lunch. Besides, our burgers are coming."

Donato gets up. "I'll ask Pat to box them up. We can take this to your place."

CHAPTER TEN

I pull my Outback to a stop behind a taxi that's idling directly in front of my apartment on Eastern Promenade. Donato parks behind me.

Nail jerks out of the taxi, hampered by that huge coat and his cast. I get out of my car, and he charges towards me. "Where've you been?"

I step back. "Excuse me?"

He jabs his good arm into the air. "I told you to get over yourself and work on caring about others. How about a dead woman? She died; you forget about that? Are you on a date? Are you gonna go inside and screw this guy on the day she died?"

I keep my voice low, hoping he'll dial it down. "The police are in charge of finding out what happened to Gilli. Not me. I'm a witness and I can't be more than that. I told you."

Donato's quietly moved to stand a few feet behind Nail. "Sir, I'm Detective Donato. I'd be happy to talk to you-"

"Not listening to you, asshole," Nail heads up the brick path that leads to my front door. "Forget rules, forget your booty call. I need to talk. Maybe you can put death and grief in an envelope and shove it in a drawer, fill your mind with 'what's next'. Ignore what is *now*." He wails. "I can't do that. She's *gone*. Don't you feel it? I *need* to talk to you."

Donato follows him. "Thing is, sir, you *need* to *listen*. I don't want to cite you for harassing this woman and being a menace on her quiet street."

"I can talk to who I want to. It's my right!"

"There are limits, sir. Right now, you're standing on the property where this woman lives, and she's asked you to leave. Technically, you're harassing and trespassing."

Nail's face crumbles, he looks like his legs are too weak to hold him up. I feel a stab of guilt, that I'm failing as a human being, that I'm letting a hurting person down.

His anguish screeches, he points at me. "I can pay you!"

Before I can inform him that G&Z is unable to take on all clients, that money doesn't open all doors, that there are legal issues, he strides back to the taxi, collapses inside, and pulls the door shut. "Go!" he shouts at the driver. The taxi drives off.

Donato goes for the understatement. "He's sort of raw."

I nod. "Gilli Wanz's boyfriend," I say. "We found her – together – this morning. He saw the body first. His name is Nail Parcell."

"Nail?"

"Like hammer and–"

"How'd he know where you live?"

"Who can keep anything from anybody these days?"

"He's harassing you?" says Donato. "You want me to send someone to talk to him?"

"I'll give him a day or two." I realize I sound like my mother – making excuses for someone's bad behavior, expecting things will work themselves out. "Grief takes lots of avenues," I say. "It was a big shock this morning. Sad. Violent. At this moment, I can see how Nail feels his agenda is more important than anyone else's."

"I don't like the look of him."

"Me neither. Abshir can't stand him. He probably rubs most people the wrong way."

"Tell your neighbors to keep a lookout for him."

"They're in Florida." The two other apartments that have been carved out of the Victorian are occupied by snowbirds; every year, right after Thanksgiving they head to The Villages near Orlando to play golf, pickleball and poker until April. So, basically, I have the whole old place to myself.

"A lot of people have anger, Rommel," says Donato. "You know that. We can't predict where they'll put it."

"It'll be okay." There I am again. And I didn't think I took after my mother at all.

* * *

Donato puts the Sparrows' take-out bag onto the kitchen counter. "Back to Croake. Here's the deal. Toxicology came back, his liver showed something the bloodwork didn't. That got Rhia looking deeper."

"Rhia's the new Chief Medical Examiner?"

"Yeah." He's rubbing his hands together and he hasn't taken off his coat. I take the hint. "I'll turn up the heat." I adjust the thermostat and flick the switch on the fireplace; the gas connects, and small flames appear. A pair of my crutches leans against the wall; I retrieve them and shove them into a closet.

Donato, from the kitchen, continues. "When this case came in – Doc Smithson, up in Augusta, was already in his Hawaiian shirt and fishing hat and half out the door. He semi-signed off on the suicide, Rhia wanted to wait for the toxicology 'cause Frank's got a high profile and thoroughness seemed wise. So, now results are in and the newbie's getting slammed with the messy case of one of Maine's most beloved citizens."

Maine is tight. Not even a million and a half people inhabit the state - people know each other or know of each other - and someone like Frank Croake, with his charm and agenda and money, was a state celebrity. Of course, his death is going to get attention, and the new chief medical examiner will get a lot of scrutiny.

Donato's looking around. "You got coffee here?"

"Instant."

"That's fine."

I open the pantry, take out packets of *Death Wish Coffee*. I flip the lever on the hot water kettle, the electric lights activate. "Hot water in two minutes," I say.

Donato grabs a pie tin that's on the counter. "Burgers will be cold by now. Gonna put 'em in the oven to heat back up. That okay?"

"I'll turn it on." We're shoulder to shoulder in the small space; I move around him, turn the dial on the oven.

He sets an alarm command into his phone, shoves the food into the oven. "I'd guess about eight minutes. That sound good to you?"

"We'll need forks for the coleslaw." I focus on the cutlery drawer. "What else did Doctor Rhia have to say?"

"Dr. Jones. Her first name is Rhia."

7 Days

"Oh. Okay." She. Didn't know that. Donato and this Rhia must've hit it off; he's on a first-name basis already.

"She moved to Maine from Chicago – Cook County Coroner Offices. First time as a chief, and she wants to be on top of everything."

"Sure. Understandable...What was in the toxicology report?"

"Codeine."

"What?"

He takes his notebook out, flips to a page. "Residue in the right lobe of the liver. Rhia says a codeine high is sort of like an exaggerated super dose of dopamine. Gives a person a good-feeling, a numbness. Nothing matters. Kids call the street version 'captain cody' or 'lean' or 'little c'. Most of it is taken in tablet or liquid form – but it can also be injected."

A decade ago, codeine became popular with a few of my peers in high school; a liquid codeine and Sprite combo was called a "purple drank" or "sizzurp". One of my teammates on the basketball team got addicted and overdosed. It was a shitty funeral. I got ballistic when Gretchen's old dentist over-prescribed a codeine mix after her gum surgery. I tell Donato about it. "After three days Gretch realized she was waking up early, watching the clock, wanting the next pill whether she was feeling pain or not. She got scared and made sure she got off it. And she switched dentists."

"Smart."

"You go over Frank Croake's medical history?" I ask.

"We requested the records. Should have them tomorrow-"

"Gordy always said Frank was Mr. Healthy Living."

"It's possible the drug wasn't taken by his choice."

"Wasn't *his* choice? What do you mean? Someone spiked his soda or-?"

"It's got a bitter taste, Rhia says. He might have noticed it in a drink. You hear of needle-spiking?"

"I read about that nutbrain walking around Paris with a syringe – are you talking about that?"

He opens my refrigerator, takes out the ketchup and mustard. "Yeah. France – that was the first place, I think, to report needle-jabbing of people on the streets, in the clubs, other crowded spaces."

"Some think it's an urban legend."

"Could be," he says. "Rhia said some docs don't believe a needle jab could penetrate clothing. Or they believe that injecting someone with a significant dose would take more time than a quick jab."

"So?"

"She doesn't agree. She brought up that anti-Soviet writer - a few decades ago - he was walking in London and got jabbed with the pointy end of an umbrella, it got through his trousers and ejected a poisonous pellet into his thigh. He died."

"She thinks Frank was injected with a poison pellet?"

"Not a pellet. But needle-spiking is a possibility. After Rhia got the toxicology back, she did another tour of Frank's body – this time with a high-powered magnifier and looking for an injection mark. She found one. On Frank's back."

Damn.

"How was it missed?" I ask.

"Because the actual cause of death was asphyxiation. Doc Smithson had determined that before he put on his Florida fishing hat. The doubled plastic bags, the tight tape, the blocking of the air supply." He checks his notebook again. "Burst blood vessels, swollen lips, blood stasis. But, on a closer look, Rhia noticed a yellowing in the eyes and blue skin under Croake's fingernails, so she took a closer look at the vomit that was trapped in the bag-"

Burgers are no longer appetizing.

Donato's still reading his notes. "Codeine can hang in the liver – doesn't flush as fast as some of the other crap. So, when the results came back, it confirmed her suspicions. She re-examined his body. Frank's tattoo had made the puncture harder to see…" He accesses a photo and gives the phone to me. "David-Beckham-worthy tattoo. Swipe through a few pictures."

I look at the photos of Frank Croake's back. A massive tattoo of a tree with a strong trunk and curving branches grows over his shoulder blades. The roots of the tree trail down towards his glutes. A lot of ink.

The last photo swipe takes me to a close-up of one of Frank's shoulder blades. "Where'd she find the needle mark?"

He points to the crux of a branch. "With a super magnifier, I could see it in the morgue. My phone couldn't catch it."

7 Days

The hot water kettle whistles. He opens a cabinet and surveys coffee mugs and delicate porcelain cups. "We doin' fancy or homey?"

"The fancy ones are used when my mother visits. I'll stick with the red mug."

He sets two mugs on the counter. I dump in *Death Wish Coffee* powder and pour in hot water.

"I liked your mother when I met her," he says.

They'd crossed paths when I was in the hospital, after Billy Payer assaulted me and locked me in a U-Tow truck. Gordy, my mother, and Donato were the regulars in my hospital room. "For some reason, she mentioned she liked you too," I say.

"I don't mind being 'liked'." He takes a carton of milk out of my refrigerator and gives its contents a sniff. "Still good."

"When did spiking drinks and getting needle-jabbed become part of a normal conversation?" I ask.

Donato stirs milk into his coffee. "We cover it as part of the PPD speeches in the high schools now. Burns me. Used to be 'don't drink and drive', then a nurse would take over and talk about safe sex and condoms. Now we add how to spot different powders and pills, how to compute dosages, how to deal with overdoses, ways to avoid being targeted. My littlest brother asked me the other day if – when he picked up his date - he should assure her he didn't have any Rohypnol on him."

"You're joking-"

"True."

I take the mugs to the table. "What did you tell him?"

"That it might *not* be the best start of a date to announce you *don't* plan to drug her."

"It'd be funny if it wasn't so sad. Is that your last little brother to give advice to?"

Donato nods. "Yeah, the baby who's dedicated to the blueberry farm. He'll be a Mainer for life." The alarm goes off on Donato's phone. "Got a hot pad?"

I toss him a kitchen towel. "This okay?"

"Yeah."

He grabs the pie tin out of the oven, transfers the burgers to plates. I find my rarely used placemats. They're burlap-y and what my mom calls 'shabby chic'. Another mom present.

"Time to start living up to the bargain, Rommel. Your turn."

I tap the file on the counter. "Okay. Here's the big picture. Years ago, Frank hired Gordy to investigate a series of robberies at the Sports Park. When the son, Cooper, started to look likely, Frank terminated G&Z's contract. Gordy doesn't know if the thief was ever identified."

"Huh."

"Frank's got a lot of property, right?" I ask. "More than just the Sports Park."

"Right. Mostly central Maine."

"And probably a healthy bank account. Are his kids getting everything?"

"Don't know the details yet." Donato brings the plates to the table, stops.

"What?"

He shakes his shoulders. "Still cold in here. How 'bout we eat by the fireplace?"

It feels too easy, almost too normal as we take our burgers to the coffee table in front of the fire. Donato sits on the couch and finally takes off his jacket. "A little over a week ago, Croake held a fundraiser in the Park's big barn," he says. "Whole thing was for the Viv Cares for Kids Foundation. Almost three hundred people showed up for free cider, donuts, a silent auction, and the Silver Arrow Band. Cooper Croake was there – for the beginning."

"Have you talked to him?"

"Trying to track him down."

"Gordy wants to talk to him."

"Get in line, Gordy." He takes a bite of his burger and points to mine. "You're not eating."

I take a bite of a pickle. "Keep going."

"Frank gave his speech, shook hands." He swallows and flips through pages of his notebook. "After he watched the final potato sack race, he gave out awards. One of the park workers, a guy named Pike, said Frank looked sweaty, kind of pale. Went to lay down in the lodge in the upstairs family quarters. Pike never saw him after that."

"So, he might've been spiked at the sack race?"

7 Days

He shrugs. "A crowd was watching the governor win it with her daughter. No one noticed anything else." He points to the accordion folder. "Let's open it." I pull at the Velcro tab, pull out a sheaf of papers. The notes are Gordy-style.

When his G&Z partner, Tony Zandrick, died, Gordy was working solo, and he was a bad typist. As cases wound down, he'd invariably shun the tedious hunting and pecking and add handwritten comments at the tops and bottoms of pages, in corners and between lines. Once I started at the office, it became my job to input old cases into the computer, but I still haven't gotten to them all.

"Gordy said Frank felt certain the old robberies were committed by someone who knew the premises," I say. "Knew the Park's banking schedule and would know likely places the safe's combination might be secreted."

The fire crackles. Our heads are close. We pass photos of the employees and the summaries of Gordy's interviews back and forth. Eighteen workers; a few full-time, most part- time. We place the photos of the workers on the coffee table. The Maintenance Head had three part-time young and muscled assistants, the Head Guide corralled seven seasonal guides, including part-time Cooper. Frank's son was the youngest and the smallest, his t-shirt reads 'Junior Guide'. The others sport long hair, chiseled faces, happy grins, and tanned bodies. There are photos of the on-call Arborist and of the office staff which consisted of Viv and Viv's mother (both now deceased). They kept the books, secured the safe, made the bank deposits.

I check the five-year-old timeline. "First robbery was in January. Viv changed the safe access code. Despite that, there was another in February. Both had occurred the night before the regular bank deposit day. After February, Frank installed two motion sensor recording cameras and Viv switched around the scheduled bank visits. But there was another robbery in April – the cameras had been disabled and Frank thought it was a computer hack. That's when Gordy was hired. There was missing money in June but after that, Gordy's presence must have made a difference. Early August, Gordy gave Frank the initial results – and Cooper was on the likely list, along with two of the others."

I read Gordy's note out loud. *"Frank discontinued G&Z Services on August 15th."* On the final page of the summary, Gordy wrote: *"No arrests."* At the bottom of the page is the G&Z *Paid in Full* stamp.

I let my finger trail down to the handwritten information on Cooper's possible motive and opportunity: he was on a boarding school holiday, working part-time at the Sports Park when the first monies were taken. February he was back in classes, but his school near Boston was only a three-hour drive from the Park. Gordy noted that it appeared Cooper was behind in payments to a drug supplier. Drug dealer's moniker: Your Man for Happy.

I look up at Donato. "You think that's on his birth certificate?"

"Ha."

Gordy's added a note on the bottom of a page and circled it. I read it out loud: *"Each time money was taken – the amount was less than one thousand dollars. The entire available amount was not taken. Smart?"*

A robbery of less than a thousand dollars is considered 'petty theft'. It'd be either a Schedule E or Schedule D crime, usually a misdemeanor and usually punished by a fine, no jail time. Maybe someone *was* knowledgeable and being careful.

Donato writes the names of the Park's workers in his notebook. "I'll have Pocket size up everyone again, see who still lives in the area."

"Still, it's a leap from an old office robbery to murder."

"Yeah. Maybe." He swallows the last bite of his burger and reaches for his jacket. He takes a piece of paper from a pocket. "This is the guest list for the Viv Cares of Kids fundraiser. All three hundred of them."

"Photographs?" I ask.

"Press was there. Lots of pictures of people patting Frank on the back, everyone crowding around Mr. Popular."

"Photos from personal cell phones?"

"I've got the team already making calls, knocking on doors asking people what they remember about the day, if they have photos - when they saw Frank, when they didn't."

"How big is your team?"

"Not big enough," he admits.

The idea of disappointing Gordy washes over me and I push my complicated emotions down. "You've been to the Sports Park? To Marker Six?"

"Yesterday."

I glance out the window, the sun's trajectory is moving towards the western sky. "I think I'll head over."

Donato's eyes narrow. "There's police tape and a cop there to stop you from going up the trail."

"Can you get me permission?"

"No."

"For Gordy?"

"Can't do that."

I grab my plate, walk to the kitchen.

"What's going on, Rommel?" He's a step behind me. "I'm talking about what's going on with *you*. Not about Croake or the scene of the crime."

There's that heat in my chest again. Maybe it's because of the tone of his voice. Or his leaning against the kitchen counter, close to me, attempting to get in my eyeline. I turn on the faucet and rinse my hands.

"Rommel," he says. "Last night, you said you recognized my 'tell'. You have one too. It's the 'no-one-is-gonna-get-to-the-bottom-of-me' look you put on."

"I don't do that."

"Yes, you do. Come on. You don't usually drink whiskey early in the day and definitely not when you're working. You don't go quiet and skitchy every time Gordy's name comes up." He's not willing to let it go. "Spill, Rommel. I want to know."

My voice is low, like this is a secret I don't want the walls to hear. "They found a tumor. Gordy's got surgery coming up in seven days. Well, closer to six days now. Dr. Frew and some robot are going to get inside him to see how bad it is – if it's a cancer, if it's spreading or…" I stop talking because my throat's too tight.

Donato takes a moment to process - then chooses the cheerleader role. "Hey, nothing will take Gordy down. Come on, you know that."

"Look, I'd rather not get all TV movie about it, no pulling at heart-string kind of stuff." I move to slip past him. "Would rather avoid the 'it'll be okay, cause Gordy's a tough rooster' bull."

Donato takes a gentle hold of my arm. "Rommel, he *is* a tough…"

I step away from his warmth and look him straight in the eye. "Hear this, please. I don't want that Pollyanna mind-over-cancer stuff. I don't want to have blinders on. Ever."

He's about to argue for positivity but stops. "Okay," he says. "No 'hang in there' empty optimism. You're good at facing facts. And I am too."

I'd like to rest my head in the hollow between his shoulders and chin but that doesn't mesh with our 'friendship zone' and besides, the last thing I want to do is cry in front of him. I get past him, move to the fireplace. "I don't want to put off anything that I can do. Gordy wants answers."

"Okay," He pulls on his jacket, goes to grab mine off the hook by the door. "Ah, I was looking for that." He's noticed his scarf on a hook.

"I forgot to give it back to you last night."

"Well, it's handy having it here." He grabs my gloves from the table, hands them to me. "It's gonna be cold at Croake Park. We'll take my car."

CHAPTER ELEVEN

We're heading north on Highway 295. Twenty minutes past Freeport, we turn onto Route 125 towards Lisbon Falls. The silence in the car is heavy. There's concern. There's the puzzle of a murder case. For me, there's sitting next to Donato. He knows Gordy. He doesn't go back as far as I do with the old grouch, but there's a respect between them. And that sports-watching camaraderie.

My mind skitters from one thought to another, from fighting feeling to feeling too much, so I concentrate on the scenery. Maine does outdoors in a spectacular fashion. Even in winter, when the hills and fields are brownish, there are the deep green pines and silver-gray waters of the bay. It's background to our silence.

Fifteen minutes later, we pass a large digital sign on the side of the road: *CROAKE PARK TEMPORARILY CLOSED. Check website for news of re-opening.* Donato turns onto Croake Road. We ride over well-patched blacktop for five miles, finally arriving at a parking lot big enough for more than a hundred cars.

A local police vehicle is parked in front of the Welcome Barn. Donato pulls up next to the SUV, powers down his window. "Officer Cussmore."

"Hey, Detective." Cussmore's got a rebroadcast of a Patriot game on the radio. "Whatcha here for?"

"Another quick look around," says Donato.

Cussmore nods. "Quiet as hell here. Oh. Is hell quiet?"

"Have no idea," says Donato.

Cussmore asks, "Need anything from me?"

"We're good," says Donato.

Cussmore powers up his window, glad to return to football.

We step out of Donato's car. In the distance, there's the kiddie park with wooden structures for climbing and crawling. Beyond that, there's a softball diamond. Beyond that, hay bales for archery practice, beyond that a volleyball pit and a medium-difficult obstacle course. The main draws of the Park have always been the lake and miles of trails; to reach them you head uphill to the trailhead.

A short, stocky man, mid-thirties, dressed in a green and brown cold-weather parka, pants, boots, and skull cap exits the Information Shed. His camouflage colors blend with the evergreens and the brown hills. "Trails are closed." He gets close enough to recognize Donato. "Oh. Detective. You here to take the 'verboten' sign down? Good. People wanna get back up there before the heavy snow."

"Not yet," says Donato. "Gustav, right? Gustav Pike?"

His name is monogrammed under the Croake Park patch. His Adam's Apple looks like a swallowed golf ball. "Been named head manager, I gotta change the identity patch."

"Named by who?" asks Donato.

"Cindy Croake. She's paying attention to things right now."

"Not Cooper?"

"Cindy's the one I talk to."

"You're the one who found Frank's body?" I ask.

"Yeah. That was a bad day. I was goin' up High Eagle Trail to clear some brush, and I saw him. Reported it to the local cops right away. They called Portland 'cause it was Frank, and they wanted that kind of doc who looks at dead bodies and we don't have a specific doc like that around here – especially for important people like Frank." He turns to Donato. "You goin' back up there? To Marker Six?"

"We'll be back down before it's completely dark," says Donato.

Pike looks at me, waiting for an introduction. I hold out my hand. "Dee Rommel."

His bushy eyebrows shoot up, as if I'm not what he expected.

"I don't think we've met," I say.

"No. Haven't." He says quickly and shifts his eyes to the flashlight in my hand. "Could need that. Gets dark fast. I'll keep lights on in the Information Shed, just in case. I might be in my staff cabin behind the lodge, heating up some chili."

"You live here - in the Park?" I ask.

"Frank liked someone on the property full time. So, I'm that person now."

A chilly gust of wind blows through. Donato takes a knit hat out of his pocket, puts it on. "Been thinking about what you told me about Frank feeling sick at the Fundraiser," he says.

Pike nods. "He was okay earlier in the day – then when he was checking all the silent auction sign-up sheets, he started looking wonky. He left the party, went into the lodge to lay down."

"Anyone else feel sick? Besides Frank?" asks Donato.

Pike shakes his head. "Don't think so."

"Anyone cause any problems at the event?" asks Donato.

"What kind of problems?"

Donato keeps it casual. "Anyone lurking. Or making guests uncomfortable?"

"No. Everyone was good people. None of the ED-ers showed up."

"ED-ers?" I ask.

"That's what Frank called the Earth Destroyers. People dumping stuff on or into the soil, people who cut down trees that should be left standing, who mess up the water and air supplies and then come by to give Frank a bad time for calling them out." Pike's attention is on me again. "I thought you weren't a cop anymore."

"How'd you know I used to be with the PPD?"

"I read about you in the papers." His curious eyes move down - past my chin to my chest, past my pelvis to my legs. "You're the one who fell off that building and lived to tell about it."

His quick bio of me - the one sentence sum-up – rankles.

Donato feels me tense. "Yeah. Well, Pike, we've got work to do," he says. He nods to the trailhead. "Before we lose the light."

* * *

We slip under the police tape and start our climb. A week's worth of fallen leaves and sleety rain make the trail slick. I used to hike here - all the way to the top of High Eagle Trail you can see New Hampshire's Mt. Washington. If you look to the right – the ocean is in view.

As the slope gets steeper, I suck cold air. Knowing there are half-buried rocks and out-of-sight gnarly tree roots, I want to land my feet squarely. Donato's ahead of me; I talk to his back. "Frank got woozy at the party. Most likely, he was drugged there. So, he'd have to be carried up here or at least helped along."

"Been thinking the same thing," Donato says.

"He was a two-hundred-and-some-pound man – couldn't have been carried by one person. What about a cart? Wheelbarrow?"

"Trail zigs and zags – it gets narrow. Wouldn't'a been easy. There's a maintenance road for ATV traffic, but it was blocked off when that Whirly Storm hit. Lots of felled trees."

Donato turns on his flashlight, skims it over the bottom branches of the trees. I sweep my flashlight's beam over the sides of the trail. There's been too much time, too much weather. Footprints would have been washed away and broken branches blown off by nature's moods.

"Why Marker Six is my question," I say.

"Good question."

Pike had told Donato the Fundraising guests dispersed just after sunset. Pike hadn't looked in on Frank, didn't want to disturb him if he was sleeping. He found Frank thirty-six hours later – with the double-ply plastic bag over his head, secured by the tape around his neck. Frank's gloves were found next to him, as well as a roll of duct tape and a Leatherman Signal knife. His fingerprints were on the knife. Dr. Stapler had been called; time of death was hard to estimate because the temperatures had dipped and gone up and dipped again – eventually hitting a few degrees below freezing.

Fifteen minutes later Donato and I reach Marker Six. Yellow tape frames a large square around the five-foot column of oak - a proud eagle's head is carved at its peak. At the base of the column are two short pieces of 2x4 nailed together to create an 'X'. It marks the spot where Frank's body leaned against the post. The woods are quiet and we're quiet. Late sunlight streams through the balsam firs' needles, through the bare branches of oaks, maples, and aspens, it creates shadows and colors, like those provided by a church's stained-glass windows.

"Gordy will want pictures. That okay?" I'm whispering – out of respect for the woods? For Frank Croake's spirit?

Donato nods permission. I use my cell phone, click a series of photos. The wind gusts and pushes against the marker, the wood creaks, sounds as if it's moaning. Sort of spooky. What about ghosts? An image floats into my mind – Frank's body collapsed against the post, the regal eagle's head watching over him.

Did someone place the double plastic bag over his head, wrap it tightly around his neck, secure it with duct tape - and then what? Stand to the side and watch until Croake stopped breathing?

It's a hideous possibility. Nervy.

I take a video panorama of the area, including the trail that gets more challenging as it ascends. Then pan up at the soaring trees. The camera view lands on a brown and white hawk atop a high oak branch. He's watching us, his eyes like black marbles. He looks arrogant, perhaps he is because he's aware he can see better, smell better, move with more freedom, detect danger before we can. He's got the grand overview.

I lower my camera. A sapling, determined to survive the winter, catches my eye. There's a lone leaf drooping from a low branch. An oddly shaped leaf.

"What's that?" I point.

Donato steps towards the scraggly tree. He replaces his leather gloves with the latex ones he's got in his pocket. He plucks the object and holds it up, it's a three-inch rip of fabric. Wool? Plaid? Hard to tell - it's sort of brownish with dots of white maybe? But it's wet, mud-spattered and has been beaten by the elements.

Donato pats at the pockets of his coat, finds what he's looking for: a plastic baggie. He drops the fabric inside it.

"From a jacket? Pants? Hat?" I ask.

He grabs a good-sized rock from the middle of the trail and places it at the base of the sapling to mark the spot. He grabs a sturdy branch off the ground, uses it to stir nearby mounds of leaves, hoping for more treasure. "Shine your light low on the trees, see if there's anything else."

Nothing.

The wind finds its way under the collar of my jacket, hits the milli-inch of bare skin between jacket cuffs and gloves. I breathe in, the frigid, clean air ices my throat. In the city – in Portland - the smells constantly change, one neighborhood to the next. The sweaty odors near Sea Dog Stadium, the yeasty ones of baking bread at local bakeries, coffee beans and bacon near the diners, fermentation near the breweries, fish at the ports, business offices heavy with scents of cologne, soap, and hair gel. There's the ancient wooden house smell – the rot, age and neglect (like on Horseshoe Lane). Car and truck exhaust of the local highways. And Portland's hundred (it seems) food trucks full of international cuisines. All contrast to this place where the air is an inspiring mix of grasses, trees and soil and the unending clean sky. I get salt, clouds, earth and space. It's the Maine that does not deserve to be disturbed.

"What else?" I whisper. "What else do we look for?"

The sun sinks below the tree line, it feels ten degrees colder. The hawk flies away. An owl hoots. A coyote's bark seers through the air. It's followed by a howling reply.

Donato straightens. My body tenses. We've both heard the crackling, crunching in the undergrowth. Something's moving through a thick cushion of leaves. We look uphill, towards the sound. A coyote hunting a deer? A fisher or a bobcat? Has a bear ever been sighted in Croake Park?

Is it the sound of a person?

Are we being watched? Thick patches of evergreens offer opportunities to stay out of sight.

Donato unzips his jacket and reaches inside to his shoulder holster. He motions to the trail leading down towards the car park – nods for me to go first.

Shadows thicken. Another rustle of movement on our left.

Then on our right.

Two people? Tracking us?

Suddenly, a battering of dry brush and a thrash of motion hurls through trees.

"Down," hisses Donato.

Collapsing to the ground and assuring loss of quick mobility is not high on my to-do list. I bend low, lean to the side, let a thick tree trunk hold my weight and jut my LiteGood out into the trail. "Police," Donato yells. "Show yourself."

Four thick-chested citizens of the wood crash through the pines, freeze four feet from us. Each whitetail has muscular, spindly legs and eyes that register pink in our flashlight beams. Two have antlers that have been scraped to points. Their faces are immobile, their eyes register annoyance. We are trespassers in their space. Suddenly, the largest buck snorts - the signal to bound off. They do – and quickly disappear.

Something from above us, or to the side of us, could have spooked them.

"Shit." My voice is mostly breath.

Donato scans the area. He keeps his gun at his side. He whispers, "Give it another second."

The wind picks up. We listen to branches shimmying, leaves rising from the ground and swirling. The muscles of my right thigh ache, my tilt is causing my back to spasm. Donato puts his gun back in the holster, wraps his arms around my waist and pulls me upright. I'm dipping against him while my body readjusts.

His lips are an inch from my ear. "You good?"

"Yeah," I nod.

"Need to hold onto me as we move down?"

"I can walk. Fine."

But we remain close for another moment, separated only by layers of clothing - shirts, sweaters, jackets, gloves, scarves, hats.

"Okay," he breathes. "Let's go."

The descent is careful. Donato's ahead of me, his flashlight on the path. We reach flat ground and see the glow of the outdoor lamps on the Information Shed.

"Everything like you expected up at Marker Six, Detective?" The voice comes from behind a stand of pines. Pike slips out of the darkness. The best hunters can light-foot stalk when they are after their prey. Maybe he grew up hunting in the Maine woods.

"Saw some deer," says Donato.

7 Days

"No big surprise, we got a lot of them here. People think they're gentle, beautiful creatures, don't think about the ticks nestling on their hides. Or about how the bucks can weigh close to four hundred pounds and if you piss 'em off, those antlers can stick right through your kidneys."

Geez. Pike's observations must fall flat on nature hikes.

"They didn't attack us," I say.

"Frank was one of those hands-off-the-deer-population-people. I told him, don't leave 'em for too long. I told 'im, you gotta thin the herd or there won't be enough food and water. If that happens, some deer'll eat or drink the wrong shit and get diseased and spread it and then other animals got problems too. We wrangled over that."

"Who won?" I ask.

Pike smirks. "Frank. It's his land."

Discussions on how to deal with Maine's deer population always ebb and flow. Those agreeing with Pike's point include people tired of having their gardens raided, getting fields of rye and wheat decimated, tired of upswings of diseases that can spread through a deer's urine and feces and contaminate the soil and other animals. This group's solutions are to lower the numbers by extending hunting privileges (mostly winter kills), administer birth control, or clear habitats so cedar swamps, acorns and chestnuts are less available, and/or relocate the does to less deer-populated areas. On the opposite side of the argument are people (like Frank) who say that poaching, severe winters, coyote attacks, timber companies stripping of the land, highway collisions and the 150,000 or so registered Maine hunters (and the 50,000 or more who show up every year from out of state) do enough thinning.

"That make you mad?" I ask. "That Frank didn't agree with you?"

Pike guffaws, his Adam's Apple jiggles. "It was always Frank's call. Big guy always got it the way he wanted. Why waste time getting mad?"

Donato points to the barn. "That's where the Fundraiser took place?"

"Yeah," Pike says. "Too cold to be outside."

Donato turns to Pike. "Open it up, will ya?"

It's a huge open space, but it's been insulated so events can be held in the winter. The dais for the band is still up. Heat lamps stand against one wall, the dance floor is still in place as are the high tables for people to perch at while drinking and eating. Large posters remain on the easels, they show kids enjoying the camp in all seasons.

Pike flips a few switches; heat pumps start to hum.

I look around the walls covered in antique tools – most have a sheen of rust. There's a row of scythes next to a dozen pitchforks, baskets are interspersed with iron wheels, ancient rakes, post-hole diggers, hatchets, shovels, and spades. They all hang like pieces of art on the shiplap walls.

"No cameras in here?" I ask.

"Nope," says Pike. "Frank was against it. We're gonna get the place cleaned up and switched out today. The memorial's here. Next week."

"It's here? I guess that makes sense," I say.

"We think Frank would want that."

"We?"

"Cindy Croake and the party planner." He catches himself. "The memorial planner. Governor's coming, lots of mucky-de-mucks. Has to be top-notch."

We walk out, Pike puts the chain and padlock back in place. Donato's cell phone squawks, he walks off to check the message.

Pike shivers. "Shit, it's cold. I'm gonna go heat up my chili if you don't have more questions."

"I do have one," I say. "Any cameras on the trails?"

"A few critter cams. We go over the tapes end of the day to check for poachers and squatters – or if someone, like a dummkopf was out solo and got hurt."

"They didn't catch Frank on camera?" I ask. "The day of the party – on Eagle Trail."

"Bad luck. You remember the Whirly Storm right after Thanksgiving? Gusts got up to sixty miles an hour and the direction of wind kept changing? Spinning counterclockwise like a hurricane does when it's up here in the North. That's why it was called Whirly - remember? Everyone was battening down, but it never got an official hurricane name 'cause it never got up to seventy something. We lost all the trail cams. Access to the back trails too.

7 Days

Weather's the ultimate dictator. Right? We think we got the control but then, weather sets us straight. Bad luck."

"What back trails?"

"A few ATV roads Frank put in – to get up to the mountain in case."

"In case of what?"

Pike shrugs. "Stupid hikers. Sick hikers. Fallen trees we need to use chainsaws on and haul off. But they're not used much in the winter and boy – not now. I'll get to clearing the trails when we get a weather break." Pike notices Donato coming back to join us. "Can I go eat my chili now?"

"Yeah," says Donato. "Thanks."

But I'm not done. "One more thing." I ignore his snort of impatience. "How connected are the trails? Do they connect to each other at different points?"

Pike crosses his arms over his chest. "Eagle to High Eagle is off by itself – pretty solitary trail. Frank liked it that way. He said it was for people who really want to go 'up'. He used to hike it two or three times a week. Cleats on his shoes in the winter, rain gear in the spring and fall, nearly naked in the summer. He'd sit at the top, look over his land and meditate." Pike grimaces, as if the word 'meditate' is too unmanly for his taste. "Now I'll go eat my dinner if that's okay with you."

"Sure," says Donato. "And thanks."

Pike walks away quickly - disappearing into the shadows.

CHAPTER TWELVE

"You hear how Pike said 'his land'?" I ask Donato as we drive back towards Portland. "Like he thought Frank was too possessive or creepy about it."

"'Croake land' always meant off-limits. Or if it could be accessed like the Park, it came with a lot of rules. No development, no hunting, no poaching. Last year he got the sheriff to arrest fourteen-year-olds – two brothers and a cousin - who were using .22 pistols to shoot snowshoe hares in the fields off the softball field."

"Kind of hardass."

"He'd caught them a few months earlier destroying nests of wood ducks and throwing the eggs at the trees."

"That would piss me off."

"Kids got community service and parents paid a hefty fine."

"You think they could be parents mad enough to kill Frank?" I ask.

"Wish it'd be that simple. We talked to them. Families were in Iowa for some great-uncle's funeral."

Donato parks in front of Gordy's house. Bert's at the window, barking, assessing the quality of the persons who might be coming up onto the porch. "I'd like to come in with you, get Gordy's take-"

"He's not going to be happy. So, save yourself."

"He wanted a miracle today? All questions answered?"

"Probably." I open the car door.

"I'd like to come in, if it'd make things easier for…"

"His bullshit detector's still working. He'd know I told you about what the doctor said, and he'd be mad."

"Okay." He drops a hand on my arm. "Rommel, try to keep a good head in place on everything. Okay? And tell Gordy I have a team working hard on Frank's case." His phone squawks again. He reads the text. "Gotta go."

7 Days

I head up the steps to the porch as Donato drives off. Marie's got the door open; Bert's behind her. She pulls me in. "I told Abshir he shouldn't stay long, but it's been an hour and he's still here." She pushes. "Is it very important? He should get some sleep."

"I'll be quick."

She steps aside, looks lost for a moment and then goes back to the television where Best Stupid Pet Videos are playing. "Marie, what're you watching?" I ask.

"Oh." She stares at the tv. "Pugs dressed up like ballerinas for a parade. They are very cute."

Marie's always been obsessed with the History Channel. Not with dressed-up dogs. She must be more worried about Gordy than she's letting on.

Bert trots up the stairs ahead of me. We move into the bedroom. Gordy sits like a frowning gray king, propped up with pillows, surrounded by water bottles, medicines, files and frustration. "Where you been?" he growls.

"Can't get a lot done unless I'm out there in the world doing it."

Gordy grunts.

Abshir closes his computer, gets ready to leave. "He wanted me to bring over more files," he says. "I did. Now he wants more."

Gordy taps his pen on his legal pad. "Whatcha got for me?"

I tell them the Viv Cares Fundraiser went great, that Cooper was there for the balloon release and then left.

"He was there?"

"Yeah. But didn't stay. Everything was good - except Frank felt sick after the potato sack race. Probably because the new coroner found a high codeine level in his system."

"What? Frank didn't do drugs," Gordy says.

I tell them about the needle-mark on Frank's back, nearly obscured by his tattoo. "Someone injected him," I say.

"Without permission? No one saw someone do this?"

I shake my head. "One of the Park's managers - Gustav Pike - said after the potato sack race, Frank went to the lodge to rest, and he wasn't seen after that."

"How does this Pike know no one else saw Frank after that?"

"I guess he meant *he* didn't see Frank after that," I say.

Gordy comes back at me. "I don't like guessing."

I continue, "Donato's team is in the process of interviewing three hundred Fundraiser attendees including caterers, parking attendants and whoever - to see if anyone remembers seeing Frank after the potato sack race."

"Looking through a haystack," says Gordy.

"The Sports Park robbery you gave me the file on – Donato and I looked at it. I don't see how it relates. Seems to be a very thin connection."

"I wanna talk to Cooper Croake."

"Thing is, he's not responding to any outreach. Donato's got people looking for him."

"Find him." Gordy makes a note on his pad. Without looking up, he targets Abshir. "You need to get on what I asked. Get those files. Time's a-wastin'."

"*Haa.*" Abshir pulls on his coat and hurries out. His footsteps descend and I hear another pair coming up the stairs – and Abshir's voice. "Hello, Mr. Walsh."

Wallace Walsh rumbles into the room, carrying a grocery bag, his face cherry red from the cold and exertion. He eyeballs Gordy and smirks. "You always wanted to sit on your butt and have everyone else do the running around."

"Brain's still working."

"You mean your brain's still cranky."

Gordy dismissed Walsh's dig. "You got something?"

Walsh unbuttons his coat. "Word is Frank Croake's last will and testament is gonna make the Ecology Council and conservation groups very happy, the Children's Museum happy and the Grieving Children Foundation very happy."

The drift is clear. "And his own kids?" asks Gordy.

"Tidy sums but not the whole hullabaloo. But you didn't hear it from me."

Walsh takes a foot-high trophy out of his grocery bag and puts it on the bed. "Gordy, it's your year to have it on your shelf."

The trophy's plaque reads "*Lincoln County Lakes. Biggest Fish. 2019.*"

Gordy frowns. "My year doesn't start 'til January."

Walsh shrugs. "Right now, you got more time to look at it."

Is this a thing with old guys? Dropping off boxing gloves and trophies when there's a reminder of mortality?

"Anything else I can do for you?" asks Walsh.

"Don't need anyone to wipe my ass, if that's what you're asking."

7 Days

Walsh winks at me and moves out. "I'll leave him to you."

As his feet land heavily on the stairs, Gordy grabs the trophy and puts it on his bedside table. He's back at me. "What else?"

"Donato and I heard something in the woods near Marker Six. Thought it was a person. Maybe two people. But then a quartet of deer bounded out."

"And?"

"We didn't actually see a person or hear persons after that."

"Why would someone be so stupid to walk through the woods to intimidate a cop?"

"We found some fabric. Torn. Hanging from a tree. Unclear, at this point, what it's from or how long it'd been there."

"You think someone was coming back for – what? Some torn clothing?"

"Donato's gonna get another team up there in the morning? When it's light. Do another look-through."

"Probably already be too late."

I point to the half dozen pill bottles on his bedside table. "Are any of those positive, happy pills?"

Gordy's got a sixth sense when people are holding back and he's not going to let me off easy. "What else?"

I decide to come clean. "Don't go nuts. I told Donato about your operation coming up."

Gordy's face darkens.

I have my excuse ready. "You said you wanted information fast. Donato didn't want to share, so I used some of the details on your health to play to his softer side. I made an executive decision."

"You're not an executive."

"If you're president, then I'd be vice president."

"My title's 'boss'."

"Come on, Gordy. Portland's a small-ish place. The phlebotomist could talk, the parking attendant at the clinic, the checkout person at the pharmacy, someone who saw you at Dr. Frew's office or saw Marie looking panicked."

"She's not panicked."

"I misspoke."

"So, you used confidential information to manipulate Donato."

"For some reason he cares about you. I thought I could use it."

Gordy sucks in his cheeks. He does this before he erupts. But I notice the sweat on his forehead. Even on his nose and chin. I dial down my defensiveness. "Sorry."

Surprise. He chooses acceptance and adjustment. "Did you get some useful stuff?"

"Some basics," I say. "No answers. From what I told you - you see any puzzle pieces falling into place?"

He shakes his head. "Always knew things didn't set well in the Croake home."

"Both of the kids have alibis for the day of Fundraiser Day and for two days after."

"Find Cooper. Tell him I want to talk to him."

* * *

I pick up a condolence card and an amaryllis plant. It's got two thick leaves and a stalk with a red bud that's about to blossom. I head to Portland's West End, the neighborhood of stately houses and groomed lawns. The Croake residence is one of the bigger brick homes and has golden glass sconces on its porch.

I ring the doorbell.

The super-thin young woman who answers the door has an addicted-to-the-mirror-and-beauty-products look about her. Milky white skin, a mouth outlined in deep red lipstick and straightened dark hair. Her blue eyes are very bright, and they're rimmed in dark pencil.

"I was asked to deliver this to Cindy Croake, if she's available."

"I'm Cindy." She motions to a credenza. "You can put that there."

It's obvious she doesn't want to take the clay pot, maybe she's worried about getting potting soil on her tight lemon-yellow cashmere sweater and slimfit cream-colored jeans.

I close the door most of the way to keep out the cold. "Chilly out there." I head to a wide antique-y chest of drawers. It's packed with vases of flowers and stacks of condolence envelopes. "You want to read the card?" I ask.

"I'll look at it later."

7 Days

I move a pile of colorful brochures out of the way and make room for the amaryllis, to give me time to get chatty. "Excuse me. Was Frank Croake your dad?"

"Yes."

"I went to summer Sports Camp when I was a kid," I lie.

Her mouth tightens as if hoping I don't have a story to tell.

I disappoint. "Learned to swim there," I say.

"That's nice." She goes to the curved staircase, grabs the suede coat with fur collar that hangs on the newel post. I continue: "Sank like a stone the first day - your dad gave me an inner tube thing so I could float and get used to treading water. By the end of the first day, I wasn't using the floaty anymore. You must've felt lucky that your dad was so great. All the kids thought so."

"Everyone loved my dad." She doesn't sound like she's part of the fan club.

I continue. "I think your brother was in the advanced swim class at the next dock – that group that swam across the lake and back every day."

"My dad always had a plan to toughen us up." She slips into her coat, cinches the belt around her narrow waist.

I keep making things up. "Your brother helped me too. Gave me lots of encouragement. Even told me some jokes. Or maybe he was making fun of me – who knows, I was just a kid. After all these years – gosh – maybe fifteen years ago at this point - I'd still like to say thanks, you know, and extend my sympathies. Maybe re-introduce myself."

"You want to re-introduce yourself to my brother?" She takes in my old but reliable puffer jacket, my scuffed boots, worn deerskin gloves and knit hat from the bargain bin at Reny's.

"Yeah. Is Cooper here?"

"No. Not right now."

"At least you two have each other," I say. "At a sad time like this. It must be hard, planning the memorial."

She tenses - as if this stranger is assuming too much knowledge and has gotten too invasive and inappropriate. I make another attempt to extend the conversation. "What was your favorite sport?"

"Avoidance."

I laugh. "I don't get it."

"The no sweat, no heavy breathing, no pain sport. Best played at the mall." She pulls on green suede driving gloves, puts the long strap of a matching bag over her shoulder. "My dad didn't like that, he said there were no trophies in shopping."

After someone's death, the living usually toss out the bad moments and elevate the good. Sometimes even try to promote the deceased to sainthood. The newspaper articles this past week did that – crediting Frank with restoring a few rare species habitats, championing forest biodiversity, and spearheading a wetlands initiative. The articles lauded him as a man with an eye out for the future health of Maine.

Cindy takes a ten-dollar bill from her bag and holds it out to me.

I put up my hands. "I couldn't take money for delivering flowers meant to honor your dad."

She puts her money away.

"But maybe I can drop a note by later for Cooper-"

"Look, I have somewhere I'm supposed to be," she says. "Good night."

I slip out the door, hesitate on the porch. "Are you or your brother going to take over the Park? Everyone loves the Sports Park. I hope it stays just the way it is."

"Stay warm," she says and closes the door.

* * *

I wait in my car at the end of the block, wondering about Cindy Croake's lack of sentiment, her non-reaction to my clumsy attempts to reminiscence about her father. Can't help but think of the hours, days, months that Gordy, my mom, and I told stories about my dad. About the hours I spent organizing his maritime books and arranging for their transfer to the lighthouse's collection in Presumpscot. Every book reminded me of a story he'd told me about the coast, about shipwrecks, about adventures and the importance of Maine's history.

Snowflakes fall on my windshield, they're heavy, the kind of wet that makes streaks across the windshield when the wipers are activated. The temperature's right at twenty-five degrees. Predicted overnight low is in the single digits. If the roads don't get sand and salt soon, it'll be like driving on an ice rink.

The Croake garage door opens. A silver Land Rover backs out of the garage and heads west. I stay a few car lengths back, then allow another car to come between us. Cindy winds her vehicle through the streets towards Brighton Avenue. Ten minutes later, she turns into the crowded parking lot at the Wandering Moose – the eatery popular for beer, wings, and karaoke. There's an orange cone in a space near the backdoor; Cindy gets out of her expensive ride, moves the cone and claims the primo spot.

She must've been expected.

I park on the street.

The thick, heavy door is painted to look like a thick forest. A portal, sketched with metallic paint, is in the door's center, where the doorplate is placed. I push in to enter the Wandering Moose world. People are two-deep at the bar. Neon beers signs sit between taxidermized heads of moose and deer. Antler trophies – plaques with horns nailed into them – pretty much take up half the wall space. It was a rite of passage to show up here on a twenty-first birthday – free drinks would flow if you showed up with a copy of your Driver's License. It used to be that simple but now the of-age kid also needs to show a birth certificate and proof of a designated driver. *Then* free drinks will flow. The ribs and wings attract a lot of types - students and profs from nearly University of Southern Maine, businessmen, construction workers, I see a few people from the courthouse. Right now, Tony Dotz and a few other guards are digging into juicy burgers in the corner. I finally spot Cindy in a booth with girlfriends, toasting each other with maxi margaritas and making sure they're being noticed. There's no vibe that this group has gathered to hold a grieving friend's hand, it looks more like females on night prowl.

Karaoke is featured on the dais in the far corner. A drunken duo belts 'Islands in the Stream' just as a barfly gives up his spot and stumbles out into the night. I claim the stool, the guy next to me is doing shots and playing *Minecraft* on his phone. The barkeep gives me a yell, asking for my order. My Trekker Pale Ale gets poured, my cash is accepted, and the twelve-ounce glass is plopped on the wide plank bar in front of me. Bratwurst-wide fingers grab it before I can.

"What're you doin' here?"

It's short and solid Pike. He leans in between me and the game guy. He's got beer-froth on his upper lip; his tongue juts out like a frog's – sticky and quick – to lap the foam off.

"I'll take my beer, you can remove your fingers," I say.

He releases my Trekker and leans closer so his breath (beer blended with recently consumed onion rings) hits me in the face. "Everyone said it was a suicide thing. How come the cops changed their minds?"

"Like you pointed out earlier at the Sports Park, I'm not a cop anymore, so not privy to all info."

He swallows a gulp of beer, his Adam's apple descends and rises again. "You were asking questions, and that cop let you do that. So, give me answers."

"All I got are questions too. Know where Cooper Croake is?"

"No."

"Gustav. Have you seen Rusty?" Cindy's left her primped-out friends and joined us. She looks like a fashionista wisp next to beefy, earthy Pike – and she's weaving a bit. Is she imbibing more than margaritas?

Pike narrows his eyes. "No. And that's good."

She looks at me. "Do you know her? She delivered this flower thing to my house like thirty minutes ago."

Pike's thick forehead wrinkles. "Huh?"

I pretend a slow register of her identity. "Oooh? Oh, yeah. I did deliver a plant to the West End. The Croake house. Was doing a favor for someone." I gulp a quarter of my beer and change the subject. "Guess it makes sense you two know each other."

"Why?" Pike likes the opportunity to step closer to Cindy, to look protective. "Why does it make sense we know each other?"

He's not the swiftest.

"Because of the Park, lug." says Cindy. "Think about it."

Pike taps my shoulder. "When did you start delivering flowers?"

"Like I said, it was a favor."

"For what person?" asks Pike.

"It was private," I say. "It's in the card."

Cindy shrugs at Pike. "I didn't read the card, lug. She was asking a lot of questions about my dad and Cooper."

He taps my shoulder again. "You're like all over the place. Don't harass her."

"I come here for the karaoke," I say. A group of college kids are on the stage, they start singing 'Happy Birthday' to a fat frat guy chugging beer and looking way too excited to turn twenty-one. "Place is full of fun and joy."

Pike cocks his head towards me, fills Cindy in. "Her name is Rommel. She was at the Park earlier today. Asking about your dad." An idea lands in his brain, he turns to me. "Maybe you're here to harass me."

"That term's getting popular," I say.

"What do you mean? 'Term'. What does that mean?"

"Harass. Harassing. Harassment. I think for it to really count, it means a person is invading the space of a person who doesn't want their space invaded." I wave him back. "You're getting too close for my comfort."

"I got a right to choose my space," Pike argues. "To go where I want."

I lean back, as if this conversation is fascinating. "But that term 'space' is up-for-grabs, isn't it? As a concept? Is it a mental or physical space we care about?"

"What?"

I feign a philosopher stance just to bug them. "And which one is worse to invade? Mind or body?"

Cindy and Pike share a 'she's a pain-in-the-ass and a waste' look.

I don't let up. "Like just showing up at a bar is not harassment but if I get too close in your face too many times and won't stop yapping at you – you might feel annoyed or threatened. I read that Americans need more personal space than people from other countries. We don't like someone standing too close to us in lines, we like our own swimming lanes. We want elbow room. Guess I'm typical." I lock on Pike's eyes and wave him back again. "So, if you don't mind."

Pike's been trying to follow my rambling. "You're whacked."

"I asked you to back your ass up."

"Oooh. Touchy one." But he retreats a step.

"Better." I finish my beer. "Time for me to go home." I nod to Cindy. "Great talking to you both." I slip off the stool, go to the front door and give it a push. But the door sticks.

Pike, trying to retrieve his tough guy persona to impress Cindy, hoots. "Not as strong as you think, Rommel."

The door gets a kick and a shoulder shove. It flies open and I stumble out onto the street. The cold grips me and I hear Pike's tipsy voice as the door closes. "Don't worry about her, Cindy. She's a gimp."

CHAPTER THIRTEEN

The temperature's fallen to the low teens. Snow has formed into a frosty crust on my car. I open the hatch, grab the long-handled scraper, use it to screech the hard layer off my windshield. Anger fuels my aggressive attack. I hate that I screwed up. Now I'll have to tell Gordy I learned nothing tonight – and that I created an animosity with Cindy Croake.

And Pike.

They're odd friends. A thick-necked chauvinist and a privileged, skinny woman who prefers malls to the outdoors.

Screw 'em. And this weather. Time to get off the roads. I'd planned to drive by Horseshoe Lane to see if lights were burning in #7 – but streets are already being blocked.

I get into the car, turn the engine on, adjust the heat to blasting and set the defrost on high. Then I'm back outside to continue scratching at the windshield, hoping the interior heat will help get the job done and I'll be able to see my way home.

Traffic moves slowly, no one wants to skid into the wrong lane and sideswipe a parked car or hit a pedestrian walking in the street because the sidewalks are un-shoveled and slippery. These are the kind of Portland nights that send the lucky-to-have-a-suitable-bank-account to warmer climes in the winter.

My pokey drive towards my place takes me by the six-story office building that was under construction the night that marked my last day as a PPD officer. I never avoid driving by here, the reminder fuels some weird determination to never be on the losing end again. To keep - at all times - a solid lookout. That luck will not always fall in my favor.

Snow was falling that night too, and the roads were icy. My partner, Marvin Payer, and I were halfway through our shift when a call came in – a report of a robbery at Doyle's Food and Brew and of the getaway car's skidding into an innocent kid on his way home from Kung Fu class. We headed to the scene but got re-routed to this building. Marvin and I were informed the assholes probably chose this place to hide because it was dark, empty, and cold - a space no one would expect. But a security guard at U-Tow Truck Rental down the block had seen a pick-up truck squealing up and parking in the darkness. He thought it looked suspicious. Officers Heckley and Shappen arrived too. Marvin stayed on the ground; the three of us ran up the concrete steps and I was the first to the top floor.

The building's finished now. There's a sandwich shop on the first floor, architect offices on the upper floors. Looks contemporary Portland-typical, which means brick, flat, utilitarian. It doesn't scream that it's a building that changed my life.

But the ghosts feel thick. Sounds seem to surround the place – the clomping of winter cop boots on stairs. The crinkle of heavy, all-weather, slick police-issue parkas. The creak of the door opening to the frosted and slick rooftop. Memories flash: seeing large metal containers destined to hold heating systems, waiting-to-be-used building materials. Heavy breathing – realizing it's mine. Was there an escape route on the other side of the building? Were the bad guys gone? Didn't know. I was the first cop on the roof. I heard – too late – a cluck, a guttural, throaty cluck of greedy anticipation. And then a length of four-by-four was coming at my face. I ducked, it whooshed through the air above me, but then whomped across my back, my boots didn't find traction and I was off the roof's edge, my weight silently falling, and me knowing (so clearly) there was nothing to hold onto and knowing (equally clearly) I had no capability to soar like a winter bird, to catch the wind and hover until a life-line could be found. My gun flipped out of my hand and side-by-side we descended and crashed into a dark dumpster full of shards of sleet-drenched dry wall and insulation, and garbage. My shoulder cracked on the metal lip; searing pain took precedence over fear. Ahh! Marvin's yell and mine blended in the night as I stared upwards and my eyes locked on a short steel beam tossed off the roof that was streaking towards me. Too fast, too heavy. It ricocheted off the wide lip of the dumpster, spun, and jetted into my lower leg.

...

And then.

...

Sirens.

...

And then white tiled hallways. Being aware of the speed of a gurney's wheels spinning on hospital linoleum, Gordy's voice yelling that the best goddamn doctor better be ready, and someone better find the shits who did this.

...

No one has yet. Despite Donato's putting in the time, working to keep the incident out of the cold case files. But no one has found the shits.

* * *

I position my Outback to hug the curb in front of my place on Eastern Promenade. If the snow continues through the night, I'll have to dig myself out in the morning and find a space in a covered car lot so the city snowplows have room to maneuver.

I flip the locks into place once I get inside. I close the curtains, tweak the switch on the fireplace and collapse on the couch. My notebook is still there. Donato has left a pen behind.

Is there new information to be listed? What fresh fact could lead somewhere? What didn't I know four hours ago? What could be important? There's no one here to engage in the discussion – and sometimes it's hard to find answers solo.

Maine cold gets under the skin, digs into the bones. It even gets into the teeth. Shivering, I head to the kitchen, fill the kettle with water. Most of my cold burger is on the counter; I take a bite, conscious that consuming calories will help create warmth. My first-grade teacher, to get us six-year-olds to zip our jackets before a winter recess session, reminded us we had no thickening of hair, no fur or feathers like animals and birds to insulate us, that we had to close our jackets and wear scarves, hats and mittens to protect ourselves. In fact, she told us, human skin gets thinner in the winter and can't hold as much moisture. That's why it dries and flakes. What's Nature telling us, she asked. Gretchen, my best buddy, shot her hand up and suggested Nature was telling us to find a corner with a tv that had cartoons on it and just hibernate. The teacher corrected her, told her "Nature's just telling us to be smart."

The water in the kettle boils. I grab a packet of tea, notice the name: *Sleepytime*. I slip the tea bag into a mug and add the hot water.

I open my laptop, decide inputting details will make me feel more productive and efficient. The licks of flame from the fireplace soothe my shoulders, they warm my face and the backs of my hands. Keep typing, I tell myself, maybe a word or phrase or idea will loop-de-loo and point in a logical direction. The tea soothes my throat and my chest gets warmer. It's only been hours since Gilli's death, getting Gordy's health news, seeing the news report on Croake at the courthouse, since exploring possibilities with Donato and wondering what the mystifying elements of Croake's death could mean. Why codeine? Why injection? Why Marker Six? Why a slow suffocation? Had someone (or someones) been tracking Donato and me on Eagle Trail? Why are Cindy and Pike hanging out at the Wandering Moose?

I activate a search engine, enter 'Frank Croake, President of the Community Ecology Council' as the subject matter. There's a photo of him - beaming - so sure of himself and his agenda for his home state. There's an article, questioning the use of personal wealth to stop progress. I wonder what progress the writer's referring to. The renewal and revitalization of nature? Or of humans using the land for personal greed and domination?

I lean back, my head settles on the couch's pillow. Is Gordy awake? Is he thinking about Croake? Or is he cursing his body, angry he's been forced to face this challenge? Has Marie crawled into the bed next to him or is she still with her Pet Videos? Is she wondering about alone-ness? Wondering if she will need to find peace with a single cup of tea?

Heat had filled the room. I decide to close my eyes to think for a moment. And then I find myself pressed against the wall in a hospital hallway and one by one, narrow gurneys speed past me. The moving beds are occupied by pale Nail, my perfectly coiffed mom, tubby Liam Grimshell, tattooed Frank Croake, gray Gordy, Gustav Pike's Adam's apple and a human body with a moose's head. There are rows of exercycles lining the walls so doctors and nurses can multi-task – participate in a spin class while scrutinizing charts and ordering overdoses of codeine. Syringes fall from the ceiling; one descends in an incredibly straight line and stabs Nail in the forehead. He holds his cast up high and wails. Donato's across the hallway from me. He waves his badge, wanting silence from all so the baby in his arms can sleep. What the hell? Why is baby Dude here – gurgling, pooping in his diaper and slobbering on Donato's shoulder? The digital sign above the operating room pops on: *"Hello Gordy, Come On Down."* I chase Gordy's gurney but because I'm juggling gnome statues, I stumble. I complain, over and over and over, shouting over the cacophony: "One thing at a time, please!" Donato shouts at me, saying, "That's not how it works! Nothing is ever one thing at a time. Unless you give things up. Put barriers in place. Save some things for the next lifetime. Don't you get it?" I want to argue with him that this lifetime is it, there's no 'next time', one must get it done *now* or live in regret, but the gnome statues crash to the linoleum. I force my eyes open, yell that someone has to turn off those lights!

I'm not in the hospital and my voice echoes in my living room.

Damn. There's a strip of bright light coming through the slim opening of my curtains.

The light has been activated by the motion sensor in my front yard. It's bright.

Could it just be the howling wind? Or is something – or someone – out there.

I lift my head off the couch cushion. The clock reads two o'clock in the morning. I take quick stock; sometime in the last few hours, I've stripped off my wide-legged pants and doffed my LiteGood; the titanium rod and fake foot lean against the arm of the couch. I've pulled the quilt off the back of the couch and covered myself.

My crutches are not in their normal place – they must still be in the closet where I stashed them when Donato was here.

I grab my LiteGood, don it quickly over the liner that's still in place on my stump, press my weight down to expel excess air between my body and the accessory.

Just then, the motion sensor light goes off. And then on again.

What's out there?

A dog. Or skunk. An old bachelor, a block away, has a shed full of chickens and coyotes have been known to show up to salivate over them. But shouldn't all animals be burrowing someplace on nights like these?

7 Days

I turn the nearby lamp off. Turn it back on. And off. And on again to make it clear to whatever – or whoever - that I'm awake and alert, that I'm primed and thinking defensively. I reach for my phone, my thumb lands awkwardly and the phone slips off the table and flips under the couch.

Damn.

And then there's a flashing blue light. I move the curtain, peek out. A PPD vehicle is moving into place behind my Outback. No siren. Just a presence.

Why?

My phone pings.

The FlickIgnite is in its place on the mantle, there in case the pilot light needs a flame boost to kick into gear. I grab it, lean on the arm of the couch for balance and sweep it under the furniture piece. The long lighter hits the phone, pushes it into the open. I grab it.

Why is the PPD vehicle here? Has something happened outside?

A text comes through. It's from Daewon Pocket. *Donato put you on the drive-by check list for tonight. Saw your lights go on and off. Everything okay?*

Is it? Seems so now.

I send the 'thumbs up' icon back. But I add a few '???'.

Why the question marks?

I text back. *Motion lights came on. Don't know why - probably just a raccoon or dog or the wind or snow or an icicle falling off the gutter.*

I'll walk around.

As Pocket gets out of his vehicle, I head into the kitchen and look out the window to the small backyard. I pulse the outdoor lights on and off and leave them on. There are no footprints in the snow. I text Pocket. *Back looks empty.*

He texts: *Bueno. You got a big broken branch half hanging off a tree on the side. No sign of any presence. No footprints.*

I text. *Must be the branch?*

Maybe. I'll stick around for a few.

Don't have to.

Another text from Pocket: *Just came from Gretchen's. She made me a thermos of hot chocolate.*

My best friend - taking care of her boyfriend. Simple and gooey and thoughtful.

Another text from Pocket: *Muy caliente. Want some?*

Aware of my state of undress, I type back: *Not presentable for company. Raincheck?*

Snow-check. Si. I will drink some hot chocolate out front for a moment.

I'm back in the living room; I watch Pocket get back into the SUV. I sit on the couch. There will be no more sleep tonight.

Another text from Pocket comes through. *You like living alone?*

This stops me. My response: *What?*

Was thinking about asking Gretchen if she's interested in us moving in together. What do you think she would say?

What do I think? My brain does not go immediately to how happy this idea might make Gretchen. I'm more aware of the tug in my stomach – is that envy?

I text: *Sorry. Losing battery. Didn't get to read that last text ... Talk tomorrow...*

I put my phone aside. Turn off the lamp.

Selfish. That's what I am.

The PPD vehicle remains. Pocket's probably sipping his hot chocolate, practicing his co-habitation proposal, and hoping for a positive response.

SIX DAYS

CHAPTER FOURTEEN

The training center in Westbrook opens at four-thirty in the morning; the early bird die-hards show up to use the swimming pool, weight room, machine quadrant and the track. A few of the Portland Prosthetics' Clinic members are among them and Wendy, my PT, is always there on the early shift, overseeing her clients as they work to strengthen the un-injured parts of their bodies. Wendy has me on a six-month schedule, wants me to peak at the right time for the Boston Marathon. Seven-mile runs three times a week, four-mile runs on the days in between and two days of rest. I'll increase gradually, and when the weather gets better, I'll do outdoor roadwork.

I wave to those going through their weight reps. Vanessa's early core exercise class is just starting, some workouts are done while sitting, some while upright and balanced on the prostheses. Austin, a high schooler who was born without a right upper limb, is showing Wendy the bionic arm his doctor has him testing. It works off batteries and is meant to blur the lines between human and machine - some computerized control system that picks up electric signals from residual muscles and creates an illusion that the brain is telling the hand to open or close. Looks like something Hogan would be perfecting in his Boston lab. Austin's chosen a neon green vortex cover for the whole thing, looks really proud of it.

I don my C-blade and bounce to test the new vacuum attachment. Stretch. Move to the outside lane that's designated for the longer distance runners. Maybe running will lighten my mind, shift facts into a new order.

I start to jog. I'll get my hips loose first. Get a rhythm going.

Do I like to live alone?
Gordy's been two blocks away.
Do I like to live alone?
Gordy's been two blocks away.

7 Days

Almost all my life.

And repeat. Second time through, I block it. Don't want to keep repeating that. Don't like the cadence. Don't like the rhythm. Don't like the question.

Frank Croake. No one even knew he was missing for two full days. Living alone. He had a house on the West End, a ski chalet in the mountains, the Sports Park lodge and cabins, a time share in the Alps and one in Hawaii. But no one to share any of the spaces with. His wife's deceased. His kid and he are not connected.

Why the injection? Why the bag over his head?

Not ready for Gordy not to be Gordy.
Not ready for Gordy not to be Gordy.

Not a good rhythm. Change that.

Sweat breaks. Heart rate's increasing. Mind clearing. I hear Gordy's voice. Just keep digging. You never know when something will be unearthed. And then there's that last thing he said to me: *Find Cooper. Tell him I want to talk to him.* That becomes the rhythm.

* * *

I head into Kennebunkport, one of Maine's picture-perfect old fishing villages south of Portland. It's got art galleries, boutiques, cafes, beaches, and sandbars. I cross the bridge over the Kennebunk River and drive towards Heron Lane. The stone walls that act as a barrier between residential properties and roads are capped with a frigid glaze.

Jade's place is a 17th century gentleman-farmer's family home. The back fifty acres were sold off to a property developer long before she moved here, but Jade's kids still have the run of a large parcel of land. The boxwoods that line her driveway are covered with burlap. She's told me it's not the snow that causes the shrubs harm, it's the hefty and cold winds and hungry deer. When Jade and her husband Sven moved here from Washington D.C. (she was part of Homeland Security) they converted the barn to a sculpture studio (for Sven) and living space where their young kids could set up their toys, tents and nerf basketball court. She set up a basement bunker and became a private criminology consultant who sorts through the minutiae of human lives, politics, unethical shortcuts, small and large businesses' hidden activities, all sorts of particles that reveal how illegitimate activity can entice and plague human nature.

Jade's just back from a short-time gig in D.C. to help the FBI flush out sex traffickers. It made emotional sense; her sister had fallen prey to them and her death haunted Jade - she wanted to honor her sister with that dedicated time. She's only been back a week, but we have her on retainer, and she slotted me into her schedule.

She opens the door, grabs the newspaper off her stoop. She's in her typical all black – jeans and turtleneck; a black headband holds back her straight, dark hair. Something's on her mind, there's no preamble: "Your mom commuted from Portland to Boston when you were a kid, right?"

We make a pit stop in the mudroom so I can shed my outerwear. "Until the daily commute became too much," I say. "Then it became the era of the weekend mom." For better or worse. It is what it was.

"Sven filled in great," she says. "He got the boys to school and Silvie, this retired teacher in town who is seventy and swims three miles a day, flies kites, roller skates and snowboards, did the after-school pick-up, covered sick days and school holidays. That way Sven could keep up with his commissions. The boys really like her."

"So, it worked out," I say.

"Except I got jealous." Jade laughs, but there's a worried self-awareness. "Hated the idea that my family might think I'm not the one-to-go-to-in-a-pinch person. In times of fun, sadness, hunger – you know."

We reach the living room; it's packed with color. Her husband's latest works are six-foot sculptures of geometric flowers and oversized ladybugs for a park up the coast, outside Boothbay. "Sven says he's in his 'cheerful' period," she says. "They do make us smile, but I'm glad they're getting picked up today; we'll get the kids' play-space back." We move into the kitchen. Banana bread's recently been taken out of the oven, and she slices pieces for us. "What I really want to ask you is this: the boys seem to be holding back. It used to be a hug fest all the time. Now – not so much."

"You think they're afraid you'll leave again?"

"I told them I wasn't."

"Maybe they're becoming more self-reliant. Kids do grow up."

"Pete's in first grade," she says. "Bori's in kindergarten. They're barely out of baby-dom."

"To you." I tease. "I read age six is the new thirty and age five is the new-"

"Very funny." Her pointer finger punches in a security code on the steel door that leads to her bunker. We descend the carpeted stairs, the coffee's already brewing. "Well, being away didn't work for me. But that's my personal biz. Your time begins now."

We're in the middle of her state-of-the-art, super secure basement. There are banks of computers, her electronic brains. I've already sent over the details: the Croake case being re-opened because of the tox screen and discovery of the injection site. "We know who benefits monetarily from his death: favorite causes and charities, his kids."

"I did a swath on Croake's businesses and holdings," she says. "We can start where you want."

"Gordy wants to focus on the family."

"Any reason?"

"Gut, I think. Might be because he never got to finish an investigation five years ago – when Gordy suspected Cooper, the son who was a teenager at the time, was stealing from the family to pay for his drug buys."

"Then let's start with Cooper." Jade opens a file on her computer. "You asked about rehab stints. I checked places in New England first and got lucky. Cooper Croake was a guest at a fancy place called 'Demarcation' near Andover in Massachusetts. He's stayed there three times."

I'm surprised. "Three?"

"These places don't have magical powers; they never guarantee success. First time, at age sixteen, he was there for six months for abuse of Class B drugs."

I read the dates on the report. "Around the time of the thefts at the Park," I say. That answers one of Gordy's questions.

"The next was eighteen months later," Jade says. "He was trying to kick a Class A habit."

"What? Cocaine?"

"Or crack or heroin – or a combo of those and others. The records noted the Class Bs he'd moved on from were oxycodone, codeine - you know, DXM - and ketamine."

"You said codeine."

"That's right. In DXM form." Jade's aware the drug had shown up in Frank's tox report.

I continue, "That means Cooper'd be aware of sourcing."

"Scoring's not much of a problem these days. Dealers are under every smelly rock." Jade checks her notes. "First two residences at Demarcation were paid for by the Croake Family Account. Last residence was over a year ago and was *not* paid for by the Family Accounts. I'm still trying to find out who bankrolled it. His trust fund's on a monthly payout, always maxed-out, he would've needed to be bankrolled."

"Does Cooper have a job?"

"Series of low-level, low-responsibility ones. When he wasn't in rehab."

Cooper Croake, on the porch of #7 looked pampered – his haircut, his shiny down jacket, high-end hiking boots. He didn't look like he was living on the edge. I move on. "Cindy?

Jade pulls up research. "She's one year younger. She boarded at Lincoln Academy in Newcastle for high school, grades were barely passing, she somehow got accepted at Connecticut College, never picked a major, and never graduated. She lives in a condo in Stamford that belongs to Croake Family Holdings and earns a middling salary at an art gallery."

"Her trust fund?"

"Got access at age eighteen, same deal as Cooper. Monthly pay-out. She's twenty-one now."

"I wonder why the kids didn't live at home during high school. And why neither kid was interested in working with Dad."

"Frank had a rep for very high expectations. That comes from a lot of different sources." She sips her coffee. "Gordy really thinks this could be patricide?"

"He usually wouldn't narrow the search so fast. Covering all bases is his usual thing-"

Jade cocks her head, curious. "What's different this time?"

I don't want to get into 'why' Gordy may not be thinking as thoroughly as usual, why he wants a quick result. "I guess he's forcing me into that role," I say.

She doesn't totally buy my response. "Okay. Means there's more pressure on you."

"Yeah."

"And you're up for it."

"Better be." I want to hand Gordy a solve. "Let's go wider. Did you find out anything interesting about Frank's properties?"

"Ninety percent of them are in Lincoln, Knox, and Cumberland Counties, within 200 miles of here. Lots of lake front, lots of forested land." Jade opens another file on her computer. "He put outstanding offers to farmers and other landowners in Central Maine who might want to sell off land. He sent monthly reminders that he'd pay ten percent over any other price offered."

"No one stopped him from all the buying?"

"It's not illegal. As long as taxes were paid, he was good. Makes sense - because of his agenda."

"You mean – environmental concerns – that stuff?"

"Frank was evangelical." She's got a stack of local magazines on a nearby table, a few have Frank on the cover. She opens one, finds an article and taps on the title. 'Don't Mess With Frank'. She gives me a synopsis. "If he witnessed people throwing beer cans or Styrofoam or trash into the lakes and rivers, he'd take pictures and get local judges riled up enough to hand out hefty fines."

"Heard about that." I flip through my notebook. "Yesterday Donato told me Frank pressed charges against three kids for shooting snowshoe hares on the edge of the Sports Park's property and raiding ducks' nests."

Jade quickly finds her research. "The kids ended up working at a community garden and manning some farmstands for an entire summer. Not bad, but they wanted to play baseball and had to forfeit being on their teams. Parents were embarrassed, kids were mad - but Frank was a guy who thought people learned better if there were significant consequences, more than a frown or slap on the wrist."

She hands me printouts from other magazines. "The one on the top reports on Frank's habit of taking drives around the country backroads. If he saw a lawn or field full of old tractors, trucks, and cars or any vehicles that might contain lead chromate paint, or cadmium residue or asbestos-"

"Asbestos? In vehicles?"

"It was banned in the late '80s, there was toxic drippings from the brakes and gaskets full of it that got on the roads. When rain hit, there was runoffo to decrease toxic runoff from the roads into water systems. But that ban was overturned; politics were put before health and safety. Frank railed against the regained permissions." She goes to the next article in the stack. "This one tells how Frank would go right up to homeowners' doors and offer to pay to have the junked things towed and dumped as responsibly as possible. If he was told to bug off, he'd go into hard-sell and remind them that Maine's already a sorry victim of Forever Chemicals. He'd remind them that since the PFAS blight took us decades to figure out – we had to keep our eyes open for dangers with other kinds of toxins." She quotes from the article: "'…from tossed machines, vehicles, refrigerators, old grills, Teflon, gas cans, chainsaws and whatever other junk that piles up in yards and barns, detrimental results can be determined.'"

When anyone mentions Forever Chemicals in Maine, it usually refers to PFAS – chemicals that were first used around the 1930s in our papermill factories to make those plates, cups, pizza boxes and other paper products that resist soaking up grease and oil. They also repel water. Maine, because of its forests, was one of USA's leading makers of paper products and that meant we made a lot of production sludge. Eventually there were outcries about dumping it into the rivers, and the big idea was to spread the waste on farmlands because it showed signs of helping soil retain moisture and encouraged slow erosion. The negative effects weren't realized for fifty or sixty years but turned out to be the transference of the bad chemicals into the crops, the wells, the water sources. There are now long lists of active lawsuits against companies that used per and polyfluorinated substances. Most famous lawsuits are probably the ones in West Virginia, with DuPont's dumping of PFOA/C-8 chemicals used to make Teflon into the water there and the increase of cancer in the population. And in Minnesota where land around 3M (and other portions in the Midwest) revealed high levels of contamination. The problem has now been found in all states, from Arizona to Ohio to Michigan to Florida. It's a shit show and Maine's been hit hard.

"You've met my friend Gretchen," I say.

"She's the one who owns Doggie DayCare?"

"Right. She tossed her waterproof mascara and waterproof lipsticks and waterproof everything when it came out PFAS was used in some of those make-up products."

Jade points to her bulletin board. "Hydraulic fluids, non-stick cookware, firefighting foam, dental floss, stain-resistant carpet - my catalog of things to avoid keeps growing."

We're descending into a rabbit hole; I put on the brakes. "Let's stick to Frank."

"But it's related. No one likes large-scale clean-up actions that affect the pocketbook. And some of Frank's proposals through the Ecology Council felt like pocketbook drains. 'Planet Versus Profit' was his battle cry." She hands me a folder. "Frank financed some clean-up experiments. Including a soil-washing company, a group touting gas fractionation, then foam fractionation companies-"

"Explain please."

She hands me a three-ring binder. "Gets technical, but all of them are different ways to disrupt PFAS toxins in the soil. Problem is, all are expensive, and sometimes a new kind of waste is created."

"Meaning we're screwed."

"Meaning the search for better ideas continues. Last year Frank hooked up with a company planting hemp fields in Lincoln County. Somehow the hemp plant draws toxins out of the soil – unfortunately it's a slow method – and again, it results in another waste that needs to be dealt with. So, he puts that experiment on hold." She gets up to pour herself more coffee. "At my kids' school, each class is required to do a yearly project on Maine's environmental concerns. Pete's class is doing one on how fish get hurt by the plastics dropped into the Bay. Bori's class is looking at the nesting challenges of golden eagles due to transitions in land use."

"Isn't that intense for little kids?"

She takes a bite of banana bread. "School wants them to know that everything's connected - food chains and survival of species and all that. I'm not against it."

"You were solidly in the Frank Croake camp?"

"Did I think some of his speeches got too preachy and antagonistic? Maybe. But, in my opinion, there's room for that voice in the social and environmental conversations."

"Let's see what we've got so far," I say, glad to jot down alternates to Gordy's myopia. "People who disagree with Frank's environmental agenda. Those who resented his land grabbing. A few pissed-offs that they or their kids had to go in front of a judge. Maybe malcontents he pulled funding from. I'll keep Cooper and Cindy listed because they don't seem to have had warm feelings towards their dad and wanted him to be a cash machine. Big question remains – why *now*? Why did someone decide *now* was the time Frank should leave this earth?"

Jade opens a computer file. "This one's recent." The screen fills with beauty shots of gently rolling farmland, a two-story bucolic farmhouse, and a large barn. She continues, "Frank was focused on acquiring two hundred acres that abuts the Sports Park. It belonged to a farmer, an eighth-generation Mainer who was son of a farmer, grandson of a farmer, great-grandson of a farmer, you get the idea. Ben Wanz was holding out because he wanted his kids – two daughters – to get interested in keeping the farm. But it turned out that was not in the cards."

I put my coffee cup down – too hard. Liquid slops onto the table. "Sorry." I grab a napkin to soak it up.

"What spooked you?"

"You said 'Wanz'." I grab the newspaper off the table. "You hear about the death yesterday at Kahta Condominiums?"

"Don't know the details, was going to read it this morning." Jade scans the front page. "Oh... the victim's name was Gillian Wanz." She's back at her computer, inputting keywords for a new search. "Wanz. Two Daughters Farm," she mutters. Information pops up. "Got it. Belongs now to Gillian Wanz and Tanya Wanz Stimm. I guess Tanya's gotten married and she's added her mate's name."

7 Days

I tell her about first seeing Nail and Gilli at Letty's Diner. About Gilli grabbing my bag. About her hoarding of goods, some (or all?) stolen, in the small house at #5 Horseshoe Lane. About Gilli's murder. I tell her Detective Banford is the lead, that I don't know where his investigation has gone in the last twenty hours. "What dealings did Frank have with Ben Wanz?" I ask.

She glances at her notes, wants to relay the story in a linear order. "Well, a year ago, it turned out Frank realized he had put too much faith in the handshake deal he had with Wanz to buy his property if and when Wanz ever decided to sell. When he heard that Ben had agreed to sell Two Daughters to a young farmer who wanted to grow grains for the breweries and raise chickens, Frank went into action."

"Why wouldn't Wanz keep the deal? Frank was paying top dollar plus ten percent."

"Tradition. Sentiment. Love of his land." She scans her notes. "Maybe the young grower reminded Ben of himself. Maybe he liked the notion of the young guy moving into the family home, raising kids there, farming the land, sort of honoring what generations of the Wanz family had built. The young farmer pulled together a down payment and was ready to mortgage himself to the hilt and it looked like the deal was set. It was quick and happened when Frank was away at some environment conference in Europe – but when he got back, he got in the buyer's ear about investigating PFAS history on the property. The young farmer didn't have concerns because Ben Wanz had no records of any use of sludge. But Frank dug into county archives and found evidence that Ben's grandfather covered fields with it for two seasons, back in the early 1980s."

"Fifty some years ago?"

"Remember, these are *Forever* Chemicals. Frank offered to pay for the tests on soil, streams and wells. The tests came back and showed the presence of PFAS. Frank shared the less-than-favorable results – along with the recent studies that demonstrate how the chemicals can be sucked up and poison new crops. Anyway, the sale got screwed up and Ben Wanz's land value dropped like a stone. Not just as farmland, but for housing development purposes too because there are still questions about the dangers of the dust and other stuff coming up off PFAS contaminated soil. Real estate people are getting more requests for tests on properties and banks are starting to drag their heels."

"Bad news for the Wanz family."

"Then Wanz's wife died of cancer. And it got uglier."

"Did Frank still want the land? Did he try get it at a cheaper price?"

"He tried, but Ben was livid and refused to sell to him at any price. Then Ben's cancer got diagnosed and he died - about seven months ago. Frank made another offer, but the daughters told him to shove it."

I only crossed paths with Gilli once, but I imagine - if she got angry - it'd be hard to get her to change her mind. How furious was she at Frank Croake?

Is Tanya Wanz as erratic as Gilli?

Jade continues. "Turned out Frank had earmarked the Wanz farm for mushrooms."

This is a total sideswipe. "What? Mushrooms?"

"Frank's latest investment. It's a company called 'Maine's Mushroom Friend'. It focuses on bioremediation genetics."

Big words.

"Mycoremediation is a subset of bioremediation-"

"Make it simple for me," I say.

"The growing of certain mushrooms. It's caught environmentalists' attention as a plausible way to pull toxins out of damaged soil. There've been successful experiments in Northern California; after one of their big fires, the soil was in really bad shape from the paint, cleaning products, electronics, propane tanks and whatever else that had been scorched or turned to ash. There was worry that rains would create run-offs and get the dross into streams and rivers and other water supplies. The mushroom guys — they're mostly bioengineers - they injected oyster mushroom spawns into planting tubes and buried them in the ground. As the mushrooms grew and matured and spread, contaminates were sucked up and the clean-up was considered a success. And so far, no extra consequences."

"How did this get figured out?"

"Someone's always thinking up something. And the world moves forward. The guy who started 'Mushroom Friend' is Carter Stround, he has an office and lab at USM. He teaches there too. Frank recently came in as a prime investor, promised Stroud money and land to use as a testing area. Seems likely Two Daughters Farm was going to be the showcase."

"And when Gilli and Tanya closed the door on him - Frank had egg on his face."

Jade nods. "Frank didn't have a rep of ever giving up. Maine's a state of 23 million acres, 18,000 of that is forested. There's only one tenth of one percent of the forest that has not felt an axe or a saw. It's getting used up. Population is ticking upwards; more people are moving here. Things are getting tighter." She looks at her charts. "There's about a million and a half acres of land used for farming and that's also decreasing. Plus, Two Daughters Farm abuts Croake Sports Park. It makes sense that Frank focused there."

I sit with this – wondering if the two deaths could really be related to a *land issue*.

Her fingers move across the computer keyboard. She mutters, "What're we thinking? Frank's death and Gilli Wanz's death are connected? That doesn't match with Gordy's gut. He's focused on the kids wanting the Croake family fortune."

"But-"

She turns to me. "But what?"

"Just thinking about a coincidence." I tell her about the brochures on Cindy Croake's hallway table. The images resembled the photos on Jade's computer. "I delivered an amaryllis plant and had to move the brochures to make room. They looked like marketing materials – photos of rolling fields and apple orchards and a New England farmhouse."

She slides her rolling chair over to her central computer and searches for "Property Development: Wanz Farm". A website – "Two Daughters Homes" comes up, the photos on the first page feature an idyllic foggy morning on the farm. Picturesque fences replete with climbing roses. A swing set and picnic table near the farmhouse. She scrolls down, there is a simple development plan for multiple homes over the two hundred acres, a community center, pickleball and tennis courts and putting greens. She clicks on the info icon and continues to mutter. "Two acre lots, a few different house designs to choose from – prices start at two million dollars. Even if half the land is dedicated to homes - that could add up to be a big chunk of change."

More than a one-time sale to Frank Croake?

"When do the lots in the development go up for sale?"

She clicks on the *Updates* icon and purses her lips. "Huh. The Project was put on hold a week before Frank's death."

Had Frank found a way to stall another Two Daughters Farm plan?

"Jade, can you print me copies?"

The printer whirrs. "Interesting that Cindy Croake would have a stack of brochures for a home development project at her place when the land decision isn't official yet." She swings back to her computer. "Let me do county records."

Jade brings up public records from the State Development Office. "Plans like this have to be registered with SLODA," she murmurs under her breath. "SLODA monitors what impact new housing communities might have on their counties. Mmm. Looks like there's a RMD classification in place – that's medium density residential data."

"Is there a developer or contractor listed?" I ask.

"Oscar Herbstrom. Portland guy."

The guy with the barrel chest, yellow tie and jewelry who thought Frank was an attention-hog. The guy who dissed Gordy's Crocs.

Two murders. About a land sale? Can't be.

Jade straightens, taps at the screen. "Oh. Wait. Wait. Here's something. Look at this. The Croake kids are listed as new investors in the Housing and Community Development project."

"Cooper and Cindy?" I ask

"But, like I said, the project is on hold. I'll need to dig deeper."

Cooper and Cindy.

And there it is. We're back to Gordy's gut.

CHAPTER FIFTEEN

Jade's buttoning up a black wool jacket and walking me to my car. "One more thing. Your personal request."

"Oh." I hadn't forgotten, I'd figured she hadn't gotten to it since I'd called last night and asked her to make Frank Croake a priority.

She's got an 8x11 envelope under her arm, she hands it to me. "There's not much on this Liam Grimshell, living in Boston, age thirty-one. Adopted into a nice family at birth. Went to good schools in the Midwest, came east for grad studies at Amherst. Stayed in New England. Lives within his means, no arrests, no DWI, no peeing near playgrounds. He has a few bowling trophies. Signs up for Weight Watchers twice a year. That's it. Why do you care about a guy working at the Cancer Research Center?"

"He got his nose out of joint because he didn't get a promotion. He blames my mom; she's one of the VPs at the Center. Sort of a harassment situation."

"Threats?"

"Not physical. More misplaced blame."

She shakes her head. "I wonder if anyone ever informed this Grimshell that we don't always get what we want? I wanted to be an Olympic gymnast. I got too tall, and my talent ended up being too small." Her brow furrows. "Why is he fixated on your mother?"

"Don't know. But she's at a conference in London for another week. She thinks the whole thing will die down by the time she gets back. Now that I know he's so squeaky clean, I can let it rest on a back burner. We'll see what happens when she's back in Boston."

"Begs the question, doesn't it," she says. "If we can't find a proper place to put our disappointments – if we can't deal with those emotions that flare up when 'we-want-but-don't-get' – then what?"

"One of life's big conundrums." I open my car door. "Thanks. How much do I owe you for the Liam Grimshell?"

"Consider it a birthday present."

"You're a professional. I am too. I don't need a freebie."

"You're a person I like and respect, you listen to me about my worries about my kids. So let me give you a freebie."

"How'd you know my birthday's coming up?"

Jade gives me a 'get real' look and laughs. "Information is what I do."

* * *

The highway's nearly empty, which is normal for an early morning in December. I bypass my personal 'wants-and-don't-gets', I don't want to spend thinking time there. I stay on Frank Croake; I want answers to the growing list of questions.

I feel the time crunch, self-manufactured or not, of getting answers for Gordy. I've called Abshir and asked him to meet me at the front door of the office building. There he is, in an orange puffer jacket, bright scarf and knit hat. I hand him two envelopes; both contain copies of Jade's research. "One to PPD for Donato and the other to Gordy."

"*Hah*. Got it."

"Tell Gordy I'll stop by soon."

"He will want to know when."

"Tell him I'm not sitting on my ass."

"*Hah*."

"One more thing." I hand him a piece of paper with contact information on it. "See if I can get a meeting with this person. Wherever he wants is fine, whenever he's free, I'll try to make it. Preferably today."

"*Hah*." Abshir's eyes land on something behind me. He steps closer to my side. I swivel and look. Nail is clumping towards us. He's still in the big coat, his shoulders are hunched, and he cradles his injured arm.

Abshir's chest juts out.

"It's okay," I say. "I left a message for Nail at the hotel he's staying at and asked him to meet me here."

Abshir frowns.

"Unfortunately," I say, "I need him."

Nail joins us. He's puffed out his chest too and he's glowering at Abshir. No love lost here.

Nail scowls. "You didn't say Abby would be here."

Abshir glares. Only his lips move. "It's Abshir."

"You need a name that'll fit in. That's not an American name. No one wants to talk foreign. What's it mean?"

"Happiness."

I hadn't known that.

Abshir shoots a question back at Nail. "What about your name?"

"'Nail' means 'gotcha'. Means 'gotcha'."

The tension in the air hangs, it feels like grade school.

I turn to Abshir. "Call me and confirm everything's done, okay?" He hesitates but I press. "Abshir, you know Gordy's waiting."

He gives me a look but secures the envelopes under his arm and punches his fob to release the lock on the door of his van. He's got final words to Nail: "I know you are here."

"Duh. I know it too, 'Happiness'. Bye."

Abshir gets into his van and drives off.

Nail's shoulders immediately slump and his neediness springs to the fore. "I can't get in the Kahta Condo to get my stuff, you gotta help me."

"You'll need a lawyer to help with that. Your relationship with Gilli wasn't clear cut enough – the hide-a-key thing didn't wash with the police."

"But I need stuff." His lips are dry and cracked. His light eyes are still red-rimmed.

"She ever talk to you about Two Daughters Farm?"

"Gilli said she could make a lot of money on that. But it was a family thing, all tied up with memories of her dad."

"What else did she say about Two Daughters Farm?"

He shivers. "I'm cold."

"Let's go inside where it's warm."

Nail stays on my heels as we enter the building. I press the button for the elevator and when it opens, the building's owner - gray-haired, gray-personality Ivan Draglo is there.

7 Days

"Dee." He waves the clipboard in his hand. "Time to upgrade the heating system. And there's a leak in the roof. I have a checklist of other things. Tell Gordy."

"Yeah. Okay."

"He's not coming in?"

"No. Soon. Soon."

Nail and I enter the narrow cube, the doors close and the elevator heads upwards.

Draglo continues his complaint track. "Tell Gordy that upgrades cost money. He'll know what this means."

"I'm sure he will."

A raise in rent. Draglo finds reasons for it every other year. Sometimes Gordy can barter our services to cover the increase – sometimes not. Since I'm in charge of the account books, I know our workload has dipped since Gordy stopped coming to the office. Another kick for me to finalize the last drags on my becoming official, getting the final sign-off on the PI license. Bring in my own clients. Maybe I will have to borrow for my bond and put myself in debt.

Don't go there. Worry about one thing at a time.

The elevator door opens, Nail and I get off. Draglo stays on – he's headed to the roof to have another look at the leak. He calls out as the doors close, "Tell Gordy."

Nail follows me down the hallway. "I'm taking charge of Gilli's burial arrangements."

I punch in the office's security code, the lock clicks open, and we go inside. "What about her sister?" I ask.

"She has no spine. I tried to tell Tanya, like a week after we met, that uselessness and spinelessness can become bad habits, but she wouldn't listen."

"Maybe it's your habit of making suggestions for personality changes that puts people off. You ever think about that?" I power up the computer.

"Tanya just listens to her asshole husband. He'd toss Gilli in a cardboard box and put her in a backyard bonfire and call it a day."

"That's harsh."

"Just 'cause Gilli's dead doesn't mean she doesn't matter anymore." He shivers. "I'm still cold."

"You want hot chocolate or coffee or tea?"

"I'll have all three."

He's like a child pouting for sympathy and mothering. I'm not a fan. But I put the mugs on the counter, get the three-drink prep going. I don't want an argument. I want information.

"You said Gilli was going to make a lot of money on Two Daughters Farm."

"She said so."

"That's where she grew up?"

"Yeah. It's only an hour and some up the coast and then inland a bit. Gilli liked to drive there and tell stories about her dad and the farming he loved." He sighs and repeats, "I need things from the Kahta condo."

"Give the police a list, they may be able to get you clothes."

"You know, you started all this."

"What're you talking about?"

"She would've calmed down at Letty's Diner. You threw your bag at her."

"She could've cracked your skull."

"She never hit me on the head."

What is his problem? "You liked being her punching bag?"

"Maybe if you hadn't interfered, if you hadn't thrown your bag at her, she wouldn't be dead now." He gulps, like a big sticky ball of emotion is stuck in his throat and he can't get air into his lungs. "She'd be here with me."

"Why would her taking my bag have anything to do with her getting beat up and killed at the Kahta Condo gym?"

"No one killed her the day before. Or the week before that. So why the day after she took your bag?"

I need to get him off this wonky idea, it makes no sense. I click on the Two Daughters Farm website, motion for him to join me at the computer. He looks at the screen. "Yeah. Her dad wanted it to stay a farm, but a sale fell through, and her dad was old, and he was sick. He put Gilli in charge because Tanya and he had the big falling out."

"Over what?"

"Tanya did the one thing she promised her dad she wouldn't do."

"Which was?"

"She married that ass. Tanya didn't find out until after her dad died that he had added some special note codicil-whatever to his will, stating if she married the ass, Gilli would be in total charge of what happened to the farm."

"Is the husband that bad?"

"Gilli's dad saw that he was. Gilli saw it too. I smelled it off him the first time I was within a hundred yards."

I point out that Two Daughters butts up to Croake Sports Park. "Did Gilli know the owner of the Sports Park? Frank Croake? Or his kids?"

"She learned archery there in the summers, she said. She liked to shoot arrows."

"So, she knew Frank Croake?"

"I don't know."

"You ever meet him?"

"No."

"Is that where Gilli met Cooper Croake?"

"Who's that?"

"He was on the porch of #7 on Horseshoe Lane yesterday."

"Renter's name is Rusty something."

"No, the smaller and younger one. In the down vest."

Nail is losing interest. "Never saw him before."

"He and his sister may be investors in the Two Daughters Home Development project."

Nail waves his arms in the air; he's done answering my questions. "Don't know. And now it's my turn."

"For what?"

"You called. I answered those questions. Don't think I don't know you wouldn't invite me here because you cared about my grief. You told that Detective to shoo me away from your apartment and you don't think that hurt?"

His ability to play the martyr is fine-tuned. "What do you need, Nail?" I ask.

He opens his wallet and takes out a folded piece of paper. "Gilli told me to always carry this with me, in case something happened to her."

There's writing on the paper. Nail continues, "In the event of her death. It says her sister has something to give me. But Tanya lives in Cape

Elizabeth, and I don't have a car." He puts a hundred-dollar bill on the desk. "I'll pay you to give me a ride."

More Nail weirdo drama. I don't want to get pulled in, but I recognize an opportunity has dropped - an excuse to meet Tanya Wanz, a chance to ask her about Two Daughters Farm and any business arrangements she might have with the Croake kids. "Okay," I say. "I figure it's a quid pro quo since you answered my questions."

"Quid pro quo. Something for something." Nail scowls. "Not out of the kindness of your heart. Sad the way the world works like that."

CHAPTER SIXTEEN

Nail's sulk is like a heavy blanket smothering the air in my Subaru. We head south towards Cape Elizabeth but it's slow-going because traffic's held up at the Casco Bay Bridge. "Gilli and I talked about death a lot," he sighs. "She didn't want to believe one day she wouldn't be here. Now I wonder if it was because she was afraid it would find her so early."

"You're saying she was afraid of someone?"

Nail wipes away a tear. "Maybe it was why she wanted me with her all the time. Not to just make sure she took her meds - but to keep death away."

I don't want to go into 'what-if' land. "You didn't tell me what kind of pills she was taking."

"Things that kept her in the middle of her highs and lows. It was like having a relationship with ice cream, she said. She loved ice cream but hated that it melted. She hated that she couldn't make it stay just the way she liked it."

"When she got too low, she'd act out? Get abusive?"

"She was like a praying mantis during sex. She wanted to consume me, but I knew to push back and not disappear. I'd get her to really look at me. Not get lost."

I really don't want to imagine it.

"What about you and that detective?" he asks.

I brake too fast. The car behind us has to brake. And the car behind that car. There's a round of honking. "What are you talking about?"

"Your coupling."

"Stop. He's a friend. We're not partners – in any way. You don't know anything."

"Well," Nail sniffs. "He wants it to be different. You can tell by the way he looks at you."

"Leave the comments about my life out of this."

"Why are you so afraid of holding up a mirror?"

"What?"

"To really see yourself. You gotta do it sometime or what's the point?"

I jerk my car over to the curb, let the traffic go around us. "That's it. You can call a taxi."

"I don't have a cell phone."

"You're a pain."

I'll figure out another way to approach Tanya Wanz.

"Sorry," he says. "It's one of the perks of being so ugly. No one wants to look at me. So I can look all I want and really see."

There it is, that annoying self-pity mixed with his know-it-all shit. I am not going to budge.

"Sorry. Sorry. Sorry. Can we drive to Tanya's house, please? She must be so sad about Gilli. I am too. Please."

Screw it. "Don't talk unless I ask you a question. Then just answer the question."

I move the car back onto the road. We travel over the Casco Bay Bridge, pass the Fire Station and turn onto Route 77. Cape Elizabeth is another seven miles down the road. The town's small, takes up about fifteen square miles and its community is proud that a good portion of it is farmland. My dad and I would cut a Christmas tree there in the winter and participate in the 'pick your own strawberries' in the summer.

My phone pings. It's Gordy. The text reads, *Call me*. He must've read through the notes I had Abshir deliver, the info I'd gleaned at Jade's.

Nail can't help himself. "You're not supposed to be reading your phone while you drive."

I speed dial Gordy. Even before he acknowledges me, I'm talking. "I'll come by in an hour. I'm with Nail. We're going to see Gilli Wanz's sister in Cape Elizabeth."

"Turn here," says Nail.

"Gonna hang up now, Gordy. We're near the house."

Gordy gives a grunt of unhappy acquiescence and disconnects.

We turn onto Bald Cypress Lane. The houses are on wide lots, they all face a fallow field. Nail rubs his forehead. "Gilli's not here to stand up for me." Anxiety's building, he smooths the note in his hand. "But this is what she wanted me to do, so I will do it."

The house is a low ranch-style, built of yellow brick. The shutters are chocolate brown. The midsize trees in the yard are bare. A mini John Deere rider mower, a snowblower, an expensive skimobile and two canvas-covered motorbikes are next to the attached garage.

"When their mom died, and the sisters got some inheritance, Gilli bought the Horseshoe Lane block. She knew the value of having property in the city. Tanya bought this 'cause Wynn told her to."

"Who's Wynn?"

"The asshole husband. Who Gilli's dad hated. Who Gilli hated. Hope we don't see him."

* * *

Foo Fighters' 'White Limo' is playing at top volume, the front door almost pulses in time with the bass. A small woman wearing a tired velour jumpsuit responds to the doorbell. She's pulling her hair over the left side of her face. She sees Nail. Tears and anger gush. "You said you would always be with her."

"Tanya. I'm sorry," says Nail, raising his voice over the loud music.

She slaps at his good shoulder. "I blame you." Another slap. "I blame you."

Nail's head drops in guilt, he sniffles, and it turns into bawling. They both cry. They're sort of communing in the pain, but not touching, not giving comfort to each other. I stand to the side of the waterworks, wonder how long it will last.

Gilli was strong and square, she had wide shoulders and hips, and aggression flowed from her pores. My first impression of her sister is the opposite. She's smaller, she looks damaged and resolved to what life hands out. Finally, Tanya slips out onto the front stoop; half closes the door. She babbles over her emotions. "Gilli shouldn't have left us. She shouldn't've. Why weren't you with her?"

7 Days

Nail points to me. "It's her fault. She got between us, and Gilli took her bag and ran away."

I hold my hands up, tired of this blame. "None of this is my fault."

Tanya pulls the sleeves of her sweater down over her hands, shivers in the cold. "Who are you?"

"Dee Rommel."

Tanya's eyes go wide. "Why are you here?" She looks over her shoulder, closes the door another inch.

"I'm sorry for your loss," I say. "I'm playing chauffeur today. Doing Nail a favor."

Tanya points at Nail. "Go."

I interrupt. "Tanya, before we do, I have a quick question."

"What?"

The music is swelling and Nail steps in front of me, pulls the piece of paper from his pocket. He wants the attention. "Gilli said I was supposed to pick up something from you if anything happened to her."

Tanya reads the note, dismisses its contents. "It's just Gilli wanting everyone to follow her directions. Just another stupid treasure hunt. Even if she's not here."

Nail's adamant. "She wanted me to have something, Tanya. I don't care if it's another treasure hunt."

Tanya's hair falls back off her face. A nasty purplish bruise is revealed below her eye.

Nail leans closer to her. "What's on your cheek?"

"Nothing," she says. "Go away."

"Tanya, Tanya," he begs. "Please get what Gilli left for me. What if it was a very important last wish?"

She relents. "Wait here. Be quiet. Wynn doesn't need to know you're here."

She steps back inside. I hold the door so it won't close all the way. I see her racing down the hallway past an open closet. There are upper shelves stuffed with hats and scarves, lower shelves where boots and shoes are tossed. In the middle are hooks for parkas. The floor is also scattered with boots. What catches my eye is a leopard-print kick boot - the heel is broken off – it's muddied and ruined by rain and sleet. It stands out against the dark brown and black winter footwear.

The music cuts off. A deep, male voice sounds from the bottom of the house. "Tanya? Tanya? Someone at the door?"

Nail groans, mutters to me. "The asshole."

Tanya's voice calls out, it's small, apologetic. "Wynn, it's just Nail. He's not staying. Gilli wanted him to have something."

There's a loud laugh. "Now I can fuckin' kill the shit worm."

A hallway door opens. A harsh wall light is revealed and a railing that leads down to a basement. A heavy footstep lands on the last tread and a big guy - red-faced and red-muscled - shows himself. This must be his post-workout look - gym shorts, compression knee sleeve and black tank soaked with sweat; the tendons in his arms popping. He comes towards us, fast, a grin on his face that holds no joy. "Slimy! Hey, it's slimy!" It's that false bonhomie that makes my skin crawl and it pairs with the barely disguised temper in his eyes. "You let our crazy Gilli down," he accuses Nail. "And someone got to her. It's sick. I was in New Hampshire looking at a boat and when the cops came here to tell Tanya, she called me, and she was screaming. That's on you, Nail. You let Gilli down. You let Tanya down. And now you come crawling here so I can kill you."

What's his name? Wynn what? Jade mentioned it when we talked about the Wanz farm – what was it? This guy likes to belittle, likes to dominate. I try to stand taller, but I feel I'm shrinking. I can't stop staring at the tattoo on his bicep: MSP 8 - with a snake, fangs out, weaving through the letters. I've seen similar tats. Maine State Prison. Cell block 8.

Nail waves the piece of paper. "Gilli wrote that she left s-s-omething for me with T-Tanya. I got a right to come get it. And why does Tanya have a b-black and blue m-mark on her face? Gilli warned you."

"Warned me about what?" Wynn puts on an innocent look, but his eyes are hard. And then he switches his focus to me. There's a clucking sound in the back of his throat - it's wet and saliva-y, as if he'd love to swallow someone whole. "You want something too? We talked to a cop called Banford yesterday, he asked us all the pertinents."

7 Days

My feet feel stuck in cement. This sense of paralysis engulfs me. What the hell? I want to disappear, to be far, far away from this guy.

Nail's voice gets louder. "She's not a cop, she's a PI. She's helping me g-get Gilli's s-stuff in order. Stop looking at her like that, she's doing me a favor like a friend."

Wynn singsongs. "Nail's got a friend. Let's all have a piece of cake."

"Have some respect for Gilli. It's not a time for jokes," says Nail.

Despite his annoying traits, I'm starting to understand why Gilli appreciated Nail. He's whiny but not a coward. Wynn could squish the pasty insides out of him in a fast minute, but Nail holds onto a sense of fair play, and he doesn't back down.

Wynn smirks at me. "Nothing to say for yourself? Cat got your tongue?"

I stare back. I want to tell him to go fuck himself, but my brain's sending me a message to stay quiet.

Tanya hurries to us from the back of the house, a shoebox is in her hand. She thrusts it at Nail. "Here. Now go."

"What's that?" Wynn intercepts the box and takes the top off. Inside is a shiny porcelain figurine of a peasant girl with a bouquet of flowers in her hand. A flat card is stuck in the side of the box. Wynn pinches it out. His mouth moves as he silently reads the note. He laughs. "What the fuck? More Gilli shit." He points to a line on the card, adopts a high-pitched 'girly' voice and reads: "Even the cross-eyed one, my love." Wynn leans towards Nail. "Congratulations to you, crud, she wanted you to have all her dainty statues." He flips the card in the air, it bounces off Nail's cast and falls to the ground. Nail crouches, picks it up with his good hand.

"Have fun whacking off to the girly statues," Wynn brays. "When Tanya and me takeover Horseshoe, all that crap will be gone."

There's that cluck-y, slippery sound of the predator in the back of his throat again. He *is* an asshole, and a stinging prickle rises up my spine.

And now he's walking away. "Tanya, shut the damn door, it's cold out there. You're letting all the heat out."

He turns at the end of the hallway and is out of sight. My lungs are free to fill again.

Nail reaches for Tanya's hand. "This is your property too. Your house too, Tanya."

She looks over her shoulder. "Shhhhhhh."

Nail continues, "You have to come to Gilli's funeral."

She puts her finger to her lips. "Ssshhhh."

I doubt we'll have her attention much longer, so I shake off the shitty feel of Wynn and point to the closet. "Did that the leopard boot in your closet with the broken heel – did it belong to Gilli? I saw her wearing boots like those – the night before she died."

Tanya turns around to look. Her brow furrows. "Yeah. She was here. She wanted to talk to Wynn, but he was in New Hampshire. She took a pair of boots of mine and left her broken ones."

"What did she want to talk to Wynn about?"

"They talked on the phone 'cause she didn't want to wait to talk until he got home."

"He was in New Hampshire?" I ask.

She nods.

"What did she want to talk to him about?" I repeat.

She avoids. "He bought a boat."

"With your money," says Nail.

"Ssshhh."

I want to get the timeline in my head. "Did Gilli and Wynn talk about what was going to happen with Two Daughters' Farm?"

"Wynn wants to sell it quick. All I know was Gilli said she wasn't going to sign off until Wynn promised."

"Promised what?" I ask.

She puts her hand to her bruised cheek. "Well, she saw this." She shakes her head. "I guess it doesn't matter anymore."

Nail leans in. "*You* matter, Tanya."

"The detectives came here to tell you - about Gilli's death?"

She looks ready to cry again.

"Wynn wasn't here?"

She gets shrill. "He was buying a boat, like I said!" She calms a bit. "But then he came home when I called him about Gilli. I have to go."

"One last thing," I say. "Did you have a key to Gilli's condo?"

"She always told me where she was putting my hide-a-key." She turns to Nail. "It was in a different place than yours."

What's with this hide-a-key? Gilli didn't trust anyone?

Nail puts his hand out to stop the door closing. "Gilli would want you at the funeral, Tanya. Don't let her down."

Tanya shuts the door.

A shiny new black Wrangler 4X pulls into the driveway and stops behind my Outback. Rusty Razer, the guy from #7 with the topknot, is behind the wheel. What's he doing here? "We're leaving," I call to him. Rusty's head is down like he's studying his phone. I shout again. "Excuse me, can you move? We're leaving."

The double garage door rises; the mechanics are well-oiled and it's almost silent. Two vehicles are inside the garage, a huge Ford Super Duty pickup and a small green Prius. Wynn, pulling a jacket on, is slipping out the interior door that connects garage and house. He waves to Rusty. "Let 'em out."

Rusty lifts his head, and his gaze is on me. That stuck in cement feeling returns – shit.

Maybe he and Wynn practice bullying in front of the mirror.

Rusty holds up his Fuji mini-camera and snaps a photo. His Rolex catches the light, glints for a moment.

"Put that away, ass. Let 'em out," orders Wynn. "Stupid family stuff, that's all."

Rusty puts his Wrangler in reverse, squeals backwards, parks the vehicle at the curb across the street. He gets out; he's carrying a large metal toolbox. He doesn't look like a handyman.

Nail climbs into my car. I back up. I want out of here. I want to get Nail out of here. I'd like to wrap Tanya up and take her with us.

"Drive faster," says Nail, maybe feeling the same way. He's holding the shoebox and Gilli's notecard to his chest.

I accelerate around a curve but then pull over to the shoulder.

"Why are you stopping?" asks Nail. "Keep driving."

"What's Wynn's last name?"

"What?"

"Last name. Come on."

"Stimm."

That's it. The name Jade mentioned. Tanya Wanz Stimm. My brain had frozen back there.

"What do you care?" asks Nail.

I lean across him, grab my binoculars from the glove compartment and open the driver's door. I situate my LiteGood foot on the pavement, hold onto the grab handle and pull myself out of the car. I stride into the brown field and hold the binoculars up to my eyes. I have a view of Tanya's house. Wynn and Rusty talk in the driveway; Rusty's still carrying the glossy toolbox.

I punch in Gordy's number. "Wynn Stimm," I say.

"What about him?"

"He's a bully on steroids and married to Tanya Wanz. She's the sole heir to Two Daughter's Farm. I don't like him. And the guy who was at #7 Horseshoe with Cooper Croake just showed up to visit Stimm in Cape Elizabeth. His name is Rusty Razer."

There's a moment. "What're you thinking?" Gordy asks.

"It's more a feeling."

"They say anything about Frank? You ask this Rusty guy where Cooper is?"

"No." I don't want to tell him I'd been in a hurry to put distance between us.

Gordy moves on. "What'd ya need from me?"

"Can you call Jade? Ask her to find out about them? Stimm and Razer? I'm still with Nail, but I'll get to your place soon."

"Don't come right here. Marie's taking me to the hospital."

"What?" My stomach jerks. "Why? What happened?"

"They gotta do some prep stuff."

"Oh." That sounds routine, calm down. "Don't let 'em jab you too much or take away your mojo."

"You know, I keep telling myself if I hadn't backed off five years ago, if I had pushed Frank to get to a logical end of that money going missing, we might not be here."

"It's gonna be figured out."

"It better be. I'll call Jade." Gordy clicks off.

I'm still watching Stimm and Rusty through the binoculars. They move into the garage. Stimm presses a button on the inside wall, the garage door silently closes.

Nail's head sticks out the open car window. "Hey! I don't want to be late for my appointment!"

I drop my phone into my pocket and get back into the car. "What appointment?"

"The funeral home."

CHAPTER SEVENTEEN

"I'll drop you off," I say as we cross over the Casco Bay Bridge and drive into Portland's city limits.

"Never works to avoid uncomfortable things."

"I'm not going to a funeral home."

"You have that detective and that Somalian I don't like to prop you up. They wouldn't abandon you if something happened to someone you loved and you were devastated - but you think it's okay to abandon me."

He doesn't realize how his words are holding up a mirror I don't want to look into. He's hitting too close to home.

He's oblivious to my silence, he's concentrating on the shoebox. "Gilli liked treasure hunts. She used to write clues all the time and liked to watch people struggle to figure them out. Once she hid notes all over the condo and I had to follow them to find surprise train tickets to Washington D.C. and the Smithsonian. Sometimes she put clues around the kitchen, so I knew what groceries she wanted."

"That was her playful side?"

"She had so many sides. She was the best, best, best at making clues."

"You think the shoebox and what's inside is a clue?" What I don't ask is if he thinks it could be a clue that relates to her murder. "The cross-eyed one? Is that a clue?"

"It's a message that she wants me to keep the statues."

"You want them?"

"What else can I do but keep doing what she wanted?" We're near Spring Street in Portland's West End. He points to a large brick edifice. It looks like a former mansion of a rich turn-of-the-century Portlandite. "We're here," says Nail. "Turn in that first driveway."

7 Days

I turn. We're in Byrne Funeral Home's parking lot. There are gigantic holiday wreaths on the double doors of the place, the red velvet ribbons make them elegant.

"Come in with me." Nail says. "Please."

* * *

Harold Byrne is in his sixties; he exudes health and hope with a pink-cheeked robustness. His starched white shirt, studded with gold cufflinks and his red silk handkerchief in his double-breasted blue suit jacket's pocket give him an aura of correctness and solid tradition. Did I see a glimpse of dismay at Nail's oversized coat, his cast, his pasty face, and liquid-y eyes? Did Byrne have a split-second of hesitation before shaking Nail's hand? If so, he covers and speaks in a warm, accepting tone. "Very pleased to meet you, Mr. Parcell. I am sorry it is under these circumstances."

"Gilli Wanz liked the pillars in the front of your building. She called them strong," says Nail. "To her that meant there was a lot of respect for death."

"And life," says Byrne. He walks behind his desk and checks the information on his computer. "I see you have filled out the online form. Gillian Wanz, twenty-eight years old. Daughter of Ben and Wanda, sister to Tanya."

Nail nods. "She wanted an open casket."

Remembering how smashed Gilli's face and body were, I wonder if this is a good idea.

Nail continues. "Gilli always wanted to be honest. You will see, when her body is released and delivered here, that someone killed her with a lot of malice. She didn't deserve that. But she'd want to be honest."

Byrne's eyes dart towards me, wondering if I'll be adding anything. I have nothing.

Nail continues, "She liked cherry wood so that's what the casket should be. And I want that silky cushion-y material inside. And lots of roses in the room where she'll be before the burial."

"And where will the burial be?"

"There's a family cemetery on Two Daughters' Farm. Where she grew up. She'll want to be there." He takes a wad of bills from his pocket and puts it on the desk. "Will a deposit of ten thousand dollars be enough for you to start making a plan?"

What's Nail doing carrying so much cash? Where does all this cash come from?

Byrne eyes the money. Maybe he's reassessing what sort of man Nail is and understanding that resources will not be a problem. He opens a drawer in his desk, puts the money inside and locks the drawer. He writes out a receipt. "There's no reason we can't provide everything you request, but you will need the county's sign-off on the burial plot. If you can send me a copy of the paperwork, that will be most helpful. Do you have an idea when we might have Gillian under our roof?"

Nail points to me. "This is my private investigator. Her name is Dee Rommel. She's in charge of getting that kind of information."

Nail's expectation that I'll be the go-between with the police and coroner and arrange the delivery of Gilli's body to the mortuary is news to me. He gives me no time to disagree, he's onto other matters with Byrne. "Sir. Can I ask a question that you must grapple with daily."

"If I have an answer, of course I will share," says Byrne.

"When you take care of a dead body, do you think of the life it once held or of its future in death?"

Byrne is soft-spoken. "Personal beliefs vary, Mr. Parcell, but we all should endeavor to make some sort of peace with a deep loss. I'm happy to give you references to grief counselors and a list of churches of various denominations in the city. It can be helpful to be guided in this journey."

Nail responds to Byrne's patience and warmth. He nods slowly. "Gilli had a fear about death. But she had to be true to herself no matter the challenges."

"She sounds like an extraordinary woman," says Byrne.

"Yeah," Nail moans. "We met when I got punched in the face at the tequila place on Bourn Street by someone who didn't like my looks. She flattened him with a whop of her umbrella. You might wonder why she paid attention to someone ugly like me, but she told me she saw I had an inner light. That it told her I was loyal and loving and that I would take care of her."

Byrne puts his hand on Nail's shoulder. "Mr. Parcell, you are taking care of her, even now. Would you like to see our chapel?"

Nail nods.

7 Days

We cross a hallway. Byrne pushes through a double door. Light and swirling colors are inside; the stained-glass windows brighten the gold carpet and chairs covered in velvet. Nail walks in, Byrne waits for me to join them. I shake my head. He nods and follows Nail. The double doors close.

Even the hallway is serene. Dark wood walls, not a flick of dust. I wonder how many unbreathing, unfeeling bodies have been mourned here.

I reach into the pocket of my puffer jacket for my phone. No texts. Nothing from Gordy or Jade.

My brain's snapshot of Wynn Stimm won't fade, won't be excised. His coal black eyes and hard jaw. The sound - that clucking in the back of his throat and how it stopped me. My ego's taken a blow. My goal's always been to be tough, stronger than I was before the injury. Hours are spent at the gym, miles on the track, lifting, going one on one with a punching bag. I've joined my gym's wrestling crew; Wendy's the coach, she says we're a no-prosthetics combat team, dedicated to learning the ancient art and mastering it with residual limbs.

Stimm's a physical threat but there's more, it's like he knows something about me. Or thinks he does.

I look at the cherubs painted on the ceiling. Clearly, Nail hasn't thought through this burial site thing. If Two Daughters Farm is sold, what will happen to the cemetery? It's not legal to dismantle graves or take out gravestones that are already there, but if the property is no longer owned by the Wanz family – Gilli's final resting place may have to be somewhere else.

I picture two young girls skipping and chasing each other on Two Daughters Farm. Gilli the ringleader, Tanya the follower. Maybe on a treasure hunt. How common were these games?

I call the PPD, ask for the detective bullpen, hoping to track down Preston Banford. I'm transferred a few times, and I find him. "Am I speaking to Dee Rommel?" he asks.

"Yeah, it's me."

"Wanting information or giving information?"

"You're still the official lead on Gillian Wanz?" I ask.

"Yes. Looks like the job's sticking to me."

"Is Horseshoe Lane and #5 still off-limits?"

"Yes. I've got a warrant on the judge's desk, hasn't been signed yet. But the crew's still working on her condo so we have time."

I tell him about Gilli's final gift to Nail.

"You think this treasure hunt could be something?"

"Nail said she collected things. Including information. I was thinking maybe this statue or the notecard could be clues to what got her killed?"

"You with him now?" Banford asks.

"Yeah."

Banford takes a moment. I know he wants to make good. Sooner rather than later. "I'll get the warrant fast-tracked. Meet you at #5."

CHAPTER EIGHTEEN

The front room of #5 Horseshoe Lane could be the site of a horror movie. The warm breaths of four people hang in the cold air like a fog and swirl around the hundreds of figurines on the wire racks – someone's idea of perfect girls, all vacant-eyed and in cream and gray peasant dresses. They hold flowers or water buckets, or baby animals. Banford and Lavonna, in coats and gloves, have divided up the room and are methodically hunting for a cross-eyed creature.

Nail holds onto his cast and complains. "I should be allowed to look too."

"From what I understand, Mr. Parcell, a lot of this is stolen property," says Banford. "We'll take care of the search."

Nail sulks and then takes notice of Banford's gray overcoat and earmuffs. He comments that the detective looks sharp and professional, and that makes him look wise and reliable. He likes his earmuffs and wants to know where Banford shops. Banford says something about Macy's and then asks if Gilli had sent Nail on treasure hunts before.

"All the time." Nail nods towards me. "I told my private investigator about it." He gets up. "If I can't be part of looking, I'll go outside. Gilli liked to sit on the porch, so I'll do that and remember her there." He pushes out the door, a wave of colder air whooshes in.

Lavonna looks over to me. "You're on the PI clock with Nail?"

"He likes to assume that, but I've fulfilled my time with him."

She's marking the checked rows with strips of blue tape. "What's your guess, Dee? That Gillian Wanz left a million dollars stuffed in one of these things? That someone killed her because she wouldn't tell them about the cross-eyed girl?"

Nail opens the door, sticks his head in. "It won't be money. Gilli believed in banks." He points to the shelves. "I remember a cross-eyed one.

7 Days

We joked about it. Gilli wondered if the painter did it on purpose or if they were drunk or…"

I move to the window that provides a view of #7. Banford lets me know there is a drive-by schedule in place – just in case Cooper Croake shows up. That there's been no sign of anyone going in or out – Cooper or Rusty Razer.

The shoebox is on the windowsill next to me. I lift out the figurine, turn it upside down. On the bottom there's a hole, about an inch in diameter. Was it in grade school artsy craft class that a teacher told us we had to put a hole in molded clay creatures before they went into the hot kiln because the moisture in the clay - as it cooked - had to have a way to escape. If the moisture didn't get released, she said, our Mother's Day statues of rabbits and happy-faced mice would explode. *Boom!* she yelled and had us jumping out of our seats. We were appropriately warned.

I tip the figurine back upright and hear something slide inside. I use the flashlight on my cell to get a look. There's a piece of cork. Was it meant - at some point - to be a stopper? Did the cork dry up and shrink and fall inside? I get the others' attention. "Are there corks covering the holes on the bottom of the figurines?"

Lavonna looks quickly at a few, makes a quick assessment. "No, don't see any corks."

I shake the figurine I'm holding next to Banford's earmuff. "Something's inside."

"Whatever it is, it's mine," Nail says as he moves back inside the house.

I take a pen from my pocket, use it to extricate the cork. It drops out, along with a thin piece of rolled parchment. It's got a thin string around it. Nail swoops a hand down to the floor, grabs it, unties the string and rolls the paper out on the windowsill. We look over his shoulder. It's a crayon drawing of a peasant girl, she's got a red kerchief over her head, and she carries a baby lamb. Her eyes are crossed.

"Okay," says Lavonna. "If there's a red scarf on the girl we're looking for, that'll narrow it down."

Nail yells: "I know where the lambs are!" He hurries to a unit against the far wall. His double-jointed body bends into an odd position and he reaches to the back.

Lavonna puts her hand on his back. "Mr. Parcell, step back."

Nail isn't listening. "Found it!" He pulls out a figurine. "Cross-eyed!"

"We'll take that," Lavonna says.

But Nail has already turned the figurine upside down. "No cork. But see what it says in magic marker on the bottom? It's in Gilli's handwriting? *Break Me.*" Nail lifts the statue over his head.

Lavonna tries to grab it. "Don't break anything, Mr. Parcell."

Nail's already opened his hands - the figurine drops to the floor and the porcelain shatters. Shiny pieces scatter and skid across the floor and under the racks. Among the shards is a crumbled wad of note paper, it rolls next to Banford's suede Bucksports. He picks it up, unwads it.

It's another drawing. Crayons used again. This one is of a Band-Aid box.

"What the hell?" Banford's looking at me.

"Next room down," I say. "Lots of Band-Aid boxes. It's like walking into Walgreens."

Nail shouts to the ceiling as if Gilli's up there, watching us. "Okay, honey. Let's go! Keep 'em coming." He tries to pass Lavonna to get to the hallway, but she blocks his path.

"Slow down, Mr. Parcell. I'll lead." She moves down the hallway, Nail follows.

Banford unbuttons the top of his overcoat, loosens his tie. "Do we think this is a treasure hunt for old times' sake – just girlfriend to weird boyfriend fun?"

"I want it to be more."

"Me too," he says.

"And there's no way to know unless it's followed to the end."

"Fuck, this is too weird."

I've never heard Banford swear. He's definitely feeling the pressure.

"You have anything else at this point?" I ask.

He sighs. "That mitten you gave me? Nail's buddy, Dalton Guffman, age fifty, weighs three hundred pounds and he's agoraphobic. He knits mittens. Hasn't been out of his apartment for four years."

"How does Nail know him?"

"He saw Guffman's mittens for sale online. Nail bought a few pairs, and they became friends. Nail started doing his grocery shopping for him. He says Nail took a taxi over to his apartment at six in the morning on Tuesday –yesterday - and went through Guffman's closet. Guffman says he keeps some old clothes in case he ever loses a hundred pounds."

Sounds like Nail's alibi is even more solid and Guffman is a dead end.

"What'd you think of Tanya and her husband?" I ask.

"Stimm was in New Hampshire until Tanya called him and told him about Gilli."

"But what did you think of him?"

Banford's deep bass voice hardens. "He's a rotten, cruel charmer. But still, he was out of town."

"Shit."

He continues, "Plus, we've got CCTV footage from the street near the gym at Kahta Condominium, from ten the night before to when you found the body. A few dog walkers, that's it. A few cars drove by, and we identified license plates. Made the calls. Nothing useful. Whole Foods, around the corner, opens at eight, that's when the traffic gets going but Doc Stapler estimates the time of death a few hours before that. There's footage of you two arriving just before ten-"

My phone buzzes. It's a text from Abshir. He's managed to make that appointment I wanted. I check my watch.

Banford does a bit of fishing: "Heard Gordy's interested in the details on Frank Croake."

"They were friends."

"Donato told me about Frank Croake wanting to buy the Wanz farm," he says. "Are we crossing over?"

"I don't know. That was all new information this morning."

Nail's voice carries from the back room, he's bragging to Detective Lavonna. "See Gilli's organization? The Extra Long Strips are on the top shelf, the next one's got the Knuckle Band-Aids and the Finger ones, the Extra Thick Patch Adhesives and a row of compression sleeves for people with bad knees."

Banford points to my phone. "That text you just got? Anything I should know?"

"An appointment's been set up. I'd like to make it."

He shrugs. "Well, we have no idea how long this treasure hunt's gonna be."

"You could've kicked us out an hour ago. Thanks for letting us stay through the cross-eyed girl."

Banford gets out his phone, uses his thumbs to jab the keys. "I'll see if I can get more bodies here." He looks up at me. "If you need to go, you can leave Nail. He might be useful."

"Trick is to keep him focused."

"You want to say adios to him?"

"No. I'll slip out."

CHAPTER NINETEEN

I park on a side street because the new-ish USM parking lot has upped its rates. I wrap my scarf tighter around my neck, pull on my gloves and walk on the street to avoid the icy sidewalks. As I approach the campus, I get another text from Abshir: Donato's looking for me. The screen's going gray; I'm losing juice. I text Abshir back, let him know that he can share my location with Donato, that my phone will be out of commission soon and, that I'll stop by the office as soon as I'm done at USM.

* * *

Carter Stround, the Mushroom Friend, wears Warby Parker glasses, the frames are the same color as the shock of his reddish-brown hair and the soul patch on his chin. He's got a 'isn't life great' look about him, a kind of positivity that rests solidly on his shoulders. His Levis are well-worn, so is his black jersey with a stencil of a mushroom on it and his cardigan sweater.

"Sorry I'm a few minutes late, I was on a call with a group in Denmark, they're using 'shrooms to clean up soil that's been contaminated with boat fuel. Frank would've loved to get in on that talk." He waves his hand around the cafeteria. "It's kind of noisy, but it's the most efficient, time-wise. I have a class to teach in forty-five."

"This is fine."

"Never talked to a private investigator before," he says, shaking my hand. Our eyes are at the same level, he's also a six-footer. "So I looked you up. You had your picture in the paper last year, running that 5K race. I'm training for the Boston Marathon."

"Me too."

"Oh. Killer training, right?"

I agree.

7 Days

"Did you go to USM?"

I nod. "Graduated eight years ago."

"We have a lot in common. What was your major?"

"Criminology and sociology. The cafeteria wasn't this fancy then."

He holds up a lunch sack. "I already ordered sandwiches just in case you missed lunch, which I did today. Or in case you need a late afternoon snack. Like I always do. Vegetarian, just in case," He points at the students waiting in the 'Whatcha Want' line. "Since you can build your own here, it can take a while. Students take time figuring out if they want lettuce or spinach, creamy mayo or sriracha or hummus or pickles…"

I plop my bag on a free table and hang my coat on the back of a chair. Framed posters of multinational, multi-religious holidays are on display; Hanukkah, Eid al-Fitr, Christmas, Kwanzaa, Inuit and Wabanaki fill the walls, along with photos of famous alumni. "If you're not hungry, you can take yours with you for dinner or a midnight snack. I need to fuel up about six times a day, especially being in training now." He takes out two cans of seltzer, hands me one. "Okay. Here we go. You're here to talk about Frank Croake."

"Yeah." I like that he doesn't find more chit-chat necessary.

"I'm a professor with a passion – not really a businessman." He unwraps his sandwich, takes a bite. His hands are rough and weathered; he projects 'outdoors'. I picture him in a forest, a walking stick in one hand, measuring land, noticing where ants are nesting, if moles and rabbits and sleeping ferns and fungi are in their proper places. He swallows and continues. "Frank said not to worry, he had all the knowledge of finances and permits for both of us. Thing is, I thought he was some angel who swooped in. We got all gung-ho. We'd hike up to the top of High Eagle and look down on Two Daughters' Farm and talk about how great it'd be to combat the PFAS Forever Chemicals - return the land to health and as a viable place to grow food in Maine." He catches a mustard glop that has settled on the side of his mouth. "Frank was a life-force. The suicide thing just didn't jibe-"

"Some people thought he was too pushy."

"Well, we agreed on a common goal. If I was on the opposite side of a pro and con argument with Frank, I might've tagged him as pushy too. But he was about supporting the growing of 'shrooms to help clean the earth in this crazy blend of efficacy, recycling, and respect for the environment. You read about any of the 'shroom experiments we wanted to do?"

"No."

"Mycelium - that's the root part of the mushroom - have these enzymes that can absorb pesticides and other pollutants. This can set up an opportunity for my coremediation-"

I only have forty-five minutes; I need to steer the conversation. "I've been told a little bit about that but-"

Carter half grimaces and blushes. "Right, there I go. The technical stuff's not primary for you. Sorry. Basically, I want everyone to get excited about the little fungi." He takes another bite of his sandwich, talks with a hand in front of his mouth. "Some not so little of course, the longest 'shroom documented – so far – is about the length of a grown-up blue whale-"

A student walks by and extends his hand out for a fist pump. "Hey, Professor."

Carter connects, knuckles to knuckles. "Fergie. Good essay."

The student, with a surge of pride, moves on. Carter's probably a good professor, he clearly loves talking about his subject and has this excitement about taking on challenges.

"I can't give any of the money back," he says.

This surprises me. "What money?"

"I can't give it back. When you had that guy call to find a time for us to talk – I worried Croake's son and daughter had hired a PI to tell me I have to give back the two hundred thousand Frank invested. It's already been spent on R&D, new equipment, upgrades on the lab. I have receipts, Frank signed off on everything."

"I'm not here to discuss anything about money."

Carter relaxes. "Frank's other big contribution was going to be Two Daughters Farm. That Park's property had never been farmed so it doesn't have a PFAS sludge history. So, Two Daughters was the perfect place. It would give us an ability to compare saturations, toxins, the whole prism. Then there was this hold-up on the sale of the land."

"Do you know why?"

"Last thing he said to me was that Herbstrom, the property developer, wasn't going to win and not to worry about it, things were going our way."

That's news. Jade had mentioned the development had stalled, but not that Croake's offer was back under consideration. "When exactly did he tell you that?"

"Right before I left for the Midwest, that would be two weeks ago. There was a Mushroom Summit in Minneapolis, and I was giving a presentation."

"Mushroom Summit?"

"Gets bigger every year. Title of my talk was 'Spore Nation'." He puts his elbows on the table. "I gotta admit, I could almost taste it. We were so close to making it happen."

"What are your options now?"

"Zilch. Until another Frank Croake comes my way. Until then, Mushroom Friendly will stay small and hopeful."

"Rommel." A shadow falls across the table. It's Donato. He grabs a chair from another two-top and sits down.

He looks pissed. What's going on?

"Carter Stround," I say. "Meet Detective Donato. He's the PPD lead on the Frank Croake case."

"Right," says Carter. "I got your call too."

Donato monotones. "You didn't return it."

"Was gonna, but I've been running all day, and I didn't want to hold up Dee. Not used to being such a popular guy." He shakes Donato's hand. "I was telling her that Frank was a great guy. As a business partner and as a person and I don't know what I can do but if I can-"

Donato takes out his notebook. "Any groups or any person find 'Mushroom Friends' a problem? Any competitors?"

"I was telling Dee-"

"I need you to tell me."

Carter's eyebrows ascend, he understands the 'cop-gets-it-his-way' thing right away. "Okay. There are others in the same lane, but we were starting out with a different approach. Frank and I had been up to Augusta to talk to ACF about licensing, permits, whatever the state might need or want to know. We were probably premature, 'cause the land question hadn't been settled but we wanted to be clear about regulations and forms. Other than that, I don't think we were on anyone's serious radar."

Donato's next question: "Did you attend the Viv Cares for Kids Fundraiser?"

"I just told–" He catches himself. "I was at the Mushroom Summit in Minneapolis, so I couldn't make the fundraiser. That was for kids' scholarships – not anything to do with 'shrooms."

Donato continues. "What dates were you out of state?"

"It was the whole first week of December and through the weekend. I got a call from one of my grad students, telling me Frank's body was found on the hiking trail. That was a blow. But how can it have anything to do with 'shrooms?"

"Why was he so focused on Two Daughters' Farm?"

"Location," says Carter. "Length of time it had been a working farm. It being close to the Sports Park. Different qualities of land, right next to each other."

Donato changes it up. "You ever meet Frank's kids?"

"No. Would've been great if I had."

"Why?"

"Maybe, maybe they'd want to carry on for their dad – in his memory or something. Maybe."

"You mean invest more money in your Mushroom Project."

"Frank sort of told me they didn't care much about what he cared about. But he was hoping they'd come around."

Donato shoves his notebook into his pocket and looks around the cafeteria. Probably, like me, he's disappointed that Carter Stround has no earth-shattering contribution.

"I get a lot of mushrooms in my yard sometimes," Donato says. "In the spring - early summer."

"Can happen," says Carter. "If the season's wet and if your drainage isn't stellar, you can get a bump in them. You pick up your grass clippings after the first mows?"

"Not all the time," says Donato.

7 Days

I've never been to Donato's house, and I've never imagined him mowing grass or planting trees or raking or doing any of those homeowner things. Carter wags a friendly finger. "Pick up the grass clippings 'cause if they're left as a cover, they keep moisture in the soil and that's what mushrooms love."

"My kid'll be walking soon," says Donato. "He's only seven months now, but he'll probably be walking by spring. I was wondering if I should find a way to get rid of those mushrooms – in case Dude grabs one and stuffs it into his mouth."

Carter laughs. "Wouldn't worry much. Only two percent of all mushrooms are poisonous. But still, you're right, no reason to tempt him. And there are a few 'shrooms containing psilocybin in Maine – in the panaeolus species. Part of the psychedelic strains."

Donato frowns. "My kid could get high if he ingested a lawn mushroom?"

Carter shakes his head. "Wouldn't lose sleep on that. Chances are yours are milkcap or meadow or boletes common varieties. If you get a lot of them, could be you're fertilizing too much."

"Some garden store guy told me it was a good thing to do."

"Only if your soil needs it. You test your soil before using it?"

"You mean did I take some dirt to a lab?"

"Not all ground soil is the same," Carter says. "You got a pet that poops on the lawn?"

"I have a dog."

"Make sure to pick up the poop. Anything that adds moisture makes 'shrooms happy."

Donato seems to be reassessing his 'to-do' list – adding the pick-up of grass clippings, checking drainage and scooping poop into his daily juggle of multiple criminal cases, traveling to Philly to see Dude, and staying up with the Patriots' win-loss record.

Donato and Carter look at their watches at the same time.

Carter turns to me. "Sorry. I gotta get to class." He wraps up the sandwich he hasn't finished. "I was supposed to meet with Gillian Wanz. She co-owns Two Daughters Farm. Frank was gonna bring her over to the lab. She hasn't returned my phone calls so-"

Donato leans forward. "When were you supposed to meet?"

"When I got back from Minneapolis."

"But you didn't meet."

Carter shrugs. "She hasn't returned my phone calls. Frank wanted us to say 'hey' in person, he even alluded that she could be convinced to lean our way and might even have money to invest."

"She won't be calling you back," says Donato. "She was killed yesterday."

Carter's shock looks real. "Oh. How? An accident?"

Donato decides not to go down that road. "Not privy to all the details yet."

"So, what about Two Daughters Farm?"

"Her sister Tanya, we assume, will be in charge of what happens to it."

"Oh."

Donato taps his watch. "You said you have to go teach."

Carter grabs his empty seltzer can, buses his food. "Yeah. Well, on that downer note, I guess I – I should get to class." He turns to me. "You know, if you want to come by the lab later, that's cool. Or we could catch a beer so we can talk more. Tonight?"

I feel Donato's eyes on me, he waits for my response.

"I'll call if I have any other questions," I say.

"I get out of the lab around six, then usually head to Lost Bear or Wandering Moose. We can meet up." He nods to Donato. "Well. This was an unusual lunch." He leaves us, drops the paper products into a recycle bin. A young student falls in next to him, and they walk off, turn a corner together.

"That was smooth," Donato says under his breath. "Eating his sandwich, talking about crime and murder, and then angling for you to get a beer with him."

"Don't forget your snagging of free lawn maintenance advice."

He stands. "Let's go. I'll walk you to your car."

"No need."

"I got a beef to pick with you."

I put my untouched sandwich into my bag and get back into my coat. We cross the cafeteria and push out the glass doors into the cold. "What's the reason for the snarkiness?" I ask.

7 Days

"Found out some unauthorized someone is talking to persons of interest that happen to be on my list."

"What're you talking about?"

"You had a talk with Stimm," says Donato.

"You went to Cape Elizabeth?"

"After you were there with Nail."

"I didn't go to talk to Stimm." I defend myself, "I was doing Nail a favor driving him there. He had to get something from Tanya. I just happened to meet Stimm."

"He didn't think it was happenstance."

"What did he say?"

"Called you and Nail a couple of choice names. And I got a few new crap titles too. Banford had been there the day before and Stimm says he doesn't like harassment."

"Geez. He didn't look like a sensitive guy."

Donato laughs. "He's got a bug up his ass now."

"Turns out, being married to Tanya, he has a stake in what happens to Two Daughters Farm. I thought Gordy would be interested in that since Frank Croake was interested in the farm too. Gordy might also be interested in the fact that the guy likes to spend his wife's money. You see the boys' toys stacked up against the garage? Motorized vehicles he can straddle and drive off road. And now he's buying a boat."

"No law against that."

"You find out if he has a job?" I ask.

"Getting a real estate license, I hear."

My boot slips on the ice. "Shit." I stop to regain my balance.

"You okay?" he asks.

"Yeah." I dismiss his concern. There are other things to talk about, losing traction on the ice is not a priority.

"I called your cell," he says. "You didn't answer."

"Battery died."

"Don't you have a car charger?"

"That died too."

"Get a replacement."

"Stop telling me what to do."

"Hate to need to do that," he says. "But you need to stay away from the Frank Croake case."

"Gordy has a citizen's interest."

"Some lawyer could make mincemeat of that defense. And the PI license committee might not see it so black and white."

"I'm not officially working for anyone. I'm doing a favor for Gordy."

"You can split the hair, others may not."

I continue, "I was thinking that I had seen Stimm's name before."

He sighs. "Where?"

"The employee records Gordy had put together from the Sports Park. The file I gave you access to. Stimm's name was on it. He worked in ground maintenance."

Donato sighs. "Right. Okay. We noticed the same thing. Stimm worked there - after a couple of juvie stays."

The wind gusts, changes direction for a moment and encircles us. In a co-protection attempt, we step closer to each other.

"Do we know what put Stimm in juvie?" I ask.

"*We?*"

"That's okay. I can dig that out."

He looks over my head, like he's studying the bare branches of a nearby tree. "What would you think of a thirteen-year-old who beat up some littler kid for a bicycle and caused the little kid to have to get his jaw wired for a year?"

I wonder what point he's about to make. "Why are you asking?"

"Or about a fifteen-year-old who had an Old Orchard Beach scam – dressing like a hot dog vendor and grabbing belongings when people headed in the water for a swim. And who threatened an old lady with a knife when she caught him with her beach bag. Who, when just turning seventeen, got chosen by Frank Croake for his Second Chance program at the Sports Park? Frank hired teens who'd gotten in trouble as juveniles and were serious about turning their lives around. They were paid to do maintenance and keep the trails spiffy. Frank took a chance on this seventeen-year-old and then finds out he's selling drugs in the Sports Park. Frank had the person arrested."

"Wynn Stimm?"

"Not mentioning any names." Donato puts his gloved hands up to his face. "Let's keep walking, my nose is gettin' frostbit."

We walk. "Do you think Wynn Stimm is the person Billy Payer's ready to talk to you about?"

Donato shrugs. "Turns out they crossed paths in juvie – they were there at the same time. Billy's moved up on my list to visit again tomorrow."

"You said he told you he'd stay tight-lipped until you gave him something he wanted. That whatever it was - it was non-negotiable."

"I'll get it out of him."

We reach my car. Donato stomps the collected slush off the bottom of his boots. "Stimm was released from Maine State Prison six years ago, left the area to work in construction in northern Maine. He met Tanya at Saddleback - skiing. Pretty soon after that, they get engaged. Then married."

"Against her dad's wishes. And Gilli's advice." I try to connect the dots. "Wynn Stimm's got a reason for a grudge against Frank for getting him arrested. He finds himself in competition with Frank over Two Daughters Farm – but he's got another problem. Ben Wanz gave Gilli the final decision on the sale because he didn't trust Stimm. Now with Gilli out of the picture, Tanya gets it all."

"Possible conclusion. Perhaps a 'maybe'."

"He hits her," I say. "Nail told me it was a bad habit."

Donato shakes his head. "Always confounds me – relationships like that. Why would Tanya give an ex-con like him the time of day?"

I shrug. "Love gets twisty. Right? Stimm might've been on good behavior at the start - his bad boy vibes might've felt like adventure, gave her a bit of freedom from being a nice farm girl. She didn't figure out 'til too late that he'd swallow her."

I open my car door, block the wind from hammering our torsos. "Maybe Pike knew Stimm from Croake Sports Park."

"And?"

"I don't know. Just thinking of who might have more background."

Donato punches a number into his phone. "I've been trying to reach Pike; he was getting me the list of who was working for the caterer during the Fundraiser. Cell reception gets iffy at the Park in bad weather, haven't gotten through. Let me try this…" Donato gets a connection. "Officer Cussmore? Detective Donato here. You on watch duty at Croake's?" He gets an affirmative answer. "Good. I'm looking to talk to Pike. Have you seen him around?" Donato listens, then: "Okay. Thanks." He clicks off.

"What?"

"Cussmore said Pike left for Portland about an hour ago, said he was meeting with Croake's daughter about plans for the Park."

"Where?"

"Cussmore didn't know."

I bury my chin into my scarf for warmth. "Would like to know when the Croakes and the Wanzes decided to talk about joining forces on a land development deal. What about Cooper? Ask him?"

"Still haven't been able to track him. He hasn't responded to our calls. You ever cross paths with Cindy?"

I hesitate but tell him about delivering the amaryllis plant last night and seeing her later at Wandering Moose. "We didn't get friendly-friendly."

"Might be better not to antagonize people, Rommel."

"Wasn't exactly antagonistic. She just thought I was odd and nosey."

"You are nosey," he says.

"Only when-"

"Save it."

He doesn't tell me not to follow his car, so I do. Under the highway overpass, up the hill past the YMCA, we reach Congress. We have to hold at a stop light. Out of habit, I reach for my phone so I can update Gordy. Remember the battery's dead. Damn.

Donato parks across from the Croake house, I pull in behind him. He gets out of his Taurus and motions me to power down my window. "Stay put," he says.

Cautious as always. By the rules.

"You have an extra phone?" I ask.

"I have a 'Dude' phone that Christine can always get through on."

"I want to check in with Gordy."

He hands me the Dude phone. "Password's his name."

"Cosmo?"

"No."

7 Days

He heads to the Croake's front door. He presses the doorbell. No response. He knocks.

If Pike is coming into Portland to confer with Cindy, I'd lay bets that the perfect house on the West End would not be his first choice to meet. He'd be uncomfortable, worry about dragging mud onto the fancy carpets or bumping into a vase or an expensive oil painting, of being reminded he was a lug.

I open Donato's phone with the 'Dude' password and search for the Wandering Moose link. I click on the venue's *Call Us* square. The bartender answers and shouts over the music. "Yeah, we're open."

I speak loud. "Looking for Gustav Pike. Supposed to meet him and I'm running late."

Karaoke blares the intro to Joan Jett's 'I Love Rock and Roll'. Bar patrons cheer. The bartender yells over the high spirits. "Pike? Gus? He's here. What's the message?" Music swells. "Do you want to talk to him?"

"No worries. I'm on my way." I yell and disconnect.

Donato's at my car; I power down the window again. "Pike's at Wandering Moose," I say.

"How do you know?"

I don't bother with a direct answer. "I'll head there now."

CHAPTER TWENTY

It's early for most diehard Moosers. We find open spots in the parking lot. The orange cone is in place near the back entrance and there's no sign of Cindy Croake's car. Donato pulls at the heavy back door, we walk down the long dark hallway past the restrooms and the manager's office, past a huge paper mâché sculpture of a black bear whose neck has been wrapped in Christmas lights. Someone's karaokuing 'I Saw Momma Kissing Santa Claus'. We reach the low-lit bar area and Donato slides into a spot at the long counter. I realize he's positioned himself right next to Pike. That's Donato, sussing out a situation and, of course, taking advantage of an opportunity.

Pike does a double take when he notices us. "You called looking for me?"

"Not us," says Donato. "Who's looking for you?"

Pike narrows his eyes. "Someone, I guess. Don't know who."

"Just here for a drink," says Donato and motions to the bartender. "Two Trekker Pales." He turns to Pike. "Can I get you another?"

Pike hesitates but gluttony wins out, he's someone who would never say no to a free drink. "Okay. Yeah." He yells at the bartender. "Detective's paying for my fill-up."

There's a sudden quieting around us. There are glances in Donato's direction. A few people slip off to the far sides of the room, pat their pockets to make sure baggies and pillboxes of contraband are out of sight.

I take the spot at Pike's other side.

"You following me again?" he asks me.

"No," I say. "Not. Why are you so paranoid?"

"Just that people are getting killed."

"You're talking about Frank. Who else are you referring to?"

"Sister of someone I know."

"Gillian Wanz? You know Tanya?"

"Her husband worked at the Park in the way-back days."

"That would be Wynn Stimm."

Pike doesn't meet my eyes.

"Did he tell you about Gilli?"

"He came in here last night."

"After I left? After I talked to you and Cindy?" I ask.

"I guess so."

"I was here until ten or so." After that, I was at home, and my outdoor safety lights were activating.

Pike turns to Donato. "You here as a cop?"

Donato shakes his head, concentrates on his beer. "Sometimes it's just about the beer."

I continue with Pike. "He a good singer?"

Pike's confused. "What? Who?"

"Karaoke. Is Wynn Stimm good at it?"

"Yeah, he'll show off on stage once in a while. Thinks he sounds like Johnny Cash."

I've learned from Donato. Keep bouncing from topic to topic. Make it seem as if there's no agenda and keep the person from thinking ahead.

"How about Cindy?" I ask. "She sing?"

"Cindy? Cindy?" He seems to like saying her name. "I haven't heard her sing."

"You have a crush on her?" I ask.

Pike looks taken aback by the question. "What?"

"I got that feeling last night. You were really protective of her. You didn't like her calling you 'lug' - but you liked that she was standing next to you."

He tries for macho jockeying. "Jealous?"

"Well, you are a catch, Pike."

"You think?"

He wants to consider it to be true, but insecurity's close by. I look around. "Cindy here now?"

"I'm supposed to meet her here."

"Does Stimm know her?" I ask. "From when he worked at the Park?"

"He only did maintenance there."

"That's where you started, right? You moved up to guide and now you've ended up the manager."

180

"That's the way the world turns sometimes." Pike finishes the beer. "How come you know so much?"

"People talk. That's all. Have you seen Cooper Croake? I wanted to give him my condolences."

"No." Pike backs up, aware he's fallen into the talk-too-much category. "There's a buddy I need to talk to." He walks off.

"You were quiet," I say to Donato as I close the space between us.

"Better I'm just a guy who came in for a beer," he smiles. "And you were doing fine."

"Now what?"

"Let's see if Cindy shows up."

There's a commotion on the karaoke dais. Someone's dragging a snare drum on the stage, he's followed by a female saxophonist. A tiny woman with a retro beehive hairdo goes to the microphone. "This is gonna be without canned-music support. Everybody ready?" The drummer leaps off the stage and drags an acne-d guy up and forces him to sit on a stool. There's cheering from the crowd. Beehive Hairdo moves into a spiffed-up, over-the-top, Broadway belt of the birthday song.

Donato talks over the strident singing. "Your birthday. It's Friday, right? Day after tomorrow."

"Oh, yeah. Haven't been thinking about it. Hard to make plans."

"Right. But you and Gretchen usually watch movies." He leans closer. "What do you think about never being able to make plans?"

"You mean 'cause people like us with 'gotta do what you gotta do when you gotta do it' jobs?"

"Here you go. Just to cover the time that might be missed." Donato starts to sing, it's at low volume, basically right in my ear. "*Happy Birthday to you, happy birthday to you, happy birthday…*"

I'm too surprised to stop him. Surprised he's being playful – and surprised his voice is Bruno Mars-y. He's got some vocal chops. "*Happy Birthday Dee Rommel, happy…*" His breath is warm on my neck, like the time we first kissed. Like in the few days of us being close – even if it was a short period of time.

"Don't mess with me," I say.

7 Days

He stiffens. "Excuse me?"

I've got my defenses up and I take a step away.

"I can't just sing Happy Birthday to you?"

"Nothing is just 'just'."

"What?"

"I'm not going to take the apologizing path here and say I'm sorry that I'm too sensitive. Not gonna do that. I didn't think you were a person to play cat and mouse, but maybe I was wrong."

"What're you talking about? What cat and mouse?"

"Stepping in and being all macho with Gordy, saying you were 'watching out' for me - worried I'd get upset about Billy Payer. Asking if 'motorcycle guy' was still in my life, lending me your scarf, standing too close, making snide comments about someone wanting to meet me for a beer. Like it *matters* to you."

"*It* matters? What's *it?* Are you asking if *you* matter?"

"The *friend* thing was what you wanted. It needs to stay in place. Okay? No singing in my ear."

"It's just a song, Rommel."

"Everything means something. I don't want hot and sexy in my ear."

He tries to break the tension with a laugh. "Geez, Rommel. 'Hot' and 'sexy'?"

"Push and pull. It gets old. You might not see it like that –but I do. And I don't want you thinking I'm over-reacting and it's my problem."

"Okay." He moves back. We gulp our beers; he wipes his mouth. "Ready to get out of here?"

We see her at the same time. Cindy Croake has her hand on the wall, as if she's wobbly and wants to be sure-footed. Rusty Razer is on her other side.

"You've had Razer in to talk yet?" I ask Donato.

"After you told me you saw him with Cooper –yeah. Says he's never been to the Croake Sports Park. Said he met Cooper at a party. They got to be friendly."

"Friendly? Drug dealer friendly?"

"We're looking into it."

"Does he know where Cooper is?"

"Says he doesn't."

I lean into the bartender. "Rusty Razer come here a lot?"

"He's one of our bouncers. Couple nights a week. Not on tonight, he's just hanging."

Cindy's not blinking. Rusty Razer leads her to a booth that has a *Reserved* card on it. She slides in, he does too, and a waitress arrives at their table with margaritas. No ordering necessary. Suddenly Pike barrels over to them, his chin extended. He takes hold of Cindy's arm. She pulls away, gives him a flirty 'bye-bye' wave. Pike turns and marches off. Razer laughs – there's a new addition to his mouth. A flashy set of bright gold teeth. Hip Hop style. Way too old for that, but he looks proud. No more missing teeth.

"A little drama," I say. "Pike thought Cindy was going to be spending time with him tonight."

"I'll be back," says Donato. He heads to the booth. Looks like he's doing a reminder introduction – probably who he is and where they've met before. Cindy puts her elbows on the table, leans over to talk, even grabs Donato's hand as if she is very happy to see him. Razer looks off, as if he's absolutely not interested. Cindy tucks a few strands behind her ear and spreads her red lips into a smile. Next comes an 'I'm thinking' gesture, a manicured fingertip to her temple, and a few more words. A yawn follows. Donato shakes her hand again; she holds on to it and smiles and then waves him off.

Donato's back to the bar. "She's on a drone flight, flying way up somewhere. She says she's pretty sure her financial consultant suggested investing in Two Daughters. That she doesn't know where her brother is. Then she cut me off, told me she couldn't talk anymore, because she wanted to get busy drinking. I suggested she Uber home, and she thanked me for caring."

"That's it?"

"That she's unhappy Cooper left her to monitor the memorial arrangements."

The family dysfunction.

Donato finishes his beer. I finish mine. Our tense conversation concerning birthday felicitations still hangs in the air.

"Well, I got things to do," says Donato. "You staying?"

"Naw. I better report to Gordy."

"You think he's come up with anything new – from old files or –"

"He's gonna be pissed I never called him back. We'll start there, I'm sure."

We push out the back door, passing hefty Tony Dotz as he comes in. He looks distracted – or on a tear to get to a beer - and doesn't notice us. Donato and I separate, get to our own cars. He raises his hand in a wave but doesn't catch my eye. He backs up first and drives out of the lot. That makes the night feel colder. I get my car in reverse and release the brake just as a pickup truck blocks me. If the driver's trying to access the space Donato just vacated – it's open. It's there, all he has to do is pull in. What is the driver waiting for?

I look into the side mirror, see the driver's door open. Stimm gets out of the car.

Damn it. I open my door and step out. "Wanna move your truck?"

"Thought you and I should talk."

He opens his mouth to show his teeth, some semblance of a smile, and emits a slick clucking in the back of his throat. It's like fingernails on a chalkboard. I want to duck and cover, get away. But I hold my ground. "About what?"

"Crazy Nail, maybe. Someone's gotta tell him he's got no part in the Wanz family anymore. Never did really, Gilli just let him hang around. He needs to stay away from Tanya. You're his friend."

"I'm not gonna be a messenger for you. And we're not really friends."

"He's an odd duck. What's going on? You like odd ducks?"

I don't comment.

He gives me a lopsided smile. "You're the one that got Payer sent up."

"Billy Payer's actions landed him at Maine State Prison. You know that place too. Know it pretty well."

"You think you're tough, don't you."

"Would appreciate it if you move your truck."

"Can I buy you a drink?"

"No."

"Why?"

"Don't need a reason. Where's your wife?"

"She's having trouble sleeping. I got her something to help."

"Special kind of drug?"

"Advil PM." He steps closer. "You got a boyfriend?"

"Move your truck. Please."

"Answer my question? Boyfriend, or no?"

"I need to be someplace. Move your truck."

"Oh, you're the kind who cuts guys off at the knees. I ask you to have a drink and you cut me off at the knees."

"Do I need to call 911?"

The half smile and the slimy cluck in his throat. "Can't handle things by yourself?"

I don't answer. There's a long silent stare contest. Then he gets back into his truck and pulls into the empty spot.

I get a good look at his license plate.

And drive myself out of the lot.

* * *

Sybil Tenant, the newly retired social worker who lives across from Gordy's house, is walking Bert. He's on a leash and looks confused when I get out of my car - he barks, sits and waits for me to come to him.

"Sybil," I say. "What's going on?

"Hello, Dee."

"Why are you walking Bert?"

"Marie called from the hospital. Gordy was there to get some tests or checkup or get something done and the unexpected happened. He had a heart attack."

"What?"

"He was rushed into emergency surgery and Marie said she had to stay. I told her there were things like stints - or -is it stents - or those bypass things to ask about."

I'm not computing it. "Wait, start over."

"I don't know if he's in or out of the operating room."

Her words keep disappearing in the cold air. I try to hold onto them, but they're slipping in and out like a nightmare. "When did Marie call?"

"An hour ago? I don't know how things are now. It was something very unexpected."

7 Days

I'm bombarded with visions of tv show operating rooms, doctors pounding on a person's chest, graphic shots of cocky surgeons in action over open chests, and purplish red, raw hearts pumping...

Bert yips.

"Marie's there," Sybil is saying. "She asked if I could keep Bert."

"I'll take Bert." I jealously reach for his leash.

She doesn't hand it over. "He's being a sweetheart, but I think he senses something's wrong."

"Gordy's my godfather and I'm Bert's godmother," I say. "I'll take Bert."

"Okay, honey."

But she still holds onto the leash, waits for me to work it out. I do. "Ummm. But I'm gonna go to the hospital now."

She nods. "Bert can't go there, honey. He can stay with me until you come get him later. If my lights are still on, I'm up. I don't sleep well at all anymore."

I race back to my car, slipping a bit, dragging my left leg a bit, just as Donato drives up.

CHAPTER TWENTY-ONE

My ragged breaths frost in front of me as I lope from the dark parking lot to the hospital's sliding glass doors. My approach is sensed, the doors open wide, it's an automatic entry into the white-walled, tomb-like lobby. Dots of people sit in chairs against the wall and in corners. Nurses in blue, wearing soft-soled shoes, pass in front of me. The reception desk is manned by two middle-aged, calm-faced, helpful ladies whose demeanors are supposed to dampen others' anxieties and fears. I give them Gordy's name and ask for directions. I can hardly hear myself. I speak louder. They ask for an ID, then give me a map to a new wing and waiting area on the third floor.

The elevator is huge, designed for gurneys and equipment and wheelchairs and dozens of nurses, doctors, lab techs and whatever/whoever else makes this place pulse. It's an off moment. I have it all to myself. The journey is silent. The doors open without a sound.

Marie's sitting, Abshir at her side, in the small waiting room. Abshir has an insulated cooler at his feet, I'm sure it's full of his mother's finest: Tupperware containers of malawah pancakes, sambusa, and spice-filled halwa that melts like jelly in your mouth. Probably a few thermoses of tea, the sweet and spicy shaah. Marie sees me, pats the chair next to her. "He's still in surgery, *brava ragazza*. It was all decided, very fast, and the doctors would not wait. You weren't answering your cell phone."

I'm defensive. "My battery died."

"It happens, *dolcezza*."

Abshir takes a phone charger from his bag, plugs it into a wall outlet. I hand him my phone and he connects it. Marie puts her head on my shoulder. She continues, "It was to be a routine visit. We came for blood tests, and I was *inattesa*, just waiting with a magazine on my lap thinking of making soup when we got home. And then there was such movement, nurses

7 Days

running in and out so fast and I could see a rolling bed down the hallway, they had a plastic breathing thing on *mia dolce uomo's* face and…"

Abshir takes a small cup from the cooler and pours me a portion of shaah. I hold it, let it warm my hands. Hold it to my cheek to warm my face.

Marie continues, "They finally took time to tell me what was happening. Now, we wait."

"Waiting will be fine," says Abshir.

Marie grabs his arm. "Gordy considers you, Abshir, a fine young man." She turns to me. "I couldn't reach you, so I called Abshir to bring some things. Gordy likes his t-shirts. And boxers. I don't know when they'll let him wear his own things, but I know my man will want to do that."

The door to the waiting room opens. Donato enters.

Marie goes to him. "Thank you for caring about us." She leans against his tall frame, and he wraps his arms around her. She motions to Abshir. "Tea for Robbie?"

Donato accepts the tea, and Abshir tells him Gordy's still in surgery. Donato looks like he doesn't know where to sit. Finally, he chooses a chair – one that leaves an empty space between us. I hand him the Dude phone. "Mine's charging now."

I lean into Marie. "All I had to do was call when I was supposed to. I could've been here."

"No, *dolcezza*," says Marie. "No one could have predicted."

"I should've been here."

"You're here now."

FIVE DAYS

CHAPTER TWENTY-TWO

Three hours later. A minute after midnight.

Abshir studies. Marie's trying to do a crossword puzzle.

I've texted my mom. It would have been early morning in London, I wasn't sure when she'd get the message, but I knew she'd give me holy hell if I kept the news from her. There hasn't been any response yet.

Donato's eyes have been closed for the last two hours. His long legs are stretched out, his arms are across his chest. Before we settled in, he'd called Gretchen to see if Thor could stay late at Doggie Day Care. I talked to her for a minute. Of course she wanted to fix things, to do something, but I told her there was nothing to do, not until we had some news.

I spent my hours with healthy Gordy - a younger Gordy, - with him razzing my dad, taking me fishing, dancing at my high school graduation, insisting I learn to box, a cranky Gordy sitting at his desk at G&Z, telling some selfish excuse for a man to just pay the alimony, that his wife had no lover and it was obvious the jerk was the one who couldn't keep his undies on. With a weary Gordy insisting we go through the fishbone-filled garbage of Mrs. Janpay, (who had been given an early dementia diagnosis) to find the diamond ring she thought her neighbor had stolen from her. (We found the ring and the neighbors became friends again.) With a funny Gordy teaching me Checkers and Cornhole – teaching me so much of what I know.

I check my watch. Three hours and fifteen minutes.

Out of the corner of my eye, I see Dr. Frew coming down the hallway. Marie feels me tense and sees him too. She grabs my hand. We hurry to him. Abshir and Donato are behind us. Dr. Frew says Gordy's been moved to the ICU, that an open-heart surgery was necessary, that a healthy blood vessel had to be taken from his leg to replace a damaged one near his heart. He explains that Gordy will not wake up until much later – probably mid-day. He suggests we all go home and take advantage of this time to get some sleep. That way, he says, when Gordy can see visitors, we won't look like shit. Having completed this part of his job, Dr. Frew nods, says goodnight, and leaves us.

Marie says she's not budging, she'll take a nap here. I'm of the same mind. But she shakes her head at me. "You know Gordy would be upset that you're just sitting here."

"Where else would I be?"

"One of the last things he said to me," she says, "Is that you'd come through for Frank Croake."

My stomach tightens. "Still working on it."

"Not sitting here, you're not. Oh, I forgot. In the car, Gordy complained you weren't answering your phone, and he wanted to tell you to call Jade."

What does Jade have? It's too late, I can't wake her and her family now.

"Please, go and get Bert," says Marie. "I've got my *preghiere* and you will distract me from talking to God."

Abshir tells me he'll stay with Marie and will call if there is any news.

Donato and I get into the elevator. He presses the button, and we descend to the lobby. "What're you gonna do?" he asks.

"Not run around treasure hunting or chugging beer."

"First of all, don't blame yourself."

"For not charging my phone? For missing Gordy's calls? For not checking in when I said I was going to? For talking about mushrooms, for spending too much time wanting to pin Croake's demise on some asshole who just might be nothing more than an asshole, for trying to solve some puzzle that won't change the big scheme of the world even if it's unsolved?"

"Second, get over yourself. Third, don't denigrate what we're doing. Fourth, Gordy believes in order and justice and appreciates you do too and counts on you to be his legs and mind now."

"Screw it."

"Excuse me?"

"For trying to make me feel better."

"I'm trying to goad you into finding your spine, Rommel. It's what Gordy wanted from you."

"Wants."

"What?"

"No past tense."

"'Course."

"Wynn Stimm cornered me in the parking lot at the Wandering Moose. After you left."

"What?" He's all ears. "What did he want?"

"To be an asshole."

"You okay?"

"I got him to move his truck. Well – I didn't *get* him to do it. But he did finally move out of my way."

Donato's phone pings. He checks his messages. "Banford's got something."

I am not up for more complications concerning Nail. "About the treasure hunt?"

"He says he's gotta meet up with us."

"Us?"

"That's what the message says. 'Us'." Donato's as muddled as I am. "He wants both of us."

I rub my face. Everything hurts. Donato waits for my decision.

"Can he meet us at Gordy's?"

* * *

Sybil Tenant's house smells like rosewater. She must spray it into the air, into the carpet, into the upholstery. It's not a fresh smell, it's like sad, musty old roses, just before they give up their petals. I've arrived to pick up Bert, he immediately gets up, mouths his leash and comes to my side.

"How is Gordy?" Sybil asks. She wears a pink terry cloth robe over flowered pajamas.

"Out of surgery, in ICU," I say. "The doctor thinks the operation went well."

"Doctors never know anything for the first couple days, they never know if a body can reset or if great damage has been done. They sometimes use robots in surgeries like this and robots can't know any more than doctors know. But I suppose it's good that the doctor tells you to be positive, better than saying he's not God and doesn't know."

Maybe she's trying to be kind, but her observations do not comfort.

Sybil continues. "How is Marie?"

"Abshir is with her."

"That tall African young man?"

"Yeah."

"Who Gordy and Marie let just walk in and out of their house. Whether they're home or not."

"Yeah. That really smart, reliable and trustworthy young man." The last thing I need is Sybil Tenant casting aspersions. If she keeps it up, I'll find every ounce of filmy, moldy rosewater in the house and dump it on her head. Or at least flush it all down her toilet.

Bert whines. The smell is probably driving him crazy too.

"Okay, buddy," I say. "We're out of here."

"Bert's a love. And I'd be happy to have him here for a few days, but my granddaughter is a mouse in the Nutcracker ballet at her school and I'm going to Boston to see the performance tomorrow."

"I've got Bert," I say. "He's my guy." I reach for the doorknob. "Marie says thanks. Enjoy the Nutcracker, Sybil."

"I'll try, but my granddaughter has two left feet."

Bert, off leash, bounds across the street. I retrieve the key to Gordy's back door, it's in its usual hiding place. We go through the gate. Bert's eyes are on the kitchen door, expecting to see Gordy coming out with his favorite chew toy. When there's no movement, he looks back at me. "It's okay, someone will always be here for you. You'll get your bone, don't worry."

He gallops up the four steps to the deck and waits for me, lifting one paw after another because the wood on the deck is cold.

"Coming, coming," I say.

I turn on the lights in the kitchen, open the refrigerator and grab one of the baggies of pre-measured, all organic doggie-food that Gordy prepares once a week. I rinse out the doggie bowl, add the food and place it on the floor. Bert buries his head in his comfort.

I move through the swinging door to the dining room and living room area, turn on a few lamps. Gordy's slippers are there, and an old sweater. A few paintings, wrapped in beige parchment, lean against the wall; must be

Marie's clients' work – paintings that she'd probably planned to get over to her gallery today.

Gordy's grandfather clock strikes two. I'm running on adrenaline.

There are footsteps on the front porch. It's Donato and Banford. I open the door before they knock. "Okay, whazzup?"

* * *

Coats and scarves are on the hooks by the front door. I'm on one end of the couch, Donato's on the other end. Banford's in the chair facing us. He's got his suit jacket off, but the tie is still in place. His notebook is in his lap. He announces. "The card that led us to the cross-eyed statue gave us the number twelve."

"What?" I ask. "What are you talking about? I didn't see a number."

Banford refers to his notes, his voice even deeper now that he's been at it all day and his bedtime is long past. "It was on the flip side of the card where Gilli wrote 'even the cross-eyed one, my love.' The number was on the bottom. Wasn't very big. We didn't notice it either until the pattern began to show."

"What pattern?" Donato asks.

"When Nail broke the cross-eyed girl figurine, there was that wad of paper that had been shoved inside and fell to the floor. Remember?" He looks at me for confirmation.

"Yeah?" I ask.

"On the opposite side of the paper –you know, where there was the drawing of a Band-Aid box - there was the number seven."

This must be going somewhere but it's taking too long.

"Wanna cut to the chase, Preston?" asks Donato, confirming he agrees with me.

"Rather not," says Banford. "Better to slow dance it, I think."

Why? To convince himself there's something here that might lead to an answer or two? Banford continues, "We didn't notice that number either until we found another note in the Extra Thick Adhesive box. That box was out of place, in the middle of compression sleeves and leg wraps, but we found it. That note was sending us to the kitchen - it had a picture of a ketchup bottle with a knife blade resting on top of it." He opens the photo app on his phone and shows us a picture of the drawing. "But Detective Lavonna was looking at the back of the note and it also had a number. A two." He shows us a photo of the '2' written with a dark magic marker.

"Okay," I say. "So, there's a twelve, a seven and a two. One thousand, two hundred and seventy-two dollars. Gilli was hiding money for Nail to find?"

"The ketchup bottle had a Gillette Super Shark razor taped to its back. There was a Post-it note attached to it also – it had the number 'zero'."

Donato's impatient. "To tell Nail not to be a 'zero' and forget shaving?"

"Nail has no hair on his face," I say. "His skin is more like a marshmallow."

Banford shakes his head. "I don't think it had anything to do with shaving."

Donato groans. "Keep going."

Banford continues. "Under the ketchup bottle there was a tearsheet from a Charmin magazine ad – you know the ad with those bears who are so proud of wiping their butts."

"Does this end up being about TP?" Donato asks.

He shows us another photo. "No. The backside of the Charmin ad had a large 'two and zero' drawn on it with a magic marker."

"And?" I look at the numbers I've written down. "We're over a million now."

Donato leans back, finally accepting he can't rush Banford. "What clue did you find in the toilet paper pack?"

"Stuffed into one of the cardboard centers of the four-pack was another clue."

Bert pads out of the kitchen and jumps onto the couch to sit between Donato and me. It's like he's interested too.

"This clue was written in dark marker," Banford's saying. "*Doyle's Brew and Food.*"

Donato leans forward. My head swivels to Banford. That was Fred Doyle's store, the man whose skull was smashed with a cast iron skillet by burglars on a snowy night in December, five years ago, right before the assailants plowed into ten-year-old Dominic Salva and his new backpack on Mayo Street.

"Doyle's Brew and Food?" I repeat.

My PPD partner, Marvin Payer, and I had responded to that call. We were headed there before we were re-routed to Mayo Street where the perps were thought to be hiding in that building that was under construction. The one I regularly drive by to remind myself to be vigilant.

Banford tears a piece of paper from his notebook and hands it to Donato. "Look at the numbers. 1,2,7,2,0,2,0. Don't think it's about dollars."

Donato takes a long look at the numbers. "Bank security box? A password?"

He hands the piece of paper to me. I write the numbers down again, without the commas separating them. I add a few slashes between numbers. "A date?" It could be 1/27/2020. January 27th, 2020.

But I know it's not. Something, deep down, tells me it's not. It's 12/7/2020. December 7th, 2020.

The night of the burglary, the night of Dominic Salva's death and the night I was slammed with a 4x4 and plunged off the roof of a building.

My breath catches in my throat. There's thrumming in my ears.

"The notecard in the TP also included a drawing of a bathtub," says Banford.

"What the hell?" says Donato. "What was Gilli Wanz playing at?"

Banford gets to the next photos on his phone. He shows them to Donato. Then shows them to me. The first photo is of the bathroom in #5 Horseshoe Lane. A close-up of toiletries. The Charmin four-pack. The clue card. The next photo is of the clawfoot tub, filled with wallets, purses, backpacks, bags of all shapes and sizes. The next photo is the tub half empty – and then completely emptied. Except for one thing left on the very bottom. A newspaper. On the front page is a smiling photo of Dominic Salva, wearing his new Kung Fu backpack. The newspaper headline reads *Tragedies in Our City*.

My eyes move to my legs, they're straight in front of me, supported by the ottoman. The thigh muscles of my left leg throb, my LiteGood feels heavy. I can sense Banford and Donato looking at me, their silent questions pop so aggressively they almost register in volume. But no one wants to voice their thoughts. Not yet.

"Nail told me Gilli collected information," I mutter.

Why did she keep this information?

Banford's not done. "We opened the fold of the newspaper, and this was there." He swipes through his phone, finds the photo.

"What is it?" I lean forward to see it better.

7 Days

"A marriage certificate, a copy of the one issued to Wynn Stimm and Tanya Wanz."

Holy shit. What was Gilli trying to say?

Donato puts his hand on my upper arm. "Steady."

Banford's still not done. "We picked up the newspaper. This was underneath."

The photo on the phone is of a balaclava on the bottom of the tub. Ski mask style – the kind that's pulled over the head and has a rectangular opening for the eyes. The polyester fabric is midnight black, the eyehole wide enough for peripheral vision, but small enough that ski goggles will fit over the space and block the wind. There's a streak of gray mud across the front, starting at the left temple and crossing to the right chin.

Five years ago. Four faces in masks, just like this one. Four guys wearing dark heavy peacoats, thick gloves, heavy boots and ski goggles. One is coming right towards me, a thick, long-as-a-baseball-bat piece of wood in his hands. And there's a sound that approaches with him. A slippery, wet clucking in the back of his throat.

The sound that had me cemented to the spot at Tanya's front porch. "Geez. Fuck."

"Steady," says Donato.

* * *

We're sitting at the dining room table, our notebooks and files on the flat surface in front of us. The clock has ticked past another hour, but there are no thoughts of falling into bed or getting rest. "What did Nail Parcell have to say about these items?" Donato asks Banford.

"Besides saying Gilli liked her games?" Banford says. "He said the date and the headline meant nothing to him. It was before he moved to Portland."

"Then why'd Gilli send Nail on this treasure hunt?" Donato asks.

I have an idea. "She hated Stimm. Maybe she wanted Nail to solve the mystery and to be a part of getting Stimm out of Tanya's life?"

Donato adds a possibility. "What if Gilli wanted to get Stimm in trouble. What if she was trying to set him up?"

"Right. If she had proof Stimm was involved, why didn't she just go to the police?" Banford asks.

"This is not proof," I say. "A newspaper and a balaclava can't tighten a noose around Stimm's neck."

Banford digs in, "But they could start a conversation."

"Like this one?" I ask.

"There are no teeth here," says Donato. "I've been over those case files a hundred times. If I add these items to the mix, it doesn't get me closer."

Banford shakes his head. "Nail might like games. I don't."

Donato leans back. "Well, you are Mr. Straightforward, Banford."

Banford doesn't take offense. "I like things to be upfront. No games." He taps his pencil on the table. "Got a team working at #5 Horseshoe now, in case there's something else. Lavonna's getting the first batch into Evidence. She's putting the balaclava in for DNA."

"DNA or not," says Donato. "It won't point to that specific date on that specific roof or that specific building. Lots of people wear ski masks. Usually when skiing."

I put my head in my hands and stare down at Gordy's dining table as if it'll have answers. "Gilli steals my bag. Sees me fall. Maybe she sees my LiteGood? Maybe she looks at my ID before she tosses my wallet and bag into the tub – and somehow puts it together that I'm the police officer injured in that December 7th crime. Somehow, she's connected that event to Stimm-"

"How?" Banford asks.

I have no answer. We need to stick to what we have. "The night I crossed paths with Gilli, she was aggressive, maybe off her meds, we don't know. She gets to Tanya's - she sees the black eye and bruises, knows that Stimm's slapped Tanya around. She screams on the phone at Stimm." I try to replay this morning's conversation. "Tanya said something about Gilli telling Stimm she wouldn't sign the Two Daughters' papers if he didn't promise to…"

"Promise to do what?" Banford asks.

I realize my problem. "I don't think she finished her sentence."

Banford taps his notebook. "She's on my list, first thing in the morning." We're well into the morning. "Well, when it gets light."

7 Days

Donato writes Stimm's name in the center of a blank sheet of paper and circles it. He draws a spider-leg-like line out from the circle and writes FC at its end. "Stimm's motive for wanting Frank Croake out of the picture. Competition for Two Daughters' Farm." He draws another line off the center circle and writes GW at its end. "Motive for the demise of Gillian Wanz: Tanya gets control of all family inheritance from her dad – and probably whatever Gilli had too. This includes the decision about Two Daughters' Farm. Rommel, you've seen it firsthand – how Stimm controls Tanya."

"He does," I say.

Donato continues, "We get him on Frank Croake or Gilli, maybe we get lucky and…" He draws another line and writes FD and DS and 12/7/2020 at its end. "We'll find the strong connection to Fred Doyle and the death of Dominic Salva and-"

They look at me.

A chill goes up my spine. I can't get my voice above a whisper. "Stimm makes this sound. In the back of his throat. I heard it when I was at Tanya's. I heard it tonight when he cornered me in the parking lot. I heard the same sound five years ago."

They don't bother asking me if I'm sure. We all know it's another observation, not hard evidence. Nothing that would accomplish a final tightening of any noose.

Banford flips through his notebook and pricks another hole into the possibility balloon. "Stimm's alibis are solid. For both timelines – Croake's death and Gilli's death. On the day of Viv's Care for Kids Fundraiser, we know Stimm was in New Hampshire with his cousin who owns a boat rental business. He and his cousin were seen at Portsmouth's Main Marina and at a storage shed that winters boats for sale; they were busy talking to boat agents about a 42-foot Grand Banks. Same thing on the day of Gilli's death. That morning, he got the call from Tanya about Gilli's death. He checked out immediately and drove home to Cape Elizabeth."

I pound my fists on the table. "Shit. Shit."

Bert pads over and puts his head on my lap. He's got a knack, a sense when someone needs a bit of comfort.

I turn to Donato. "What was the non-negotiable thing Payer wanted?"

Donato shakes his head. "We can do this without Billy Payer."

"But we want the fastest way."

Banford perks up. "Payer's got something about Croake? I don't know about this."

Donato weighs the pros and cons of sharing. Finally, he caves. "Okay. Here's the deal. Payer wants *you*, Rommel, sitting across from him. He wants to give *you* the big info that could pertain to the death of Frank Croake. He wants to be face-to-face with you and plead his case."

"Manipulative son of a bitch," says Banford.

Donato continues, "He wants you, Rommel, as one of his last victims to agree to write a letter that conveys your belief that he's turned a corner and should be granted this transfer to a new circumstance in a sunny Florida lock-up."

"Don't trust him," says Banford.

"Agree," says Donato.

Banford continues, "Payer's got a thing about you, Dee. Thinks you two met in some personal battle and you won."

"No one won."

"He thinks you pulled out in front."

If so, by a hair's breadth. Payer had me locked in his U-Tow hideout, surrounded by his knives and cages. I thought I was going to die. Marvin Payer, my PPD partner, found a way to upset the plan. "I didn't win."

Banford disagrees. "Payer thinks Marvin, his own brother, chose you over him. Big betrayal."

"And he's got thirty years inside to keep thinking about it," Donato says.

They wait. Leave the decision to me.

I don't hesitate. "For Gordy. For Frank and Gilli. To get these things closed."

"You sure?" asks Donato.

"Set it up. Tomorrow."

CHAPTER TWENTY-THREE

Donato's gone home, so has Banford. Bert's on the floor at my feet. He looks up at me. He's good at sensing moods, anxieties, and muddled thoughts. "Yeah, Bert. It's all a jumble."

He barks his agreement.

"I'll be back in an hour.

* * *

I'm back at the hospital. Gordy's still in ICU, the anesthesia hasn't completely worn off and he's in a neverland. Marie's been allowed to sit in his room. I take her place. Abshir says he's going to take Marie home so she can shower and change clothes. She says she'll be back as soon as she can.

Gordy's never looked smaller to me. His shoulders look bony, his hands are half-curled, his skin looks tight and transparent on his skull. There's a tube in his mouth that goes down his throat. The bedside monitors tick and hum and record their findings – the electrocardiogram stats, breathing rates and oxygen levels. A nurse whose name tag reads Guido comes into the room and changes the IV unit.

"What's in there?" I ask.

"Things he needs. Some of it is pain medication. He's not in pain."

"When do you think he'll wake up?"

"Every patient's different. The doctor wants to give Mr. Greer extended time, to make sure the fluid in his chest drains properly."

"What about the breathing tube? How long is that staying in?"

"Depends on how Mr. Greer's doing. A few days. Then he'll be able to talk. The catheter could come out a few days after that. Once he's able to swallow pills, we'll nix the IV and transfer him to the cardiac unit."

7 Days

"How long would he stay in the cardiac unit?" I catch myself. "Forget it. I get what you're saying - it all depends."

"Right. Different pace for different people." He moves out of the room.

Come on Gordy, get it together. You never put things off - you accomplish, you always get things done. "So why change now?" I mutter under my breath. "Get the tempo up. I need you."

Marie's back sooner than I expected. She's convinced Abshir to attend his morning class, told him he could have a stint sitting by Gordy's bedside while she got lunch (only one visitor is allowed at a time). She looks revived, ready again to plan life for Gordy and everyone else around her. "Go do what you do well, Dee. *Andare via.*"

Get going. Yeah.

I head back to Munjoy Hill and pick up Bert. Gretchen's just opening the doors of Doggie Day Care and I'm first in. "Thor stayed overnight, he'll be happy to see Bert," she says. Bert licks her face and jogs off to claim a doggie bed. Thor joins him; they situate themselves in back-to-back comfort and look content. It's a bro-mance.

Gretchen grabs my hand. "Can't you stop for a day? You're looking like a dragon's coming at you."

"Have to do something that turns my stomach."

"Don't do it." Gretchen can put on blinders if unsavory reality gets too close. I don't mean to sell Gretch short. She knows there's a dark side, but she'll choose optimism until there's no other choice. "I gotta go," I say. "Talk to you later."

"I want to help in any way I can."

"Taking care of Bert and Thor is what we need right now. Thanks, Gretch. Later."

* * *

Letty's Diner is full of early morning breakfast regulars. Jade waits for me in a small booth; we'd planned to meet for a quick hand-off of files. I slide into place and Allison, working the morning shift, pounces, tells me she'd read about the death of 'that wild woman with the baseball bat'. She asked if the 'alien-looking' boyfriend did it. I told her everything was in flux. She said the whole tragedy made her sad.

I agree. "Sad and angry."

Allison hears the 'ding' of a ready order from the kitchen. "I've never served someone the night before they died," she says and hurries off.

"Anger's your fuel, Dee," says Jade. "Just keep it under control." She pulls a card from her bag; it's made of thick ivory cardstock. "Gordy get one of these?"

It's the announcement of Frank Croake's memorial service. It's scheduled for Monday, at Croake Sports Park Barn. At noon.

"That's three days from now," I say. "His body hasn't even been released yet."

"Don't need the body for the memorial."

"Seems like it'd be better if all questions were answered before-"

"Cases can go unsolved for years. Forever. Better to get the memorial done, honor the person no matter the circumstances. The Governor will be there, Portland's City Council and other movers and shakers in the state. Everyone's probably lined up to give eulogies."

"Political opportunities?" I ask.

"I'm sure some people will be speaking from the heart."

I see Donato's car arrive. "Here I go."

Jade hands over the files. "Billy Payer doesn't deserve your emotion. Keep it chill."

"Thanks, Jade."

I have her files under my arm as I settle into the Taurus' passenger seat. Donato's got the heat blaring. I hand him a coffee-to-go.

"Thanks. Latest on Gordy?"

"No change."

He looks at the files. "Whatcha got?"

"Two backgrounds from Jade; one on Stimm and one on Rusty Razer. She said she didn't see any smoking guns relating to the death of Croake, but maybe we'll see something."

"Okay."

I hold up the last file. "And one on Oscar Herbstrom."

"The financial consultant?"

7 Days

"She said Gordy asked her to collect the latest."

"Why?"

"I'd like to be able to ask him."

Donato hears the edge in my voice. Ignores it. He drives onto the entrance ramp to merge into traffic on Highway 295 - heading north. An unspoken agreement seems to be in place. We stick to business.

I open Rusty Razer's file first and share Jade's research: Rusty Razer grew up in a big family in New Hampshire. They owned a few pizza shops, and all the kids pitched in. Except for Rusty who got into drugs and dealing early. When Rusty was seventeen, his dad bought him a one-way bus ticket to California and told him not to come back. So Rusty was off New England's radar for two decades and then ended up in Portland a few years ago. I read: "He rents #7 Horseshoe Lane and 'hangs'."

"Like he was 'hanging' at Wandering Moose?" asks Donato.

"Guess so. With people like Cindy Croake."

"Do we think Rusty supplied Cindy's 'high'?"

"To be determined." I tell him about the beaten-up old Chevy that slowed down on Horseshoe Lane. And Rusty ambling to it for a chat. For an exchange of drugs? Unclear.

"He must've met Stimm along the way. Does the file tell us where?"

"No." I look at the next file. "Most of this we have, except for Stimm being a person of interest in the disappearance of a woman named Amelia Jurner up in Greenville. She had a boat on Moosehead Lake and in the summer, she'd take tourists out to enjoy the lake. She disappeared three years ago. Her place was cleaned out, her car was gone, her boat and boat trailer were gone. Her friends didn't believe she'd take off without telling them."

"Stimm was a person of interest?" he asks.

I keep reading and summarizing. "They'd been dating. A few people thought Stimm got her hooked on something because there had been a significant personality change."

"What kind of change?"

"Got dependent. On Stimm."

"I know a sheriff up there," says Donato. "I'll call him. What's the third file?"

"Oscar Herbstrom."

"Right. Gordy wanted the info."

"Jade said Gordy was curious because the kids locked on with Herbstrom pretty quick. He knew Frank had used Herbstrom in the past, but they parted ways because they didn't see eye to eye on some things. Herbstrom called the kids the day after Frank was found and offered them any help they might need."

"Quick on the opportunity. That's the secret to success."

"When did you attend 'How To Make Money School'?"

"Ha."

I go back to the file. "He's recently started a property development company. Are we assuming Herbstrom was the one who talked to Cindy and Cooper about investing in Two Daughters Farm?"

"We assume nothing."

We take the exit to merge onto Route 1 and drive through Brunswick. We're only twenty or so minutes out of Portland, but the temperature has dropped, the recent snows have stuck. Now is the time of year that each new snowfall starts to build on the last - snowbanks establish themselves on the roadsides and fill the forests.

"Recommend closing your eyes," Donato says. "Get some sleep. You can drive on the way back and I'll sleep."

He doesn't add that it'd be a good way to avoid other conversations. Safe and careful Donato. Sounds good to me.

I don't intend to drift off, but the heat is on in the car and my parka's warm and the sun's sparkling off the snow...

When I open my eyes, it's an hour later and we're on the outskirts of Thomaston, a historic town full of well-preserved stately homes of those who, in the early 1800s, made fortunes in shipbuilding, shipping and lumber. Another big money-maker was quarrying lime rock and transforming it into cement for construction materials. The remnants of the massive kilns on the Georges River that were needed for this transformation are visible. They're no longer pushing the 'forever' carbon emissions into the atmosphere. The nearby looming Dragon Products Plant does the job today - it produces most of Maine's cement.

7 Days

Route 1 becomes Thomaston's Main Street, and we slow to 25 mph. We're getting too close to Payer. I distract myself, concentrate on checking out the cafes, antique and jewelry shops and the Maine State Prison Store where Mainers and tourists can buy tables, chairs, chess boards, desks and other polished woodworking handcrafted in the prison's workshops.

I run through the history of Maine State Prison as told to me by my dad. Built in 1824, it was a few miles off this Main Street – near LimeStone Hill and the quarry. The original prisoners worked the quarry during the daylight hours. At night, after the limestone dust attacked their lungs, they were infamously lowered into stonewalled holes that were covered with tarps. Iron bars were locked into place. It wasn't until a big fire in 1923 destroyed the first buildings and the prison had to be rebuilt, that the 'holes' were replaced with above-ground, two-bunk cells. When the quarry was used up, the prisoners' daily routines changed. At first, they made carriages and bridles, then when the motorcar changed those needs, they were kept busy making furniture or upholstering chairs and couches for many of the nearby towns' residents. Some worked in a print shop during the winter and the prison farm in the summer. Overcrowding became a real problem, and prison reform articles were written. After seventy-five years, a new MSP was built. That was in 2002, it was not even ten miles miles from the former prison, on a twisty road close to a quiet village called Warren.

We're about to make the turn onto that twisty road.

Donato sees I'm awake. "You sure about this?"

"Yeah."

Route 97 – we're on it. We're in Warren in fifteen minutes. Three fences protect the prison's perimeter; the outermost is a forty-foot wall of chain link topped with Razor wire and alarm points. The middle is made of Taut wire and embedded with sensors that will also activate alarms if touched. The innermost barrier is called the zone fence, it's a web of stainless steel and another set of alarms.

Donato parks. I take in the complex where Billy Payer's serving consecutive sentences for kidnapping, assault and second-degree murder. He'll be in his sixties before he gets even a ghost of a chance at freedom. I want it to be a forever sentence.

The entry for visitors, lawyers and others wanting access to the prisoners is a boxy and modern building; the word *Integrity* is stamped above its doors. Is it a warning? An admonition? A blanket statement that all who enter must put on their honesty and responsibility hats?

* * *

The two chairs in the interview room are made of molded plastic, one is placed on either side of a heavy oak table. Cameras - in two corners of the room - are activated, as is a recording device. Billy Payer's lawyer, Davie DeCambero, a weasel who probably paid someone smarter to take the law boards for him, stands with Donato and a prison representative on the other side of the reflective glass. He's armed with a quickly slapped-together proffer – a document stating that should Payer's information be useful, Donato and I would be compelled to recommend to the Prison Board that Payer be given all consideration for a transfer to the Florida lock-up.

Payer and DeCambero have concocted the details. We'll see.

I've requested Payer be handcuffed.

It's time for me to enter the room and my breath catches in my throat.

Even with the buzz cut, he's still got a golden-boy glow. The chiseled chin. Wide cheekbones. Straight nose. Payer's taken advantage of gym time, his white t-shirt and prison-blue overshirt are stretched tight over his biceps and chest. Today his cockiness is paired with a cool confident smugness. "Dee Rommel," he purrs. "I'll take this opportunity to introduce the improved Billy Payer." He holds up his cuffed hands. "Would love to shake hands."

"I wouldn't."

"But there's no need for these." He shakes his manacles. "I'm a new man. Don't mean any harm."

"Let's get to why I'm here." I don't sit. I lean against the wall as far from him as possible.

He notices and smiles. "First, give me the lowdown. Is Robbie Donato here too? And Gordy Greer? I know my lawyer's watching." He waves at the glass.

"I'm not here to give you information."

7 Days

Payer smiles as if he pities me. "Slow down, Dee Rommel, grab a little joy in life. This is a highlight of my day. Highlight of my week, of my last two years here. I'm pumped to show you I'm doing my best to make sure the taxpayers paying for my housing, laundry, new socks and food get their money's worth."

"Not interested in hearing you pat yourself on the back."

"And that I'm taking advantage of educational opportunities and also securing my place in the Lord's tribe. A pastor from Cushing started volunteering here and we clicked. We're getting super-great Billy-stuff done." He pats the mini-Bible in his shirt pocket. "Once I truly heard Pastor Phil's message - that the best thing I could do was to get through those big stages as fast as I could and get to Acceptance, I had a revelation. That I'd have a fuckin' chance, finally, to realize my potential." He taps the heels of his hands against the table and points to the chair. "Why don't you sit down?"

"What big stages are you talking about?"

"The ones people go through when they lose a loved one. Some famous person wrote the stages in a book." He closes his eyes and recites. "Denial, Anger, then False Bargaining..." He opens his eyes and continues his lecture. "A prisoner goes through the same things, when his freedom dies. Lots of us get stuck in False Bargaining, even if we know there's no drug or money or selling of your firstborn that'll change your sentence. So, you gotta get past Bargaining. And deal with the next in line. That fucker is called Depression and it wants to suck you in. Angry Depression, Sad Depression and Self-Harm Depression. Get past that, it can be clear sailing. Pastor Phil coached me, told me to race my butt to Acceptance. He said that's where growth starts to happen. So, I did. Race. Got there. Been a productive boy since."

"Pastor Phil sounds like a cheesy church bookmark."

"He's worth his shit."

"He rehearse that little speech with you?"

"When I got here, I was lashing out like hell – kicking, screaming, all foul-mouth, hocking up big balls of glop at the guards. All that got me was staying in ACU."

"The Controlled Unit."

He points a finger at me. "You named it. Twenty-two hours a day in lockdown, two hours hallway walking time *with chains on*, and no mixing with the general population. Meals in my cell. I had to make my daily dump sweet and long and extra meaningful just to have some purpose to the day. Then Pastor Phil visited and explained the route into Level One – where a guy can get some breaths of choice. I got on the road, buried the anger and followed the rules and learned to Accept and got to Level One. Then Level Two. Now I go to meetings, join programs, and get access to electronics. Pastor Phil suggested I take classes to prepare me to give back to others who find themselves in my situation. He told me taking those classes will help me get to Level Three." He looks up at me for applause, gets none. His nostrils flare. "You don't need to look at me like I'm a turd on the bottom of your shoe."

"I don't arrange my face. It arranges itself."

"I'm a different Billy Payer. New and improved. Learn to live with it."

"Your change of spots won't give your brother his life back. It doesn't help Karla. She had to move back in with her parents, she doesn't go outside, and she shakes all day. You set her up to be gang-raped and you're responsible for screwin' up her life."

"I wish for Karla a different story. Pastor Phil says we can write our stories anew, get over our pasts. It's all about the rewrite."

I'd like to shove his nose deep into his skull and watch his brain explode.

"You're lookin' good," he says. "Look at you and your re-write. Fallen PPD. Rising to getting a 'well-done' from the mayor as a junior P.I. star. Too bad Karla doesn't have your spine."

"Screw you."

"Would love to accommodate you, Dee Rommel, but tut-tut, we have people watching." He lowers his eyes, as if I've flirted with him and he wants to be demure. "My new story is about transformation. I was a taker. Now I'm a giver."

"Then give me information. You told Donato you had something on the murder of Frank Croake."

Payer straightens his back, ready to get down to business. "Okay. Okay. When I was getting out of my last visit in juvie I was sixteen and put in an application to work at the Sports Park. Croake didn't hire me. He made a mistake and hired another juvie from the detention center."

"Wynn Stimm?"

Billy's surprised. "Dee Rommel. So fuckin' smart." He flicks his eyes to the reflective glass, maybe sharing a realization with his lawyer that he might have lost a bartering point. "You know about Stimm?"

"We've met."

He leans forward. "Yeah, you have."

Adrenaline makes my heart push against my chest. My mind goes to Detective Banford's photos of the balaclava, the newspaper with the December 7th date, and the copy of Stimm's wedding certificate. "What do you mean by that?"

Billy recognizes the flush that has filled my face as an opportunity. His confidence returns. He slides his cuffed hands across his lips, as if he's zipping them.

Stick to the plan. Donato, Banford and I agreed on that. Don't get sidetracked by Gilli's obtuse clues. Stay on the recent events. Billy contacted Donato with a promise he'd have something on Croake's death. Stay on Croake.

"If that's all you've got – some juvie jerk-off together - I'll leave you to Pastor Phil."

"Oh, I have more. When we served time in juvie, Stimm and I had each other's backs." He taps a scar on his neck, a thin white gash just under his jaw. "After this. This is a scar that's never gonna disappear. But I got him back – kneecap decimation. Perfect hit. He was in a brace for a year."

I fake a yawn. "Bored with your biography."

Payer continues. "Frank Croake thought Stimm had more potential than me – 'cause Stimm's got that smile and swing going on all the time. Croake couldn't see he was a liar and a cheat. When he hooked Croake's son up with drugs-"

"Cooper? Stimm is the one who got Cooper started on drugs?"

"Yeah. The teenager took to it like it was the air he needed to live. Stimm would take the ATV up the back dirt and meet people on the trail to High Eagle. Cooper got to be a regular."

"At Marker Six? That's halfway up."

Billy shrugs. "Marker whatever. We called it Eagle One Take-Off."
"What kind of drugs? Codeine?"
"That was popular for a while."
"Is that what Cooper took?"
"At first, I think so. Good entry drug, you know."
"No. I don't."
"Such a goody goody Dee Rommel. Yeah, it's a good entry. That pop singer – Justin B, somebody – he was addicted to it. All about relaxation and euphoria. Unhappy kids like it."
"Okay. Start with codeine. What else? Cocaine? Heroin? Meth?"
"Sure."
"Complete with needles?"
Payer nods. "Injectables. Snortables. Lickables. Happy Man Pills for the starters. Anything that suited. Toolbox full."
"A lot of needles?"
"Stimm liked to educate his clients. What's the fastest way a high gets into the system, he'd ask. What's the most efficient? It was like he was teaching and everyone was a student, and they had to try different stuff. He'd start them with some pot, since smoking speeds to the brain and you feel it right away. And if your brain likes what smoking or vaping pot does, he'd say – why not see how other availables might make you feel. Try a MDMA tab on your tongue. Try to snort coke up your nose. But know this, he'd say. The second fastest high comes with the injectable. Needles can get you into the higher-powered mind-alterers fast. You inject directly into a vein – in the arm, in between your toes. If you go for the femoral vein in the groin, you gotta get it just right or you're gonna hit the artery. He'd have everyone strip down and have them feel for the sweet spot in the groin area."
"He was a drug dealer and teacher all in one. Gives me the whelps."
"And as always happened, someone gets hooked. They like it and then they never want to wait. It's Eagle One Take-Off and everyone wants up in the air. Want it powerful and fast."
"And addiction was the goal."
"That's where the dealer's money is. But who knows who's gonna get addicted fast and who's got the bucks to support it. Cooper fell fast – and he

had access to money. He liked the injectable. Stimm explains it this way: lots of people like the *drug*, but they also get hooked on the ritual too, on preparing the needle and cleaning the injection site. Get hooked on the anticipation. So Stimm really makes out if it's a needle fixation *and* the drug addiction."

"You were there for this?"

"I'd show up once in a while. But drugs-" He puts his hand to his pretty face. "They can mess this up. I'm not gonna mess this up."

"How'd Frank Croake find out?"

"Don't know. But he did and he set a trap with local cops. They waited for Stimm to hand out the supply and take the money, then bam, busted the druggie party. Frank had Stimm arrested right in front of the people he'd convinced he was so cool. Humiliation never sets well. Cops also found his extra stash under one of the staff cabins. Stimm was max-sentenced. And since he'd aged out of juvie, he served his time here."

"We knew Stimm was in here for drugs, you're not giving us any fresh news about that."

"But you see I have details. You need me to fill other stuff in."

"Like what," I challenge.

Payer scrambles a bit; he's wondering what will soften my resolve. "Thing is, I bet you didn't know this. When Stimm got out, Croake didn't let up on him, he gets someone to watch Stimm's ass. Doesn't want him anywhere near his son or the Park. Ever. So just to ditch that constant surveillance, Stimm had to move north."

"We know he moved up near Moosehead."

"'Cause he was getting harassed by Croake's hire. And I got more. I got more." He smacks his lips. "But done giving you info for free."

"You and Stimm stayed in touch?"

"We always know where each other is."

"What about when Stimm got married last year and moved into a house in Cape Elizabeth? That's close to Portland. Did Frank Croake still keep a watch on him?"

Maybe there's someone to talk to - someone who was tracking Croake recently.

Payer turns coy. "Maybe."

"Where are you getting your information?"

"Prisons use info as grease. For every orifice."

He gives me a sly look.

I stay on him. "Is Stimm still dealing drugs?"

The slyness morphs into a Cheshire Cat grin.

"Is Rusty Razer involved?"

Payer raises an eyebrow. "Dee Rommel. Knows of the Appendage Man. You're always the show-off. You could be a great cop." He laughs, leans back, waits for my reaction. "But that ship has sailed, right?"

I ignore the dig. "Appendage Man? What does that mean?"

"What you get yourself when you need something done but you don't want to touch it yourself." He leans back. "Time to put on the brakes. I gave you free shit to prove I got it. But now it's time to pony up. Did Donato explain the deal? My lawyer's got a draft ready. It calls for a letter from you, agreeing the old Billy Payer is gone, and the new guy deserves the chance to pursue his potential in Florida lock-up."

"You're not worried you'll lose friends here when it comes out that you're a snitch?"

"I'm covered. I let it be known I have a doctor's appointment."

"You just said prisons are gossip machines. You think a false appointment will hold up?"

"I got it covered. So, deal?"

I shrug. "Well, you really haven't given me anything, except that Stimm is a waste of space and he and Croake didn't get along."

His eyes narrow. "You gotta sign a promise letter first. You know, I got a lady professor in Florida who believes in me, aching to be my sponsor."

"I heard about that. I did a little research on women who suffer from this disease."

"What do you mean 'disease'?"

"Women who connect with guys behind Taut wire fences, alarms and iron doors. It's called hybristophilia. They get into it because they never have to put up with any of the tough stuff of a real relationship. They can feel like a saint, a mother, a sex object but hold all the power in the relationship."

"Bull fuckin' shit. My lady prof's into me. I'm not a disease. And I got power. I don't need to accept her phone calls."

I press. "Who shot Frank Croake up with codeine?"

"Sign my lawyer's document."

I continue, "And when lady prof realizes Billy Payer is incapable of real transformation and isn't worth her time? And you can't go over to her place and beat the daylights out of her to change her mind, what's going to happen? When you can't stop her from ghosting you and your sponsor disappears?"

"Won't happen. You want to know what I know or not?"

"Who shot up Frank Croake with a drug? Who got him halfway up High Eagle? Who put the bag over his head and watched him suffocate? If you have *proof* it was Stimm-"

Billy 'zips' his mouth shut again.

I finally sit at the table. "Your lawyer didn't tell you how this plays out? You sharing stories and possibilities doesn't complete the process. Promising to come forth doesn't complete the process. Once you actually give up something and once your snitching pans out and once the cops grab the killer and charges are made, and evidence is in place – *then* and only *then* does the proffer go into effect. It's no overnight thing; every step takes time. Your lawyer didn't tell you that?"

Payer turns his head, glares at the reflective glass and his middle finger shoots up. Looks like the process was *not* made clear and dipwad Davie DeCambero could get a new asshole ripped into his backside.

"But still," I continue. "The sooner you tell us what you know, things *could* start to move forward."

"How do I know you won't take what I got to give and get your arrest and then say I didn't have anything to do with it?"

"It's called trust. But then, you've never been trustworthy, so you might not understand the word. Do you have any idea what real 'trust' means?"

"I gotta talk to my lawyer."

"You do that." I head to the door, knock on it. I turn back to Payer. "But you know what? I think you have nothing. You wanted some attention. That's what all this was about."

His eyes narrow. "Careful, Dee Rommel. You should respect me."

"Why?"

"'Cause you shouldn't be too sure you'll be able to pull another rabbit out of the hat."

"Meaning?"

"Losing half a leg is one thing. You got a lot more to lose."

"Is that a threat?"

Payer 'zips' his mouth - runs his fingers across his lips again.

CHAPTER TWENTY-FOUR

"Failure before lunch never feels good," I say as we cross the prison's parking lot.

"It could be like you said in there, Payer just wanted to get in your face again. But let's look at what you did get."

"Marker Six, as the place of death, makes some sense now."

"Could be the place where Croake got the better of Stimm. But, Stimm's got an alibi for when Frank was taken up to Marker Six."

"The injection makes more sense now. Reflects on how Cooper took to the needle. That could mean something."

"Still. Stimm has an alibi."

"Maybe the alibi's got holes." I continue to make my case. "Frank Croake got Stimm arrested and he did time. Cooper was sent to a fancy rehab, didn't spend a day in juvie. That probably burned Stimm. And then, Stimm's out, he's done his penance, but Frank leans into harassment and has someone on his tail at all times. Never lets the guy alone. Do you know who he hired to follow Stimm?"

"No."

"Was it a PI? If it was - it wasn't Gordy. At least I'm pretty sure it wasn't, Gordy didn't mention it."

Donato nods. "That was new information. Payer did give you that."

But what do we do with it? How do we find out who Frank hired? "This person could've been watching Stimm during the last few weeks."

"Frank Croake and Stimm's paths crossed badly – years ago, says Donato. "But Stimm had five years to get back at Croake. Why would he wait? And remember what I've been repeating. The alibi. So don't get stuck on Stimm, keep the options open."

"Is this a teaching moment?"

Donato frowns. "I don't want you misinterpreting everything I say or how I say it." He kicks at a chunk of slushy ice.

He's right. I have my edge on. "Okay. Sloughing the chip off my shoulder. I'm bright and amenable again."

"That we will see."

I hear the sarcasm but move on. "Okay, okay. What about that piece of fabric that we found on the Sports Park trail?"

"Silk and flannel wool combo," he tells me. "Could be from a shirt or a jacket lining or – lab's working on it. We'll see if we get any DNA results."

"Stimm's particulars are in the system. As a felon."

"Yeah. But, as you know, DNA takes time. Could be a week. Or more."

"Stimm is deep in this," I say. "If he's back in the drug business, could he be brought in on distribution charges?"

"You said you weren't going to be stuck."

"Sorry."

Donato continues, "I already have a task force on the drug angle. If there's been any sign of recent activity, we'll find it."

We're ten yards away from the car. Donato presses his fob, unlocks the Taurus. I look at my phone.

"Anything on Gordy?" he asks.

"Text from Abshir." I read it aloud: *Gordy still in ICU. Not out of surgery fog yet.*

I move to the driver's side of the car.

"I'll drive," says Donato.

"We made a deal. You get to sleep."

"Got a call from Detective Banford. He's at the Medical Examiner's office in Augusta for the autopsy of Gilli Wanz. Asked if I could swing by - if it worked with our schedule."

"Why?" I check my watch. It's noon. I want to be at the hospital when Gordy wakes up.

"Not sure. But Augusta's close. I check in, then we take the 95 back to Portland. That's faster than Route 1. Won't add that much time."

He heads west on Route 17. "Talked to Sheriff Robinson up near Greenville. He communicated his condolences that 'charming' – as he called him - Wynn Stimm was now in our territory. He said that the woman who disappeared, Amelia Jurner, was popular, maybe liked to party too much, but she was a good neighbor, good worker. He's pretty sure she's at the bottom of the lake or buried in Baxter Range and her car and other property were quietly sold off."

"By whom?"

"Sheriff's got his ideas, but there was no trail. He couldn't nail Stimm for anything 'cause Stimm had a strong alibi. Stimm said he was staying with a cousin, looking at boats, in New Hampshire."

"That cousin and looking at boats comes in handy."

Donato must've been busy multitasking while Payer and I talked. He continues, "Stimm's time in Greenville had caught the attention of the Drug Squad up there. They could never nail him as a user or on distribution. He finally left town and moved up to Saddleback for the winter ski season."

"That's where he met and romanced Tanya."

* * *

We pull into a lot off Hospital Street. Rhia Jones meets us in the lobby of the Medical Examiners Building. Donato introduces us. She's slim, medium height, has dark red hair and green eyes behind wire-frame glasses. Donato asks if Frank Croake's body is ready for release. She shakes her head. "Should be soon." She turns to me. "If you'll excuse us. Detective Banford is waiting."

She motions for me to take a seat in the waiting area and leads Donato to the elevator that will take them to the lower-level morgue. Rhia presses the button, and they wait. I'm close enough to see her show Donato a photo on her cell phone. "My daughter's birthday party," she's saying. "Two years old."

"Her name's Daisy, right?"

"You remembered."

"She's cute," says Donato. "Has your red hair." He's got his phone in hand; he accesses a picture of Dude. "Look, he's holding himself up on the couch. Getting ready to walk."

The elevator door opens, they step inside, bonding over kids' pictures. Totally off-business and I resent it. But then, she's with dead bodies all day,

7 Days

maybe she takes every opportunity to appreciate the living. The elevator doors close, and they're out of sight.

I check my phone. Nothing new from Abshir. I get out my notebook, I want to jot down thoughts from the meeting with Payer.

- Marker Six (Eagle One)
- Codeine. A toolbox of drugs. Needles/injectables.
- ATVs. Back dirt tracks
- Frank Croake (FC) harassing Stimm after release from prison
- Stimm feeling FC's reach – resenting constant surveillance
    o Who, at FC's behest, was keeping an eye on Stimm?
    o Another PI? Or? Who could it be?
- Rusty Razer and Stimm – in a drug business together now?
- Stimm's charm - dangerous
- False Bargaining
    o Do we all do it?
- Acceptance
    o Is it possible?

Items standing out to me:

- Control of Two Daughters Farm
    o Mushrooms
    - Carter Stround
        o Tanya now sole heir
        o Gilli wanting Stimm out of Tanya's life
        o Oscar Herbstrom
    - Housing development
- Stimm – did he slip through the fingers of the law in northern Maine? Amelia Jurner
    - Connection between murders of Gilli Wanz and FC?
        o In common: Stimm. Razer. Croake kids. Tanya. Rusty. Herbstrom.
    - Connections? Alliances?
    - Stimm's alibi?

I use my phone to look up Best Boats in New Hampshire. I find the listing and punch the 'Call' option. A live person answers. "Yeah. Here."

I start my story: "Hi, I'm calling from Hangley Boat Decor, we're making new cushions and window curtains for a boat that was recently bought at your yard. A 42-foot Grand Banks. The measurements seem off. If you have the information, maybe I can check them with you before I start cutting fabric."

He laughs. "We don't get into interior decorating measurements. You want to know engine sizes, water pump health, condition of deck, I can help. Oh wait. The 42-footer? Only Grand Banks we have. Boat's still on the market. There's no signed sale."

"Must be close to it," I say. "I've got the cushion order in front of me. The new owner told me there was a big celebration at the Oar Room, lots of champagne."

"Who are you again?"

"Hangley Boat Decor. We're new, out of Scarborough, in Maine."

"There is no new owner yet."

Why is this not adding up? "I've got an order from someone named Wynn Stimm."

"Ahh. That guy. Check didn't clear so we're still showing the boat. Not that you heard it from me, but you might want to cover yourself. Stop the work till you get a fat deposit from that blowhard. And I recommend *cash*. Anyway, I gotta go. Good luck."

He hangs up.

* * *

An hour later, I'm behind the wheel of Donato's Taurus. He's got the passenger seat back as far as it can go, his hands are clasped over his stomach and his eyes are closed.

"You and Rhia Jones look like you've gotten friendly pretty fast."

He doesn't open his eyes. "Got kids in common. That becomes a sort of shorthand."

"Huh."

7 Days

"And that single parent thing."

"Huh. She's divorced?"

"Husband died in a plane crash. A year ago."

Now I can't be snarky.

"Are you going to tell me why Banford wanted you at the morgue? Were there drugs in Gilli's system?"

"I'm gonna concentrate on my nap."

He's clearly not going to share.

"Stimm's alibi - that he was buying a boat-"

"What about it?"

"He wrote a bad check. Boat's not his."

He looks at me. "You know this how?"

"I happened to call the boatyard in New Hampshire."

"You tell them who you were?"

"I made up a story."

"Geez, Rommel. So what if his check bounced? Stimm was still in New Hampshire. The night of the Fundraisers, he got towels delivered at nine, and chatted up the maid. Got an extra blanket from the front desk at midnight. He's on their security camera. Then again at three a.m., he gets three bottles of water from the desk, said he had a hangover. He was eating breakfast in the hotel restaurant at six, even spilled hot coffee on himself and flirted with a waitress."

"He really wanted to be seen."

"And he was."

"I didn't know you had checked all that."

"And yep. Banford's got him on the same hotel security cameras for the morning Gilli Wanz was killed too."

He puts a glove over his eyes to block out the light. It takes only a moment and he's snoring.

Screw him. This avoidance of each other while being a foot apart sucks. I might have been supersensitive last night with the birthday song. Maybe I overreacted.

No. Not apologizing.

But, before, when we were thrown together, there was always a warmer companionship.

That's gone. Too many things are slipping through my fingers.

CHAPTER TWENTY-FIVE

Eventide's approaching. We stop at Letty's to retrieve my car. Donato drives off, he hasn't told me where he's headed. Not that he owes me insight into his schedule.

I pick up Bert at Doggie DayCare and I take him for a walk to the park by Oceanview Gateway. The building is cold, leaden and gray tonight, there are no events scheduled for the evening to brighten the windows. The ancient pylons of an old pier stand up through the water. They'll be at attention 'forever' due to the worry that pulling them out could release long-buried toxins from way-past railway coal and grease and manufacturing residue. Nothing we can do. City is stuck with them.

Bert leads us down the sidewalk towards Fore Points Marina. The fancy new floating docks are empty for the season. The all-weather picnic tables are glazed with ice. Guard stations are empty. Talking to Bert is always easy because he never disagrees. "It's good to rattle the cage a bit, isn't it, Bert. To remember that nothing stays the same…"

Bert turns around and leads us back to the doors of G&Z. "He's not here, Bert. Soon. We just gotta believe he'll be in his office again. Soon."

Abshir's van pulls into a parking spot in front of the G&Z building. The plan is for him to take Bert to Gordy's and stay with him until Marie gets home.

I haven't gotten real sleep for almost forty-eight hours. But now is not the time to worry about that. It's my turn to sit with Gordy.

* * *

Winter gloom hangs like a specter outside the window of Gordy's hospital room. His eyes are glued to my face, they look bigger and buggier because his skin has sunk into the hollows between cheekbones and jaw. He can't talk because the tubes are still in place, but his chin moves upwards a mill-inch, a command for me to keep talking. I've filled him in on Jade's information on Wynn Stimm, Oscar Herbstrom and the property development of Two Daughters Farm. I've taken him through the treasure hunt at #5 Horseshoe, the newspaper and balaclava, the information from Carter Stround and Frank's hope that mushrooms could aid in getting rid of the PFAS toxins in the soil. We've gone through the events at Wandering Moose and my pretty solid assumption that Cindy Croake was skimming on a high and the fact that Cooper Croake is still missing.

I finish with how Donato and Detective Banford and I talked through the night and the visit to Billy Payer - the information gleaned at Maine State Prison - especially that it was Stimm who introduced Cooper to drugs and how Marker Six and the injection could have horrific resonance. And how Billy intimated at Stimm's antipathy towards Frank Croake. And me.

He finally lifts his hand (barely) to stop me, then opens his palm and settles it on top of the heavy sheets. His fingers move, like he's beckoning me. I skootch the chair closer so my knees are against the side of the bed. I put the tips of my fingers into the bowl of his hand, and he moves his around to touch them. It's not a firm hold, and the effort seems to take his full concentration.

"You need something?" I ask.

His fingers curl in to touch my hand.

"Do you need me to call a nurse?"

His fingers pull back.

"You want to give me some direction?"

His fingers curl towards mine again.

I take a pen and notebook from my pocket. "Can you write down what you want to say?" I put the pen in his hand. His fingers can't hold it. His eyes demand my understanding. "Okay. Let's do 'yes' and 'no' questions." I put my hand back into his palm. "Let's do the good old reliable squeeze for 'yes' stuff."

His fingers touch mine.

"First, do you want to yell at me for not calling when I said I would?"

He presses.

"That's a strong 'yes'. Okay, I get it. My terrible bad." I duck my head so he won't see me press down a pitiful, self-centered glob of sorry guilt. "It was selfish of me to wait until I had more, to want to move it along by myself, find Cooper, get you all the answers, want to present you with a gift-wrapped 'solve'."

He presses my hand.

"Got it. Another 'yes'. Okay. Selfish. Unprofessional. Let's move past that. I should tell you that the plan is to go forward with Frank Croake's memorial on Monday. Three days from now. It's not going to be postponed." His fingers stay steady on my hand. "The send-off will be at the Sports Park in the barn." His chin rises, his eyes narrow. "I know you don't want anyone to stop looking for answers. Not for a second. I promise, no one will stop."

Am I imagining it? Do Gordy's eyes get narrower? Is this disbelief?

"Let me ask you some questions," I say. "Do I trust Billy Payer?"

His fingers move away from mine.

"That's a 'no'. Obviously. But do you think he *might* have something that *might* help figure out what happened to Frank?"

He wiggles his fingers.

"Yeah, I can't tell if he's wasting our time either. You think I should concentrate elsewhere for now?"

He squeezes my hand.

"Wynn Stimm? Donato thinks his alibi is airtight. What do you think?"

Gordy closes his eyes. I feel his frustration, clearly this was not a 'yes' or 'no' question.

"Sorry. But consider this. Someone could be doing his dirty work. Payer calls it being an 'appendage' man. Stimm's pushing this 'turned over a new leaf, married a nice farm girl', has this 'smart entrepreneur' moving into real estate work thing going. But he's not a good guy. Billy Payer said Frank Croake hired someone to keep an eye on Stimm after he finished his time for the drug charges. To keep him away from Cooper. I told Donato it wasn't you - but am I wrong? Did you do that for Frank?"

His fingers fall open. That's a 'no'.

His eyes widen, turn steel-ish. It's his 'listen-to-me', 'get-back-on-track' stare.

"You want to stay on the Croake kids?"

He presses my hand. Three times.

7 Days

"Donato and his team are looking for Cooper."

His other hand slaps at the bedsheet, sharp. Like I haven't been listening.

"But you want me on it too. Okay. Okay."

His fingers press my hand again.

"I need to think about where he could be. About where he'd go." I ask. "Where would he go to stay out of sight?"

Gordy's eyes circle the room.

I look around. The walls are blank. The TV is dark. His hand taps the hospital bed. He's trying to move his head from side to side, but the tubes and paraphernalia hold him hostage.

"I don't get it."

He lets his eyes circle the room again.

"Don't want to make excuses, Gordy, but if you're trying to tell me something, I-"

Two of his fingers grab at one of mine. Takes a moment. And then he opens his fingers again.

"Yeah, okay. No excuses. I'm listening. I'm really tired, but I'll sleep later."

He turns his hand over, it's on top of mine now, acknowledging my tiredness. His fingers tap on the back of my hand. "What, now we're gonna do Morse Code? I'm rusty on that."

He pats my hand softly. There's a long moment. His breathing slows and his eyes close. Sleep has drawn him away again.

"Gordy?" He's asleep. "Gordy. I'm not ready for anything to happen to you."

The lights are low, and the hospital hallways are quiet. I put my forehead down on the edge of the bed. It's good to have the weight off my neck. I close my eyes. Maybe the thinking will be easier.

Jule Selbo

FOUR DAYS

CHAPTER TWENTY-SIX

There's a hand on my shoulder. I raise my head to see Nurse Guido next to me. "Morning."

I check on Gordy. He's still in his intubated dreamland.

"What time is it?" I mumble.

Guido answers. "Almost five in the morning."

I lost an entire night?

Guido continues. "Marie wants me to tell you she's here if there are things you need to do."

Hint. Hint. Marie's never subtle.

I look out the window. The sky is black. Snow falls softly past the outdoor lights.

Guido checks Gordy's stats, interprets the messages on the machines. "No surprises. We'll see what the doctor has to say later today."

Okay. Right now, I have to figure out how to find Cooper Croake.

* * *

I stand in front of the hospital, zip up my parka and let the cold jolt me into full wakefulness. A Blacklane Mercedes pulls into the nearby drop-off area.

"Dee?" The heels of knee-high leather boots hit the ground. My mom, in a maroon coat, hat and scarf, gets out of the car. Blond hair frames her face looks like a halo, the heat of her breath in the cold air makes it look like she's encased in a cloud. She hurries to me. "Honey." She's almost a foot shorter than me, but her hug is strong. "I don't want you to be alone in this."

My dad had his heart attack when he was fishing with Gordy. Gordy had gotten him to a hospital in small town Damariscotta, sixty miles from Portland, it took me over an hour to get there. Gordy and I sat watch. My mother had to drive up from Boston. She got there too late.

"How's Gordy?" she asks.
"Sleeping. Doctor thinks things went well."
"Is Marie with him?"
"Yeah. We traded places."
We step apart.
"What about London - your conference?" I ask.
"I gave my excuses and regrets. This is where I need to be."
The driver has gotten out of the luxury car, he's holding my mom's briefcase. He's wearing a black overcoat, and he's got a Jamaican accent. "Ma'am? No forgettin', uh?"
"Oh, thank you, Jamari."
"Like me to wait?"
"No, thank you."
She takes her briefcase, and he gets back into the car. My mother waves as he drives off. "There were no planes from Boston to Portland until this afternoon, and Chester didn't want to wait for the first Concord Express Bus, so he called the car service he uses. It was the fastest way here for us."
"Where is Chester?"
"Jamari dropped him at the hotel, he wanted to get us checked in. Let's get out of the cold." She leads me back to the hospital entry. The sliding doors open as we approach, and we move into the lobby. "Fill me in, honey."
"Gordy's had spurts of wakefulness. He's intubated so he can't talk but we got in a little communication. I know what he wants me to do, so I've gotta be off to do it."
"Does that man ever stop?"
"There's something he needs done and it's still very primary - even with all this."
"Yes, his need to keep you on-the-go."
"Mom."
"That's Gordy, I know." It's a loving acknowledgement. She puts her hand on my arm. "We know."
"The doctor says Gordy will need time," I say. "Of course."
"You need time too, honey. Let's get you something to eat. No one does well while running on empty."

"Mom, my refrigerator's got zilch-"

She takes her phone from her coat pocket, texts. "Katy will be up. She's two blocks away. Let's walk, there's no wind. After the plane and the car, I need to stretch."

She slips her hand into the crook of my arm. She smells like sea air and lavender even after ten hours of travel. I didn't inherit her ability to always look good. When I'm baffed, I look it. "No need to over-think," she says. "You used to love to go to Katy's through the side door."

Delicate snow swirls. We head down the gentle hill past darkened houses and storefronts. There's a gas station at the end of the street, colorful readouts of gas prices pulse and there's a slim harsh light illuminating the pumps. No one is filling their gas tanks or leaning their heads back to let the snow touch their cheeks. We pass an old brownstone; it's got a gated front lawn. The streetlight's glow reveals three rabbits emerging from under an evergreen hedge - heads down, they lick at the fresh snow. Their heads jerk up, they've smelled us. They're off - quickly hopping around a corner. Maybe there's a nest against the brownstone's foundation where they burrow for warmth.

We reach an aged clapboard house wedged between a modern bank and the recent construction of a workout gym. The old house is part residence, part business. The lights in the back kitchen are on, and the side door is unlocked. There's the smell of rising dough, butter, cinnamon, lemon and cooking fruit. We enter and Katy, one of my mom's oldest friends, is rolling out thick scone dough on a marble board and cutting it into triangles. She doesn't break her rhythm when she sees us. "Gayle. Dee. Help yourself to coffee." This has been a family operation for two generations; Katy's sister will come down from the upstairs living quarters after the scone dough has rested, in time to put them and the muffins into the oven and to make the frosting for the cooling cinnamon buns and blueberry turnovers before customers arrive and she starts to man the sales counter. We sit at the small kitchen table and Katy puts slices of quiche in front of us. "Have this. It's best when it's warm from the oven."

"Thanks Katy," my mom says.

7 Days

Katy hurries off to take the bacon out of the refrigerator. She calls over her shoulder. "Feels like old times. Hope you're staying a few days, Gayle, so we can catch up after my workday."

"I am Katy. I am staying for a while. Don't let us disturb you."

"I won't. I can't."

My mom reaches for my hand, keeps her voice low. "What about Gordy's pancreas?" she asks.

"When they had him on the table, they did some laper-laser something, got some tissue or chunk for a biopsy."

"This is no time for fear. Gordy's a fighter, we know that."

"Yeah."

"What is it that Gordy wants you to do?"

"Find Frank Croake's son. Maybe he can help get to the bottom of why Frank was killed."

"I thought it was suicide."

"The case was reopened on Tuesday – just two and a half days ago. It wasn't suicide and Gordy's non-stop about finding out who's responsible."

My mom nods. "Because Frank had his back for all those years. Gave him the seed money for G&Z - if Gordy promised to give up the gambling."

News to me. "Didn't know that part of it."

"Your dad and Frank kept Gordy honest about it. Let's eat." She forks a bird-size portion for herself, encourages me. "Come on, honey. You were never a good eater as a baby either. Too busy doing anything but."

The creamy quiche, filled with ham and cheese, wakes my stomach. The rest of my body perks up too.

My mom sips her coffee. "Your friend, that detective with the new baby - Robbie Donato - is he involved?"

"Yeah."

"You trust him. Let him take care of Gordy's hunches."

"Donato's got other hunches. And the investigation is going in a lot of different directions. Lots of moving parts."

"Is Frank's son dangerous?"

"No." I say it too quickly and my mom raises a suspicious eyebrow.

Mom takes another bite of the quiche. "What else aren't you telling me?"

I don't want to get into Stimm, what the newspaper and balaclava could mean or how Stimm's presence has affected my equilibrium. The wet cluck in the back of his throat. Why worry her? "Nothing. Really."

"I want you to get some sleep, but I assume I'm not going to win on that." She's got her phone out again. "I'm texting Marie that I'm in town, that I'll be by the hospital in an hour. Let's go to your apartment. You'll feel better if you shower and change clothes."

She's always believed if you feel good about how you look and smell, life will go better.

"Will you get your car and pick me up?" she asks. "Five minutes?"

It's easier to fall into her timetable. "Sure."

* * *

I roll the iWalk out of the shower and quickly don the LiteGood and find clean clothes and an unwrinkled sweater. When I come into the living room, the flames in the fireplace are blazing. My mom is leaning her head on the arm of the couch, her feet are tucked under her.

"You're the one who needs to rest," I say.

She shakes her head. "I'm fine. Happy Birthday, honey." She waves at the coffee table.

Half a dozen Katy-made cupcakes are lined up. One has an unlit candle on it.

"Oh. I didn't think about it." She must've asked Katy for the cakes when I went to get the car. "Chocolate. The best. Thanks."

She starts to put her boots back on. "We'll celebrate later."

There's a knock on the door. I look out the window, see the morning light has arrived. It's Nail. Damn. His skin looks even whiter and more dewy damp. His arm is in the cast, his eyes are still red and sunken. But he's added a new look. Earmuffs. Just like Detective Banford's. They may warm his ears, but they leave his bald head open to the cold. "Nail, it's too early," I say. "Whatever it is you need, I can't help you."

I notice the taxi outside - it's pulling away from the curb and driving off. Shit.

7 Days

"The police let me go into the Kahta condo," he says. "They stayed with me the whole time while I got some clothes and my favorite toothpaste. I didn't get everything I needed, but I wanted to let you know."

"Okay. Good for you."

He looks around me, sees my mother. He waves. "Hi. I'm Nail. Like hammer and-"

"Hello." My mom smiles.

"Are you her mother? I can see the resemblance in the nose. And the hair color. The lips too."

Mom shoots me a look: 'who is this odd person?' But she's always polite. "Have you visited Dee before?" she asks.

I interrupt. "Nail, we're just leaving." I go to the dining table to retrieve my bag.

Nail slips inside, slips the puffer coat off his injured shoulder and arm. "Warm inside here. Feels good. I like fireplaces." He puts his coat and scarf on the chair.

"Hey, don't do that, we're not staying," I say. "Don't take your coat off-"

He pushes the earmuffs off his head, lets them circle his neck. "Ahh, this is my first time in your place. Last time I came by, I wasn't invited inside." He turns to my mother. "Even when I hired her, she never invited me inside."

"You hired Dee?"

I pick up his coat, try to usher him back towards the front door. "Nail, you hired me for a few hours to find Gilli. When we found her, our business arrangement was over. You asked me to take you yesterday to Tanya's, and that task was also completed."

Nail smiles bravely, fills my mom in. "I used to spend all my time with my girlfriend. Did your daughter tell you my girlfriend was beaten, kicked, her hair pulled out and her head bashed in and killed?"

My mom's skin pales. "When?"

"Two days ago."

"Dee and I haven't had a chance to talk about everything. I am sorry for your loss."

"You're very kind," says Nail. "And she's responsible for this-" He points to his arm. "We're trying to find out…"

I jump in. "There's no 'we', Nail. The police are investigating." And since Donato didn't share any news on Gilli's post-mortem, I have nothing new. I grab my jacket and car keys. "I'm leaving now, Nail."

Nail turns to me. "Where are you going? Can I come with you?"

"No."

My mother flicks the switch on the fireplace. The flames die. "As it happens, I need to visit someone at the hospital. Dee's going to drop me off."

Nail puts his hopes in my mom. "Maybe you'd like some company at the hospital?"

My mom shakes her head. "I'm fine, thank you. I will be with others."

Nail has cut a hole in the black sweatshirt he's got on, to give room for his cast. The sweatshirt has a stencil of a mushroom on the chest - what the hell? It's the same design I saw on Carter Stround's jersey. 'Maine's Mushroom Friend Project' is written below the artwork. "Where'd you get that shirt?"

"Gilli gave it to me." He turns around so I see the back. "She got interested in this company. See the autographs?"

The art features a cluster of mushrooms. Three people have added their signatures over the white caps. Carter Stround, Frank Croake and Gilli Wanz. Carter told me he'd never met Gilli. "What did she tell you about it?"

"Nothing. We didn't talk about her business stuff."

"Did you meet the people who also signed their names?"

"No." He lifts the earmuffs back into their intended place. "Okay, you both have places to go, and I don't. Where am I going? Where am I supposed to be? When Gilli was alive, I knew where to be. Now, I don't know. Ahh. I have to find a place where it feels – right. Not the hotel, that's for sure."

My mom's got her coat on. "Do you have a family, Nail?"

"I don't want to be somewhere where I'm judged."

"You have that friend," I say. "The knitter of mittens."

"Doesn't feel right invading his space. He takes up a lot of room."

Banford's description of obese Dalton Guffman made me think of Jabba the Hutt. Maybe he does fill the entire apartment.

7 Days

Nail puts one arm into the coat, lifts the rest over his shoulder. "Tanya, she knows I care about her, and she doesn't mind me. But she's married to the ass so I can't visit. Wynn makes it feel not right for everyone."

My mother ventures, "What would feel 'right', Nail?"

"Where it's safe. Where no one sticks their nose up in the air, where I could maybe have a purpose. It's good to have a purpose, like I did when I used to take care of Gilli."

A place to feel right.

Where would Cooper Croake feel 'right'? The family's ski condo in Sunday River has been checked and found empty. The local police continue to monitor it. He's not at the family house in the West End. He's not at #7 Horseshoe Lane (was he just visiting Rusty Razer that morning or is there a relationship there?) His apartment in Boston remains empty. He's not at the lodge at Sports Park or in one of the staff cabins. Donato's team has checked all the hotels and motels around Portland. No Cooper Croake. Where would he feel 'right'?

Where no one judged him.

I realize there's another place to check out.

CHAPTER TWENTY-SEVEN

Highway 95 is a straight stretch that dips and rises and dips and rises between Scarborough and Kittery. I'm in the middle lane, sticking to the speed limit. I pass the tractor trailers in the right-hand lane, there's a trio of SUVs passing me on the left. On both sides of the highway, evergreens shoot fifty feet or more into the cold, clear sky. Winter hawks are flying this morning, alighting on the treetops, then taking flight again.

Why did Carter Stround tell me he'd never been introduced to Gilli Wanz? He said they had an appointment and that she'd never showed. Wait. The signers of the sweatshirt didn't have to add their signatures at the same time. Maybe Carter and Gilli didn't meet. Maybe he didn't lie to me. Maybe someone who grows hero mushrooms doesn't lie. I wonder if Carter is already in his lab this morning. Testing whatever. Or if he's on the phone, looking for new backers. Or taking a hike, being uncomplicated.

A dark pickup truck crests the low rise behind me. It's been there, traveling at the same speed for the last ten miles, staying about the length of a football field back. Maybe the driver doesn't want to focus on jockeying for position or besting everyone else on the highway. Maybe he's making mental lists - like me. A green car passes the pickup, the car moves into the middle lane to take a position between us. It gains on me, gets too close, as if to intimidate and make me go faster or shift over into the slower lane. Screw him. Semis continue to rumble in the right lane and I'm not moving over. The faster lane is clear, there's plenty of space to pass. The green car finally gives up on the gamesmanship and passes me on the left. Then the pickup is in plain sight again, still at that steady distance behind me. The hairs on the back of my neck prickle. I speed up. The pickup does too; the distance between us stays the same. I drop below the speed limit. The pickup driver does too - keeps the same distance.

7 Days

Exit 25 is coming up, it leads to the southbound Kennebunk Service Plaza. I make the turn, follow the curve that leads to the FoodMart and the gas pumps. Paranoid, I use my side and rearview mirrors to watch the pickup's progress. The driver doesn't take the turn-off; the pickup continues along the highway.

Hypersensitivity can happen. Like when I'm in the middle of a puzzle, when there are no clear answers. Like two nights ago, when the sensor lights went off in the yard of my apartment building. Billy Payer's warning: *Don't be so sure you can pull another rabbit out of a hat.* Wynn Stimm's throat cluck. I shake my shoulders. Forget it. My job is to find Cooper Croake. For Gordy. Focus. Keep it simple.

No one's after me. Unless. Unless someone else knows I'm looking for Cooper – and they want to find him too.

I drive through the FoodMart parking lot, head back towards the highway entry road.

I see it.

A rusted, vintage white Chevy in a spot in front of an entrance to Dunkin' Donuts. The same as the one that stopped in front of #7 Horseshoe Lane? My stomach drops. I raise my foot off the gas, slow down. I don't see anyone in the car. I drive a hundred yards, pull into a parking space and walk back towards Dunkin'. No driver or passengers in the car. I click a photo of it and its license plate. The front passenger seat is full of maps and take-out food cartons. There's a blanket tossed onto the back seat. Inside Dunkin, there's a line at the ordering station. A few older couples view the wall menu above the counter, six guys wait behind them, they all wear Highway Patrol vests.

I hadn't gotten a solid look at the guy driving the Chevy on Horseshoe Lane; Rusty Razer and his mini-Fuji camera had blocked my view.

Well, I'll take pictures too. Photos of the t-shirt rack and the pink/gold/white Dunkin' sipper cups. A few casual shots of the menu above the counter. Just happens the customers are also in the shots. No one takes notice of me.

I slip through the open archway and walk through the aisles of junk food, motor oils, batteries, paperbacks and sundries. I don't see any topknot hairdos like Razer's, no one who looks like they'd be his friend (or business partner). But then, what would that look like? I continue past the hot dog and pizza stalls. A guy's ordering five hot dogs, he starts scarfing down the first one right away. For a split second, I worry about his stomach.

"Need help finding something?" It's a FoodMart employee who must have a bad dental plan. He's all crusty teeth, nose hairs and a real bad shave.

"No," I say. "Thanks." I push out the front door, back into the fresh air.

The vintage white Chevy is gone. Damn. I wanted to see who would show up. Lost the chance. I should've stayed put.

I drive through the lot again, past the gas pumps, the air compressor station, the electric car charging towers. I don't see the Chevy heading towards the exit or merging onto the highway. I drive to the rear of the service plaza.

Just dumpsters.

I text the photo of the car to Abshir, ask him if he can trace the license plate.

* * *

I cover the last sixty-some miles to the outskirts of Andover, Massachusetts. The old Chevy does not reappear. The exit takes me to a country road, and it leads me, eventually, to a high stone wall and tall iron gates. I stop at the small bronze sign that announces the name of the location: *Demarcation*.

A paved drive edged with pines winds through the landscape for a half mile. A sprawling, cream-colored brick building comes into view - three stories, a few low turrets, a bright red tiled roof. Two tennis courts are close by, they're covered in a light dusting of snow. There's a gazebo, and a smaller building that has a sign – *SPA* - written above its door.

The guest parking lot is near the main entry. I press the doorbell, look up at the camera mounted in the overhang. Smile. I'm buzzed in.

The lighting is soft, it falls on caramel-colored carpet and groupings of wingback chairs surrounding low round tables. It looks like a high-end, expensive hotel. A severely elegant woman in a navy-blue suit sits behind an antique desk. Her dark hair is pulled back into a low, tight ponytail, her ivory skin is wrinkleless and her mouth shines with purply-pink lipstick. Her name tag reads 'Ms. Blaine'. She could be mid-thirties or forty – maybe even fifty if she's had the help of a plastic surgeon. The fact that I can't tell makes me distrust her.

7 Days

But she's the only person in sight. "Welcome. How may I help you?" Her voice is like thick honey streaming off a spoon – smooth and slow-syrupy.

"I hope so. I'm here to see someone."

The sharp nail of her pointer finger taps on the glass covering on the desk. A digital screen and keyboard appear. "May I see the doctor's permission and proof of our guest's acceptance to be visited?"

"Excuse me?"

"We require those two documents."

"This isn't official in any way. Just a quick stop. I don't need much time."

Her pitying look tells me no amount of 'just-give-me-a-break' in my voice will sway her.

"Cooper Croake is the name," I say. "I think he's been a guest here - a few times."

"All I can do is advise you to go through the necessaries and get those permissions."

"Could you just look him up on that computer you have right there in the desktop? I want to make sure I'm in the right place. I don't want to do extra work if I'm in the wrong place."

"You're not sure you're in the right place?"

I try another smile. "It's important that I find him. A family matter. Could you just let me know if-"

Ms. Blaine opens a drawer and lifts out a brochure. "My function is to check the passes of potential visitors and/or offer introductory information about our facilities." She pushes the brochure towards me.

Well, I can be tenacious and annoying too; I take a tearsheet from my bag. It's from a local magazine, the picture is of the Croake family with a ski slope behind them. "Cooper is the one on the left. You could let me know if you've noticed him. As a guest here."

She opens another drawer and takes out a sheet of thick bonded paper and a slim ballpoint pen. "If you would like to leave a message, I will give it to Administration, and they will consider your request. Please include your contact information."

"Does that mean Cooper Croake *is* here?"

She uses the fingernail on her middle finger to flick at an itch on the corner of her mouth. "Your name please?"

"Dee Rommel."

She presses a *Note* icon on the computer screen and types. "I have inputted your visit."

I grab the fancy note paper and pen. "Any idea what the response time might be? For someone to take a look at my inquiry?"

"It's not in the description of my position's perimeters to predict."

The note gets written. There's nothing left to say to Ms. Blaine.

I walk outside. The temperature is still close to freezing but the sky is crystal blue, no sign of snow. A gardener is picking up broken branches and placing them in a wheelbarrow. Two men in dark blue pants, coats, knit hats and gloves, pushing small carts of hanging files, pass me. They turn down a walkway. I hang a moment, then move into position to see where they're going. The path dead ends at an entrance marked *Guest Quarters*. The two men go through the door.

I check over my shoulder. The gardener has stopped his work and is making it clear he's watching me.

"Are you looking for me?"

I turn around. There's the slim physique, the sharp chin, dark hair, shiny puffer vest. Cooper Croake is coming out of the Guest Quarters door, pushing a small cart; this one contains board games and books.

"I am. I'm Dee Rommel, I work for a private investigator named Gordy Greer."

"Is this about my dad? Do they know who killed him?"

"Investigation is ongoing."

He takes a moment to register my face. "You were at Horseshoe Lane. Tuesday. Three days ago."

"That's right. The Gilli Wanz property."

He looks over his shoulder at the Guests Quarters door. Is he going to flee?

"Do you know people have been trying to reach you?" I ask.

"I turned my phone off. Too many reporters. TV stuff. I couldn't do it. I needed quiet time."

"Coop? Everything okay?"

7 Days

That voice comes from close behind me. I turn back around, face a broad-shouldered man. He has green eyes and a perfect dark mustache and looks determined to be a savior or a shield.

*　*　*

We take off our coats and sit in a corner of Demarcation's two-story library. A librarian sits behind a desk on the other side of the room, she's focused on her computer. No 'guests' appear to be interested in books this morning - the place is quiet, somber. Green-eyed Ernesto has pointed me to a massive armchair designed to support readers and nappers. He joins Cooper on a small velvet couch, crosses his legs. His shiny black loafers gleam.

"I remember Gordy Greer was a boxing champ in Maine," says Cooper. "I met him a few times with my dad. You work for him?"

I nod. "And he'd like to talk to you."

"People need to leave Coop alone," Ernesto says. "He's grieving. The memorial's on Monday. He plans to be there."

"Of course I'll be there," adds Cooper. "He was my dad."

"I'll be with you," says Ernesto. "It'll be a tough day. But necessary. To make sure the healing process is facilitated."

I'd rather hear from Cooper, so I aim at him. "Maybe there's something you can do to help," I say. "If you want his dad's killer brought to justice."

Cooper takes a deep breath. "The last time I saw my dad was when we let loose the welcome balloons at the yearly Fundraiser – the one named after my mom. You know, the one for camp scholarships."

"Gordy thought you and your dad weren't on good terms."

Ernesto answers again. "Cooper decided to put in the effort to identify base familial problems. To try make fresh, adult connections. Right, Cooper?"

Cooper nods. "My dad and I started meeting up. And talking. About mom and the reasons – well, maybe they could be called the *unhealthy mistakes* made on both sides that caused our family's dysfunction. The lack of support that was experienced on both sides. Kids to parents. Parents to kids."

Sounds like he's parroting talking points in a group counseling session. But not my place to judge.

Cooper continues, "My dad and I wanted to fix the rift."

Ernesto nods at Cooper. "And you were getting there." He turns to me. "Cindy, his sister, was not ready yet. Cooper encouraged her, but she wasn't ready. Now it's sad because she's missed her chance. But Cooper made the effort."

"I've been wondering," Cooper says to me, "If I had stayed through the whole fundraiser?"

Ernesto stops him. "We can't bargain with the past. You had to get back to work in Boston."

I know there's CCTV footage of Cooper going through toll booths on the way back to Boston. And street footage of him entering the Nike Shoe Store on Newbury Street and in-store footage that shows he put in a full day of work as a salesman.

"I gave notice that day," says Cooper. "The day of the Fundraiser. They asked me to finish the week. I agreed, but when my dad's body was found – they didn't hold me to it. Really what they didn't like was the media coming around."

"You quit your job? Why?" I ask.

"We offered him one here," says Ernesto.

"It's probationary," says Cooper. "We'll see how it works out."

Ernesto's hand drops onto Cooper's shoulder. "You're committed to helping others. Of course it will work out." Ernesto turns to me. "I'm his advocate at Demarcation, sort of a mentor."

Cooper's eyes flick over to Ernesto's. There's gratitude in them.

I stay on Cooper. "But I guess you aren't committed to helping your sister take care of the arrangements for your dad's memorial."

Cooper, surprised, shakes his head. "Oscar Herbstrom's office is doing all that. If Cindy told you she was… she may have mis-spoke."

A look passes between Cooper and Ernesto. Some tidbit of knowledge they don't want to share.

"Oscar Herbstrom?" I ask. "Why would he offer to plan your dad's memorial?"

"He told us he has a staff that wants to help. And Cindy and I can't agree on much right now. It's easier. My dad and he worked together for a while. He's got knowledge of the family finances and that'll be helpful when we get around to dealing with dad's stuff."

"Stuff?"

"Plans. Investments."

"Did Oscar Herbstrom mention the Two Daughters' Farm?"

"The land next to the Sports Park? I think so, but we're not making decisions. My dad just passed, there's a lot to talk about."

I change the subject. "Cooper, when we crossed paths at #7 Horseshoe Lane – that was the morning it was announced your dad's case was reopened."

"Yeah, I didn't even know about it then. I was on Horseshoe because I had to take care of something."

"What?"

He chooses avoidance. "Family stuff."

"With Rusty Razer?" I ask.

Ernesto's surprise is clear, and it's not a happy surprise. He turns to Cooper. "You didn't tell me that."

Cooper looks guilty. "I went there for Cindy. Sorry I didn't tell you."

Ernesto's lips, half-hidden under his mustache, frown.

Cooper turns back to me. "When I was driving back to Demarcation that morning, I heard on the radio that my dad's case was reopened."

I take out my phone. "Look, I gotta do this - pass along that I located you. I'm going to call the detective in charge."

"You're calling the police?"

I punch in Donato's cell number. "It'll save us both some headaches."

Cooper's face flushes. "Is it true they found drugs in my dad's body? My dad didn't do drugs." He looks like he wants to throttle someone. "Someone put a bag over his head and left him to die. I can't get that out of my head, it's a daytime nightmare. What do the police know?"

"It's best if you talk to them about the details."

"My dad didn't do drugs," he repeats.

"You need to share that - and whatever else - with the investigative team."

Cooper's hands rub circles on the front of his vest; is this some attempt at calming himself? "When it was discovered it wasn't suicide, I didn't know what to do. I didn't want it to be suicide but-"

Ernesto soothes him. "You made the right choice to come here."

My phone connects. Surprise - Donato answers. I get up and walk towards a wall of books. "Thought I'd have to leave a message," I say.

He sounds distracted. "Dropping Thor off at Doggie Daycare. How'd you hear about Billy Payer?"

"I didn't hear anything – haven't heard anything since we saw him yesterday. What happened?"

"Got the living shit kicked out of him. He's in the prison infirmary, his jaw wired shut."

"Who's responsible?"

"No one left their calling card. And Payer's not giving out any clues."

"He thought he'd covered his ass. Guess that didn't work."

"You calling about something else? Need something?"

"I'm visiting with Cooper Croake."

A moment. The news sinks in.

"Where?" he asks.

"Massachusetts. Demarcation Rehab. He says he didn't know anyone was looking for him. Gordy wouldn't give up on wanting to talk to him and I followed a hunch that Cooper might have come here."

I wait. But Donato's silent.

"Gordy's moving to the cardiac recovery unit today," I say. "So I want to set a conversation up with Gordy and Cooper."

"I'm in first place," he says. "Please give your phone to Cooper now."

I walk back to the sitting area and hand Cooper my phone. It's his turn to move to the other side of the room and keep his voice low. Ernesto leans towards me. "Cooper's been clean for over a full year but finding out his dad was murdered, that could throw anyone for a loop. He doesn't want to regress. So, he came here, where he feels supported and safe."

"What's your position here, Ernesto?"

"Chief Relations Officer of the Demarcation Group."

"Sounds important."

"We are committed to support our clients' recoveries and to provide tools for a continued, productive life."

"Good soundbite."

Ernesto ignores my comment. "Cooper needs to feel good about himself and this is the time for him. You know, research shows that genetics - DNA - can make some people more prone to addiction. Genetic make-up can indicate a predilection to the disease."

"Cooper's?"

"He was very susceptible," says Ernesto. "And it takes great fortitude to buck addiction. It wasn't until he paid for his own stay here that it was clear *he* knew he needed help and *wanted* help. Sold his nice car and got a junker, emptied his own bank account and figured out how to take a loan against his trust fund. He's pretty broke - in a monetary way. But he's in it for the long haul and we think we've got to an emotional base. Cooper lacked a sense of family and unconditional love, and it made him vulnerable. We all hope for that in our lives, don't we? He wanted it from his dad. He was on a journey to see if it was possible."

Cooper walks back to us, he's looking at Ernesto. "Detective Donato wants me in Portland. He says it's a voluntary interview, to see if there's anything I know that could help. I'm not in trouble."

Ernesto stands. "All right."

Cooper continues, "So they won't have to fire me here? Take my job away?"

Ernesto puts his hands on Cooper's shoulders. "If you're not in trouble, why would that happen?" He doesn't wait for an answer. "I'll clear it in the office. For both of us. And I'll drive."

CHAPTER TWENTY-EIGHT

I follow them in my car. It's easy. Ernesto does not speed.

I call my mom and ask her to get word into Gordy, to tell him that Cooper Croake has been found. That he's on his way to talk to Donato and he's agreed to see Gordy after, if the doctor will sign off on it.

"All right, honey, I'll try to grease the wheels for that." She tells me the move to the cardiac recovery area has taken place. The intubation is over and Gordy's already rasping out orders. "Why do we put up with him?" She half-laughs.

"Bad habit?" I joke.

"Oh, I don't know," she says. "Oh. Do you have a minute?"

"Yeah, just driving."

"Chester wants me to tell you I received an email from the employee at Cancer Research the one that was unhappy with my decision about the promotion? He apologized for being unprofessional."

"Liam Grimshell?"

"How did you know his name? Oh, you're just like Gordy. Always snooping. You and Gordy are a pair."

"I guess that's good."

She laughs. "I'm sure." She clicks off.

A moment later my phone pings. It's Abshir. The white vintage Chevy belongs to Tab Razer. Brother to Rusty. He's got a record of arrests for distribution of drugs and three assault charges. His official residence is listed as Kittery, Maine, very close to the border of New Hampshire.

Maybe it was a coincidence that Tab Razer stopped at the Kennebunk Service Plaza today. The plaza is between Portland and his home. He could've just been visiting his brother.

That could make sense. Or, it wasn't a coincidence.

I turn on the radio for company - and find out there's a snowstorm moving across Canada and heading our way.

7 Days

* * *

I call Donato when we reach Portland, tell him we're about to get off the highway at the Franklin Street exit. Three minutes later, we're parking on Federal Street, between the courthouse and the PPD. Donato's there, his scarf wrapped around his neck, ducking his chin down against the cold. Cooper gets out of Ernesto's car and joins him. They walk towards the PPD's rear entrance. The doors close behind them. Donato doesn't even send a 'thanks' my way.

So it is.

Ernesto steps out of his car, holds up a set of keys. "Cooper asked me to check on Cindy. I'm going to see if she's at the West End house." He dips back into his car and drives off.

It's noon. I figure I have at least an hour to wait. Maybe more. Highroller's close, lobster rolls are their specialty. But I'm not in the mood to eat. Mmm. Oscar Herbstrom's office is a block away on Milk Street. His name keeps coming up. My own curiosity's high - plus I can predict the questions Gordy's going to have - most of them starting with 'why'. Why has Herbstrom stepped up to be Cooper and Cindy's support? Why is Two Daughters so central? Why? Why?

What can be the harm of asking about the latest news on a housing development? Maybe I'll tell Herbstrom I want to leave urban Portland and move to the bucolic countryside someday.

Right. Fat chance.

* * *

The elevator opens directly into the Herbstrom Offices. A file clerk is arranging folders, he asks if he can help me. Oscar Herbstrom's massive voice comes from the large office just off reception. "Who's here and how can I make money for you?"

The barrel-chest is first to appear in the doorway, it covers a polka dot shirt and shows off a pink tie. The rest of his body comes into view, the gold is sparkling: the rings, the cufflinks, the tie clip and the gold earring. He sees me. "Oh, Gordy's right hand. Heard your boss is in the hospital. Ticker problem."

Small city. Hard to keep the information mill quiet.

He gladhands me, it's a meaty, overfriendly handshake. "What can I do for you?"

I smile. "Wanted to ask about Two Daughters' Farm."

"What's your interest?"

"Heard about it through some friends of the Wanz's I think." I'll try to walk a slim line of truth.

He adopts a solemn face. "One of the daughters is recently deceased, unfortunately."

"Yeah, I heard." I slip into the fib lane. "Heard the farm might be the host of a new development for homes and that you might be involved. Since I was nearby, I thought I'd drop in and ask about it."

"What were you doing in this neighborhood?"

Now an outright lie. "Dropped something off at the courthouse." If he follows up with another question, I'll tell him my life is none of his business.

"Well." His grin is wide. "Good for you girl. Good plan. I've got a few development options that are coming close to fruition, all of them good investments. Real estate. Can't go wrong with investing in real estate. Let me show you some options."

"I like the location of Two Daughters Farm."

"Well, I can't make any promises on that one yet. I'm getting the ducks in a row, need a few signatures and release of some investment funds. We'll get there. Check back in a few weeks, maybe a month."

"Heard Frank Croake's kids might be investing."

Herbstrom takes a moment. "Where did you hear this?"

"Scuttlebutt. Bar talk. That you were advising them. And that since the land's next to the Sports Park, and the Croake kids knew their dad was wanting to acquire it, that they were thinking of following his wishes."

He tugs at the earring in his ear. "Well. You hear what you hear."

Not a confirmation or denial.

Herbstrom goes on. "Good for you, though, girl. A lot of people your age these days put blinders on, don't want to think ahead, don't accept the benefits of future planning. Some think this world us old folks shaped is a mess and it can't be fixed because greed and egos and the almighty dollar have become monsters, and the status quo is too hard to crack. Doomsday's a 'coming they think - so why invest time in hopes or dreams?"

"I think the world's worth fixing," I say. "Worth looking after."

"Good girl."

"Haven't been a 'girl' for a while."

"Figure of speech. Forgive. Forgive." His white teeth sparkle and he continues. "Frank Croake was all about that. Didn't mind being called 'Mr. Woke'. Thought he'd use Two Daughters as some lab for mushrooms to get PFAS out of the soil. But let's get real. That land's worth 'x' millions if it's used as a laboratory, it's worth triple that as a housing development. Plus, building new homes means jobs are created – for plumbers, electricians, construction guys, tractor and excavator rentals and, down the road - gardeners, sanitation workers, mailmen and whoever. A housing development helps people."

"Or - you invest in growing mushrooms to clean the soil so the land can feed people again."

He dead-eyes me. "Well, there's that, I guess. But, where's the most money for Tanya Wanz? That's what she needs to think about, and she's got a husband who's getting her to see where the real money is."

"You know him? Wynn Stimm?"

"Smart guy. Turned his life around, credits Tanya for that."

"He does? You mean because he gets to buy stuff with her inheritance money, control her properties?"

He tuts, shakes his head. "That sounds small and judgmental. Relationships all have their perks. Let me say, he's got a vision. We pointed these truths out to Tanya - if toxic land doesn't get us, the rapture could come, the sun could explode, people on the other side of the world who hate the USA could blow us to smithereens. We told Tanya – why not pocket the cash now, do some social good with it if that's your thing - and at the same time, be able to buy everything that catches your eye, live the got-rocks life?"

"You and Wynn Stimm, sounds like you're close."

"We happen to think the same about this development."

"You think Tanya'll follow the advice?"

"All she needs to do is sign. She's only dragging her heels because she's mourning her sister. That was a rotten death thing, but life goes on and ducks will align."

"I heard that Gilli was talking to Frank Croake about the Mushroom Project."

Herbstrom's well-practiced smile finally fades. "Young *woman*, you don't think I see what this is? Gordy's right hand comes in, tells me with sweet eyes she's dreaming of a future home on some farmland. I can see through it. You're doing some Gordy sneak – being his conduit while he's busy staying alive. Wanna tell me what's really going on?"

"Just thinking about the fact that two of the people interested in the Wanz deal are dead."

"Unrelated." He sounds positive about that. And now he's got other things to do. "I've got phone calls to make. When the Two Daughters Development moves forward, come to me with a bank statement that shows you have the wherewithal to continue this discussion."

He punches the elevator call button for me.

"Thanks for your time," I say.

The elevator doors open, and I step inside.

"Give Gordy my regards," Herbstrom says.

The doors close.

And a minute later, they open in the lobby. Tanya Wanz stands, waiting. She is in a white parka and pink hat and looks small and timid and afraid to look unhappy. Probably because Wynn Stimm is beside her, one hand holding her arm.

"Hey! It's one leg." Stimm says.

I keep my focus on Tanya. "You okay?"

"What's going on? Does wifey have a new friend who cares about her? Time to celebrate with a piece of pie?"

"I was in with Oscar Herbstrom - in his office," I say to Tanya. "He told me he's discussing business with you, but that you wanted to take time to mourn Gilli. He thought that was a good idea, for you to take the time."

Stimm's smile grows too big. "It's none of your business if there's real estate my wife and I are talking to Herbstrom about."

7 Days

I continue, as if Stimm is not there. "It's your family's place, Tanya. Gilli wanted to be buried there."

"What?" Tanya looks startled.

"She told Nail," I tell her.

Stimm jumps in. "We're not interested in that weird guy."

"You mean the weird *kind* guy?" I ask.

Stimm puts his arm around Tanya's shoulder. "Real estate is my area of expertise now."

The *ding ding* - signaling that elevator doors have stood open too long - sounds. Stimm waves a hand at me. "You don't hear that noise? Move, okay. We're going up."

I let the elevator continue to *ding.* Just to bug him.

He smirks, figures he'll bug me too. "Heard you visited Maine State Prison. Looking for a career opportunity there?"

"No," I say.

"Why not? You got a shitty job now with some old geezer stickin' your nose in where it doesn't belong. And from what I see, you're shitty at it."

My turn. "You must still know a lot of people up in Warren at Maine State. People who may, in recent hours, have crossed paths with Billy Payer?"

"Payer gets selfish sometimes. He knows better. I just don't think Florida's for him." Stimm breathes in and I hear the wet cluck in the back of his throat. "Move, pleeeeease," he says.

I step to the side and let the elevator doors start to close. Stimm shoots his hand forward, holds the doors back and pulls Tanya in with him. "Don't get in the way, Rommel."

* * *

Betsy, a young cardiac nurse, is leaving us in Gordy's room. "Remember, Dr. Frew says five minutes. No more."

Gordy motions to Cooper to come closer to the bed. He's free from intubation, and his voice is raspy. "Good talk with Detective Donato?"

"They still don't know who did it, Mr. Greer."

"You couldn't help them?"

Cooper shakes his head. "No."

Abshir slips into the room, takes out a notebook. Gordy does the introduction. "Cooper, this is one of my team – Abshir – he's going to take some notes on our conversation if that's all right. That way I can review it all later, in case my brain's not working full tilt. Okay with you?"

"That's okay," says Cooper. "Sorry you have this - health thing-"

"Working fine now. Could go twelve rounds, no problem."

"Maybe take some time, sir, before boxing in the ring again." Cooper nods towards me. "She said you want to talk to me about my dad."

"Wasn't easy for him sometimes," says Gordy. "Sometimes Frank got sad 'cause he thought his kids didn't get him - but he knew it went both ways. You thought he didn't get *you*."

Cooper's hand rubs circles on his chest; reliving this truth hurts. "After my mom died it got to be that my dad's favorite place was sitting on some mountaintop, being quiet, waiting to see a moose walk by. Just breathing in the clean air got him high. He made it a priority a lot of times and forgot about us." He goes for a positive. "But a month ago, we started talking, Mr. Greer. I was going to learn everything he was into, all his projects. Maybe help, maybe start some of my own. Keep the Sports Park going. He asked Cindy and me to come to the fundraiser - in respect for my mom. Cindy didn't make it. But I did."

"Sure that meant a lot to him," says Gordy. He points to a calendar on the table near his hospital bed. "Sorry I won't make your dad's memorial."

I notice the same Monday is circled – the one originally designated for the medical procedure to check out Gordy's pancreas. Now, it's circled for Frank Croake's memorial.

Gordy continues. "You know, your dad hired me once. When there was money missing from the Croake Park safe. Years ago. You were sixteen."

Cooper swallows hard but acknowledges it. "Yeah, I know."

"When I told him I thought it might be you - he told me to back off. Didn't want you to get a mark on your record since you were so young."

Cooper hangs his head. "My dad and I talked about all that."

"Sit down," says Gordy. "Tell me."

7 Days

Cooper sits in the chair by the bed. "Not like I'm making an excuse, I know I had things wrong, but sometimes, with my dad, I just wondered where I fit in. There'd be fifty or more scholarship kids whose dads wanted to feel great about themselves – he'd encourage them and teach them and puff them up and all I got told was to be grateful, because I had so many privileges. Told me I should be the encourager, the guy running equipment, let all the other kids shine. Felt like I never got the pat on the back. Stupid, I know now."

"You started taking drugs to get your dad's attention?"

"You know how *really* stupid I was? I got off on having my *drug dealer's* attention. He kept telling me how good I was doing. How I could handle the drugs better than any kid he'd known. He elevated me to using the needle before anyone else. I was the youngest, but I was the star of the group."

"Kind of warped," I say.

Gordy's eyes shoot over to me, he raises a finger. He wants Cooper to talk.

"I see that now," says Cooper. "He was saying all those things because he wanted my money."

"It wasn't your money," says Gordy.

"I know. I know."

"And it was about more than money, wasn't it."

"It was so he could have power over me. Keep me coming back. I get that now." Cooper's sharp chin is jutting out even more, he's angry with himself.

Gordy's next question: "You steal that money from the safe at Croake Park?"

"I gave the combinations and the keys to the office - to someone I owed money to."

"Who?" My gut knows it, but I want him to say the name out loud. "You don't have to be afraid. Statute of limitations is up," I say.

Cooper looks confused. "What?"

Abshir chimes in. "No one can be charged for a petty theft that took place over a year ago."

"Unfortunately," I say. "Unfortunate because there'd be no consequences to anyone for that crime because it took place too many years ago."

"Oh." Cooper still hesitates.

I press. "Did this person go by 'Your Man for Happy'?"

"You know that name?"

"We know your dad had Wynn Stimm arrested."

Cooper rubs at his chest again but still he doesn't confirm. "It was a long time ago and I'm ashamed. You know what the drugs did for me? Made me not care. About my dad, our family, my grades, shitty people. Made me think I could just drift off into a zone and not care."

"What changed your thinking?" asks Gordy.

"Finally, it hit me. I wanted to care. About life. People. Things. That it was too lonely if I didn't. I looked in the mirror. Looked really hard and I didn't want to feel lonely anymore. I begged Demarcation to give me a bunk, I emptied whatever I had in my bank account, and signed up to clean toilets, make beds, and wash vomit off the walls. I'd sit outside rooms while someone else was screaming their head off just so I could participate in the sessions, go through the rehab program again. I knew I had to make it work this time. Didn't see a future if I didn't. And I did, I stuck to it."

Gordy nods. "Well, that's good to hear, Cooper. But I'm still asking. Who was the person who stole the Sports Park money from the safe?"

"I don't want more trouble. Mr. Greer, can I tell you what I'm afraid of?"

"Sure."

It takes Cooper a moment to find the words. "I wonder if the person who put those drugs into my dad - if they did it as a message to me."

"What would the message be?" asks Gordy.

"That I was a lucky rich little shit and..."

"And what?" I ask.

"Other people aren't, and why should I get off so easy?"

"They wanted to get back at you for that?" I ask.

Cooper's voice is barely above a whisper. "Or at Cindy."

Gordy puts a hand on Cooper's arm. "Your dad was a good friend. He stood by me and helped me set up in a new life. I owe him. And 'cause you got your new life going now, I want to help you. I'm laid up for a bit – as you can see but I want Dee and Abshir to be there - in my stead." Gordy snaps his eyes over to me to make sure I'm listening, and then continues, "We don't want the memorial for my good friend to be held when there are still questions – 'cause then it becomes about who did this? We don't want people

7 Days

talking or wondering about a possible killer. Because then the murderer wins again. We want the memorial to be about the good things about your dad."

* * *

Ernesto waits for us in the lobby of the hospital. "Cindy's not at the West End house. Coop, I checked with those friends you told me to check with. They told me she went off to meet with a guy who wears his hair like a bun on top of his head."

Cooper goes pale. "That's Razer. I gotta find her," Cooper starts to bolt for the door, then stops and grabs my arm. "Mr. Greer said you would help."

"Yeah. I'm right here."

Cooper's breaths get shorter, anxiety is building. "Razer was why I went to that place on Horseshoe. I went there to pay him to stay away from Cindy. He said I didn't have enough money, that he wanted another thousand. I sold my watch and all my tech stuff and gave him the money. He said he'd leave her alone."

Ernesto has a question. "If she's not with her friends, Coop, where would she go?"

"I don't know," he says. "I don't know."

A place comes to my mind. "There's somewhere we can try."

CHAPTER TWENTY-NINE

The Wandering Moose and its parking lot is chaotic. Swirling blue, yellow and red lights shed odd-angled brightness and shadows into the darkening day. PPD officers hold back neighbors and patrons who have gathered in clumps on the sidewalks and street, gawking at the ambulance parked outside the rear entry. EMTs unload equipment and medical kits out of the back of the vehicle. I slip between people, get to the edge of the lot, skirt around a tree to get a better view.

Tony Dotz, the overweight guy from the courthouse, is leaning on the tree's other side. Lately he's been here every time I've set foot on the property. Is this his regular hangout? He doesn't try to hide the fact that his eyes are full of tears. "It's Cindy Croake," he says.

"What happened?"

His parka's unzipped, his face is red, his triple chin is shaking. "I messed up. It happened right under my nose."

"What do you mean?"

"I told Frank I'd keep an eye on her. Wasn't gonna stop doing that just because Frank was gone. He worried about her."

"What happened?" I ask.

"Overdose. Pretty sure."

My stomach drops. Cooper's nightmare.

Dotz goes on, "Ever since she came back to Portland after Frank died, she's come here a lot. Started to meet up with that creep Razer. He got real handsy, real chummy. One of her friends hates Razer and knew her dad and me were trying to keep Cindy on a good road, she called me to say Cindy changed her plans with her and said she was going to the Moose. I hurried over; Cindy was sitting alone in her favorite booth. I got a beer; I see her get a call. She puts a napkin over her margarita, tells the waitress she'll be back, that she's going to the Ladies'. Razer shows up five minutes later, sits at their booth, gets served his margarita and settles in, a big grin on his face. Then this woman comes screaming into the bar that someone's on the floor in the Ladies' room, screaming that she doesn't know if the woman's dead or not-"

There's a flurry of movement at the back door. EMTs guide the gurney out. We're close enough to see the oxygen mask over Cindy's mouth, her dark hair, the top of her cashmere turtleneck. I catch a flash of rings on a hand that slips off the side of the gurney. A medic checks the safety straps, tucks the hand back under the sheet. Cindy is lifted into the ambulance.

I look over my shoulder. Cooper and Ernesto must've had to park on another street, they're racing towards the crowd. The ambulance takes off just as Cooper, almost hyperventilating, nearly crashes into me. "It's Cindy, isn't it?"

"Yeah, your sister," says Tony. "I'm sorry."

Cooper covers his mouth like he's gotta hold back a scream racing up from his chest.

"Razer's inside," says Tony.

Ernesto reaches us. Cooper turns to him; his voice is thin. "It's Cindy."

"Which hospital is she going to?" Ernesto asks.

Tony's already asked. "Maine Med."

Ernesto wants Cooper to leave the scene. "We'll go there."

But Cooper's watching a PPD officer who has taken a few steps away from the Wandering Moose's back entry to help a medic with a bag. He dashes to the door - what the hell? I reach out, but Cooper's already passed me. "Damn it." The officer's still busy, I skim by and follow Cooper.

Can't see him. The black walls make the hallway a dark tunnel. There's the silhouette of the massive bear statue, the Christmas-lights necklace glows around its neck. I lope past the dim bulbs over the restrooms and the door with the Employees Only sign, go to the archway into the main room. Allison, the waitress from Letty's, is standing with the bartender, they're hunched over, ready to duck behind the bar. Suddenly a beer bottle flies, I lurch back so my ass hits the wall – the bottle misses me by an inch. "Crap!"

Cooper's adrenaline is peaking, he's yelling "Fucking bastard! I paid you, I *paid* you to stay away from her! Liar. Cheat. Life destroyer! I'm killing you. Now!"

Looks to be five or so people taking cover in the room, afraid to move because more beer bottles are whipping through the air. Some hit pillars, some hit tables and chairs. They all explode and liquid sprays and shards of glass fly. Sconces on the wall are hit and shatter, a row of antler trophies crash to the floor.

And then there's a sickening thump, the sound of a heavy bottle hitting flesh and bone. There's a howl of pain and a loud stream of curses. I peek around the corner and see Rusty Razer. Blood is gushing from his forehead, streaming into his eyes and dripping off his nose. But he's still got an ugly grin on his face, maybe because he's got three inches and fifty pounds on Cooper and he's holding a heavy bar stool over his head.

Cooper's crazed. "Fuck you! I'm all she's got now, and you didn't keep your word. I'll kill you!"

Razer charges. Cooper kicks over chairs, creating obstacles. Razer, licking blood off that new set of gold teeth, jibes at him. "You spoiled little prick-dick. Daddy's money, daddy's money." He heaves the stool. Cooper leaps backwards to avoid the stool but Razer gets to him, his fist clenched, close enough to strike. I hear the bridge of Cooper's nose crack and see a tooth shoot out of his mouth. Cooper's feet land on half-broken bottles, he loses his balance and she's on the floor. But he's not done, he grabs at a fallen antler trophy – the rack is a three-pronged fork, the middle kicker is the longest and has the sharpest point. Razer's only thinking of his next punch, doesn't see Cooper's arm come up to sideswipe him. The points of the antlers connect with Razer's ear and rip across his cheek. Cooper jerks the piece upwards and the pointed end gouges into Razer's eye.

"Faaaaaaahck!" Razer's pain fuels him, he wipes at the blood, his spit sprays as he curls to his side and reaches into his heavy boot for a weapon.

"Knife!" I yell. I clutch the closest thing to me – the Christmas necklace on the bear statue. I yank it free, zing it through the air, it hits Razer's face – it only takes a split second for him to flick them off and re-focus but it's enough – a half dozen cops have pushed through the front door, and a trio through the black hallway behind me. One of them is Pocket, he grabs me by the shoulders and pushes me against the wall. "Stand back, Dee." He joins the voices hoping for de-escalation, they tell Cooper, who has bottles in both hands, and Razer, with his knife ready, to stand back, to hold off, to stop moving, to settle down. But Cooper's not registering the voices and

7 Days

hurls a bottle at Razer just before Pocket knocks him against the bar and immobilizes him. "Cooper Croake. Don't move."

Razer sees he's outnumbered. He clears a thick red glob from his eyes, allows two cops to disarm and quickly cuff him. Pocket pats Razer down, checking for more weapons. Another officer is checking Razer's coat on the back of the booth. He feels something – and holds up a small, shiny handgun – a Stinger .38. Cheap, chunky, but capable of serious damage.

The crazy ambulance night for Wandering Moose continues. Razer gets loaded into one, Cooper into another. EMTs examine the wounds, officers step inside as ride-alongs. The doors close, and the ambulances are driven away.

My phone pings. It's Ernesto. "Where are they taking Coop?"

I look around. "Where are you?"

"Outside. Across the street. Where are they taking Cooper?"

"Emergency Room first, I'd bet. Cumberland County Jail, probably, after that."

"This is not good." Ernesto sounds distressed. "I'm gonna need to share this with the Admin at Demarcation. Thing is, they knew I was driving him, that I was going to be with him in Portland and then this happens."

His concern seems to be about how Cooper's plight will reflect on him. "Maybe you can just share that he went after a slimy drug dealer to avenge his sister," I say.

"That's a good way to spin it." He coughs and continues. "I'd like to keep my name out of this."

What about that unconditional support Ernesto thought was so important? "Well, we'll see how that falls out."

Ernesto clicks off.

It's a waiting game now. I stand against the black wall, hoping no one's paying attention and orders me outside. Tony Dotz has moved in next to me. "Lucky the asswipe didn't boot-holster his gun," he says.

"Yeah." Cooper could've been shot – maybe others.

"Did you look inside the Ladies'?" he asks.

"Haven't had a chance."

We're a few feet from the restroom. I slip inside. It smells of urine, oversweet perfumes and fried bar food. People Magazine covers of pop singers have been tacked on the graffitied walls. One of Cindy's green suede gloves is on the floor. There's a transparent vial half-rolled under the stall. It's empty. A spoon is next to it, there's black residue in its well. Did it hold the potent hit of horse or coke or meth that went into Cindy's vein? The hypodermic needle has settled under the sink. I can guess who put the rig together. Small wads of toilet paper, all with dabs of bright red blood on them, have been tossed on the floor.

The door opens. "What're you doing?" It's Officer Vera Sandrich. Last person I want to keep an eye on me.

"Thought this door was the exit," I say.

"When there's a picture of a toilet painted on it? Very funny, Rommel."

"I didn't touch anything – if you were about to ask."

"You need to go sit with the others," she says. "We have an area set apart near the window. We'll take your statement there. You got that?"

"Sure."

She wants me to add her title. "Officer."

"Sure, officer."

"No use of cell phones. No messaging, no pictures."

I follow Sandrich into the main room. She points me to a seat next to Allison just as Detective Latifa Lavonna and her forensic team enter through the front door. Sandrich hurries over to Lavonna to suck up. Allison grabs my arm, she's still shaking. She tells me about walking into the Ladies room and seeing Cindy on the floor. "Her eyes were all icky, glazed and bubbles of saliva were in the corners of her mouth. I just came here tonight for a little karaoke – I thought I'd pee first so I could give it my all. When I saw Cindy, I thought I was gonna pass out, but I put on my big girl pants and ran out and yelled at the bartender to call 911."

Tony Dotz is next to Allison. A realization hits me. "Tony," I say. "Years, back, when Wynn Stimm got out of prison, and moved back to the Portland area, did you follow him around?"

"Wynn Stimm? Yeah. Did that for Frank. Guy couldn't move without me on his tail. We celebrated when the creep-shit moved north."

"What about when he moved to Cape Elizabeth just a few months ago?"

7 Days

"At first. But Coop wasn't living around here and Coop had taken a good turn, wasn't using. I told Frank it looked like Stimm had changed too. That he was living a Mr. Clean life with a rich new wife. Going into real estate. And I'd taken on more shifts at the courthouse, so we cooled it. Then Frank started getting worried about Cindy and drugs – he asked for a name of someone in Stamford to keep an eye on her in Connecticut where she worked. When she was up here, which wasn't much, I stepped in."

We're sitting close to the booth that Cindy and Razer favored. His coat had been tossed over the back of the booth, next to her suede coat with the fur collar. There's a distinctive lining in hers - chocolate brown flannel with white snowflakes. It's the same fabric I'd first thought was the last leaf on a tree on the High Eagle Trail. That ripped material had been muddied and it was sopping wet, but it's the same. Donato had put the torn piece into a plastic bag, had sent it into the lab to see if DNA could be determined.

There's a bad taste in my mouth. Don't want to think about it. Cindy? Had she been on the High Eagle Trail? Had she been there when her father suffocated? I stand to get Sandrich's attention. "Officer." She's standing not far from us, and she purposefully ignores me. "Officer, I need to talk to the detective." Sandrich is not interested.

I look around, want to find Lavonna. She's coming back into the main room. Gustav Pike is at her side. Where had he come from? Does Lavonna think he has insight? Information? Was he outside and she brought him in? They finish their conversation, she points to our group and wants him to join us. I stand again. "Detective Lavonna. A word?"

She hears me. "One minute, Dee. I'll be back." She walks to the bartender. Pocket joins her. I can't hear the conversation, but Pocket, Lavonna and the bartender head down the dark hallway.

Pike takes the empty seat next to me. His Adam's Apple is sliding up and down as he struggles to deal with his emotions. "You think Cindy'll make it?"

"I don't know."

His shoulders slump. "I told her Razer was bad news. Women never see the guys who really care about them. Who would be good for them."

I keep on my track: "Gustav, I've been thinking about this. You said the back ATV trails at the Park have been closed since the Whirly Storm brought a lot of trees down. You said the back trail to High Eagle was closed when the Fundraiser took place."

Pike shrugs. "I finally told the detective I'd clear 'em."

"You did?"

"I don't need to answer your questions."

"Why did you lie the first time we asked?"

"Razer told me if I cared about Cindy, I'd keep my mouth shut." He takes off his Sports Park knit hat, stuffs it into his jacket's pocket. "But it was my job, so of course I cleared the trail as soon as I could after the storm. I had to make sure there were no bald wires or trapped animals."

"Who has access to the ATVs?"

"They're in a shed near the staff cabins. Pretty easy to access. I told Detective Donato that too, you can talk to him."

"Where are the keys kept?" I ask.

"In a drawer in the manager's cabin."

"Your cabin."

"Since I became manager. There were a lot of cop types at the Park yesterday, going over the ATVS with brushes and tape and they took photos, checked the tires. So, I had to 'fess up. I told the detective that I had dragged some trees over the trail a couple days after the Fundraiser – so it would look like it hadn't been cleared."

"Razer said he'd do something to Cindy if you didn't do that?"

Pike hangs his head. "Yeah."

I think he's going to cry.

Allison leans into me. "How long do you think we'll have to stay? I have an early shift at the diner in the morning."

We don't have long to wait. Lavonna walks back into the bar area. Pocket is behind her, carrying a large metal toolbox. Shit. My stomach clenches. Looks like the same one Razer was carrying when he arrived at Tanya and Stimm's house in Cape Elizabeth. Another cop brings up the rear, he's got his hands on the bartender. He motions for the bartender to sit, the bartender complies, and the officer cuffs him. Life has gotten much more complicated for Wandering Moose employees and patrons.

7 Days

Lavonna motions me over to her, we stand next to Cindy's favorite booth. I tell her why Donato might find Cindy's coat interesting, how the lining might match a clue Donato's sent to the lab. And where I've seen the glossy-sided toolbox before.

"You ever look inside it?" she asks.

"No," I say.

"It's a real candy store. Paraphernalia. Pills, powders, vials of God knows what. It'll take a while to identify it all, make matches to what might be in Cindy's system, what might have been in Gilli Wanz's body."

Gilli was also drugged? Ahh, there's the information Donato didn't share after her autopsy.

"What drug was identified in Gilli's system?" I ask.

"I'm sure that'll come out at the appropriate time."

Lavonna won't share either. Cop code.

"Thanks for the observations, Dee," says Lavonna. "Excuse me."

She has forensics take pictures of the coat and its lining and they pack it into an evidence bag, just as Donato walks in. Lavonna brings him up to speed. I'm getting really tired of trying to read lips. Donato looks over to me, excuses himself from Lavonna.

"Lining of the coat," he says. "Looks like a match. You okay?"

"Don't like thinking Cindy was up on High Eagle Trail when her dad died."

"Agree."

"Cooper told me he paid Rusty Razer to *not* provide Cindy with drugs. Apparently, money changed hands and promises were not kept. That's why Cooper went nuts here."

Donato nods.

"Pike told me you've checked the ATV trail."

He nods.

"That Razer threatened him. That's why Pike lied about clearing the trail."

Another nod. It sucks playing catch-up. I guess it goes both ways.

"One more," I say. "Are you focused on Razer now for Frank Croake's murder? Razer and Cindy?"

Donato takes a moment, knows it's not the time to share. He asks his own question. "How's Gordy?"

"Doc says his body is doing what it's meant to do. Gordy will want to know about Cooper."

"They tell me Coop's had to be sedated, that he'll be on mental-health watch. I'll see him in the morning."

* * *

Seems like my life is now centered at Maine Med. I check on Gordy first. Abshir's in the waiting room, studying. He tells me my mom has gone back to her hotel, that he's just left Bert, that he'll be taking over from Marie in a few minutes. "Is Gordy awake?" I ask.

"They want him to sleep, so a little drowsy was added to his IV."

"Okay."

I tell Abshir about Cindy's overdose, about the arrests of Cooper and Razer. We decide Gordy doesn't need to know the specifics until tomorrow. By then, hopefully, I'll be able to tell him what the damage is – if Cindy Croake makes it, what the charges against Cooper will be.

"You sure you want to stay?" I ask Abshir.

"*Haa.* I have a test on Monday that I need to study for. I would like to do that here."

"Okay."

It's a lonely ride down the elevator. I know Donato's got a cop outside Cindy's door. Another one is in the ER where Razer's being worked on. Cooper's being watched too. Donato and Lavonna and Banford will be at the PPD where the team is logging in evidence, with special attention to the contents of the toolbox.

Where am I supposed to be?

Bert could use the company.

A text comes through: *Got time for birthday night?*

CHAPTER THIRTY

Bert sleeps in the corner of Gretchen's living room as the *Barbie* movie plays. Gretchen has Cheetos, potato chips, dips, Two Fat Cat pies, and chicken wings from Tomaso's. My mom has dropped the cupcakes off, they're lined up on her coffee table. Gretchen had wanted an update, so I did my best and then felt completely tired of my life. "Okay, enough. How are you and Pocket?" Had he ever broached the subject of them moving into together? I haven't heard.

Gretchen "Good." She grabs a potato chip, swipes it through the onion dip. She crunches it, takes the time to swallow – but I can tell she's dying to get into her news. "There's a major question in play."

I don't want her to know Pocket asked my opinion about the next step in their relationship and that I had sidestepped the issue because I was feeling alone and sad and ungenerous. "What's the question?"

"You have a lot going on right now. Gordy and the Croake thing. This can wait."

"What's the question?"

"It's of a serious nature. You know – about people who work, grocery shop, do laundry, cook food, see friends, and sleep on their own most of the time. It's a question about if they want to change things up and do a lot of those things - as a pair."

"What's the exact question, Gretch?"

"Pocket has floated the idea of us living together."

I thought she'd be jumping for joy. She actually looks nervous.

"The question is under consideration," she says. "Your thoughts?"

"Consideration is good."

"And?"

I toss a kernel of popcorn into my mouth. "Remember what 'consider' means. Means you don't have to make a quick decision."

"Oh."

"You can take as much time as you need. You can consider."

"Dee, help me."

"What do I know?"

"You know him."

"I like Pocket," I say.

"He is a good one, isn't he." She grabs another potato chip. Smiles. "So, I will consider. With joy."

"With joy." I repeat. Good for her. I didn't want to weigh in too heavily - too much responsibility. "I have no expertise, as you know. I love you. I want you to have everything that will make you happy."

She leans over and kisses my cheek. "A lot of people love you too, Dee. Sometimes I don't think you accept that."

"I'm not in love with love the way you are."

"Mmm," she says. "I'm not so sure about that."

"I'm not."

She laughs, reaches behind the couch to give me a wrapped gift. "It's from your mom. I invited her over to join us, but she said she knows this is our tradition."

That's my mom. Giving me room. She's convinced I want (need?) it.

Gretchen continues. "She dropped it off."

I open the box. Inside is a red silk shirt and drapey, wide-legged black velvet pants. There's a note. *So proud of you. We are all so happy Gordy has made it through. These presents are for you, honey. For your birthday and for the holiday coming. And when invited – please GO to a party.*

She never stops. Hoping I'll enter a social whirl. There is a large heart drawn on the card.

"I have a birthday wish for you too, dear buddy," says Gretchen.

"That's backwards. I get to be the one making the wishes - when I blow out a birthday candle."

Logic won't stop Gretchen. "I wish, in this year of thirty, you'll accept stuff and not turn away when you feel you can't control the outcome."

"Gretch, it's my birthday. Not a time to try shrink me."

She slaps my arm playfully. "You don't have to hold on so hard to your discontent. I say let your marshmallow squishy show - your dad was right, you know. You are kind of soft and squishy inside, but most people don't get past the crunch."

I laugh. "There's this guy – Nail. I met him just a few days ago. He was Gilli Wanz's boyfriend."

"The one who's dead?" She looks worried.

"Don't worry, I'm not gonna get gory about it. Nail - he's odd – has some disturbing ultra wet white skin thing and talks too much. But he's so clear about this huge need for people to connect."

"I agree with him."

"He says if you look hard enough in a mirror that the need becomes clear."

"I don't know about the mirror but-"

"He's too needy. So needy it makes me uncomfortable."

"Dee, being a little uncomfortable isn't bad. It usually means you're taking a chance."

"No more analyzing, Gretch. I know you want to dance the happy dance because Pocket's basically told you he's crazy about you. Let's get squishy about that."

Gretchen jumps up and dances in front of the TV. Onscreen, Barbie is realizing she's been arched up on her toes for too long, wants to put her feet solidly on the ground. Gretchen pulls me up and I join her and the Barbie cast in bopping to 'Dance the Night'.

By the time Barbie realizes her pink and perky life isn't as great as she thought it was, Gretchen's asleep, curled up on one end of her couch. I leave her a note, telling her thanks for the Two Fat Cats pie and the new TrackRun shirt and that I'll talk to her in the morning. I pat Bert on his head and whisper, "Time to go." He gets to his feet.

* * *

I crank the heater on high, steer the Outback towards Cape Elizabeth. Something's pulling me there.

* * *

7 Days

The Wanz-Stimm home is dark. The garage door is closed. There are no cars on the street, the empty field across from the house is quiet. I guess this is harassment. Watching someone's home who doesn't want his home watched. But I'm on a public road, so technically I'm not trespassing. Still, it's a form of invasion. If it's not a slam dunk for harassment – then it's definitely a sneaky lay-up.

The garage door opens. A slim safety light comes on.

I slip down in my car seat.

Stimm steps out the door that connects house and garage and walks to the driveway. He lights a cigarette. The red glow of the burning tobacco is laser small; his bulking body is in shadow. But his head turns my way, and he looks right at me. In my gut, I know he recognizes my car.

A long minute goes by. He extinguishes his cigarette on the side of the garage slider. Drops the butt on the driveway and goes back into the house. The garage door closes.

Just then, a Cape Elizabeth patrol car, sedan style, approaches. It slows as it gets near to me. A window is powered down and the driving officer cocks his head. I power down my window. "Hi, Sergeant. I was just leaving."

"Why are you here?"

"Ahh. Driving around."

He notices Bert in the back seat. "With your dog."

"A friend's dog who really likes car rides." They wait for more, so I embellish my falsehood. "I thought if I saw my friend Tanya's light on – I know she's been through a lot lately with her sister's death, I thought I'd stop in, see if she wanted company. But it looks like she's asleep."

The officer in the passenger seat of the car leans forward. "Hey, Dee Rommel."

I don't recognize him. "Ahh. Hi," I say.

"We played basketball at the Academy together. On Donato's team."

"Oh. Yeah. Didn't recognize you." And I don't remember his name.

The driver keeps staring at me. "You said you were leaving?"

I get his hint. "Yeah."

"Now."

"Yeah. Guess so." I start the Outback and drive off.

THREE DAYS

CHAPTER THIRTY-ONE

I wake up, groggy. I've slept in my clothes. Bert's taken over half my bed. My hip socket hurts. My LiteGood must've ended up at an odd angle on the mattress. I'll pay for not taking it off last night.

It's getting unattached now. I bend to grab my shoes, pull them off the real foot and the fake foot. I unzip my pants, push them down to my ankles, kick them off. I doff the LiteGood, and the liner on my stump. The air on my skin feels good. The sweater's next, then I unhook my bra and fall back onto the bed.

I tell myself I've accomplished Gordy's primary 'ask'. I found Cooper and he and Gordy connected. I know Gordy's not satisfied. Neither am I.

Frank Croake's memorial is two days from today. Seems a lot of people have accepted that Frank will be eulogized and buried before his murderer(s?) are charged. Is Donato focusing on Razer and Cindy? A piece of fabric will not be enough. Razer's threats to Pike, telling him to keep the clearing of Sports Park back trails a secret or Cindy would get hurt – those will not be enough. A match to a kind of drug in a toolbox will not be enough. Opportunity to inherit, the Croake kids' dislike of parenting style will not be enough.

I check my phone. There's a message from my mom: she'd like to sit with Gordy this morning because she and Chester need to leave for Boston at noon, she hasn't been able to re-arrange two important meetings. I text her back. *Sure. I'll talk to Marie about the afternoon. And thanks for the presents. I'll wear the shirt and pants. Somewhere. Promise.*

I open the back door for Bert, he races out. Time to make some instant coffee. Better yet, get good coffee at Sparrows. Shower first. Wash hair. Rub off the groggy.

An hour later, I notice I've missed another text. This one is from Carter Stround, he must've left it when I watched Bert do his laps around the yard, when I was feeling guilty that I wasn't doing mine.

7 Days

The text reads: *Dee. Good news? Maybe? Maybe it's not over? Tanya Wanz wants me to meet her at Two Daughters at noon to hear about the plan. I'll meet her. Your Mushroom Friend. PS. Dinner soon?*

* * *

The Nor'easter was supposed to exhaust itself in New Hampshire's White Mountains, but Abshir's still following the news. "The weather people say it has changed course, that the winds are getting stronger, and it could be moving towards Maine later this afternoon."

I'm driving my Outback, he's in the passenger seat in his orange parka. We're on the 295 North and snow is falling. "We should get there and back before it hits, if it does," I say. "Carter's note said noon, we'll get there after that, but they might be taking a walk of the property."

The clouds are getting darker and thicker and are moving lower, like they're about to land on the roof of the Outback. "Route 125 should be coming up, quarter of a mile, *hadda*," Abshir says. He's got his phone open, the GPS is activated, but the weather's affecting the vocal support. There's a gust of wind, the top layers of the nearby snowbanks loosen; icy particles rush up into the air.

"There's a gas station on the left. Right before the turn-off," I say. "Keep looking for that."

"There it is. Turn."

We do, and there's a clear Route 125 sign. We're on the road to Two Daughter's Farm. If Tanya wanted to meet with Carter – does that mean she's made a decision about what she'll do with the Farm? Will Wynn Stimm be there? Does he know? I'd texted Carter back, asked him to alert Donato and that I was on my way to meet him at the Farm.

I didn't add 'just in case'.

* * *

The home's simple. Two story, a plain gray shingle roof, yellow shutters on the windows. The barn is nearby, its wood siding has gone gray from decades of exposure to weather, but the bones are strong. There's also a long low chicken coop; it has a worn sign above its door, it's of a rooster followed by three hens, they all strut under a setting sun.

The fields stretch out in all directions. Was all the soil contaminated with the PFAS sludge? How could something so idyllic be the victim of the Forever Chemicals?

No sign of anyone. When I step out of the Outback, I notice tire marks on the lawn, just to the side. The rime-ice crust on the brown grass has been crackled and pressed down.

No cars here now. But someone's been here recently.

I trudge to the front door. I'm sure the electricity's been turned off, and the pipes must've been drained so water won't freeze in them over the winter. The home looks cold, bereft – but I sense an expectation there too. As if the house is sure (or at least hoping) someone will come back, warm it again, bring it to a vibrant life again. Maybe that's Tanya's plan. A small doorbell is on the side of the door. I press it. It's no longer connected. I knock on the door.

No response.

I notice a metal mailbox to the side of the door. A thick card sticks out of it. I pull it out, it's got USM engraved at the top. There's handwriting: *Tanya, I waited for almost an hour. Maybe the impending storm changed your mind about traveling here today. Can't get a signal on my phone. Let's reschedule soon. I'll try to reach you when I get back to Portland. Carter Stround, PhD. The Mushroom Friend.*

Abshir waves at me. "Dee! Something is banging in the back."

I move around the side of the house, to the backyard. There are overturned metal lawn chairs and tree trunk stools around an abandoned fire pit. I hear a steady screak and thump. *Screak and thump.* The aluminum and heavy glass storm door is moving back and forth, opening nearly all the way and then crashing back to close but never properly latching.

There's a scuffle of footprints in the ice-snow layer on the concrete steps leading to the door. Large boots. Smaller ones. There have been people inside in the last hours.

Are they still in there?

"Dee." Abshir's on the other side of the steps. "See this."

7 Days

There's a boot on the lawn. Made of rabbit fur, lined with fleece and decked out with thick pink laces. Probably a woman's size seven. There's only a light coating of snow on it; it hasn't been languishing long in the elements. *Screak and thump. Screak.* The metal storm door is getting louder. The wind is picking up. Out of the corner of my eye I see a movement - a curtain flapping out of a window into the air. An upstairs window is wide open, the sash is raised to its maximum, not a screen or weather protector in place. Who opens a window in a house at this time of year? I look at the placement of the boot. Right under the window. Has it been tossed out? Nearby is a lump, thinly-skinned with snow. "Abshir. What's that?" We move to it. It's a rolled-up blanket, the bottom half has fallen open. Wrapped inside is a pink leather bag with a bamboo handle - very girly. Not the normal bag a woman carries in the middle of winter. And another rabbit fur boot, it matches the one on the lawn, but this one has no laces.

Abshir points to the bushes next to the house. A pink puffer jacket is pressed into the dry branches.

A boot, blanket, bag and jacket thrown out the upstairs window? Why?

Abshir tries his phone again. No connection.

Had Carter alerted Donato that he was planning on a meeting with Tanya today? That I had mentioned meeting them? If so, had he also sent word that the meeting was off – that Tanya had not shown?

No one with knowledge of Maine's snowstorms would be venturing out now. Abshir and I are it.

I step close to a first-floor window, look inside. Rugs are rolled up; worn, flowered sheets cover the furniture. No sign of life.

I motion to Abshir that we should try to get inside. Abshir catches the swinging storm door and holds it open. I turn the knob on the wood door.

Simpler than I thought. The knob turns.

Our breath enters ahead of us. We're in a hallway, a stairway can be seen at the end of it. A family room is to our right. That room's walls are full of photos in crafty handmade frames - Tanya and Gilli and parents in a cornfield, the family at a picnic table in the summer, high school graduation pictures of Tanya and Gilli. We tread lightly, see the kitchen through an archway.

There's a muffled sound. Scraping of a chair? Someone's heard us? Hiding from us? Wanting attention? We step into the kitchen.

More distressed grating, it's coming from a closet. Abshir grabs one of the metal kitchen chairs, holds it up. There's a cast-iron skillet on the counter. I pick it up.

I grab the handle of the closet and release the door.

It's Nail. His legs and the hand that is not in the arm cast are tied to a metal chair, a brown grocery bag is over his head "What the hell?" I pull off the bag. His skin is sweaty and a terrible shade of white-gray, and he's still got his earmuffs on. His mitten is stuffed into his mouth. "Nail, what are you doing here?" I take the mitten out of his mouth and his drool drips.

"I s-sent hope out t- there - that you – or s-someone would come-"

"Who did this?" I ask.

"I didn't s- see," says Nail. "I got hit on the back of the head." His lips quiver, he's cold, scared, relieved.

"Why are you even here?" I repeat.

He holds his injured arm, looks pitiful. "I t- told Tanya she didn't have to be lonely all the time. She listened to me for the first time. She wanted to drive to the farm this morning and I said I'd come too, so she picked me up in her car."

Abshir's untying Nail's legs. "Where is she?" he asks.

"You got ears, why don't you listen? Someone came up behind me and hit me. I don't know where Tanya is." He moves his legs after Abshir's freed him. "Took you long enough. It's f-freezing in here."

"*Soco*," says Abshir.

"Talk English. You're in America."

Abshir keeps his temper, but I hear the edge. "I said, walk around: *soco*. That will help warm your body."

Nail has another idea. "Tanya has a blanket in the back seat of her car. She hates to be cold too." He gives an order to Abshir. "Go get it."

"Where's her car?" I ask.

"Outside. We parked right outside."

I shake my head. "We just got here, there is no car on the drive."

More sweat springs from Nail's overactive pores. He's looking more like a sponge. "Did Tanya leave? Did she leave me here to freeze?" Nail wipes wet from his face. "No, she wouldn't do that, because she'd know Gilli wouldn't want her to do that. She's not a mean person. Just a weak person." He gets an idea. "The barn doors were open. I told her to park in there, but she gets stubborn like Gilli, and she said we wouldn't be long, that we'd leave the car outside so the Mushroom Guy could see it."

The barn doors were closed when Abshir and I arrived. Who had opened them? Who had closed them?

"The Mushroom Guy came and went, Nail," I say. "He thought no one was here."

Where's Tanya? Obviously, not in the kitchen. It's a simple square and the shelving is open. There's one door next to the refrigerator. A heavy iron hook holds it shut, it's slipped into an industrial-strength eye attached to the wall. A cellar? "Stay here," I say.

I pull up on the thick iron hook.

The stairs are narrow, the space below is small. Tiny windows shed a bit of light over a boiler, water heater, a workbench full of old tools, and a pile of logs. Small canisters of paraffin lamp oil are next to standing tiki torches - the kind used for lawn parties. There's an old dresser, probably used as a catch-all for nails and screws and odds and ends. There's no place to hide. "Tanya?"

Nothing.

I go back upstairs. Somehow Nail has gotten Abshir to give him his scarf and he's draping it around his shoulders.

"Abshir, let's check out the second floor," I say.

"*Haa.*" He tells Nail to keep watch out the windows, to yell if someone arrives. Nail gets his back up and says Abshir can't tell him what to do. I tell Nail if he's not into helping, we'll tie his good arm to the chair again and stuff him back in the closet. He sniffs and looks nervous, says he'll yell if he sees anything.

At the top of the stairs, a linen closet faces the landing. It's small, full of empty shelves. Two hallways stretch out from the center. It looks like there are two bedrooms and a bath on each side.

Abshir and I go in different directions. I head to the left.

The hallway wallpaper is flowered – small yellow roses entwined with green stems and leaves. Framed photographs hang close together, most are dedicated to 4H memories. The girls holding ribbons for perfect pumpkins at the annual Windsor Fair, Tanya holding a basket of baby chicks, Gilli balancing on a rolling log in a pond, Tanya as soloist in a tiny girls' band, Gilli maniacally grinning and eating a stick of fried butter. I pass the first bedroom, there's an iron bed frame, sans mattress. No closet, just a standing wardrobe. Its doors are open. Nothing - nobody – is inside. I continue down the hallway.

Creak. Was that a result of my stride? Or Abshir's on the other side of the house? Are we alone? The wind is slipping through crevices that all old houses get as wood expands and contracts over the years of summer heat and winter chills.

I reach the next doorway. Flurries of snow hit me. It's the room with the open window.

Tanya is face up, her head and torso on an old, thin mattress; her legs, in heavy snow pants, dangle – they're too short to touch the ground. Cold flakes and ice have gathered in her hair, on her chest. I touch her neck, there's a pulse. But her chest is barely moving. "Abshir!" I yell. I've got my phone out, punch in 911. A warning appears on screen, an alert that a connection cannot be made.

Tanya's eyes are half-open, but her pupils have slid back, they're almost invisible. The sleeve of her sweater is pushed up, a pink shoelace is tied tightly around her arm - a crappy tourniquet situated above the needle that's still in her arm. There's blood in the syringe's base, just under the plunger, a sign that a vein had been struck and whatever was injected was mainlined straight into her bloodstream.

She moans. "Hellllllllllllllp."

"Abshir!" I yell again.

I run through old training. Get her sitting up, make sure nothing is blocking her breathing. Pull out the needle. Gently. Gently. She's gotta stay conscious. I need to watch for a seizure. I prop her up, she's limp. I vigorously rub her back. What I need is naloxone. I want to get the opioid analgesic into her body, but don't have it. "Come out of this, Tanya."

Abshir rushes in.

"She shot up," I say. "Or was injected, I don't know. Your phone?"

"*Maya*. No. Not good."

"Close the window."

7 Days

"*Haa.*" He slams down the sash.

"We're going to have to get her out of here," I say. "Androscoggin Medical is the closest. But it's a half hour away."

"*Haa.* Snow is getting heavier," he says. "If we are going to go-"

"Get some of those sheets from downstairs. We can wrap her up, get her a bit warmer and carry her to the car."

There's the sound of a car engine and an approach of tires on the gravel driveway. Abshir goes to the window. "Who is it?" I ask. "Recognize the car?"

"No," says Abshir. "It looks very old."

Nail is calling up the stairway. "Car! Car! Car!"

"Go tell him to be quiet," I say. "See if you can bolt the back door, then get out of sight."

Abshir's still at the window. "It's parking behind your car, so we're blocked in."

Nail calls from downstairs. "Car! Car!"

Abshir rushes off to quiet Nail – and, hopefully, stash him somewhere.

I try for positive: Maybe Carter Stround turned around, decided to check if Tanya had arrived at the farm late. But that doesn't make sense, and I'm not getting suckered into false hope. I lean Tanya against the bed frame, go to the bedroom door to see if there's a lock. No lock. Back to the window. Through the thick snowfall, I make out the old-style car shape.

It's the vintage Chevy.

This feels totally wrong. A lean, unshaven man in a long, runway-model-worthy fleece coat and a thick knobby fleece hat pulled low on his face, is getting something out of the trunk. I don't even have to check the photo library on my phone – it's something about his height and shape and the way he holds himself – it's the hotdog eater from the Kennebunk Service Plaza. He lifts a long, pointed spade out of the trunk, it's wrapped in brown paper and has a tag on it, like it's been newly purchased.

I should've told Abshir to bring Nail upstairs. At least we'd all be together.

Another person gets out of the car. He's got his parka's hood up; it hides his face. He's not in a hurry. He goes to the open trunk, takes out a heavy shovel, this too has a big yellow tag on it. He walks to my car and smashes it against my windshield. Another smash. Another smash. The glass finally breaks, and the shovel crashes through. He bats it deeper into the car, it's probably cutting into my gear shift. He leaves it there, the handle, with its *Sold* tag waving, sticks halfway out of the car. He walks back to the Chevy's trunk, lifts out a small cooler, big enough for a six-pack of beer. I recognize this man's gait, the arrogant hold of the head, the self-love.

Wynn Stimm and Tab Razer walk, side-by-side, to the back entry of the farmhouse.

I grab Tanya under her armpits and get her standing. "We gotta move."

Tanya's small body collapses against mine. Her head flops onto my chest, she's dead weight. I half drag, half carry her to the hall and into the bathroom. This door does have a lock. I settle Tanya on the floor, let her huddle against the toilet. "Helllllllllp me Gillllllli," she moans.

The room is puny. Tub. Toilet. Sink. A metal towel bar is attached to the wall. A shower curtain rod is in place over the tub, no shower curtain. A plastic toilet brush. Linoleum floor. That's it. I open the medicine cabinet above the sink. There's a bottle of Listerine and a half-crumpled Mouse Motel.

I'm in deep shit.

Where are Abshir and Nail? The cellar? There was a hook and eye on that door, but it's on the kitchen side. It's not going to stop anyone from going *down* the stairs.

Suddenly, there's a crazed and petrified yell – and scraping noise of scrambling feet across the first floor. A man's voice: "Fire! Fire!"

I hear the downstair's back door crash open. *Screak and thump*. Louder than before. Then the screak is gone. Has the storm door been ripped free of its hinges and is it flying and tumbling across the ground? A human *roooooar*. I peek out the bathroom window. Tab Razer is racing across the lawn - his thick, long fleece coat is on fire. "Shit! Ahhh! Faaawwwk!" he yells as he tries to get the fancy coat off - but either the zipper or buttons or whatever are too strong or his frantic movements are preventing him from getting it off. He bats his hands against the curly dense fabric but yelps as the skin on his hands burns. He dives, lands on the cold snowy ground – rolls around - anything to put out the flames. Thick fleece coats can hold onto fire and fleece burns hot.

7 Days

Tab Razer's body stops moving. Flames continue to dance on the coat, yellow hot, even as the snow starts to cover him.

How the hell did this happen?

I see Stimm stride onto the lawn, but he doesn't even go the distance to Tab. He takes a moment, turns around and heads back into the house.

Abshir and Nail? If they're in the cellar, what did they do to cause this fire? Will they – can they attack Stimm too? How? Will they wait for him to come to them? Or will they charge up the narrow stairs? Has Stimm already trapped them? Connected the heavy hook into the iron eye?

If so, will Stimm be on his way up the stairs to find us?

My phone is on the sink. I press the *Record* command. I have no idea if it will activate - but just in case all goes south and my phone is found, there will be a record of it. I put it under my sweater, in the V of my bra. Maybe it will only record heartbeat.

I have nothing else. Zilch. My eyes survey the space again.

What about that high shelf above the sink? Just below the ceiling. From my vantage point it looks empty, but I can't see all to the way to its back. I step, with one foot, onto the side of the tub, position the LiteGood for balance and hold onto the shower rod for help. I stretch to look, just to make sure - ahh! Is that a forgotten canister of hairspray, rolled back to the wall? No way I can reach it. I grab the shower curtain rod, compress the two ends together so the inner spring collapses. The rod is freed from its holder and it's in my hand. I use the length of it to sweep at the shelf, the hairspray canister rolls forward and falls to the linoleum floor. It looks rusted, the cap is no longer in place. It could be empty. But maybe not.

Heavy footsteps move up the stairway. Whistling begins and a familiar singsong: "Tanya has a friend. Weeping willies, Tanya has a friend." The steps take the corner and steamroll towards the bedroom where Tanya had been left. Every ounce of his two-hundred pounds causes a creaking of the floors. "Where is wifey? Where is wifey?" Whistling again, he's coming towards the bathroom. Light knock. Light knock. "Let's get this moving, girls." There's that clucking, self-satisfied noise, it's magnified in the empty house. He kicks a heel at the door, taunting. "I said, let's get this moving." Tanya rolls her head, still disoriented. She makes herself smaller in the corner.

Stimm jiggles the door and laughs. "Oh Dee Rommel, you were supposed to be gone years ago." Another jiggle – it's another tease, because we both know it's a courtesy lock, and that he's got the muscle to get past it. But he likes the scaring, the intimidation.

"Suggest you take off, Stimm," I call through the door. "Police are on their way."

"Don't think so."

"By this time, Rusty Razor's probably spilled it all, he'll be trying to save his own neck. About you hiring him to take out Croak and Gilli."

"Guessing games. Guessing games. Who doesn't like 'em?"

"What'd you pay him? A new Wrangler 4X for taking out Croake? New dental – all that gold teeth shit – was that for Gilli? Payment in *things*. Keeping cash out of it."

"People want what they want."

"Rusty's brother gets a fancy coat. Didn't do him much good."

"No. It didn't." He's matter-of-fact, no sentiment. "You keep getting in my way, Rommel. Don't like it."

Keep him talking. "You suck at picking your partners. It was Rusty who jabbed Croake with a needle at the Fundraiser, right? With a needle just like the ones they'll find in that toolbox he had with him at your house."

"Like those needles available at any drugstore near you."

"The cops have the toolbox now, they'll find something."

"Rusty's not going to talk-"

"About how he took Croake up in an ATV to High Eagle? With Cindy?"

"Fishing fishing, who's got the fish."

But this feels right. I'm sure now. I know I'm right. I continue, "And then Cindy. What was Rusty going to get for taking her out? Was he going to get a better place to live than Horseshoe Lane? She'll talk too, it'll all come out."

"She won't talk. 'Cause she can't. She didn't make it."

What?

He sounds so sure. "Rusty made sure she got the extra extra spicy sauce, and she was a little skinny thing. Too much for her."

"She died?"

7 Days

"She was starting to love the needle too. Just like her brother. Spoiled Croake girl takes a final breath, too bad, she'd been looking ahead to having all that money. Too bad, so sad."

Is it true? I don't want to believe him. Don't want to think about Cooper's anguish when he finds out.

Stimm bangs on the door with his fist. This time with a little more force. "Let me talk to my wife."

"She doesn't want to talk to you."

"She alive?"

"Oh yeah. Sure. She'll have stories to tell."

"She's a mouse." He sighs. "I got time. We've got time. No one's coming to the rescue. And you probably noticed, Dee Rommel, there's no dumpster to fall into this time. No super-save."

A dark fury grows in my gut and starts to rise.

Steady. I hear Donato's voice. *Steady*.

Stimm gives the door a medium-sized shove - it's still a taunt, a way to say there's more where that came from, but he's almost ready. "Let's get this over with, girls. And Tanya, hear me, sweetheart, I told you. Never mess with my plans."

Tanya's head drops, her chin is on her chest. Her body slumps, has she lost consciousness?

"You mean Two Daughters Farm?" I ask. "It is Tanya's. Did you know Gilli was starting to talk to Frank Croake?"

"Fuckin' Frank Croake, big hero. Thinking he was anointed as the clean-up guy. Money, money, money, and his driving around in his shiny new electric pickup that costs more than most of those people he's calling out as polluters can make in five years. Like he had the right to tell people what was trash – poison trash - or not."

"Why codeine for Frank?" I ask. Have to keep him talking.

"His kid liked it - it was his starter drug. I was educating Dad about how the right drug made his own little Cooper not care that his dad was a shit. I had to *instruct* Dad."

"Why'd you have to take out Gilli?" I ask.

"'Cause she's loud and crazy and thought she could control Tanya and she's always played the big sister card who thought she knew best. Like Croake. People who think they know best should get off this earth."

"You think you know best."

He laughs. "Gilli didn't plan on me, did she."

"That you'd be tossing Tanya out the window? Was Tanya set to follow her boot and bag? Were you going to dig a hole with the spade and shovel? Somewhere to make sure she wasn't found 'til spring?"

"She wasn't listening to me."

"Which one of the Razer brothers got into the gym at Gilli's condo? Was it both of them? How'd they do it?"

"Not like I never saw where crazy Gilli put Tanya's hide-a-key. Like I told Tanya – no secrets from hubby. I handed the key card off to Rusty and one day - when Gilli was out of her place - he went in, got hold of the gym entry, and the brothers waited for the right time."

"Killing for a fancy fleece coat. Sounds really, really sick."

"People want what they want."

This time he kicks his boot at the locking mechanism. It breaks. The door swings open and I'm there, with the ripped open Mouse Motel box. I toss the contents at his face. Loose powder, some kind of rodenticide shoots out and gets into Stimm's nose and eyes. His yelp sucks more shit down into his throat. He steps back in shock. I balance on my LiteGood, press my hands against the bathroom walls and whip my good leg forward and crash my boot into his right knee. Hope it's the one Payer damaged years ago. Stimm grunts and stumbles and drops the cooler he's got in his hand. It clatters to the floor, falls open. A dozen syringes, all pre-measured and ready to go, roll out, cascade down the hallway. Baggies of powder and pills fall into clumps on the floor. Asshole. Fuji camera insta-pix have floated out, they've fluttered onto the floor.

Concentrate. I've got the shower rod in hand. It's thin aluminum, it can't hurt a lot so it's all about the placement. I go right for his esophagus. Right above the trachea. Jab it down.

Hard.

Twice.

7 Days

Stimm makes this scary growl, it's followed by a snuffy and wheezy attempt for breath. I stand above him, land a kick on the other kneecap. The left one this time. Just to make sure I get the one that was going to destroy him the most. He buckles in pain.

I stand above him, get close to his face. "One more thing, you sad fuck, I want to know." I'm breathing hard, the words are sticking in my throat. "Tell me it was you who pushed me off that goddamned roof."

His eyes bug. His face is wracked with physical agony.

"Tell me that it was you who killed that boy. Ran him over. I need you to say it was you."

Stimm's in respiratory distress. His face is raw, his skin is peeling, there must be an acid in the rodenticide of the Mouse Motel, it's eating his flesh. One eye is swollen shut, the other is just a slit.

"You were on the roof," I spit, I'm growling, my voice so raw. "You whacked me and shoved me. Say it."

His lips move, he's only got choking gasps to get air into his lungs. But he grabs my LiteGood, he takes hold right at the ankle joint and pulls hard. I grab at the wall for balance. And I've got the hairspray canister in my hand. I slam it against his knuckles, his fingers jerk loose. I aim the aerosol at his mouth, press the nozzle and - nothing. Fuck. Nothing.

Stimm's hand snares me again – but there are two guys flying through the air and they land on Stimm's chest. They exacerbate the open stab in Stimm's throat. I've never heard that violent discharge of breath before. I think his windpipe exploded.

Stimm's mouth moves. Just aching air is going out, not much going in.

No time to waste. Tanya hasn't moved. There's been no moan or groan from her. I frantically rummage through Stimm's cooler and get Abshir's attention: "We gotta get to the Medical Center-"

"I'll try Emergency again" he says. Frustrated, he practically tosses his phone. "Nothing."

"Someone go see if one the cars is usable."

Nail's moved to Tanya, he's not listening to me. "Tanya can't die."

Abshir races down the stairs. "I will look at cars."

"Found it!" I yell. There it is, at the bottom of the cooler. The naloxone. Stimm probably showed it off to clients – egging them to try larger and more dangerous doses and assuring them he could bring them back from madness or the brink of death with a quick injection of the palliative. I get back to the toilet and Tanya, push Nail aside. I draw a dose into a syringe, flick it with my finger to dispel bubbles and inject the serum into her arm. "Come on, come on." Thirty seconds later, like life has decided to come back with full force, Tanya's eyes flash open wide. Her body spasms, she screams. Her scream is loud and long and echoes in the empty house.

Abshir has rushed back up the stairs, his dark hair is crusted with snow. He tells me he's taken a look at my car and its crashed windshield. "It is not drive-able." He says there are no keys in the Chevy, they're probably in a burned-out fleece pocket.

Stimm is unconscious, but his chest is moving, barely, up and down. I search the pockets of his parka to find the keys to Tanya's Prius. "Check the barn. Stimm's gotta stay alive. I'll stay with Tanya here, I've got enough naloxone if she needs more."

"No, he doesn't have to stay alive," says Nail. "Let him die for what he did to Gilli."

"He's not getting the 'easy out'," I say.

Abshir retrieves the Prius from the barn. Nail and I drag Stimm down the stairs and outside. We have to pull him into the back seat. We cover him with a blanket. Abshir's ready to drive off towards Livermore Falls to the Medical Center, hopes the snowplows are active on Route 125 and Route 17; but we can't access a minute-to-minute weather report, so who knows.

Nail insists on riding with Abshir – he's all puffed up, convinced that a Nail/Abshir team is indomitable.

CHAPTER THIRTY-TWO

I don't want to disturb the detritus of the fight, the spilled contents of Stimm's cooler. But the insta-pix are there, and I can look without touching them. There's a series of Frank Croake against Marker Six, slumped. Then with the plastic bag over his head. Of hands putting the duct tape around Frank's neck to make sure no air gets in. A picture of Cindy in her suede coat. Looking away, doing nothing to change the course for her father. And four more shots of Gilli - beaten and crashed against the Kahta Condo Gym's glass wall.

I help Tanya downstairs and pull the sheets off the couch and chairs in the family room. I wrap her in them, wind them as tightly as I can. She's quiet but alert, she sits on the couch near the empty stone fireplace - in the place where she grew up. "I'll be right back," I say. I leave her and move outside. I grab the wet and near frozen blanket that held Tanya's bag and boots and take it to Tab Razor's body. His face is blackened with burns, his lifeless eyes stare at the sky. The fleece is still smoldering. I cover him. Why? It's not respect for him, it's respect for the end of a life, I guess. It just feels right.

Now, back inside, it's just me and Tanya. In the cold cold house.

Just then the storm magnifies. It consumes the flat land, full force. In less than a minute, it's a whiteout. I can't see the barn from the house anymore – can't see my wrecked car – can't see the chicken coop. I move to the kitchen window. I can't even see the backyard trees.

I hope Abshir and Nail have reached the Medical Center. But even if they did, there's no way they'll be able to turn around and get back to Two Daughters' Farm.

* * *

I use my cell phone flashlight to guide me down the cellar stairs. There's a gun on the concrete floor – a Stinger .38. It's a match to the one

7 Days

that Rusty Razer had on him at the Wandering Moose. Did the brothers do their gun shopping together? A two-for-one deal? An empty lamp oil canister is on its side on the top of the dresser. Next to it is a small box of matches. Abshir (or Nail?) must've seen no other option – be shot or toss the lit lamp oil at Razer. So, they did what made sense, and the fleece ignited.

There are ten smallish logs in the cellar. At least they're dry. There's one stubby candle.

I pull open the drawers in the dresser. I was right. The top drawer contains small plastic bins filled with carefully organized screws, nails, washers and more. All separated by sizes. The second drawer houses small tools, all sizes of screwdrivers, wrenches, socket sets, pliers, and small drills. The final drawer, at the bottom, is stuck. Weather has warped the wood, and I can't get it open. Not even using the largest – or smallest – of the screwdrivers.

Back in the kitchen, I find old coupons in a drawer by the ancient stove. Grocery coupons, drugstore coupons, a few from gas stations. More torn out from the local newspapers. These won't be enough to get a fire going. The furniture left in the family room is upholstered. If I put cushions on the fire, I'll be filling the room with toxins.

I carefully extract the family photos from their thin, homemade wood frames. I put the pictures in front of Tanya. She's on the worn couch, her feet tucked under her. She stares at the images of her family.

I light the stubby candle, it's one of those forest green ones with the pine needles embedded in the wax. Hopefully it's not a quick burner.

I'm careful. I baby every piece of wood and paper and place them on the fireplace's grate. Use the matches sparingly. Add the smallest log – I don't want to smother my base. The log finally ignites. The fire is started.

I close the doors of the family room to contain the heat in one place. Tanya will get warmer. I consider heading to the barn to see if there's more wood, but the two hundred yards to the barn are impassable. For now.

I sit close to Tanya. "We're gonna share body heat," I say. "Let's get really close."

She leans on me. Her eyes close.

And I wonder about feeling so alone. If only I could conjure up that special person that would be here, alongside me. Who would appear? Whose hand do I want to hold? Who do I want by my side?

Something has to change, so I don't feel so separate.

TWO DAYS

CHAPTER THIRTY-THREE

It's past midnight. I slowly open my eyes. Didn't expect I'd fall asleep. I listen to Tanya's soft snoozy breathing. I go to the window, stare out. The blizzard has not let up. There's one log left; the rest have become ash.

How much longer can this storm continue?

There's thirst. Hunger. Cold.

I've put a bucket outside the back door to collect fresh snow. My dad always warned me against getting too fond of eating it, melting it and then drinking it. That its beauty is full of airborne pollutants. And here I am on an idyllic farm whose soil is full of pollutants. I want to hold onto the surface beauty, not see what's underneath.

Tab Razer's spade leans against the kitchen counter. I use it to shovel a clump of snow out of the bucket and move it to the kitchen sink. I've already got the stopper in place. I let it melt. And drink.

I've checked the floors. All have been varnished – with polyurethane probably – multiple times (by the look of it) over the decades. I know the finish is like a sort of plastic in liquid form it's spread over the wood with a brush. It hardens after it dries. Something like that. I know if it gets burned, there are crap fumes and chemicals that get released. I check the open kitchen cabinets. Same thing – even the backing wood has been varnished.

I troll the upstairs. The doors and door frames have layers of paint on them. The dry wall behind the wallpaper? Can't use that. This old stuff could be full of asbestos and sulfur and I don't know what else.

The whole place is feeling like my enemy.

I hear a buzz. It's my phone, letting me know the battery is now completely dead.

Back to the cellar. Have I missed something? I look at the underside of the narrow stairs. The wood looks raw – but the tops of the treads have been painted with thick, drippy paint.

7 Days

What's that? There's a cooler tucked behind the boiler. It's got black sides, that's maybe how I missed it before. Maybe there'll be a soda inside. Or a beer. I ease up the top. It's empty.

The lowest drawer of the dresser. There could be nothing in it. Or at least, nothing of value to Tanya and me today. But it's not going to get the better of me. I grab a hammer, lean down so I can reach past the dresser's short legs to the underside – and pound upwards. Maybe I can loosen the stuck drawer this way. There's a little give. I grab the handles and pull. Still stuck.

I hammer at the bottom again. Then I hammer at the sides. A chunk of veneer falls off. I start to sweat, and I don't want that. I don't want to release any heat, any moisture. I take a moment. Then give it two more swings.

I yank - hoping for scrapbooks, diaries, old newspapers, old letters. Anything to burn. The drawer opens halfway.

Enough for me to see jars and jars and jars of pickles.

* * *

I sit on the couch in the family room. Who knows when Ben Wanz's wife put up the cucumbers. These pickles could be five years or ten years old – maybe they were forgotten once she passed. The lid of the jar in my hand is on solidly. I hold it next to the warmth of the last log, tap the side of the metal top with the back end of the screwdriver. Twist, twist. The top cracks open and I used the tip of the screwdriver to pry loose the suction rim. Ahh. The smell of vinegar, sugar and dill rises.

Sweet and sour dill pickles. Thank you, Mrs. Wanz.

I feed Tanya. The taste must remind her of happy times on the Farm. A slight smile spreads across her face.

I sip the pickle juice. It's good.

* * *

I wake. My watch says it's noon. The storm has calmed. The air is no longer thick with white. I can see a patch of sky. The winds have dissipated too. There's my car – it looks like a mound; it's completely covered with snow.

"Thank you," says Tanya. I thought she was still asleep.

"How do you feel?" I ask.

"Cold."

"Have another pickle?"

She half-laughs. "I wouldn't put meat in my hamburger bun. I'd just pile on my mom's pickles and homemade mustard and ketchup. Gilli made fun of me." She notices she's been awarded all the sheets. "You want to wrap one around you? You must be cold."

"Storm's letting up," I say.

"Will someone know where to look for us?"

"Sure. Sure." I'm hoping Abshir and Nail made it to the Medical Center. That someone has been told about us. "I think it's clear enough to go check the barn. I'll see if there's firewood in there."

"I should help."

"Better you stay here."

I grab the spade. I'll use it for balance and if I need to dig myself out of somewhere. I've crossed the field and am halfway to the barn when I hear the snowplow. Its diesel engine is loud, it's moving slowly. I start to see the safety lights swirling. When it comes into view, I see it's huge. It makes the turn onto Two Daughters Road – and trudges on its massive tires into the yard.

All right. Okay. My shoulders fall. Relief. Exhaustion's close behind.

Nail jumps out of the cab, keeping hold of his cast. "We came as soon as we could! My guy Abshir stayed at the hospital. There are cops around Wynn, but Abshir wanted to keep an eye. Said you'd want him to do that. How is Tanya? Is she okay?"

"She's in the house. She's okay."

Nail's still wearing those earmuffs. "Wynn's gonna be a vegetable, they say. Didn't have enough air to keep his brain going. I don't know where they keep people that are brain-dead in jail. But the good news is now I can visit Tanya at her home and he won't be there."

ONE DAY

CHAPTER THIRTY-FOUR

We stand on the frozen earth of Two Daughter's Farm, in the small cemetery on the edge of its woods. Gilli's headstone is on the ground, next to her family members who settled the land in the early 1800s. Her actual grave will be dug in the spring, today, the granite will be left to mark her spot.

I stand with Tanya, Detectives Banford and Lavonna, the funeral home's Mr. Byrne, Abshir, a Unitarian minister, and Nail.

Doctors saved Stimm's life, but he'll never set foot here again. Tanya will be alone. It'll feel weird and scary for her, probably, but she'll have a chance to build a new life. Nail has told Tanya he'll be around when she wants him, because he owes it to Gilli. That he'd even taken an apartment down the road from her in Cape Elizabeth, moved all his things from the Kahta Street condo into it. That he'd watched the *For Sale* sign go up on the front lawn of Kahta Condos.

The minister finishes his prayers. "We are here, with longing in our souls. Gilli left us too early. I am sure, that she would want us to be strong, to who we are, to embrace who we will become."

Tanya and Nail set bouquets of roses on the headstone.

Carter Stround waits in the kitchen of Two Daughters Farm. He's set up some space heaters, brought in a thermos of coffee and pastries. Tanya thanks him and she turns to me. "This feels right. My family is not leaving Two Daughters. The cemetery will stay, the land will stay in the family. And we'll make the farm healthy again."

I look at Carter. There's no triumph on his face, it's more a deep, serious sense of responsibility.

* * *

7 Days

Abshir heads back to Portland and his scheduled political science test. I don't have far to travel to the Sports Park. Back onto Route 125, another two miles and I turn onto the long drive. The parking lot is nearly full, but I find a spot to leave Gordy's car. Mine will be in the shop for a while. I look over the field, where summer softball is played. At least three inches of snow covers it. The branches of the pine trees droop because heavy snow rests on their tips.

Carter's Jeep pulls up beside me. He gets out and we watch a trio of deer bound across the field.

"Looks like the four-legged buddies are showing up to pay their respects too," he says.

"Yeah. Yeah."

"Thanks for what you did," he says.

"I didn't do anything. I showed Tanya the sweatshirt Nail had – the one you and Frank and Gilli signed. That's all I did."

He takes in the landscape, breathes deep. "No reason to ever leave Maine."

A sentiment I share.

"Shall I wait for you two?"

We turn around. It's Jade, bundled in her black coat and oversized faux fur hat and mittens.

"Jade, have you met? Ahh – this is Carter Stround," I say.

"Mushroom Friend?"

"That's me," he says.

We walk into the massive barn. Heat lamps are on high, the heat pumps that line the walls are also blasting. There's got to be two hundred people there already, all are mingling, gawking at the huge wreaths of flowers and video screens of talking heads that relay messages from people around the country – and the world – that Frank had connected with over the years.

Gordy has sent the biggest of those oversized horseshoe wreaths. Marie would've been a bit more tasteful, so Gordy must've been able to put in the order himself. I see Cooper; Oscar Herbstrom is right at his side. I'd heard Herbstrom put up bail, that he wanted to make sure Cooper could make the memorial.

No sign of Ernesto.

Cooper's pale. He's walking tentatively, avoiding eye contact. Herbstrom's doing a good job at making sure no one gets too close to him.

* * *

The wide and narrow window in Gordy's hospital room has louvered blinds. They are mostly open today; I take this as a sign he's 'back' and wanting to know everything that goes on. Marie is doing her crossword puzzle and I'm watching the Monday Night Patriots game with Gordy. Out of the corner of my eye I notice a man moving in the hallway, he's pushing a baby stroller.

He's headed our way – straight to Gordy's room. It's Donato. He pushes through the door. He takes a soft yellow bundle out of the stroller.

"Is that yours?" asks Marie, forgetting her crossword.

"Dude." I say it at the same time Donato says it.

Donato continues. "Yeah. My son. Dude's his name. I got special dispensation from the nurse. We can only stay a few minutes." He unbuttons the baby parka, pulls the knit hat from the mini-man's head.

I'm speechless. The kis has blue-gray eyes, pink skin, chubby cheeks, and a plumpish body. Donato extricates Dude from the parka to reveal a yellow and orange striped sweater with a teddy bear on its front. Baby Ugg booties are on his feet.

Dude, happy kid, kicks his short legs, points to the ceiling, interested in the fluorescent lights.

"So, that's yours," is all Gordy has to say. Then he adds, "The Patriots are getting their butts kicked."

"What's new?" laughs Donato. Then he feels like he needs to explain: "Dude's visiting his grandparents, Christine's folks, in Kennebunk. Christine's shopping with her mom today. The dentist husband is off playing pickleball with Christine's dad. And since it's my day off, I get Dude for a whole six hours. I was going to take him snowboarding, but thought I'd wait a few years for that. This was my second choice."

"You get the recording off Dee's phone?" asks Gordy. "The Stimm confession?"

"Yeah. Tech was able to do that. We got him for Frank Croake and Gilli. Rusty's going away too."

Gordy yells at the TV, there's been another interception, and the Patriots are cooked.

Dude hoots and flails his arms at the hospital machinery near Gordy's bed, maybe he likes the clicks and beeps and colors.

I keep my voice low, talking just to Donato. "Wynn Stimm was one of the guys on the roof. He pushed me off. I couldn't get him to say it. But I know."

Donato leans close. "We'll get him - and get him to name the others. That night's not getting forgotten."

Dude, in Donato's arms, bends his body towards me and grabs at my hair.

"Hey, hey, little guy," says Donato. "Not cool."

Dude squiggles in Donato's arms, tries to twist loose. "We don't grab a girl's hair, little guy."

Dude keeps reaching his arms towards me. "Huhoh ooo ga ga oooh," he says. Or something like that. His eyes are bright and his soft pudgy cheeks glow.

"Dude. Dude," says Donato. "Leave the lady alone."

I feel Marie and Gordy watching.

Then Dude uses his chubby legs to launch himself off Donato's stomach and he falls right at me. I grab him so he doesn't take a header, I've got him under his tiny armpits, and he buries his face on my chest. I get the whiff of baby laundry detergent, baby shampoo, baby food, baby everything. He raises his head, and his roly-poly hands grab my long hair again. Bubbles of drool collect on his lips; he gurgles and laughs.

He's a charmer.

Donato's watching too, ready to take Dude back at any moment. "You okay?"

The End

ACKNOWLEDGEMENTS

7 DAYS is the fourth book in the Dee Rommel Mystery series and the community of support keeps growing. There's the amazing Maine writing community, its independent bookstores, the book clubs (from Higgins Beach to Willard Beach to Freeport to the island of Vinalhaven), book gatherings helmed by old friends and new friends across New England and its libraries and community centers. And thanks to the national and international fans who want to know the challenges Dee Rommel will face next.

Thanks to Biff Brady, private investigator and polygraph expert, Mark Read for his knowledge of land conservation in Maine, former Assistant Police Chief Joe Loughlin for reminding me that crimes (and criminals) come in all shapes and sizes, to Brent DeMichael for all his introductions and to J.A. McIntosh for her sound knowledge on disability challenges.

I want to thank my writing group - I call us the "Sea Dogs" because it was the name of the bowling alley bar where we first started to meet. Also, thanks for the close reads by fellow authors Lara Santoro and Susan Merson. Of course, thanks to Elgon Williams and Pandamoon Publishing.

I'm a writer who writes "wherever". Favorite places are coffeeshops and bar stools that give me new perspectives and a respite from my (beloved) desk. Here's to Becky's Diner, Bard, Lenora's, Porthole, AC, and my 'standing reservation' in the far corner of Portland's Regency Hotel's watering holes, helmed by John and Liz.

Finally, to Mark Winkworth for keeping me sailing and to avid reader Sally Reinman who wants Dee Rommel to shine.

> *"A book is made from a tree. It is an assemblage of flat, flexible parts (still called "leaves") imprinted with dark pigmented squiggles. One glance at it and you hear the voice of another person..." Carl Sagan (1934-1996)*

About the Author

Jule Selbo, produced screenwriter and playwright, moved from Los Angeles to Portland Maine to focus on writing novels After writing three award-nominated historical fiction novels, she's now in her favorite genre: crime-mystery. *7 DAYS*, A Dee Rommel Mystery is the fourth book in the crime/mystery series that has made the Kirkus' Top 5 from Indie Publishers List, has been awarded a Silver Falchion and award nominations from Foreword Review, the Clue Award, Maine Literary Award and more. The series begins with *10 DAYS*, is followed by *9 DAYS*, then *8 DAYS* and now *7 DAYS* (ahh, yes, the pattern is clear). Quoting from reviews: "Dee Rommel is one of today's most compelling detectives";"A hero unlike any other in crime fiction"; "Fans of Lisa Jewell and Lisa Gardner will enjoy these suspenseful thrillers". https://www.juleselbo.com

Your purchase of *7 Days by Jule Selbo* supports our growing community of talented authors.

If you enjoyed this book, please let the author know by posting your review at https://www.pandamoonpub.com and register today to receive advance notice of new book releases, special bundles, and discounts.

Growing good ideas into great reads…one book at a time.

Visit http://www.pandamoonpublishing.com to learn about other works by our talented authors.

Mystery/Thriller/Suspense
- *A Flash of Red* by Sarah K. Stephens
- A Rocky Series of Mysteries Book 1: *A Rocky Divorce* by Matt Coleman
- Ballpark Mysteries Book 1: *Murder at First Pitch* by Nicole Asselin
- Ballpark Mysteries Book 2: *Concession Stand Crimes* by Nicole Asselin
- Bodie Anderson Series Book 1: *Code Gray* by Benny Sims
- David Knight Thrillers Book 1: *The Amsterdam Deception* by Tony Ollivier
- David Knight Thrillers Book 2: *The Tokyo Diversion* by Tony Ollivier
- Dee Rommel Mysteries Book 1: *10 DAYS* by Jule Selbo
- Dee Rommel Mysteries Book 2: *9 Days* by Jule Selbo
- Dee Rommel Mysteries Book 3: 8 *Days* by Jule Selbo
- Dee Rommel Mysteries Book 3: 7 *Days* by Jule Selbo
- *Fate's Past* by Jason Huebinger
- *Graffiti Creek* by Matt Coleman
- *Killer Secrets* by Sherrie Orvik
- *Knights of the Shield* by Jeff Messick
- *Kricket* by Penni Jones
- *Lama With A Gun* by Seth Augensein
- *Looking into the Sun* by Todd Tavolazzi
- *Mile Marker Zero by Benny Sims*
- *On the Bricks* by Penni Jones
- *Project 137* by Seth Augenstein

- *Rogue Alliance* by Michelle Bellon
- *Sinai Unhinged* by Joanna Evans
- *Southbound* by Jason Beem
- *Suicide Souls* by Penni Jones
- *The Juliet* by Laura Ellen Scott
- *The Last Detective* by Brian Cohn
- The Moses Winter Mysteries Book 1: *Made Safe* by Francis Sparks
- The New Royal Mysteries Book 1: *The Mean Bone in Her Body* by Laura Ellen Scott
- The New Royal Mysteries Book 2: *Crybaby Lane* by Laura Ellen Scott
- The New Royal Mysteries Book 3: *Blue Billy* by Laura Ellen Scott
- *The Ramadan Drummer* by Randolph Splitter
- The Teratologist Series Book 1: *The Teratologist* by Ward Parker
- *The Unraveling of Brendan Meeks* by Brian Cohn
- The Zeke Adams Series Book 1: *Pariah* by Ward Parker
- The Zeke Adams Series Book 2: *Fur* by Ward Parker
- *This Darkness Got to Give* by Dave Housley
- *To Kill a Unicorn* by DC Palter
- *Countdown to Decryption* by DC Palter

Science Fiction/Fantasy
- Children of Colonodona Book 1: *The Wizard's Apprentice* by Alisse Lee Goldenberg
- Children of Colonodona Book 2: *The Island of Mystics* by Alisse Lee Goldenberg
- Dybbuk Scrolls Trilogy Book 1: *The Song of Hadariah* by Alisse Lee Goldenberg
- Dybbuk Scrolls Trilogy Book 2: *The Song of Vengeance* by Alisse Lee Goldenberg
- Dybbuk Scrolls Trilogy Book 3: *The Song of War* by Alisse Lee Goldenberg
- Everly Series Book 1: *Everly* by Meg Bonney
- Everly Series Book 2: *Rosewood Burning* by Meg Bonney
- Finder Series Book 1: *Chimera Catalyst* by Susan Kuchinskas
- Finder Series Book 2: *Singularity Syndrome* by Susan Kuchinskas
- Fried Windows Series Book 1: *Fried Windows (In a Light White Sauce)* by Elgon Williams
- Fried Windows Series Book 2: *Ninja Bread Castles* by Elgon Williams
- *Humanity Devolved* by Greyson Ferguson
- Magehunter Saga Book 1: *Magehunter* by Jeff Messick
- Magehunter Saga Book 2: *Priesthunter* by Jeff Messick
- *The Bath Salts Journals Volume One* by Alisse Lee Goldenberg and An Tran

- The Crimson Chronicles Book 1: *Crimson Forest* by Christine Gabriel
- The Crimson Chronicles Book 2: *Crimson Moon* by Christine Gabriel
- *The Grays* by Dave Housley and Becky Barnard
- The Phaethon Series Book 1: *Phaethon* by Rachel Sharp
- The Phaethon Series Book 2: *Pharos* by Rachel Sharp
- The Phaethon Series Book 3, Phantasma by Rachel Sharp
- The Sitnalta Series Book 1: *Sitnalta* by Alisse Lee Goldenberg
- The Sitnalta Series Book 2: *The Kingdom Thief* by Alisse Lee Goldenberg
- The Sitnalta Series Book 3: *The City of Arches* by Alisse Lee Goldenberg
- The Sitnalta Series Book 4: *The Hedgewitch's Charm* by Alisse Lee Goldenberg
- The Sitnalta Series Book 5: *The False Princess* by Alisse Lee Goldenberg
- The Thuperman Trilogy Book 1: *Becoming Thuperman* by Elgon Williams
- The Thuperman Trilogy Book 2: *Homer Underby* by Elgon Williams
- The Thuperman Trilogy Book 3: *Thuperheros* by Elgon Williams
- The Wolfcat Chronicles Book 1: *Dammerwald* by Elgon Williams

Women's Fiction
- *Beautiful Secret* by Dana Faletti
- *Find Me in Florence* by Jule Selbo
- *The Long Way Home* by Regina West
- *The Shape of the Atmosphere* by Jessica Dainty

Non-Fiction
- *Marketing for Freelance Writers* by Robyn Roste
- *The Writer's Zen* by Jessica Reino

Made in the USA
Middletown, DE
08 May 2025

75259681R00186